THE SWORDSPEAKER SAGA

GRIMBRIAR

DJ EDWARDSON

GIRRAFIX

KNOXVILLE

Contents

1. A Dark Arrival — 1

2. The Shepherd's Crook — 12

3. A New Kalvar — 21

4. Into the Summerlands — 30

5. Ghost Trail — 38

6. The Final Record — 49

7. The Lost Hylls — 60

8. Chitter Chatter — 73

9. Flawed Sight — 82

10. A Feast of Crumbs — 94

11. Messenger — 105

12. Dishonorable Men — 117

13. Of Grief and Memory — 130

14. Ring of Fire — 138

15. Contest of Manners — 146

16. Snow Glaze — 154

17. The Furls — 167

18. Where Fires Burn Cold — 177

19. Rumblings in the Dark   187

20. Trapping Rats   196

21. Different Paths   204

22. Drench and Drudgery   214

23. Fister the Magister   221

24. Dark Waters   234

25. Adrift   243

26. When the Strains Run Dry   250

27. The Night Comes Alive   256

28. Cornoc's Tale   262

29. Bramble Eyre   269

30. A Servant's Ears   278

31. The Marshal's Plans   292

32. Beranskyre   300

33. Bed of Sorrow   312

34. Hunting for a Cure   320

35. The World of Sun and Moon   330

36. Mortar and Pestle   336

37. The Broken Welnod   346

38. Thorns and Thistles   356

39. Grimbriar   361

40. Secret in the Water   369

41. False Heart   381

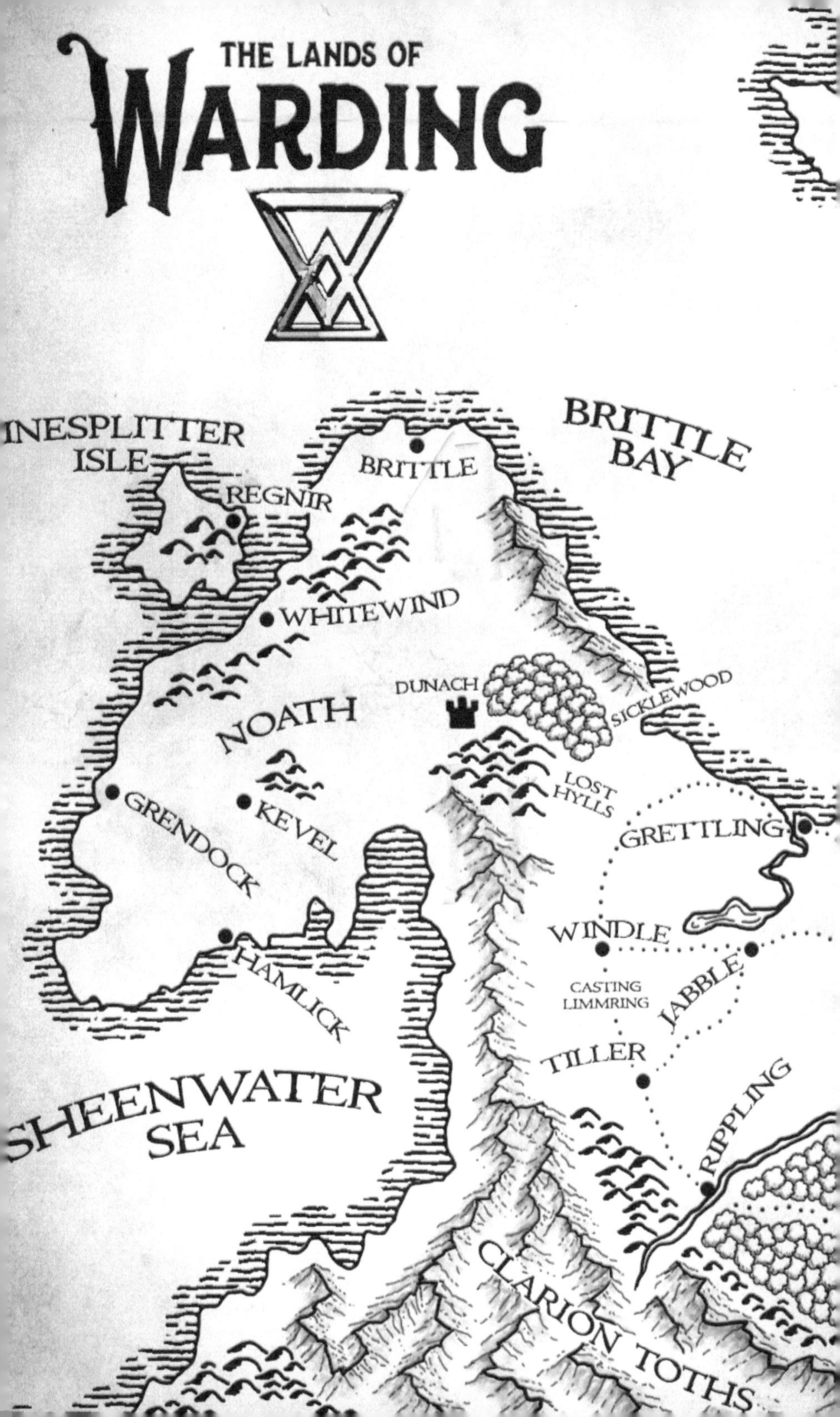

THE LANDS OF
WARDING
INESPLITTER ISLE
BRITTLE BAY
BRITTLE
REGNIR
WHITEWIND
DUNACH
SICKLEWOOD
NOATH
LOST HYLLS
GRETTLING
KEVEL
GRENDOCK
WINDLE
HAMLICK
CASTING LIMMRING
JABBLE
TILLER
SHEENWATER SEA
RIPPLING
CLARION TOTHS

42. Duty Does What it Must   395

43. Quarry in the Quarry   407

44. Noble Lies   416

45. Truth and Justice   423

46. Shared Vision   432

47. Hope and Dread   439

48. The Hour of Hard Places   446

49. Voice of Doom   457

50. Until the Battle is Over   472

51. A Tear in the Fabric of Night   488

52. The Battle Is Not the War   498

TETHER
HAUKMARN
DIREROC
MARRED WASTES
AVAR
GAVEL
CHOR
LATHETHICKET
DIRING SEA
ROVING
THE CLEFTS
FENNIGAR
FURROW
INRIS
WINDSTERN
SEABRIM
CASTING SELVEDGE
CASTING URLISH
QUELLING
HEMMING HYLLS
CHARRING
DUNSKEIN
NICKLING
MAVRIN GAZE
CASTING ALDRIC
MERRILING RIVER
MADRIGAL
FATHOMWOOD
BRAMBLE EYRE
THE HOWL
GLENWITHER
TOTHS

Chapter 1

A DARK ARRIVAL

S hadows, shadows everywhere. No matter where he looked, Kion's eyes met with shadows pooling upon the ground in liquid darkness, black wounds upon the land. The full moon did little more than deepen the stains. Its wan light shrank from the edges, unable to penetrate the darkened wells.

They had arrived late into the night. Trekking to Whitewind across Rimewinter's bridge of crystal blue ice had made for slow going. They had to watch their footing to avoid slipping into the sea. Tinesplitter Bay had been easier to cross when covered by snow.

The travelers had expected to arrive in the dark, but not a darkness like this. Kion unsheathed Truesilver shortly after the sun went down. A familiar reddish glow enveloped the sword. Beside him, Tiryn's dagger, Rimewinter, shone with a clean blue light of its own, though of a lesser degree, for the naked blade remained strapped snugly across his sister's chest. Where the two glaive-lights met, they blended in purplish harmony. The light brought Zinder's canary-yellow hat into vivid contrast against the encroaching darkness. The fashionable nyn had wanted to look especially striking for their triumphal return, and the giant bulbous headpiece was nothing if not eye-catching, but the way the brim drooped almost to his shoulders after a long day subjected to sweat and sun made him look like a tulip with wilted petals, giving quite a different impression from the one he'd intended. Behind these three, and towering over the nyn, though they were all of fourteen years old, came the twins, Trik and Trak, their Frin guides. These two scanned the dark patches of the village with troubled eyes, but could tell no more of them than the others. Scriff, their pet frost fox, circled their legs. The animal's milk-white fur stood on end. A low growl rumbled in its throat. Not since the clash with the snowwinder had the frox (as Trik and Trak called him) displayed such agitation.

"What black arts are at work here?" Zinder pushed his sagging hat up away from his eyebrows.

"I thought the curse was lifted," Trak said. "The snow's gone, but something else has taken its place, something even more unnatural than endless winter."

"Maybe we're just…tired," Trik said and faked a yawn. He was as wide awake as any of them. "Sometimes my eyes see spots when I've gone too long without sleep."

"Everything looks so different. Not at all the way I remembered," Tiryn said, trailing the others down the paved street, her eyes roving the darkened houses.

Whitewind, once gripped in the unending snow and ice of the Longwinter, had been released at last to summer's healing warmth. The thatched roofs of the triangular, timber-framed houses lay exposed to the air for the first time in centuries and the stone paths between them showed no trace of winter's touch. But a new kind of chill now permeated the air, invisible and daunting, and it sank its talons deep into the bone.

"It must be Vayd," Kion said. The leader of the haukmarn had come into possession of the axe Shadowriven two days past in the caves of Tinesplitter Isle. Tiryn had found Rimewinter there as well, along with five other ancient glaives. The others had yet to awaken the way Truesilver and Rimewinter had, despite Trik and Trak's best efforts to call them to life. What mattered now, though, was not the glaives, it was finding Vayd. They had been following him ever since they escaped the caves, but the swiftest runner in the Four Wards could not overtake a haukmar on the march.

"This feels indeed like the work of Shadowriven and its thrall, though how Malix has wrought such a thing is beyond my ken." The sage voice of Kithian, which came to Kion through his sword, helped to quell the unease stirring in Kion's heart. No matter how hard the road before him, Kion could draw strength from that voice, ageless and understanding, which he and Tiryn alone could hear. If not for that voice he would have lost all hope by now, for his mother's recent death hung over him as dark as the shadows now covering the village. He forced down the surge of memory before it could blossom into grief and take hold again. This was no time to give in to his private pain. Vayd was on the move and the fate of Whitewind was shrouded in doubt.

Tiryn touched Rimewinter's hilt, her brow knotted, as she listened to Kithian's words.

"What do you think, Nurien?" she said.

"These shadows forebode much evil for the people of this village, indeed to all who cross Malix's path. Fear tells me that something terrible has happened here, but all is dark to me, as if the very pools themselves veiled my Sight." Nurien's soft voice, ever tinged with sorrow, was even more somber than usual.

"We must find Kalvar Chaw," Kion said.

"Of course. His house is just off the central plaza." Trak hustled up beside Kion and took the lead.

This deep in the night, it was not unusual that no one stirred, yet the quiet felt as unnatural as the pools of darkness themselves. It was as if the village were still covered in snow. The farther they went, the more unsettling the scene became.

"Kithian, you said these shadows are a mystery. What is Shadowriven capable of?" Kion said.

"The answer to that is bound up with the grief and loss of the Shattering. It saddens me even now to repeat it." Truesilver's light dimmed. *"Malix was granted the ability to give his glaivebond tremendous strength and endurance. Greater still, he was the only glaive who could impart his gifts to others, though to a lesser degree and for a shorter time. But through the twisting of the Spark, and with*

his glaivebond Talinyon's help, Shadowriven's gift was altered. After that his power did the opposite. It drained the strength of others and gave it to his glaivebond, so much so that if he took enough he could bring about the death of those he afflicted."

"And these pools? Is that what he uses to drain people's strength?" Kion said.

"No. These shadows are something new. Never before have I seen their like."

"Nor I," Nurien said.

Trak stopped at the edge of a circular plaza and pointed to the opposite side.

"There. That's where our uncle—I mean the kalvar—lives."

It was a house like all the others. It gave no impression of belonging to the leader of the village, but then again all the houses looked more or less the same, small with respect to length and breadth, yet with tall, precipitous roofs, and built from thick beams.

The shadows were especially thick in this plaza. Indeed, there were so many that the only way around them was to head down another street and hope to reach the house from another direction. If the moon had not been so full they might have seemed more like stains or ordinary shadows, but there was no mistaking their unsettling nature under the cold silver light.

"Do you think, Swordspeaker…do you think it's safe to walk through them?" Trik said.

Kion hesitated, but refused to give in to fear. "They're only shadows," he said. "Right, Kithian?"

"Perhaps it is time for us to find out. Tell the others to wait while you go forward," Kithian said.

As was his custom, Kion conveyed Truesilver's words to the others.

"You're sure, lad?" Zinder said, pinching the end of his neat little beard. It was so white it looked as if it were coated with snow. "What if you fall in? Shouldn't we tie a rope around you, the way we did on Tinesplitter?"

"I don't think they're actual holes. How could Vayd have possibly made so many in such a short time? But even if they are, I won't just go striding right into them. I'll be careful. No need to worry."

Zinder wrinkled his nose. "Fine. Go off brave as a badger if you like, but I'll worry all the same. It's all well and good to be courageous when your enemy is flesh and blood. But these shadows give me the trembles." He set down his pack and the dormant glaive he'd been carrying and fished out a span of rope. "Best to have this just in case."

Tiryn laid a hand on her brother's arm. "Zinder's right. It doesn't hurt to be safe."

"As long as I have Truesilver I'll be safe," Kion said. But seeing Trik and Trak huddling together, along with the look in Zinder and Tiryn's eyes, he gave a nod and allowed Zinder to tie the rope around his waist all the same.

Kion stepped to the edge of the closest shadow. Standing before it, the blackness looked deeper than ever. It was not mere shadow, but the complete absence of light. Shadows have some variation to them, but these were utter darkness, a place where the light could not go. They absorbed all sound as well. Kion scraped his foot on the lip of the pit and it made not the faintest whisper.

"Touch my blade to the shadow," Kithian said. His voice showed no fear, but Kion wavered. What was down in that pit? And how far did it go? What if he lost hold of the blade?

With great care, he lowered his sword into the gash of darkness. When it reached the shadow the tip disappeared. A haze of black wisps rose like smoke along the metal. Instinctively, Kion yanked it back. Dark streaks slid off the blade, slowly, as if composed of thick oil.

"Press in further," Kithian said, the firmness in his voice shoring up Kion's doubts.

Kion dipped the sword once more into the darkness. The shadow rose higher this time. Sinuous tendrils enveloped the blade. More than a quarter of it disappeared before Truesilver struck something solid. The sensation was faint, but it had to be rock. It wasn't a pit after all, though Kion's eyes still struggled to accept what his mind told him.

He drew back the sword. This time he had to exert some force. The blackness clung to it through some mysterious strength, but Kion won out.

"The shadow seeks to draw all things into itself, like its master. I wonder, though, whether it can endure glaivefire."

A hum of expectant energy passed through the sword.

"Glaivefire." Kion spoke the command, his voice rising above the muffling darkness. Red tongues of fire rippled along the silvery metal. He plunged the flaming sword back into the shadow. Rather than rise up to cover the blade, the darkness shrank back this time, as though something alive. The moment the fire touched it, it burst into a puff of ashen smoke and then was gone.

"Unnatural as it is, it is only a mockery. It cannot stand against the true Spark of the Mastersmith," Kithian said, well-pleased.

The others rushed up on either side. Scriff gave a rousing chorus of yips which, through his glaive, Kion understood to mean, *"Nothing can withstand your red fire, not even the deepest shadow."*

"Do it again, lad," Zinder said, undoing the rope around Kion's waist as though he meant to unleash a hound to the hunt. "Banish these blots back into whatever foul malice spewed them forth."

Kion swept his sword into another pool of shadow and it vanished like before.

"You are right, Kithian," Nurien said. *"It cannot endure the presence of the Spark. Tiryn, try the glaivefrost and see if it works the same."*

Tiryn set down the dormant glaive she carried, an ancient double-bladed sword, and unstrapped Rimewinter. The sky-blue gems on the hilt and pommel flashed a welcoming glint when she gripped the handle.

"Glaivefrost." Tiryn said the word in her quiet, unassuming way.

Shards of blue ice flashed along the hilt and streaked into one of the pools. As with Truesilver's fire, the darkness scattered into nothing in an instant and was gone. More shards leapt from the blade, like a swarm of wintry hornets. Between the ice and the flame, the shadows of the plaza were banished as from night to day.

"I don't know what those shadows were, but I'm glad they're gone," Trik said. "I don't have the trembles anymore like Zinder."

"Well, I was never *that* afraid of them," Zinder said.

"The air feels fresher now," Trak said, "more like the way it did on the island."

"You're right," Kion said.

"It's still awfully quiet," Tiryn said, fastening her dagger back under its straps and picking up the other glaive she'd set down.

"Yes, that's odd. This close to his house, I would expect to hear Uncle Chaw's snoring," Trik said.

"Maybe he's already up and making breakfast. He is an early riser," Trak said.

"Let's hope so. I could use a good meal after that long walk across the ice." Trik tried to sound chipper, but the ominous silence was hard to ignore. They may have banished a few shadows, but they still had yet to see a living soul.

"Breakfast? Well, let's get moving then," Zinder said, mustering more enthusiasm than Trik, but not by much.

At a word, Kion quenched Truesilver's fire and they made their way to the door of the kalvar's home. It stood ajar. Kion pushed it open and walked inside. A sparsely furnished room awaited, with a hallway leading away from the other end. In the corner, the hearth stood cold and ashen, as lifeless as the village outside. A squat table surrounded by four barren stools made the room seem all the more empty. Kion stopped in the middle of the wolfskin rugs covering the floor.

"Kalvar?" he shouted. "Are you here?"

A sinking silence was all that came back.

"We brought the swordspeaker back, Uncle," Trik said. "And we found another glaive, too." He had been rehearsing how he would announce their arrival all the way from Tinesplitter, but his words now had little in common with those fair-weather speeches.

Trak stepped into the hall. "I'll see if he's in his room," he said, his voice unsteady. He disappeared into the shadowy passage. There followed a knock upon thick wood. "Kalvar? It's me, Trak. Are you in there?" After a pause, a door creaked open. Trak gave a shuddering sigh. His feet dragged as he returned. "He's not in his room."

They all stared at each other, desperate for answers that would not come. The shadows, the silence, the missing leader. What had happened in Whitewind while they were gone? It had to be Vayd, but how? Trik sniffled and hung his head. Tiryn wrapped an arm around his shoulder.

"We'll find him," she said.

"Uncle Chaw must have left to hunt down that haukmar monster," Trak said.

"Yes." Trik perked up. "That's it. He went after that brute. Uncle's the strongest warrior in Whitewind. If anyone could beat that haukmar it would be him."

Kion withdrew from the others back toward the door. It was hard to shake the feeling that the kalvar wasn't just gone from his house, but gone forever. Vayd was formidable even without Shadowriven, and who could stand against a swordspeaker unless they had a glaive of their own?

"Come. It's no use staying here." Kion motioned for the others to follow him outside.

He set off in another direction. He didn't know where he was headed, but moving was the only thing that made sense. Staying in the house would not yield the answers they sought and would only deepen their sorrow. Kalvar Chaw was a good and wise leader and Kion could not bear to think that he was gone.

Kion and Tiryn banished more shadows as they went, slowly cleansing the village of the mysterious blight. And yet the absence of the shadows did not dispel the deathly silence which gripped this place. Every house they passed and every street they traveled remained as empty and lifeless as the one before.

Until they heard the cry.

It was a soft cry, barely noticeable over the shuffling of their feet upon the pavement. Zinder noticed it first for he had the keenest senses. He raised a hand and the others stopped and listened.

"It's coming from the barn behind that house," he said.

Wordlessly, they made their way to the building. A little stone path led around the side to a wooden structure nearly the same size as the house in front of it. They tried the large double doors, but they held fast, bolted from the inside. The moment the doors shook, the crying stopped.

"Hullo. Is anyone in there?" Zinder said.

No answer came.

"All the barns in Whitewind have a side door," Trak said. "I'll try that." He disappeared around the corner. Then came the sound of wood rattling against wood. "It's locked as well," he said, returning.

"Please open the door," Kion said, raising his voice. "We're here to help." They waited a few more moments in silence. "I am Kion, the swordspeaker. I've returned with my friends."

After another long silence came the soft padding of feet over packed dirt. The wood swayed as the bolt slid away and the door opened just wide enough for two large, tearful eyes to appear out of the darkness. They belonged to someone very small, shorter even than Zinder.

"Hullo there, little one," Zinder said, doffing his cap. "May we come inside?"

Soft as a mouse, the little girl pushed the door open and stepped back into the shadows. The companions slipped inside. Truesilver's gentle light bathed the entrance in flickering shapes. The girl stared at the blade, transfixed, eyes unblinking. Her face was soiled with a mix of dirt and tears. Her hair, which must have been long and beautiful once, was tousled and flecked with bits of straw.

"Hello, there, Pinna," Trak said. "Are you all right?"

Pinna's eyes drifted into a sightless stare and she swayed ever so slightly back and forth, her mind far away.

"Your brother says you're shy, so we understand if you don't want to talk," Trik said. "You look a lot like him." The girl's face tightened at the mention of her brother and she looked down. She was about to cry again. "You're much prettier, of course."

Her head rose and her eyes glinted with an echo of happiness, but it fled as soon as it came.

"What are you doing here, Pinna?" Kion said. When she didn't answer, he added, "Where is your family?"

Her mouth trembled and she burst into tears. Tiryn knelt down and drew her close. Scriff let out a sympathetic whine.

"There, there, little one. It's all right. Cry all you want," Tiryn said. She smoothed her hair with a light touch, just like Mother.

Zinder pulled Kion aside. "The little girl is frightened out of her wits. There's little hope of getting her to tell us what happened in this state. Perhaps after she's had a bit of a rest and a good meal she might feel more like talking."

"Good thinking. Tiryn and Trak, you take Pinna to the kalvar's house and cook up some breakfast for her and the rest of us. Zinder and Trik and I will take Scriff and keep searching for survivors. We'll join you once we're finished."

Little Pinna met his eyes. She struggled to stave off her tears, to be brave before the swordspeaker, but sorrow overmastered her. Kion knew how she felt. Her mother and father were gone, just like his. There was no other reason why she would have locked herself alone in a barn like this. The revelation brought his own loss and his failure to save his mother crashing back against him. The grief was only ever kept an arm's length away at best. But the need to care for Pinna and find the others helped him stem the tide again for now.

"I fear you will find no one left." Nurien's voice cut into his thoughts. *"But make a pass on the outskirts. You may find there what you seek."*

Kion led the others from the barn, Tiryn cradling Pinna in her arms. He hoped Nurien was right. He longed for this nightmare of shadow and sorrow to be over, but some nightmares linger long after waking.

Chapter 2

THE SHEPHERD'S CROOK

The Whitewind of before was no more than a memory. Its people seemed to have melted away with the snow. Kion, Zinder, and Trik passed many houses and everywhere it was the same. Empty echoes were all that remained.

Beyond the blots of shadow, there was no sign that Vayd had ever come to the village. No dead bodies, no wounded. Even the animal pens were empty. Kion made a point to check the kalvar's stables on the edge of the village, but Smokewind and Cyprian, the fine horses which had carried them here, were gone along with all the rest.

"This will be hard on Tiryn," Kion said.

"We can only hope that they fled to safety. Let us search outside the village, as Nurien said. It is always wise to heed the counsel of those gifted with the Sight," Kithian said.

"So that dagger can see the future?" Zinder said in response to Kion passing along Kithian's words.

"That is one of Rimewinter's gifts, yes."

"I'm not sure how I feel about that. It seems like the future would best be left unknown."

"At times that is true. But the Mastersmith does not give his gifts in vain. The challenge comes in using them wisely. There are times to use a gift and times to put it aside."

"I don't want to know the future unless it's a happy one," Trik said. "And right now, I don't see how any of this will turn out to be happy."

"Happy or sad, we cannot avoid it. Let's go see what's on the outskirts," Kion said.

From the stables, it did not take long before they reached the edge of the village. Scraggly rowans grew there. A few precocious buds peppered their limbs. The first glimmerings of dawn could be seen through their branches as the night shed its black scales, exposing patches of gray. Unseen denizens of the forest scuttled in the underbrush. Off in the distance, the shrill piping of a lone nuthatch floated upon the air. The unexpected sounds, after the long night of silence, lent swiftness to their feet and spurred the little party on.

Finding no sign of any villagers, they ventured into the trees on either side of the road. Zinder and Scriff hunted for any trails they might pick up. Trik wandered, aimless, wondering aloud how they expected to track anyone when there wasn't any snow.

"There are ways, my friend," Zinder said, and he pointed out little details to the bewildered young Frin. He noted not only the tracks of several wild animals in the mud, but broken twigs and other telltale traces. Still, none of the tracks had been made by humans.

As they returned from their third foray into the trees, a great tumult erupted from the underbrush. Before they knew what was happening, half a dozen Frindalian warriors surrounded them, long-bladed spears pointed at them from every side. Scriff alone escaped the gauntlet, yipping and whirling around the men and puffing out clouds of white mist which coated the legs of some of the warriors in ice. But it was not thick enough to hinder them. When one of the warriors raised a spear to skewer the animal, Trik cried out.

"Don't hurt him, you oaf! That's Scriff! He's my pet!"

"Stay calm, Gim-dor-ren," Kithian told the frox. *"This is only a misunderstanding. We shall resolve it shortly."* Scriff heeled at the side of his master, though his eyes still flared with a deep and threatening light.

"Drop your sword." One of the men aimed his spear dangerously close to Kion's throat.

"But I—" Kion started to explain, but was cut short when the flat of the spear pressed against his skin.

"I'll only warn you once."

"It would be wise to obey for now."

Kion slowly lowered Truesilver to the ground.

"Minjar, you can't treat the swordspeaker like that," Trik said, batting away the spear in front of him and coming to stand beside Kion.

The warrior menacing Kion gave a start. "Trik O'Trannon? Is that you? You look changed somehow."

"Of course it's me. I'm the personal guide of the swordspeaker and I won't have you treating him like this." Indignant red splotches swelled beneath his skin.

"Swordspeaker? As in the legends?" The man pulled his spear back tentatively. "Don't talk nonsense. If this is another one of your foolish tales, you will answer for it to the kalvar."

"Have you seen the kalvar? We're looking for him—for anyone, actually—and well, I guess we actually did find someone—you! Only we didn't expect to get this sort of a welcome. But I suppose these are strange times we're living in, what with the curse being lifted and all."

The man beside Minjar motioned Trik to silence. He had a hardness to his gaze reminiscent of Dunwik, the other Frin guide who had taken them to Tinesplitter. The others, including Minjar, paid close attention to his words. "Slow down. What do you mean you don't know where the kalvar is? I'll grant that the lifting of the Longwinter is a mystery—that's why we came back early from our hunt—but your words add to the confusion. Tell us—plainly and directly—what has happened since we left the village."

"Right!" Trik slapped the side of his head. "You weren't here when the swordspeaker and his companions came to Whitewind. Well, then, have I got a tale for you!" As briefly as

Trik could manage (which was not that brief at all, for he could not resist interjecting numerous asides and remarks about the "grand happenings," "momentous legends," and "song-worthy feats" performed by the swordspeaker and his companions) he related to them the story of Kion's arrival and near death on the judgment post before they discovered that he was a swordspeaker. Once that unfortunate misunderstanding had been cleared up, Trik and Trak and Dunwik had guided them to Tinesplitter Isle to find Kion and Tiryn's mother. Sadly, their mission had failed, and Dunwik was slain, buried in a fall of ice.

The hunters took the news of his death heavily, though none more than the man next to Minjar.

"I am sorry, Carik," Minjar said.

"Dunwik was a great warrior. It was an honor to know him," Kion said.

Carik's eyes softened and a newfound respect settled there.

"He was my father's sister-son," Carik said. Kion nodded, sharing a moment of quiet understanding with the once dour warrior. "If you were a friend of Dunwik, you have my friendship as well." He gave Kion a deferential nod, which Kion returned.

"Kion Bray, at your service."

"And I'm Zinder Hamryn, his guide and guardian."

Carik regarded Zinder with a suspicious eye, his face growing stern once again. "Are you an actual nyn from the legends as well?"

"Of course. And what of it?" Zinder thrust his pointy beard forward, bristling. "Nyn are quite real I'll have you know."

"Oh, I know what you're thinking," Trik said to Carik. "But don't worry, he's not a sorcerer. Not all nyn are corrupted, apparently."

"Not all—? Why, we're no worse than anyone else I'll have you know. At least we have enough manners not to go sticking spears in people's noses when they're perfectly innocent—and trying to help, I might add!"

"It's all right," Kion said. "I think they understand that we're friends. But let's let Trik finish his story, in case there's any doubt. Go ahead, Trick."

Trik needed no prodding to resume his account, though he began in a somewhat more subdued manner. He recounted the discovery of the glaives in the Tinesplitter mines and how Tiryn had become a swordspeaker. Vayd, the haukmarn leader (he had to explain what haukmarn were as well, calling them "enormous gray sausage-armed brutes with the wits of an ice block"), had found a glaive of his own, though one that chose to rebel against the Mastersmith who forged it. They had followed Vayd back across Tinesplitter Bay on a bridge of ice made by Tiryn's dagger since the bay had unfrozen. But Vayd had proved too swift to catch. When Trik ended by describing the empty village and the strange lingering shadows, alarm broke out upon the faces of the hunters.

"The kalvar is gone? But how? How could one warrior have defeated the whole village?" Carik said.

"We don't know. That's why we've been searching for survivors," Kion said.

Carik stared down at the magnificent blade, glowing softly in the predawn grayness. "A swordspeaker. Can it really be true? I suppose if any sword were a true glaive it would be one like that." Reverently, he picked up the sword and placed it back in Kion's hand. The other men regarded the weapon with mounting wonder.

Carik knelt before Kion and the others followed his example.

"You have our allegiance, Swordspeaker. How may we serve you?"

Kion shifted his feet. "Please, there's no need to bow. We are all equals here."

When they did not rise, or even look up, Trik nudged him and whispered in a way that was far too loud, "It's no use, you have to order them to do it now."

"Very well. All of you, please rise." The Frin obeyed at once, standing taut and ready for the next order. Kion hesitated, but need drew him on. However unnatural it felt to be advising these older men, Whitewind was in trouble and they were the only ones left to try to save it. "The first thing we need to do is find out if any of the other Frin survived."

"I have an idea where they might be if they fled the village," Carik said. "The Shepherd's Crook. That's where we shelter our herds during storms. There are many hidden cracks in the cliffs there which are difficult to find unless you know where to look."

"The Crook! Of course, why didn't I think of that?" Trik said.

They fell in together and marched farther away from the village. Zinder clapped Trik on the back.

"You did well with your story back there. You have the makings of a fine talespinner in you," he said, adding with a sparkle in his eye, "once you get the part about the nyn right."

For the second time that morning, a reddish sheen flooded Trik's face, this time not from indignation, but from pride.

The Shepherd's Crook was the name of an old dried riverbed at the bottom of a sheer gorge. It ran for less than half a mile and traced in rough fashion the shape of its namesake, a staff curved at the end for wrangling wayward animals. Kion and Zinder would never have found it without the help of Carik and his men. Even Trik had forgotten where it was, though he pretended otherwise. For all his vaunted claims, the young Frin was sorely lacking as a guide. But, as Zinder said, he showed promise in other things.

The newly unfrozen gorge was a morass of wet silt and rubble. Puddles dotted the ground everywhere they looked. Several giant stones stood upright in the center of the bed, worn smooth from the time when a river had run through. Nestled in the cliffs along either side, a smooth shelf cut into the layered rock. Toward the back it disappeared into shadow.

Carik whistled calls as they wove their way along the riverbed. His calls sounded very much like the nuthatch they had heard earlier that morning. After the fourth call, a high whistle came in answer. It lacked the skill of Carik's, but was clearly an attempt to mimic one of the dawn-singing birds.

Carik whistled again and another call came in reply.

"Someone's here! Maybe a whole group of someones!" Trik said, surging toward the sound with Scriff at his heel. Trik would have soon outdistanced the rest of the party, but the muddy floor made it impossible for him to break into a run. Scriff padded on ahead with a light step, soon disappearing from view.

The others followed, eyes alert for any sign of the survivors. A moment later, Scriff re-appeared, yelping near the base of the cliffs. A young Frin about Trik's age darted out from one of the dark nooks above the frox.

"Skol! It's you! You're alive!" Trik shouted.

Skol's hair was a lighter shade of brown than most of the Frin. A smattering of freckles brushed his nose. He gave a solemn nod, staring blankly at the company as they clambered onto the rock shelf. Whether from surprise or confusion, or the natural Frin reticence, the boy watched their approach without saying a word.

"Ho there, Skol. It's good to see you," Trik said. "Whatever happened, it's all right now. We've got the swordspeaker here, and Carik and his hunters."

"The same fear haunts his eyes as the little girl's. They have both seen something they cannot forget," Kithian said.

"Greetings, Skol," Carik said, his tone far more serious. "The swordspeaker and his friends tell us that the village is abandoned. Can you tell us what drove you to the Crook?"

Skol took a moment to gather his strength before answering.

"We fled here to escape from the shadows…Most of the children came…" He spoke slowly and in soft tones, still half-dazed by whatever it was that he had seen.

"We found your sister. She was hiding in your barn," Trik said.

Skol's head snapped up. "You've seen Pin? Is she all right?"

"Yes! She's safe and warm at the kalvar's house."

Skol choked back a cry of relief, tears hovering at the edges of his eyes. "Thank you for taking care of her. We were separated when we…during our escape."

"You did well to come here," Carik said. "But where are the others who fled with you?"

Skol spoke back toward the caves. "It's all right. You can come out. It's Carik and a hunting party, and the swordspeaker and his friend are here too."

Dozens of children slipped out from the deep shadows behind Skol, venturing out with bewildered steps. The terror upon their faces gave way to relief and awe as they came into the light. Most could not keep their eyes from Kion's glowing crimson blade.

"And Trik! I'm here too, and so glad to see you all! Skol, this looks—this looks like nearly all the children of the village."

"Yes, all but a few who got lost along the way," Skol said. "Like Pin."

"We'll find the others," Kion said.

"Skol." Carik addressed him with care, but also firmness. "I read much pain in your eyes, but you must be strong and tell us what you know in order to understand the nature of the threat against our people. What happened in the village?"

Skol took a long, difficult breath, his mouth quivering. Another boy came to stand alongside him.

"I can tell them," he said.

"No, it's my place," Skol said, forcing himself to grow calm. "I led us here. I…I can tell them what happened." He took one more deep breath. "A gray giant came in the middle of the night. It…attacked without warning. I never saw it, but some of the others said that it looked like a man, but was taller and stronger and with cunning eyes, like a wolf's. The warning bells rang out.

Our fathers went to fight and our mothers fled with us from the village, but…they didn't make it. Sheets of darkness, darker than the darkest night, came upon us. They washed over us and when they had passed our mothers were gone. Some of the children who had been in their arms fell to the ground and were hurt. We didn't know what to do so we picked them up and ran as hard as we could. Once we were far enough away to catch our breath, I remembered the Shepherd's Crook and thought we would be safe there. We thought the gray monster had left, but weren't sure, so we stayed here and waited for our parents to come and find us until…until you came."

The only sounds as he finished were of children sobbing as they relived the terrors of the night they had passed through. Many did not cry at all; they only stared unblinking at the swordspeaker and his company. But their eyes were lost, seeing neither him nor anything else within the Shepherd's Crook. They were trapped in a dark prison of memories which no child should ever have to endure.

"The evil of Malix has only deepened with time. I do not pretend to understand what happened here, but clearly this is his doing. We must find Vayd and Shadowriven and put an end to his madness." Kithian's words were honed to an edge.

"Shar's dome, what in the Four Wards is happening?" Zinder said, taking his hat in his hand, his eyes as dull as the gray rock walls of the gorge.

Chapter 3

A NEW KALVAR

The fane had fallen. Antirith stood over his body, defending it. The fanewardens and their archblades fought bravely beside him, selling their lives to the last. That is what I saw as our company burst forth from the gates. I often wonder if I still would have made the charge down the Winding Rise if I had known what I know now. If I had known how petty the nobles and highgilds could be. If I had known how much they care for their own power and influence above the good of the people. If I had known how they value gold more than the lives of the men who defend their lands.

Once I believed that we fought for the Four Wards, for the dream and the hope of seeing it restored to its former greatness. Perhaps under Fane Galbraith that was true. But what do we fight for now, now that so much blood has been spilt and so many have gone down to the grave? The leaders of our armies fight now for prestige, for a higher seat at the table during the fane's feasts or a private audience to curry more favor. I could not save Antirith that day at Roving and I cannot save the Four Wards now. Not from the vultures who roost within its gilded halls. Our greatest enemy is not the haukmarn, it lies within. At times it is all too much. At times I grow weary of it all.

The entry in Strom's journal ended there. Kion was about to turn the page to discover how Strom had found a reason to keep fighting, but Tiryn called to him from down the hall.

"Hurry, Kion, they're starting to gather outside."

Kion closed the worn leather-bound book and stepped out into the hall. He would have to find the answer to his questions some other time. For Strom had found the will to fight on in spite of his doubts. Kion had seen it in the dying bladewarden's eyes. Strom had gone to that death willingly, spilling his blood in one final sacrifice not only for his men, but for all of the Four Wards. Kion would need that same clarity and strength to face what now lay before him.

He greeted Tiryn with a light embrace and strapped True-silver to his waist.

"Has Zinder already gone?" Kion said.

"He doesn't like to be late," Tiryn replied.

"That's a kind way of saying he's impatient." Kion enjoyed a brief chuckle at his friend's expense.

"Twice the reason for him to go early, then."

Tiryn wore a teal tunic and trousers and a black leather vest, which the Frin had given her. Rimewinter hung in a polished leather sheath across her chest. Zinder and one of the older Frin had worked to craft it the day before. The leather had a rich beaver-brown hue and was fitted with silver framing.

She tugged nervously on the ends of her shoulder-length braids. "Do you know what you plan to say?"

"Honestly, no. I wish Kithian would just tell me the words so I could repeat them."

"Your own words will be more than enough," Kithian said.

Kion paused with his hand on the door handle. He ought to have taken encouragement from his glaive's words, but found his doubts hard to shake. The village of Whitewind needed wisdom in this hour. They needed a true leader, like Strom. All Kion had done was best Vayd once in battle, and then only because of Truesilver's fire. He was no bladewarden. He had not even fought in the Warding army.

"Kithian's right. The words will come," Tiryn said.

That was just what Mother would have said. Echoes of her presence sounded everywhere he turned. The world was cold and hollow without her. No amount of warmth or goodness could fill that emptiness. It seemed impossible to go on at times.

But go on he must. He swept aside his dark thoughts and forced his way into the shining sun beyond the threshold.

The plaza outside swelled with people. The village had not met like this since Vayd's attack. Besides the survivors they'd found in Shepherd's Crook, they'd discovered another four children hiding in empty houses and barns like Pinna. Not a single child remained unaccounted for. Yet, the sight of them milling about, talking and smiling amidst the pleasant rays of the newly restored summer, could not erase the haunting absence of those who were lost. Only a few older boys and girls, and the men from Carik's party, passed Tiryn in height. The rest were mere children. Vayd had captured or slaughtered all the others, down to the last man and woman. It was unthinkable that a lone haukmar could have killed them all, even one with a glaive. But neither could he have taken them all prisoner. The shadows may have vanished, but a pall of secrets still cloaked the village.

How could these children go on without knowing their parents' fate? At least Kion knew his mother and father were dead. These children would live in the shadow land of uncertainty for years to come, clinging to a hope that would slowly wither and die with each passing day.

Trik and Trak ran up as soon as they caught sight of Kion.

"Swordspeaker," they said in unison and gave exaggerated, awkward bows.

"We're ready to hear what you've decided," Trak said.

"You know, some of the older girls will be of marriageable age soon," Trik said.

Trak swatted him on the shoulder. "Trik! Don't be so forward. The swordspeaker has to make his own decisions. I'm sure he'll make the right one."

"Yes, well, thank you for the advice," Kion said with a shake of the head. He never had to wonder what Trik was thinking. "Now, where is Zinder? I'd like him to be there when I address the village."

"Oh, he's over there in the middle of the crowd, telling the story of your battle with the dreadwulfs for about the fifteenth time," Trak said. "Did he really jump into the jaws of one of those beasts?"

"He did. He may not look it, but Zinder is braver than any of us when the hard hour comes. Tell him the time for stories has ended, though. We need to get started."

The twins ran off, weaving recklessly through the children, but managing not to bowl any of them over.

Skol and Pinna came rushing up right as the twins left. Pinna gave Tiryn all the embrace her little arms could offer and Skol made a sincere bow. He had not left his sister's side since he came back to the village.

"Swordspeaker, Pin has something she'd like to give you and your sister—sorry, I forgot that both of you are swordspeakers." Skol's eyes dropped to the ground at the mistake.

Tiryn waved away his concerns. "That's fine. I still don't think of myself that way most of the time either. It's all so very new."

Skol managed a nod and nudged his sister forward. She held out two tiny hands balled into fists.

"This is for sending the shadows away," Pinna said. Her wispy voice was as tender and dear as her glimmering brown eyes. Even after Skol returned, she rarely spoke, so it was a treat to hear her now. She turned up her hands and opened them with great care, revealing a bunched up leather cord in each. She gave one to Kion and the other to Tiryn. Unraveling the cords revealed a piece of driftwood hanging from each, carved in the shapes of their weapons: a sword for Kion and a dagger for Tiryn. The shapes were rough, but the wood had been sanded smooth. They were surprisingly artful for having been fashioned by one so young.

"Oh, they're lovely," Tiryn said as she and Kion draped them about their necks. "Just like the one who made them."

Pinna hid her face in her brother's shirt, but peeked out with one eye, her face a-flush.

"Wherever I battle, I shall have this around my neck," Kion said. "And it will make me braver, remembering the brave little one who made it." No treasure in the fane's palace could have been worth more than this little trinket, born amidst sorrow and loss.

Carik and Minjar arrived and Tiryn gave Pinna one last embrace and Kion saluted them. The children bowed and slipped back into the crowd.

Carik carried with him the kalvar's staff of office, its beads and feathers and bits of fur dangling from the carved antlers branching out from the head.

"Swordspeaker, it is an honor as always," Carik said.

"A true honor," Minjar said.

Kion cast a quick glance at the pommel of his sword. He endured their show of respect knowing it was Truesilver whom they were honoring as much as him.

"Thank you. I'm just waiting for Zinder before I begin. Ah, here he is. What's the point of being early if you don't plan to start on time?"

"The point, apparently, is to wait for stragglers like you," Zinder said. "Besides, a good story waits for no one. I couldn't leave them hanging without the ending." He tweaked his tall wool cap. The day was far too hot for such attire, but Zinder said that he wanted to wear it anyway since it was in the "traditional Frin style."

"And I'm sure none of the retelling involved making your part come out better than it actually was," Kion said. There was nothing to take the edge off his nerves like a good back-and-forth with his dearest friend.

"I almost died, I'll have you remember! I think that earns me a little artistic freedom." Zinder rose as tall as he could, which wasn't much. "Besides, what's the point of telling a story if it doesn't get better each time around?"

"Well, I'm sure the children enjoyed it. But I have my own

story to tell now, and I don't think it will be quite as well received."

Kion looked out across the aimless crowd. The children still chattered on. Some played with Scriff, tossing a ball and cheering as the enchanting little frox raced to fetch it. The ball got more and more icy with each trip until it barely fit in his mouth. The children marveled at the way the creature's dark eyes glowed blue whenever he drew near the glaives. Others played a game involving the arranging of stones upon pavement inside lines of chalk. Still others sat and enjoyed the sweet candy sticks Tiryn and some of the older girls had made yesterday. Despite all that had happened, they were still children. Yet, without parents to guide and protect them, they would not stay children for long. Would they still know how to laugh a year from now? Would they even be alive? How would a village of children survive?

"It's time," Kion told Carik.

Carik raised the staff and called out, "Silence! Silence!" The children quieted with remarkable swiftness. "Hear the sword-speaker's words."

Kion gripped the handle of his sword.

"They will understand. They are far stronger than they appear," Kithian said.

It was one thing to know what to do, quite another to do it.

Kion took the staff from Carik and stamped it on the ground, the sign given before a kalvar addressed his people.

"People of Whitewind. Most of you are children. And yet you find yourselves where no children should be, bereft of father and mother. I, too, have lost my parents. My father died when I was the same age as some of you. And my mother died a few days ago. The grief is still fresh." He paused, gripping his sword all the more fiercely. He had not anticipated saying these things. The words came out unbidden. But when you did not know what to say, it was best to speak what was on your heart. "If I could bring my parents back, I would. If I could bring your parents back I would. But there are things even a swordspeaker cannot do.

"You did not ask for the burden of these losses. But you are not alone in what you face. Nor was I in making my decision. I am not as wise as Kalvar Chaw. But I have drawn upon the wisdom of both Truesilver and Rimewinter, Tiryn and Zinder, in making my decision. And we are all in agreement.

"Your village needs a new kalvar. You need a leader who will guide you through the darkness to brighter days. You have suffered a terrible tragedy, yes, but there are fair tidings as well. The Longwinter has ended. Summer has returned. Is it not comforting to feel the warmth upon your cheeks, to cast aside your heavy coats, and listen to the trickle of water running through the streams once again? Let these be signs to you that the time of shadow has passed. A new day has come to the land of the Frin."

Here he paused. The anticipation was so bright upon their faces he could scarcely look at them.

"Sadly, I cannot share in the coming days with you." An audible gasp arose from among the older children, whose dreams of being led by one of the swordspeakers from the legends vanished in that instant. "Though Carik and the others have asked me to stay, the enemy who desolated your village roams free. And he will not stop at the destruction of one village. He will ravage all of the Four Wards if left unchecked. He must be defeated. And only a swordspeaker can do this. Or perhaps two." He shared a quick look with Tiryn, who gave a little shudder, but met his eyes with a quiet strength.

"After much thought, I have chosen Carik as your new kalvar." Kion expected some reaction from the crowd, or at least from Carik, but the look upon the hunter's face was the same as the one on most of the other faces: grim resignation.

Kion placed the staff in Carik's hands. "Your cousin, Dunwik, served us well on Tinesplitter Isle. I believe the same courage, strength, and wisdom runs in your blood. You will lead

Whitewind into the world beyond winter, into a time of seasons and change."

"It is the best choice," Kithian said.

"It is the only choice," Nurien said.

Trik and Trak wrapped an arm around each other and Trik sniffled and wiped his nose. They had not spoken of the loss of their uncle, Kalvar Chaw, but that perhaps more than anything showed how deeply they were hurting, for the twins were rarely at a loss for words.

"Now, don't be sad, it's time to show your gratefulness and loyalty to the new kalvar!" Zinder let out a tremendous whistle between his teeth and began to clap and whoop and holler. Tiryn joined in, but her clapping was soundless by comparison. The other hunters added respectful applause, looking unsure of themselves. Trik and Trak managed solemn nods, but none of the children made so much as a sound. Perhaps the Frindalians expressed their approval in other ways. Knowing how quiet they tended to be, perhaps they were not accustomed to showing approval at all. Zinder soon caught on to the fact that his enthusiasm was not shared by those around him and his clapping and clamor died a red-faced death.

"My friends and I will leave on the morrow," Kion said. "But I promise you this. We will hunt down Vayd Mokán and avenge your fathers and mothers. We will drive this shadow from our lands. It falls to you now, children, to grow up quickly. Your new kalvar and the village of Whitewind will need all that you can give in the days ahead."

Carik knelt before Kion, his gaze clear and sharp, as a hunter who at last spots his prey after a long and weary trail. The rest of the Frin knelt with him.

"I must confess that I had hoped otherwise, yet in my heart I knew that you would choose this path," Carik said. "I am no swordspeaker, but I do love my people. I will serve them as best I can and together we will rebuild our village without fear, knowing that you and your sister go to make these lands safe. Only one thing I ask of you as you set out on your journey."

"Whatever you ask, Kalvar, I will do if I can," Kion said.

Carik made a tight fist, and pressed it against Kion's chest. "Bring this monster Vayd to justice. May your vengeance be swift and final."

"That I will do, Kalvar. You have my word."

"May it be even as this man says," Kithian said. *"Justice swift and final."*

"And yet I fear it may be otherwise. Justice is often long in the coming," Nurien said. *"If it comes at all."*

Chapter 4

INTO THE SUMMERLANDS

Their last departure from Whitewind had taken place upon ice-bound docks with the whole village out to see them off. Families had stood huddled together, fathers and mothers standing with their children along the frozen shore. This time they had gathered in the plaza outside the Feasting Hall. The whole village had come as before, but it was only a splintered fragment of what it had been. Instead of their mothers and fathers, the children clung to dolls and trinkets and other echoes of their once unmarred innocence. And they clung to each other. Most of all they did that.

Dunwik's three children stood at the front along with Skol and Pinna. The five of them had been friends from birth and that friendship had only deepened with the loss of their parents. Dunwik's two boys often hunted with Skol, and Pinna treated his three-year-old daughter like her very own sister.

The impact of Dunwik's death upon his children had been lessened by the fact that they were not the only ones to lose their parents. Shared suffering lightens even the hardest burdens. And yet, for Kion, bringing the news of their father's death had only deepened the tragedy. For it is one thing to see a man suffer a needless death, struck down when so much of his life lay yet before him, but to have to tell of that death to those who loved and needed him most only multiplied the bitterness of the loss.

Trik, Trak, Scriff, and Kalvar Carik stood near the front as well. In them lay Whitewind's best hope for the future. Since the day of Kion's decision to leave, Carik had taken the mantle of kalvar with both hands. In that short time he had already appointed several others to lead the children in the doing and making of the various things they would need to survive. Minjar was put in charge of forming new bands of hunters and training them in the way of the spear and the bow. Another of Carik's companions gathered groups of children to forage for herbs and food. One man took on the training of several of the older children at the smithy. Zinder joined him, teaching them all many new and marvelous things. Trik and Trak, though not as old as the hunters, were put in charge of woodcutting and went with a few of the taller children to fell trees and replenish the village's stores of wood. And on and on it went. Whitewind became a flurry of activity after the terrible silence following Vayd's assault. Fishing, tailoring, tanning, gardening, cooking, washing, carpentry; the fresh winds of industry blew away much of the gloom afflicting the village.

Kion had spent most of the previous afternoon with Carik, discussing the defense of Whitewind and what lay ahead for the small village. The Noathryn would eventually come now that the Longwinter had ended. Carik decided to lay up supplies in Shepherd's Crook and escape there should invaders come. For there was no hope of overcoming a force of any size with the few warriors they had left. For now, the Noathryn aggression would be focused eastward, toward Inris, as they fought alongside the haukmarn to conquer that land. But if the war ended in the Warding army's defeat, Whitewind would not long remain free.

Kion sounded Carik on the possibility of the Frin passing through Noath into southern Inris and leaving their troubled land behind, but this Carik staunchly refused. Whitewind was their home. They had been there before the Noathryn and they would live and die there, no matter what befell. Kion took comfort knowing that, though Whitewind's light flickered weakly, surrounded by a nest of shadows, it had not vanished altogether.

"While there is life there is always hope," Kithian reminded them.

The children wiped away tears as they waved good-bye. Trik and Trak made no effort to hide theirs. The two held on to Kion, Tiryn, and Zinder for as long as they could, unwilling to part.

"We'll never forget you," Trak said.

"And…and…" Trik struggled to get the words out through his sobs. "And we'll make sure your legend lives on. You're the most…the greatest…"

"The greatest heroes of the age." Trak finished what his brother could not.

"You are heroes in your own right," Kion said. "One day you will both be great warriors like Dunwik. Grow strong and defend your people."

"And keep at it with those stories of yours," Zinder said.

Tiryn joined them in their tears, but Zinder stood with his mouth shut tight and his lips aquiver. Kion alone remained grave and outwardly unmoved. He would not allow sadness to take hold, for fear that he might waver in his resolve. For they had to leave; they could not stay.

"Take care of Scriff," Tiryn said, ruffling the frox's fur amidst pleasant growls. Scriff nuzzled her cheek and danced and yipped around her, attempting to lighten her mood. Scriff had grown dear to her in the short time they had been together, with Rimewinter helping her speak to the frox.

"Do not fret," Scriff said. *"I will guard my masters until you return."*

The frox's words only made her cry all the harder and his breath turned the tears into glittering blue gems upon her cheeks.

The Maid of Ice sometime appears
Her face a-glitter with diamond tears

The words of the Frin song drifted through Kion's memory.

He glanced down at the glaive Tiryn wore on her belt. His sister was not meant for war. Even if she had wanted to fight, or the leaders of the army allowed her to, she had no skill in battle. How then would she be able to help him defeat Vayd? Yet, he could not leave her behind. Furrow was gone. Mother and Father were gone. Where else was she supposed to go? As Zinder had told him once, the safest place in the world would be at his side. But if Kion went off to war, that would no longer be true.

"The twins are right," Carik said, laying his hands upon Kion's shoulders. "You are living, breathing legends and the wind will carry your deeds back to us. When you have brought peace back to the Four Wards, we will rejoice along with you."

The three companions took up their things. The villagers had given them a handcart which Kion would use to pull their supplies. Besides food, bedrolls, and Zinder's tools, it carried the oil which Truesilver needed for its fire. The oil added considerable weight, as did Kion's armor and the dormant glaives. What would happen with the other weapons only time would tell.

As they turned to leave, Skol's voice arose in song. He was joined by Pinna and Dunwik's children at first, and then the others.

There is a place along the shore
A place of wonder, a place of lore
It sits within a wooded dell
The land wherein the Frin do dwell

Long forgot they do not forget
The world may change but hope lives yet
In legends which the Frin hold dear
Guarded down throughout the years

Should you find the land of the Frin
Their stories you will enter in
And fables that once seemed untrue
Before your eyes will live anew

The Frin still dwell beyond the hills
The world may change, but hope lives still
Though memory fades they linger yet
Though long forgotten they do not forget

As the song drifted over the rooftops, Zinder could hold his tears no longer. The pleasant voices lifted high and true, lighter than air, warm as a hearth fire. Knowing the brokenness carried in that melody made the sorrow of leaving all the more keen. Zinder and Tiryn could barely see the road ahead. They wandered, dream-like and dismayed, into the land beyond the village, into the world known to the Frindalians as the Summerlands.

How dear those children had become to them in a few short days. And yet, how fragile was their fate. They had lost so much. Long, lonely nights awaited them, dark nights, uncertain nights. Nights without consolation, without relief. Nights of tears and terror. Nights ruled by that most cruel of all questions, "why"?

Kion knew what lay ahead for them. He had walked that road before and he walked it again now. Though he held back his tears when he said good-bye, and held them even as the children and the village became lost from sight, as the last notes of the song faded from hearing his resistance broke at last and the tears came, fierce and merciless as the wind. Tears for Whitewind and tears for its children.

Whitewind had been the closest thing to home the little company had known since Furrow burned to the ground.

Leaving it now was all the more troubling because they had no home to go to and no prospect of finding one anytime soon. Their home now was the weary wandering of the open road. No hearth awaited them there. No stout walls to protect them and keep the elements at bay.

Silence reigned long over the company, but in time, the wind dried their tears and the fair sun coaxed their downcast spirits back into some semblance of life. A long journey lay ahead, perhaps one fraught with many perils and trials. Without horses, they had little hope of overtaking Vayd, but they hoped to pick up his trail somewhere in Noath. Kion gazed down the rough dirt road before them. Rowans lined either side, their limbs newly awakened from the long sleep of winter. A red-breasted bird flashed through the canopy, too swift to mark its kind. Sunlight dripped through the trees, a sweet nectar which brought nourishment to the long neglected land below. The return of summer was at least one turn in their favor.

"What if we can't pick up Vayd's trail?" Zinder said. He wore a pine-green cap with a flap at the back to keep the sun off his neck. An ashen cloak hung from his shoulders, framing his vest and cloud-gray trousers. The neutral colors were not his usual style, but when traveling, fashion gave way to practical concerns, even for someone of Zinder's sensibilities.

"Then we make for Dunach Fortress," Kion said. "We may need to head there in any case. They will have horses and may even aid us in our search." But even as he said it, he was not so sure. He had promised the varlance of Dunach Fortress that he would return and join the Warding forces once the search for his mother had ended. Once he set foot back there, his path would no longer be his own. But there would be time to consider such things later. If they could find and defeat Vayd quickly, the war would end before he ever reached that place.

Tiryn's brow darkened at the mention of Dunach, but she did not speak of it for now. "I do miss Smokewind and Cyprian," she said. "What do you think happened to them? I can see why Vayd would attack the people of the village, but the animals? What could he have wanted with them?"

"*Remember the dim-touched creatures we met on Tinesplitter Isle,*" Kithian said. "*It was never known how Talinyon and Malix created them. That it was through some twisting of the Spark was clear, but it was thought that it would take time in the defiling. The Mastersmith's work is not easily marred. But in truth, we do not fully understand how Malix warps these poor creatures, nor how swiftly he is able to do it.*"

"Shar's dome, are you saying that the axe created and commands whatever beasts of the night are out there?" Zinder said.

Nurien answered, "*Indeed, it was out of fear that Malix would return with a fresh army of the dim-touched that I convinced the other glaives to help me imprison him in ice. The Four Wards were still devastated by the War of the Shattering and I foresaw that until Malix was finally and forever defeated, he would only grow stronger and the armies of men weaker.*"

"*Ill-fated as your course proved to be, there was reason to your fears. Had Malix but possessed the patience to wait before he struck, it is likely his armies would have overwhelmed the Four Wards' defenses and even the swordspeakers would not have been enough to oppose him.*"

"But we don't even know for sure that Malix did anything to the horses," Kion said, seeking to instill what hope he could. "It may be that he only captured the animals or drove them away in fear."

"Whatever he did, I'm sure it was vile and loathsome," Zinder said.

"Perhaps there is a way that it can be undone."

"*You are right to hope, glaivebond,*" Kithian said. "*Though evil may not be wholly mended, good will always come from the attempt.*"

The crystals in Rimewinter's hilt glimmered, as if Nurien considered adding words of her own, but she said nothing.

"Malix was defeated before. He will know defeat again. But

just now, I feel the same as you, Tiryn. I miss Smokewind and Cyprian. I was looking forward to speaking with them more now that I've come so far in the beast speech."

"Aye, they were fine animals, those two. But I imagine after lugging that cart a few dozen more miles, you'd settle for a mule," Zinder said.

"I miss Crusty, too," Tiryn said.

"There's not a day goes by that I don't." Zinder shook his head and scuffed his boot in the dirt. And in somber thought, the three companions trudged their way eastward, the day crisp and clear, but the road as unsure and treacherous as if they were still walking on ice.

Chapter 5

GHOST TRAIL

They passed through the gap in the hills between Noath and the land of the Frin late that afternoon. A strong wind arose, blustery and harsh, to beat against the sallow plains. Kion sought to press on past dark, but Zinder called a halt after his hat had flown off his head for the third time. They slept that night in the open with only the cart for protection.

By the next morning, the wind had abated and Zinder no longer had to fear for the fate of his headwear. But the rugged plains made for slow going. The cart grew heavier and heavier with each mile. It bounced and bobbled over the clumped and caked terrain. Clods clung to the wheels. After a while, the wheels were more dirt than wood and they had to stop and knock the clods free.

At midday, they rested in the Yemmel Grove. Here they partook once more of the bulging purple hourglass fruit which hung from the trees. This delicacy and the inviting shade caused them to tarry longer than they otherwise would have. But despite lingering for more than an hour, they never saw the amiable shepherd Haiza or his brescan herd whom they'd met on their last trip through the grove.

The following day brought them in sight of a whiff of steam to the north, deep within the Hot Spring Hills. That is what they called the heather-covered rises to the north, though none of them knew the actual names of the places within these unfamiliar lands. Few Inrisians ever traveled here and the few towns marked on the map Varlance Aonar had given them lay far from their present path. Drawing near the hills, they came across a trampled pathway. On their previous journey, they'd hidden from Noathryn slavers traveling this same road. It must have rained several days ago and quickly dried, for the ground here was crusted over and unworn, as though the road had not seen much use since then.

Zinder stopped and made a curious sound. "How unusual," he said, twiddling the end of his knife-point mustache.

They were due for another rest so Kion lowered the handles of the cart.

"What do your sharp eyes tell you?"

"A very strange tale. Unless I am mistaken, a large band of booted men came through here not more than three or four days ago."

"What's so unusual about that?" Tiryn said. "I'm sure many bands travel along this path. It's the fastest way north or south for miles around."

"Yes, but that's not all." Zinder teased his mustache from a knife into a needle. "They came here, but they didn't go on. The tracks just stop. They don't even leave the path. People don't just stop and go nowhere. It's hard to imagine, but it looks as though close to forty men came here three or four days ago and simply vanished."

Kion did not have Zinder's skill at reading tracks, but there were an awful lot of them both here and to the south. To the north the prints were faded and older and far fewer. His mind went back to the silent village of Whitewind on the night they had arrived.

"Is it possible that Vayd came here and did the same thing he did in Whitewind?"

"It does strike a fellow as frighteningly similar."

"But there are no shadows the way there were in Whitewind," Tiryn said.

"It may be that the shadows only endure for a time," Nurien said.

"From what you've told me, these haukmarn can cover half again as much in a day as a man on foot. If Vayd did not slow—and we have no reason to believe that he would—he would have passed this way four days ago if he was headed east."

"The same time Zinder judges these tracks were made," Kithian said.

"But those who traveled this road would have been Noathryn. They are haukmarn allies. Why would Vayd do to them what he did to the Frin?"

"Evil is only ever a half step from betrayal," Kithian said. *"Now that Vayd has a glaive, his purposes for the Noathryn may have changed."*

"That monster is getting more foul-hearted by the day—no, by the hour!" Zinder yanked his mustache so hard that he winced.

"Evil desires are only limited by the ability to perform them. No one is as evil as they could be, nor as good. Now that Vayd possesses Shadowriven his power to do evil has only magnified."

"No doubt Malix's counsel fans the flames of those desires and gives him fresh designs," Nurien said.

Kion knelt and fingered a dirt clump, part of one of the dozens of tracks stamped in the path. Zinder's keen eyes had left them with another terrible mystery. Was Vayd truly killing all of these people? There were no signs of battle to speak of. Did he take them unawares? Or through some clever trick? The more they learned of Vayd's deeds, the darker the shadows surrounding him grew.

The fourth night from Whitewind they slept beneath one of the ancient hovar trees. These solitary giants, each of whose trunks could have formed the masts of a whole fleet of ships, rose with unchallenged majesty over the small moss-coated islands dotting the tufted plains of central Noath. They were as far above common trees as oak, birch, and walnuts were above the measure of men. Though as fir trees they offered little shade, their size invoked a sense of awe in the same way as the fortresses at Dunach and Roving. The mere sight of them made the whole world larger. Walking beneath such lofty creations reminded Kion that there would always be things far greater and more enduring than whatever terrors threatened the land of men and beasts. Wars might rage and countries fall, but the mountains, the seas, these great pillars of living wood, they would endure. They were the fabric that wove together the ravelings of wayward men.

Kion's eyes fluttered open the next morning, gazing toward branches that seemed to soar a league above him. His calloused hands and sore limbs throbbed with the memory of the previous day's journey. Another hard day of travel awaited. He woke Tiryn and only then noticed that Zinder was missing.

"Have you seen Zinder?"

Tiryn was still half-asleep and shook her head with a yawn. When Kion repeated the question, the alarm in his voice forced her fully awake.

"Perhaps he went to do some hunting," she said.

"I'm up here, you tiny little dreamers!" Zinder called out. "Now who's the short one?"

Kion had missed him before, but sure enough, there was Zinder, perched at a dizzying height, clinging to the smooth saddle-brown wood of the hovar with only two pickaxes, the boot teeth on his shoes, and a headful of foolishness.

"Fire and ice, Zinder, have you lost your senses? What are you doing up there?"

"You have no rope! You could fall at any moment," Tiryn said.

"Ah, never you worry, lass. In my youth I *lived* in the trees, though never one this enormous. Look at this beast, just look at it! This is the only place in the world they grow. Something like this, well, it's just made to climb. I may never see another."

Kion laughed, half from fear, half from the absurd bravery of his friend. How Zinder had the energy for such reckless feats after walking so many miles under the unforgiving sun, he couldn't say.

There was no laughter for Tiryn. She bit her lip and fiddled with the ends of her braids. "It's not safe, Kion. If he goes any higher, he'll disappear."

Zinder let out a rakish chuckle. "Oh, my. Well, would you look at that?" His high-pitched voice carried over their heads.

"What is it? Have you spotted something?" Kion said.

"Why, yes. I can see the fane's closet from up here," Zinder said. "And he has terrible taste in clothes!"

"If you're going to risk your neck, at least tell us something worthwhile. The fane's fashion tastes won't help us find Vayd."

Zinder twisted around to gaze out across the wide Noathryn landscape, shielding his eyes against the rising sun. He stared long across the slumbering countryside before speaking again. "I can't see Dunach. It may be too far away or it may be locked in the haze covering the eastern plains. Of what I can see, there is scarcely a living thing that stirs, only a few flocks of birds wheeling to the south."

Noath was said to be even more unpeopled than Inris, with most of the towns scattered along the shores, but the absence of beasts was troubling.

"You don't even see any shepherds or cattle?" Tiryn said.

"No cattle, no bresca. It's all empty or hazed over. A giant yellow quilt of the unknown. It is beautiful, but the loneliest beauty you could ever imagine," Zinder said.

"Remember the way the frost fox acted before we arrived in Whitewind?" Kithian said. *"He skittered about, sniffing for something. He said the air had lost all smell. It made him feel the way a human might if he lost his sight or hearing. The animals may have fled at Shadowiven's approach and not yet returned."*

"At least we know there's no danger of running into Noathryn soldiers," Tiryn said.

"Let's hope that holds true for the rest of the journey. All right, Zinder. Enough playing squirrel. Come down before you fall and break your neck."

"Yes, well, I've had my fun and I'll be a good nyn from now on, smith's honor," Zinder said.

While he scampered down, Tiryn and Kion finished loading up the cart, though Kion did most of the work. Tiryn was too distracted watching Zinder's descent, making sure he got down in one piece.

Once the packing was done, Tiryn redressed the bandage she'd put on Kion's hand the day before. He had opened up a painful cut on his left palm. She coated it with some grettlespice ointment to ease the pain and wrapped it up tight. The ointment had a burnt smell to it, but the relief far outweighed the unpleasant odor. Tiryn had one of her braids in her mouth as she worked.

"You're still shaken over Zinder. He's down now. No need to keep worrying," Kion said.

Tiryn hesitated, but then, succumbing to Kion's insistent stare, she took the braid out. "No, it's not Zinder. It's Varlance Aonar. I've been thinking about the promise you made to him at Dunach. You said you would fight for him when you returned."

"Yes. I have to stop Vayd and stop this war."

"I know…It's just that…you know what happened to Father in the war. And now Mother's gone, too. I'm afraid you might not come back."

Kion took Tiryn's hand in his. "I can understand that. But Mother and Father did not have a glaive. Truesilver will protect me. And someone has to fight this war. Aonar and Roardin and Endrith are all risking their lives for Warding. I put this off to try to save Mother. But she's gone and now I have to fight. I only hope it's not too late."

Tiryn went back to chewing on her braids. "I know someone has to fight. I just wish it didn't have to be you. I won't know a moment's peace until you return. Something tells me this war is going to break my heart, and there aren't many pieces left to break."

Kion wrapped an arm around her shaking frame.

"Did you have another vision? Have you seen something that I ought to know?" he said.

"No, it's just that I can't help but worry. After all that's happened…Oh, Kion, I miss her so much."

The words stung, plunging sharp and deep. He missed Mother, too. Their family was being whittled down so that what had once been a towering hovar was no more than two naked roots, exposed to harsh and bitter winds. The old life with all its golden joys and ringing laughter had fallen away.

Tiryn was right to fear. Even with Truesilver, he was not invincible. He might not come back. And then their family would be nothing more than a memory. The days on the Tors, the days of wandering among the hawthorns with his sheep, of hearing his father's pipes by the fire, of opening the cottage door to his mother's warm smile and the smell of her cream potato soup, of sneaking up behind Tiryn and frightening her half to death while she was hard at work in the garden…so much had already faded. Nothing could bring Father and Mother back, or Furrow, or the life they had lost. But though much was gone, they still had each other. And if Kion fought in the war, he would be risking that. Yet was that not a risk worth taking? To save the world for some might mean losing it for others.

"Aonar is a good leader and a good man. If not, he would not have let me go in search of Mother. The Warding army needs my blade. Think of all those who still have their mother. Should I not fight for them, though mine is lost? Think of Endrith's mother and Aunt Lizet and a thousand people we don't know and will never meet. I have to fight so that they don't suffer the same fate we have. You understand that, don't you, Tiryn?"

Tiryn gave no reply. She only trembled all the more.

Seeing the somber air that had fallen over the two of them, Zinder kept quiet until Kion let Tiryn go and took up his place with the cart. As they headed out from under the great hovar's branches, the cart had never been heavier.

"Well, it was a magnificent view," Zinder said, his voice touched with wonder. "I wish you could have seen it."

"I believe you," Kion said. But after his conversation with Tiryn, none of the marvel in Zinder's voice could find its way into Kion's heart. He plodded forward, his feet weighed down, shackled with uncertainty, as the company journeyed forth into the morning haze.

By midmorning the next day, they reached the bouldered downs west of Dunach. They had failed to track down Vayd. They had no choice now but to set their feet toward the fortress. Perhaps the scouts there had seen some sign of him or Aonar could be persuaded to renew the hunt. But that would be for the varlance to decide.

The rocky ground slowed them once again, but that was just as well. Every step now was a struggle between weariness and resolve. Kion could no longer remember a time when his hands did not ache. He had half a mind to load the cart onto his back and see how long he could endure it, just to give his hands some relief. Tiryn and Zinder would have helped if they could, but neither could manage the oversized cart for more than a few steps over the rough terrain. Zinder, seeing his plight, encouraged him that the end was near and yet over and over again they wandered into paths blocked by boulders or hills too steep for his spent legs to ascend and they had to retrace their steps until they found another way.

Despite his blistered and aching hands, the burden of the cart, and the futility of the false trails, what weighed upon him most were Tiryn's words from the day before. Perhaps it was foolishness, but he did not fear what might happen to him in the war. He had promised Aonar that he would fight and he had meant it. This was his path. Kithian had even told him as much. But whatever his fate, whether he lived or died, joining the war would mean separation from Tiryn, and that he did fear. Zinder would go with Kion, and his smithing and weapon-making skills would no doubt be invaluable for the Warding forces, but Tiryn would have to endure the long lonely nights of uncertainty on her own, with no one there to comfort her.

But perhaps it did not have to be that way.

"Tiryn, I've been thinking…The varlance might allow you to stay at Dunach, and even if he sends me off to fight, he might let you travel with the army as a healer."

They had stopped to catch their breath at the top of a rock strewn hill. Tiryn slid her pack to the ground. Dust stained her cheeks and brow. She looked as if she'd just come in after a long day in the garden.

"Do you really think so?" Her eyes opened wide, standing out all the brighter against her sooted skin. "Aonar is a fair man. I suppose he might let me go with you…But I've been thinking about something else as well. What about Rimewinter? I don't want to fight, but then why am I a swordspeaker? What am I supposed to do with my glaive?"

"Oh bother," Zinder said. "I was wondering when we'd have to sort this out. It's a fine fettle, isn't it? Girls with daggers, hurling darts of ice everywhere. What are we to do? It's certainly handy in a pinch, but all it takes is one stray arrow or one howling haukmar to get through and then what? You're not trained for tooth and nail, toe-to-toe, hammer and tong battle. And a dagger is a poor weapon for that sort of thing even if you were. The thought of you out there on the battlefield is enough to worry the hair right out from under my hat. And that's saying something, because nyn never go bald."

"Each glaive is different," Nurien said. *"Each of us was created for a particular purpose. Though my blade is as sharp as Truesilver's, it is not as long or as well-suited to open battle. Tiryn and I were meant to serve in a different way. My ice is best used to protect and defend. But*

beyond my glaivefrost, my gift of foresight is singular among the glaives. Through me, you will gain wisdom that the greatest warrior cannot match, nor overcome. A single fight may be won with strength of arms, but a war is not won by might alone. Knowing the designs of your enemy is a weapon more telling than any blade."

"That is true. Physical strength is not the only kind of strength," Kithian said. *"Your wisdom and foresight will be sorely needed if we are to win this war."*

Kion stared off toward Dunach, but it lay still shrouded by the dust clouds and crags. The gift of foresight was one he did not pretend to understand. It seemed to offer as many questions as answers, and yet he could not deny that it might prove invaluable in this war.

"Let's hope Aonar sees it that way as well and lets us stay together."

"I'll back you up," Zinder said. "Whatever happens, we'll find a way to walk the same road. We're all in this to the end."

"You must not face Vayd alone, Kion," Nurien said. *"Terrible things will come of it if you do."*

Vayd's shadow loomed over everything, stretching out from somewhere beyond the eastern hills. Kion imagined the haukmar leader waiting for him even now, plotting how to exact his vengeance with his newfound power.

"I fear putting Tiryn in danger, but I trust you, Nurien," Kion said.

Tiryn's hand clasped the driftwood necklace given to her by Skol and Pinna. Her face tightened, and when she spoke, her voice was strained. "I don't want to fight any more than I want to be apart. I despise war. Those it doesn't kill it leaves wounded and scarred, like walking a path of shattered glass…" Her voice broke and she said no more.

Kion offered his shoulder for her to lean on. Grief ate away at their will to go on, but it also drew them closer. He needed his sister to walk through this path of shattered glass along with him.

"We cannot avoid this war, but we will face it together."

"I will keep her safe, swordspeaker," Nurien said. *"If I achieve nothing else in this war, I will do that."*

"You shall achieve far more than that," Kithian said. *"You and Tiryn both. It takes no foresight to see that."*

"And I'll be there, too. Don't forget your wonderfully witty and fabulously fashionable friend," Zinder said, drawing a hard fought smile from Tiryn. "I'll give that old gray mountain a pair of crossbow bolts to the kneecaps and you two can finish him off."

Tiryn wiped away a trickling tear. Though she spoke no words, a spark flashed in her eyes. She would find the strength to fight in her own way when the moment came, even if she never ventured onto the battlefield.

"It will not be easy," Kion said. "But as Kithian says, 'We can only fight the battle in front of us.'"

He pulled up the handles to the cart once again, his hands throbbing in protest. Yet far worse pains seemed to lie before him. They set off up the rock-littered slope as the sun tumbled toward a blanket of haze. It was doubtful they would reach Dunach by nightfall, but they would arrive soon enough. Whatever the varlance had in store for them, and whatever the war beyond might bring, they would face it together. With fire and ice. Through darkness and light.

Chapter 6

THE FINAL RECORD

Dawn failed to break in full upon the land. Granite clouds trapped the sun behind them and refused to offer a single crack for it to break through. Motes of dust settled upon the hills and clung to the skin and clothing of the little company toiling up the ascent to Dunach. The fortress hovered atop a promontory, a vague shadow, obscured by haze, great cliffs guarding it on three sides. No torches lit the walls to burn away the shroud of dust. No soldiers manned their posts. No sound stirred within the brownstone defenses.

Morning birds ruled the hour, their songs issuing forth in a high, fluted joy which belied the forlorn air. *"It is here. It is here. The day is here. The day at last is here. Oh, praise the Master of the Day."* They kept repeating it over and over again. A note of relief rode upon the sound, as if it meant something more today than it had the day before.

The last half mile before the gates was like swimming upriver. Kion had to fight for each step. His legs buckled under the strain. The patchwork of cuts and blisters covering his hands screamed at him to stop. Several times Zinder and Tiryn had to help keep the cart from slipping back down the rise.

Just a few more steps. Then he could rest and be rid of his burden.

Each step was a victory, and as he rose, his will to join the war rose with him. Soon he would fight under Varlance Aonar's command. He could almost see the proud emerald-and-gold banners of Inris fluttering down the line. Hosts of men in glittering mail standing at the ready. And there sat Kion, atop a great black steed. He raised Truesilver to the sky and its flame blazed forth, a beacon for Warding, a promise of their coming victory. Zinder rode into battle beside him, his crossbow cocked and ready to pick off their enemies, his eyes bright as sparklight. And somewhere off behind them, safe in some impervious tower, Tiryn stood watching, guarding the stronghold and awaiting his return. Step by grueling step the dream grew until at last they came before the gates of Dunach. And there the dream died.

The gates lay torn asunder. Beams and splintered boards sat in a ruined heap. Deep rake marks gouged the wood, shredded by some powerful rending force. Scattered arrows surrounded the wreckage, though from the look of it none of them had hit their mark for not a single body could be seen. Kion drew True-silver from the cart. Tiryn took Rimewinter in hand. Zinder cocked an ear as his sharp eyes searched the dust-filled light of the bailey. But beyond the shattered gate lay nothing but a terrible silence.

"Blast! The enemy has sacked the fortress," Zinder said. "But where have they got to? This place is still as death."

"*I do not believe that either the haukmarn or the Noathryn did this,*" Kithian said. "*They would not have left this fortress undefended once they captured it. It is far more likely the work of dreadwulfs or some other dim-touched creatures.*"

"*The dim-touched serve Malix,*" Nurien said. "*It should be no surprise that he has drawn them out to menace the world once again.*"

"Are you sure?" Tiryn said.

"*As his creations, they are bound to him and no longer possess a will of their own. Yet if this was their doing, they are here no more.*"

Kion returned Truesilver to its sheath. "Then, as in Whitewind, we will search for any survivors, as well as any sign of how this happened."

They left the cart at the ruins of the gates. More arrows littered the outer bailey, most of the shafts broken, but no other signs of battle disturbed the well-worn flagstones. The gate to the inner bailey lay broken and shattered as well.

"This was certainly not the work of men," Zinder said.

"The markings on the wood look too thin for dreadwulf claws. Perhaps we shall find answers inside," Kithian said.

They scrambled over the ruins of the second gate.

Buildings lined the walls of the main bailey; the barracks, stables, smithy, and storehouse all looked abandoned, their doors smashed open. The doors of the great keep were splintered and mangled as well. They chose to search there first.

Inside, heavy walnut tables and chairs cluttered the great hall, toppled or broken as if dropped out of some tempest. Of the six doors within, two had been ripped off their hinges, one to the left and one to the right of the entrance.

Zinder, who, the last time they were here, had spent his time in the barracks recovering from his wounds, took in the rough-hewn stonework and the arched ceiling with a wondering eye, but there was no time to stop and admire the craftsmanship. Kion and Tiryn pushed through the debris and passed through the open door to the left. This led to a set of spiral stairs.

Up they went. Kion's weariness slipped away. All thoughts of pain and discomfort fled. The fate of Aonar filled his mind. What would happen if he was dead or gone? How would they defend western Inris without his leadership?

Most of the doors on the second floor had been forced open or torn from their hinges. Many rooms showed signs of struggle —upended chairs, fallen candelabras, broken pottery, gashes in the floorboards. One room had a bent spyglass on the floor. Zinder examined it, but with a sigh pronounced it beyond repair.

They hurried from room to room, seeking some hint as to the keep's fate, and also of Aonar's. They banged on the closed doors and called out to see if anyone would answer, but no answer came. Soon they arrived at the door to Aonar's office. They found it locked, but this time they stopped so that Zinder

could pick it. Using a clever little hook and a long metal needle
that he kept on his belt, they gained entry almost as quickly as if
they had had a key.

The varlance's chambers were in perfect order. War banners
hung from the walls. Great bay windows looked out to the west,
but the haze surrounding the fortress obscured the view. The
only change from before was that one of the two lanterns
hanging from the ceiling was gone and there was a map on the
desk. Markings on the map showed the major settlements and
features of Inris and Noath, though Inris had other markings for
hills, mountains, rivers, and forests, and in general had far more
detail. Clay tokens painted in white or gray rested upon the map
like pieces from a game which nobles might play. The gray
pieces were etched with a claw and showed the places the haukmarn had conquered. The white ones had the design of a shield
and occupied the strongholds that Warding still held.

Grettling had fallen to the gray, as had Fennigar and Roving,
but this they already knew. To the south of Fennigar, Quelling
still had a white marker upon it, but a gray one touched it.

"The city must be under siege," Zinder said. "The war has
marched on since we've been gone."

"The fane will send his men soon," Kion said. "Veris is far
away. The pass through the mountains is no easy journey."

Zinder offered a grumbling scowl which said all he needed to
about his trust in the fane.

They turned to leave, but Kion hovered in the doorway. This
was the place where Aonar had first received him when he came
to Dunach. Aonar had given him a warm welcome, praising him
for his defeat of the pack of dreadwulfs. Kion had never spoken
to someone of such high standing before, yet Aonar had shown
him more respect than the people of his own village ever had.
Kion had expected an aloof tyrant, like the varlance he had read
about in Strom's journal. But Aonar carried himself with honor.
Wisdom tempered by suffering glimmered in his one good eye.
The other he had lost in battle. He spoke with great sorrow of the

son he had lost while battling a dreadwulf. He was a man who knew both the glory and the terrible price of war. Yes, Aonar would have been a man worth fighting for, but Kion would never get that chance.

Their search continued without result until they came to the dining room. Here they had eaten with Aonar the night before they left. The door lay flat on the floor, wrenched from its hinges. The thick oak table inside was thrust against the far wall and the chairs were in disarray. A few of the banners had been torn from the walls. The fragments of a lantern littered the center of the room. Many books had been knocked from the shelves which ran along the left-hand wall. A few of the covers had rips and scratches. Loose pages added to the disheveled mess. Tiryn knelt to recover them, but it was a pointless task. The books would never be whole again.

"They may only be old records," she said, her voice low. "But it doesn't seem right to leave them like this."

Kion joined her on the floor. "You could take one of the books if you like. I don't think anyone will need them now. There's no one left to read them."

"We haven't looked in the barracks yet," Tiryn said, her tone rising with a hint of hope.

"Hold on, what's that book over there? It looks different," Zinder said. He went over to the table and lifted one of the fallen chairs. Underneath lay a book, face open to the floor. Blotches of ink stained the cover and the edges. A quill lay beside it, snapped in two. Zinder rubbed the stain with his finger. "The ink is fresh. And look, there's the smashed inkwell in the corner."

He set the book on the table and Kion and Tiryn gathered around. The book was leather-bound, like the others, but though it had been battered and trampled, the pages were crisp and unfaded. Zinder leafed through the most recent entries, each of which had a similar appearance, with a date and a name, followed by the summary of that day's events.

"It's a journal, like Strom's," Kion said.

"Yes, but more official," Tiryn said. "See how the name is signed, along with the rank: Wardmark Dengril."

"The last entry is dated four days ago, the fourth of Sabrand," Zinder said. He read the entry aloud:

The fortress is taken. The enemy roams free within our walls. All resistance is broken and I have fled to this sanctuary to record our final defense. This will likely be my last act in service of the Four Wards.

The attack came in the middle of the night. The guards of the watch neither saw nor heard anything until the enemy reached the gate. Dark beasts, so black they were almost invisible, rent the gate asunder, tearing through it with great screeching and wailing. A large band of nyn led them, but unlike any I have ever seen—here Zinder paused and made a dour face, reading the line twice more before continuing—*Our archers slew dozens of them, but there were too many. The bells stirred the fortress to life, but to little purpose. For each enemy they slew, five more poured through the gates. Though I never laid eyes on their leader, Swordswain Moril sent word that a haukmar led the charge.*

Varlance Aonar and the swordswains sought to draw them off so that the rest of us might escape. Brave man. I shall never see him again. None of us will. I can only hope that I may face death as bravely when my time comes. As a soldier, one lives in death's shadow each day. But I never thought I would die alone here in the room where I spent so many hours studying old records and writing new ones. It is fitting that my life expires now onto this page, to join so many others whose lives are recorded within.

Though Dunach is lost, the Four Wards shall stand. If any should find this, the last record of the long history of this great fortress, I entreat you to bring these words to the margrave's men or the fane's.

The enemy has reached the hall—*silent they move, but I can hear when they break down the doors. I lay down my pen now and take up my sword. Strength fades, but the will grows stronger.*

Zinder turned to the previous page in hopes of learning more, but found only the report of scouts roaming the surrounding lands the day before. They had seen no sign of any enemy. The only thing unusual was that several of the long-hounds seemed restless and troubled.

"This must be a mistake. A band of nyn and dark beasts? Led by a haukmar? I don't believe it." Zinder flipped through page after page searching in vain for answers. But all he found were records of the life and deeds of the soldiers at Dunach, nothing more.

"I don't believe it either," Kion said. If the account had said that a herd of cattle attacked the castle, it could hardly have been more believable. "There are probably not fifty nyn in all of Inris. And what reason could they possibly have to assault a fortress like this?"

"This was written in the middle of a battle. The attack happened at night. Dengril's eyes must have betrayed him," Tiryn said.

"One thing is certain," Kion said. "Aonar and the rest of his men are gone. Dunach is an empty ruin. We must bring word of this to the Warding forces."

"What are we going to tell them?" Zinder said, pacing up and down the room, rifling through pages. "That the fortress fell to Vayd and a host of nyn and invisible beasts?"

"No, only that it has fallen. Tiryn is right, the wardmark could not have seen what he claimed. Nyn are craftsmen and merchants, not raiders or mercenaries."

Zinder took several long deep breaths, slowly regaining his calm.

"Yes, we cannot give full credit to that account. There are no dead within the courtyard or at the gates even though he claimed they slew several. The nature of the attacks remains unclear, but at least we now know that Vayd no longer travels alone," Kithian said.

"Even in the last war, when the nyn fought on the side of Malix, they never ventured into open battle. They worked in building Taliny-on's defenses and provided him with machines of war. Whatever sacked this fortress was something else," Nurien said.

"Your Sight tells you nothing?"

"Much remains dark to me, as with the shadows of Whitewind. I am certain of nothing beyond what you have read in that record: that Vayd was here and that he was not alone."

"But what sort of army travels with him?—that is what I should like to know," Zinder said, still leafing through more pages. "Shar's dome, this is like nothing under the sun. This fortress was undermanned to be sure, but even a small force could defend it for a time and Aonar was a varlance—a varlance! That dark glaive is at the heart of this or I'm a widow's husband."

"I wish we had more answers, but somehow I don't think we'll find them," Kion said. He passed over to the bookshelves, touching several of the spines to see if any other books might be of help. But they were only annals and records of past battles, nothing more.

"Maybe if we study Dengril's book further something will reveal itself," Tiryn said.

"Yes. We'll take it with us," Kion said. "Let's go now and search the other buildings. We have discovered all we can here."

Tiryn picked up the book and gave it a lingering look. She slipped it into her pack. "Thank you, Dengril," she said. "You were faithful to the end."

Indeed he was. Strength fades, but the will grows stronger. It was the ancient battle cry of the fanewardens.

They were Strom's last words as well.

The whir of bloated flies warned Kion even before they opened the stable doors. He had smelled dead sheep before, but the stench wafting through the building was different. It assaulted him the moment he entered, reeking like rancid vegetables. It was the smell of withering and rot, and it summoned a wave of bile to the back of his throat. Zinder covered his nose with his kerchief. Kion and Tiryn used their sleeves, but it did little good. Having once smelled it, Kion would never forget it.

"A body lies around the corner," Nurien said. *"It belonged to a young man. He has been dead for several days."* Though immune to the reek, a current of disgust ran through her voice.

"So, Vayd didn't capture them, at least not everyone," Kion said.

"Ack!" Zinder said, half-choking. "The stench! I don't think I can go any farther. I'll...I'll just stay here and guard the door in case we...well, we don't want to get surprised from behind."

"Yes, stay here," Kion said. "Tiryn, you should stay back too. This won't be pleasant."

"I can manage. I visited Mistress Shona once when she was preparing Old Man Nobbler for burial. I've seen a dead body before."

Kion shifted Truesilver to his left hand and took hold of Tiryn's. Together they turned the corner, the light of their glaives bathing the woodwork and floor with soft tints of red and blue.

When Kion laid eyes upon the body, his stomach lurched. The once vibrant form of an older boy lay face upward in the muck of one of the stalls. Flies hovered about him, slow and fat and shameless. His skin had turned unnatural shades, but in places it was still tight, though it bulged in others. But for the deformities, the face could have belonged to Kion or any of the young men from Furrow. A pitchfork lay at his feet.

This was what happened to people in war.

"He died fighting," Nurien remarked. It was the best thing that could be said.

"Oh, Kion." Tiryn looked away and covered her mouth with both hands. "Mr. Nobbler was old and shriveled, but he was not left to come to this."

"We will give him a proper burial," Kion said.

"There are more," Kithian said, his voice even more solemn than usual. *"Another lies in the stall at the end of this aisle."*

A flash of heat burst inside Kion's chest. This was all wrong.

The fortress had fallen. Aonar was dead or gone. Boys were dead in the stables. All because of Vayd. Never had he loathed the haukmar leader, or anyone else, more than he did in that moment. "We have to stop him. We have to keep Vayd from doing this again."

"He has evaded us once more, but the persistent hunter catches his prey. We will find him," Kithian said.

Kion looked down the length of his blade. How many more would die before that happened?

"We can't let this go on," Tiryn said. The usual softness of her voice was gone. She pulled her hand away from her mouth, breathing the stench full on. She stared at the body, her eyes locked upon the gruesome display. Her jaw worked back and forth in a helpless grinding motion. "And the only way to stop it is to fight." Hurrying over to a nearby stall, she yanked up the bar and flung the door open. After a quick search, she emerged with a saddle blanket and a shovel. She handed the shovel to Kion. "We'll cover the body and bring it outside. We can bury him beyond the walls. There's no place in the courtyard. Then we'll come back and bury the others. And when we're finished we'll leave here and you'll join the war and I'll help you—I—I don't know how, but I will—and then we'll stop this war so that boys like these can die in peace, after long and happy lives, surrounded by the ones they love."

Kion lowered his blade. Tiryn had never spoken like this before. The quiet girl he knew had been carried away. A new one stood before him. He stared at her, the flies buzzing, the stench festering, searching for the old Tiryn behind her eyes.

"Are you all right, Tiryn? We don't have to do this right away."

"Yes we do," Tiryn said. Her face hardened along with her voice. "They cannot be left here to rot like beasts."

Tiryn was right. War broke everything. Lives, homes, hearts.

"We will stop this, Tiryn," he said. "It's like you said, you and

I been given these weapons for a reason. They will show us the way."

"We have passed a threshold here," Kithian said. *"You may not yet have joined the ranks of the fane's men, but you have seen the true face of war for the first time."*

"Hold on to this sight," Nurien said. *"Unpleasant as it is, you will need it in the days ahead. Recall it to memory whenever you feel yourself losing the will to press on. Let it remind you of what we are fighting for. We will ensure that these young men did not die in vain."*

Chapter 7

THE LOST HYLLS

They buried three young men that day in the bramble north of Dunach Fortress. Kion lifted the bodies into a wheelbarrow and brought them one by one. Zinder could not stomach the smell, and Kion's hands were too wounded to be of much use so Tiryn did most of the digging. She set to it with a fierce will, anxious to cover their bodies so that at least the boys could have the dignity of a quiet grave, their deaths no longer visible to the wider world. But though their splotched faces and misshapen limbs were now hidden, they were forever engraved in her memory. Nurien had urged them to remember the sight, but she would not be able to forget it if she tried.

> *From light to light, and through the dark*
> *The hammer stroke ignites the spark*
> *The spark may fade, the glow remains*
> *It does not leave the world unchanged*

Zinder spoke the ancient words over the graves and silence fell. He had nothing more to say.

Tiryn did not sing "The Halls of the Fallen," though that was the custom as well. Ever since her mother's death, the music had left her. She had not lifted her voice once in song. How much less could she lift it now amidst such senseless suffering? Silence was the only song her heart now knew. Neither had she touched her pipes. They lay buried deep in her satchel. She had lost the music before, at the death of her father. How long had it taken her to sing or play again then? She could not remember. But she had learned to make music again. With her father it had been a way of healing, of bringing him back in some small measure. Music was his gift to her, and recovering it had been her way of honoring his memory, of cherishing what he had passed down.

Cooking and gardening had been her mother's gifts. Tiryn had loved working alongside her in the garden especially. Her mother had a way of nursing the seeds to harvest. No matter the frosts or the droughts her gardens flourished. It was as if the things she planted rose out of the sheer love she had for them. But there were no gardens to tend now. Their little patch of land in Furrow lay fallow and forgotten.

As for cooking, the road was too long and weary to bother preparing anything now. The dried meat and oat cakes of the Frin were all that they could manage. And even if they had something to cook, it would not be the same as cooking back home in Furrow with all its spices and the glowing hearth and the well-worn clay cups and bowls which held the lingering smells of a thousand nights of laughter and good cheer.

No, her mother was gone, and there was nothing Tiryn could do to fill that void.

They slept that night out under the sparklight. A night in the fortress would have given more comfort, but Tiryn did not feel safe there and the others agreed. An emptiness pervaded the fortress now, a gaping black, as if the whole place were one large open grave.

Dark dreams troubled her. But they had nothing to do with Dunach. The same dreams had troubled her ever since the return to Whitewind. She could not say what happened in them, only that they were full of shadows and that she awoke each morning troubled and spent, barely rested. Something was pressing in on those dreams, trying to tell her something. It was the clamoring of thunder, a warning of the true storm to come. But did she even want to know what the storm was?

She had spoken with Nurien of her dreams more than once. If anyone could understand their meaning, it would be her.

"It is one thing to have the Sight, but another thing to know its proper use," Nurien had told her. *"The Sight is a murky glass at first. It takes time to see anything clearly."*

"Are you sure I have the Sight? I've only had three visions that I know of. And none of them came true, at least not fully."

"Even when you master your Sight, the visions will never be as clear as things are in the waking world. There will always be an element of mystery to them. Most visions are not to be trusted the first time. It is only if they come a second time that they become more sure. And when they come a third time, that is when you know they are all but inevitable."

Tiryn couldn't remember how many times she'd had her vision of Charring. She'd been in the grips of the wistering fever then and the days had run together in a whirlpool of pain and weakness. The vision of Kion leaving had only come once. Perhaps that was why it had been so easy to avoid. The vision of the Maid of Ice had happened twice, though, and that was the one that brought her Rimewinter.

"Have you ever had a vision three times?"

"Yes. The last time it led me to imprison Malix on Tinesplitter." Nurien's voice hitched with regret. *"And you have seen what terrible things came from it. It led to the death of my glaivebond and five others. That is one vision I wish I had never had. I had thought it was given to me to end a great evil, but to do one evil to stop another is the path of folly. I see that now, but that lesson has been bitter in the learning."*

The sorrow in Nurien's voice at her failure reminded Tiryn that humans were not the only ones who walked paths of pain and regret. Though Nurien's suffering had happened long ago, she had been asleep for hundreds of years, so to her it was as fresh as Tiryn's.

"It's hard for me to imagine you doing something like that.

You're so wise and gentle. But Kithian has forgiven you, so that must mean a great deal."

"That is Kithian's way. He is quick to forgive and even to forget. But it is not mine. For those who See it is hard to unsee."

Tiryn placed her hand upon the dagger's handle. It was cool to the touch, but vibrant life hummed within. Yet the stain of doubt and misgivings marred its vibrancy. It was as plain as if she could have looked into Nurien's eyes. Emotions flowed from the shining blade into the pit of Tiryn's stomach, the same place where her own grief had taken up residence. How odd that she could feel something so strong coming from a piece of metal. Then again, how strange that she was even a swordspeaker at all.

She still knew very little about Nurien. But the one thing she was sure of was the bond between them. Of that, there could be no doubt. It had formed all at once, and yet now that it was there, it felt as if it had always been. That bond gave each of them strength to bear the other's burdens. Nurien had led six swordspeakers to their deaths, including her own. Tiryn did not fully grasp the depth of Nurien's sorrow at this. In the same fashion, Nurien had not known Tiryn's mother, or even what it was like to have a mother, especially one as tender and loving as Tiryn's. But she did not need to understand the loss to help Tiryn endure it. Her presence alone was enough. And that protective presence would never sleep or slumber, never fall away in tragedy or death. As Tiryn cradled the weapon's handle and drifted off to sleep, she vowed to remain as faithful to her glaive as it was to her, whatever dreams and sorrows might come.

The company set off from Dunach on the ninth of Sabrand. The city of Grettling lay to the east, but had already been overrun. Though they were certain that Vayd must have been the one who assaulted the fortress, they could find no trace of where he had gone after that, though they searched for several hours.

"To the town of Windle we must go now," Zinder said. As the only one among them who had traveled widely across Inris, it fell naturally to him to guide the company. "We have to bring word of what happened at Dunach."

"We've lost Vayd's trail and also my chance to honor my promise to Aonar, but I don't see that we have much choice." Kion adjusted his grip on the arms of the cart for the hundredth time. Both hands now wore bandages. Beyond warning the forces of Inris of what had happened at Dunach, they needed to get to a place where he could rest and his hands could heal.

"Are you sure that there will be soldiers there?" Tiryn said.

"Yes, and I imagine that just as before, they'll take one look at Kion's sword and ask him to charge into battle the next day," Zinder said.

"If so, this time I will take up the call. Aonar may be gone, but my pledge to him remains. My path lies with the Warding army. And from there back to Vayd."

Tiryn suppressed a shudder. Burying the stable boys may have stirred her to want to end the war, but a day later, when her passions had cooled, the awful cost of that desire came rushing back to her. Fighting in the war still meant the chance of losing Kion. Though her mind had reconciled itself to his decision, her heart had yet to conform. She doubted it ever would.

High summer blazed across western Inris. The Lost Hylls offered little protection from an imperious sun which now ruled the barren sky. They wandered through a maze of low, stony humps and graveled valleys. Long years under the scathing rays had dried up any rivers or streams that might once have given life to these lands. In many places the soil had weathered away, exposing the fractured bedrock beneath. The loose pebbles and patches of silt made Tiryn miss Smokewind and Cyprian even more. For all her love of dance, she was frustratingly clumsy whenever she had no music to guide her feet, and she stumbled often and fell more than once.

Unrelenting heat dogged the company as long as the sun showed its face. It was so bad that Kion had to borrow one of Zinder's hats. Zinder lent him a floppy brown one that made Kion look even more exhausted than he was. Tiryn alone bore the heat well, for she held on to the handle of Rimewinter as she walked. The coolness of a mountain snow emanated from the blade, shielding her from the sweltering heat. But Rimewinter crafted shards of ice for Kion and Zinder and they let it melt upon their tongues and faces, which brought some relief.

"It tastes quite good," Zinder said when he first tried it. "Better than normal ice anyway. I'm still waiting for the ice cream, though."

Tiryn shook her head at him, but could not hold back a smile. Even tired and haggard as he was, Zinder never gave up his hopes, though sometimes they were as silly as wishing for ice cream from an ancient glaive.

On they journeyed. Though the sun blazed all the hotter, a more pressing problem soon arose: they did not know the way. Though they turned to the south and to the east whenever they could, the way was often barred unless they mounted one of the many hills. While that meant some trouble for Zinder and Tiryn, for Kion and his cart, most of the slopes were too steep or rocky to get over without emptying the cart and hauling up their baggage by hand. Often they found themselves forced back west or north. They grew so desperate that they discussed abandoning the cart and divvying up the supplies and the dormant glaives, but Zinder and Tiryn could only carry so much. Even if they abandoned most of their provisions—which hardly seemed wise—their pace would slow to a crawl under the weight of such burdens.

"No wonder they call them the Lost Hylls," Zinder said,

sliding a kerchief embroidered with marigolds across his fore-head and mopping up puddles of sweat.

"If only we still had Endrith to guide us," Kion said.

"On horseback we made it through in only a few hours," Tiryn said. "But we've lost almost a whole day now."

"If we don't find a way out soon, we may have to camp here for the night."

"And risk being set upon by dreadwulfs or Noathryn or whatever in the Four Wards swept through Dunach?—and don't say that it might have been nyn, I don't even want to hear that mentioned!" Zinder said.

"Of course, none of us think that," Kion said.

Zinder snapped the excess dampness from the kerchief, giving a satisfied nod. "Good. Now with that settled, I'd rather walk until I drop before I spend the night here. These hills make it easy to walk into an ambush. We would never see it coming."

"That's true, but I don't know how much farther I can go today."

"Yes, better to rest and take our chances than risk you collapsing." Tiryn held out her waterskin and Kion eagerly slaked his thirst.

"Thank you." He wiped his mouth on his shoulder. The sleeves were already drenched so it did little good. "Kithian, can you find us a way out of here?"

"You know as much of this land as I do. But Nurien has passed this way before."

"That was an age ago," Nurien said. "The land is much changed. A road there was that ran through these hills, fair and well-kept. It traveled all the way from Grettling to Grendock. But with the coming of the Noathryn, that road is lost."

"Yes. Much has changed." Kithian's voice carried a shade of lament. *"But though all has turned strange and we are strangers here ourselves, there are others who call these hills home. Unlike in Noath, animals still dwell in these lands—hares and deer and the birds above,*

but they flee at the rumor of our approach. They are not accustomed to the presence of men."

"Most beasts may have fled, but there are others who remain close and yet hidden," Nurien said.

A quickening flutter rose inside of Tiryn. "The creatures are close by?"

"None at this moment, but many creatures live below ground. If we keep our gaze below the surface we may discover a beast who could help us."

Of course. Tiryn had forgotten about that. Kithian and Nurien's glaivesight allowed them to see through soil and rock and other solid things as if they were little more than wisps of smoke. Though they could not see far, most burrows would be close to the surface.

"So it's up to the animals to save us." Zinder let out a deflated whistle that sounded like a strangled flute. "If this keeps up by the end of the war we'll have an entire battalion made up of dogs, chickens, and rabbits."

"Zinder, that's actually not a bad idea." Tiryn absentmindedly took the waterskin back from Kion, but did not drink. "But I think bears or lions might be a better choice."

"Somehow I doubt even dragons would fare well against whatever Vayd and Malix did in Whitewind and Dunach," Kion said.

"Yes, well, it was only in jest, Tiryn," Zinder said. "Animals are capable of many marvelous things, but fighting together on the battlefield is not one of them."

"That is true. The animals that still understand the beast speech do not like to fight against men. Most fear them, and rightly so. But that does not mean that they cannot help us in other ways," Kithian said.

"Could you show me what you see, Nurien?" Tiryn said.

The hills passed away and Tiryn found herself hovering well above the ground, only it wasn't her that was hovering, it was just her sight. Her body shimmered below, small and wraith-like. Kion and Zinder stood nearby, white outlines against the milky, transparent ground. Colors faded into a twilight luminescence. Though her vision now rested beyond herself, she was still able to walk, as if her body were some puppet moved along by strings of thought. Indeed, she was more sure-footed in this strange fashion than when she was inside her own skin.

Beneath the ground emerged glittering rocks and worms and all manner of tiny, scurrying things. From time to time dark pockets appeared in the soil, small cavities of nothingness, but no animals could yet be seen. How different the world looked through the eyes of her glaive. Here they were, striding past wave after wave of stony hills at the height of day and yet Tiryn might as well have been walking in moonlight. Since she only saw the outline of things, their shapes grew in prominence. It was like looking at a living sketchbook where the drawings moved. She would have to attempt to make her own drawing of the scene in her notebook when she got the chance, though she doubted that she would be able to do it justice.

They had gone less than half a mile when Nurien called a halt.

"There, beside those bushes, lies the entrance to a burrow."

Tiryn had missed it, but now that Nurien pointed it out, it was unmistakable. A dark opening lay cleverly shielded by a sheet of exposed rock. A tunnel about the thickness of her leg ran underneath it. Not far down the snaking channel a bright creature huddled in quivering anticipation. It could not see Tiryn or the others, but it knew they were there. At first it seemed a white glowing ball of fur, for the glaivesight obscured the details of things, but Tiryn soon made out two little eyes and a squat snout. It had the look of a beaver, with two long front teeth, but the fur was shorter and the nose smaller and it lacked the beaver's hard flat tail.

"What is it? A groundhog?" Tiryn said.

"No, it is one of his cousins, the marmot," Nurien said. *"They prefer rocky places such as this, though it is rare to find them so far from the mountains."*

Kion set the cart down. "I see it too. Should we call to it, Kithian? Will it hear us down there?"

"If it is within my sight, it will hear my voice," Kithian said. He addressed the beast with gentle command. *"Creature of the ground, my name is Kithian and I am one of the Mastersmith's glaives. I travel with friends whom you need not fear. We come seeking your aid, for we are strangers in these lands and know not the path that leads out of these hills. Will you help us to find our way?"*

The nose of the furry little beast bounced in six different directions and its head tilted in surprise. The next moment its whole body burst into motion, undulating and scuffing its way up the tunnel until it plopped out of the hole, its fur all aquiver, but more from excitement rather than fear. Nurien ended the glaivesight for it was no longer needed now that the creature was in plain view. After a brief moment of blackness, all the colors and fine details of the ordinary world returned.

The creature was about as big as a farm cat but thicker. Soft yellow fur dusted the belly of its otherwise hazel-brown coat. Eager black eyes no larger than a fingertip roved wildly from one person to the next and the creature's nose never ceased to wiggle. It burst into a chittering, chirping riot of noise, as eager to express itself as they were to receive its help. The sounds had the cadence and tenor of an oversized mouse. The beast went on and on, scarcely taking a breath until Kithian interrupted—

"Hold, good marmot. Do not fret yourself over having been discovered in your hiding place. That was no fault of yours. For the eyes of a glaive see differently than those of mortal creatures. But before you go on, we would know your name."

"What's it saying?" Tiryn said, disappointed that her ear had failed to pick out any of the smattering of words and phrases Nurien had taught her.

"That it is honored and humbled to be in our presence, among other things," Nurien said, with a slight hint of amusement in her voice.

"Many other things," Kion said. "I've never met such a talk-ative animal."

The marmot erupted into another chorus of cheeps and chirps until Kithian had to stop it once again.

Zinder crossed his arms and made a sour face. "That marmot must be reciting the whole history of the Four Wards for all its blabbering. Did it give us an answer yet? Is it going to help us or not?"

"Bur-gan-dor, please be patient while we consider your words," Kithian said. The jittery creature stopped speaking at once. It stayed still as a stone after that, though its nose kept twitching and its eyes never once ceased to flit about, studying each one of them.

"What did he say?" Tiryn said.

"I will tell you briefly some of what he said," Nurien replied. *"He began with great surprise, saying, 'Oh my, a glaive! So that's what they look like. Somehow I pictured them more like sticks made of stone. Forgive me, forgive me, I'm a simple marmot, and a silly one to tell the truth. At least that's what the rest of my clan tells me. Always making a racket, that's what they say. Especially when the rest of them are trying to sleep. But you didn't hear me just now, did you? I can be quiet when I want to. How did you find me, after all? Was I chittering away without realizing it? Oh, don't tell me they were right about me after all—' At that point Kithian interrupted him and asked for his name."*

Nurien paused to allow Kion to relate the words to Zinder. Tiryn found herself trying hard not to chuckle. The poor beast seemed a delightful, if rather silly, little creature.

Nurien continued, *"The marmot grew even more flustered at that point and said, 'Oh, my. I've done it again. Gone chattering on and forgotten my manners. My name is Bur-gan-dor. And I'm from the Gan family, as you surely must have guessed from my name. We have burrowers all throughout these hills. It's an empty land, which makes it a good land. No foxes or badgers. Only the occasional great-hawk we have to watch out for. And, oh, dear, you're the first men I have ever seen. And of course the first glaives. And there are two of you! Why, this is an honor a simple marmot like myself surely does not deserve.'"* Nurien's tone grew lighter the longer she spoke, so that after a while it felt less like her own voice and more like the flighty marmot's.

Bur-gan-dor, though not understanding Nurien's words to her companions, gathered from the long pause that the glaive had finished her summary and so began squeaking and squealing once again.

"Why, this marmot is as chatty as my grandnyn at tea-time," Zinder said, fanning himself with his great gray hat. "I wonder, though, if it's as good at pathfinding as it is at talking? We'll be here until sundown if we let it go on like this. Does it know a way out of these hills or not?"

"Yes, that is quite unusual, Bur-gan-dor," Kithian interrupted the marmot again. *"But perhaps you can tell as about the beetles you ate for breakfast some other time. The people traveling with me have no burrows to rest in and have traveled long in the heat of the day. They need to reach the open plains where they hope to find trees and shelter and the path back to their own homes. Do you know of a way out of these hills?"*

Again Bur-gan-dor went on, his nose quivering, his paws rubbing together, his furry tail swishing, and all the while his little mouth chirping away.

"He will help us," Kion said. "He speaks so fast it is hard to catch everything he says, but that much at least I understand." He stepped forward and dropped to a knee before the marmot, who once again went stock-still, as if he were one of those windup toys Tiryn had read about. "Thank you, Bur-gan-dor. We will gladly follow you to the ravine you speak of. My name is Kion, and this is my sister Tiryn and my friend Zinder."

The marmot's head swiveled back and forth several times as it struggled to grasp what had just happened. A human had addressed it! Poor Bur-gan-dor seemed not to know what to make of it all.

"It can understand you!" Tiryn said.

"Yes, as long as a swordspeaker has his glaive close by, and has learned enough of the beast speech himself, he can make himself understood by any animal willing to listen. Bur-gan-dor is overcome with surprise, that is all," Kithian said.

Bur-gan-dor shook himself from head to toe and at last recovered. To Zinder's dismay, he chattered on again for some time until Kithian interrupted him again.

"We are so very glad that you have agreed to help us, and we would love to hear all about the new burrow you are working on, as well as the rest of the names and deeds of your family. But perhaps you can save your tales for our travels, for darkness will soon come and we must be underway."

The little furry fellow jerked into a standing position for half a moment, then spun like a whirligig and off he went, blathering away in his frenetic manner. And after that it was all Kion and Tiryn and Zinder could do to keep up.

Chapter 8

CHITTER CHATTER

Bur-gan-dor was both the best and the worst guide they could have asked for. His senses were sharp and his knowledge of the Lost Hylls unassailable. But he chattered incessantly and ofttimes got so carried away that he took them in the wrong direction, forgetting even the knowledge that he was leading them anywhere at all. They had to ask him several times an hour whether he was certain they were headed the right way just to keep him on track.

The party would have pressed on long after dark in order to take advantage of the cooler air, but the marmot's bungling and forgetfulness only worsened with the setting of the sun. Bur-gan-dor had the remarkable ability to doze off while still moving—and talking at the same time. After he'd nodded off the fourth time they decided to call a halt to their journey.

The moment they stopped, the marmot fell dead asleep. But that did not keep him from continuing on with his tale about the time he'd almost forgotten to wake up from his "winter-rest" as he called it. Apparently this was due to the overabundance of grass he had used to make up his bed that winter. "You shouldn't overdo it on the straw" had afterwards become a phrase he used whenever tempted to do something in excess. Though Kion and Zinder found the marmot's unending chatter tiresome, Tiryn thought it charming. Her only frustration came from not being able to understand what Bur-gan-dor said on her own and having to wait to hear it through Nurien. But a curious thing happened just before dark. She found herself understanding certain words and even phrases which the marmot used over and over, common words like, "no," "then," and "how" but also short phrases like "oh my," "not sure," "they say," and "simple marmot." That last phrase in particular was one of Bur-gan-dor's favorites. The little marmot did not have a very high opinion of himself it seemed, which endeared him to Tiryn all the more, and made it that much easier to overlook his inability to keep quiet.

"The more you hear the beast speech, the easier it will be for you to learn it," Nurien said.

Bur-gan-dor's chattering at last dwindled into what sounded like suffocated snores, as if the creature was constantly on the verge of ceasing to breathe. Tiryn lay in her bedroll on the leeward side of the large hill where they had camped. Kion and Zinder had gone to sleep some time ago.

"I hope you won't think me foolish," Tiryn whispered to Nurien, "but of all the things swordspeakers can do, the ability to speak with animals is the one I like best."

"That is understandable," Nurien said. *"For it is the most natural of the gifts. It is in fact the restoration of a gift once enjoyed by all men, and so the longing for it lives on inside of you. Given how great your desire to understand what they are saying, you will grasp the beast speech quickly, I perceive."*

"I will miss Bur-gan-dor's chatter when we have to say good-bye to him tomorrow. He's been good at teaching me without even knowing it."

"I do not believe the others share in your opinion of him. But that, too, is understandable. Silence is the world at peace and its most natural state. It is its own language and wise are they who can hear what it has to say." They were the last words Tiryn heard before she slipped off into what dreams awaited her, dreams dark and terrible and which she would not remember.

It was still dark when Tiryn awoke to Nurien's voice. Nurien was not speaking to her, however, but to Kithian.

"I believe we have been followed since Dunach. I sensed a stain upon the fortress, and something like it has pursued us ever since. A shadowy presence with ill intent," she said in a low voice.

"So now the hunter becomes the hunted. Does your sight tell you anything as to the nature of what pursues us?"

"No, it is something strange, something I have never sensed before."

"Nurien, what are you and Kithian talking about? Are we in danger?" Tiryn's hand went instinctively to her dagger and she unsheathed it. The normally soft blue light flared like fireworks in contrast to the predawn darkness, but there was no immediate threat in sight.

"Not at the moment. Whatever things follow us are either too distant or too cautious to test us yet."

"Sometimes visions don't come true. Could it be the same with what you're sensing now?" Tiryn said, staring out into the pitch-black hills around them. Only the barest glimmerings suggested the shape of the land. Everything beneath the sky was cloaked in darkness.

"The taint of Malix's corruption is not like the visions given by my Sight. It is that which I sense now. It is a disquiet, a rot, and a reek, and taints all my perceptions. It is something born of darkness and lack, something hollow and restless, that moves among the shadows. What-ever it is, I believe it only moves at night, for during the day, its presence is hidden from me."

Kion and Zinder both stirred, and Kithian did not delay in sharing Nurien's warnings.

"Oh, bother, it sound like more of this dim-touched mischief," Zinder said. "Whatever it is, if it so much as twitches within a league of us, I'll spot it. Of that you can be assured."

Hopefully, whatever it was would get as lost in the hills as they had. But if it truly was as dark and mysterious as Nurien made it out to be, would even Zinder's sharp senses be able to warn them of it?

Tiryn tried to quell her forebodings as they broke camp, but with little success. Her imagination worked against her, conjuring up the ghosts of the slain from Dunach, risen to haunt the living, waiting for the right moment to overtake them. She had read harrowing tales of monsters and mysterious creatures, but ghosts had always been the most frightening, for there was nothing that could be done to stop them. They were spirit only and against such things the flesh had no defense. She told herself that ghosts only had the power to strike fear in the living and could do no true harm, but she only half-believed it.

They had some difficulty rousing Bur-gan-dor, but, like one of those wind-up toys he kept reminding Tiryn of, once he got moving he would not stop, nor did his talking.

They set out after their strange little guide. Dawn had yet to come, but traveling in the dark would help them avoid the heat of the day.

"Bur-gan-dor says 'It's going to be a big, bright, beautiful day,'" Nurien said.

"How can you tell that in the dark?" Kion said.

In answer, Bur-gan-dor went on for so long that it was too much for Nurien to relate, but she summarized it by saying that he described his intuitions regarding such things as "inner quiverings."

"I had hoped to practice speaking the beast speech with Bur-gan-dor, but I can hardly get a word in edgewise," Kion lamented as the marmot continued on without pause and seemingly without a breath.

"I have been told on more than one occasion, perhaps even by certain persons with whom I share present company, that I have the tendency to talk too much," Zinder said. "After having encountered this marmot I shall never give credit to any such claims ever again. If someone ever complains that I am too talkative, I shall simply tell them, 'It could be worse, I could be a marmot!'"

"Kithian, are all marmots like this?" Kion said.

"I have not had the occasion to ever meet one before," Kithian said.

"Something tells me this tendency might be particular to Bur-gan-dor," Nurien said.

"I don't mind his talking," Tiryn said. "It's helping me learn the beast speech."

"Well, at least some good will come of it," Zinder said, punctuating his words with a loud puff.

They wound their way through the labyrinthine hills, following their chirping, chittering, chattering guide. Bur-gan-dor wandered off the path three times before the sun came up, once heading up a steep hill before Kion reminded him that he could not push his "gatherings" that way. Bur-gan-dor did not understand the word for cart, or even the idea of it when Kion explained it to him.

"Why would you ever need anything more than what you can carry in your paws?" Bur-gan-dor asked, but he stuck to the valleys and lowlands after that.

When the sun lifted at last above the horizon, it ventured into a sky far less barren than the day before. Though the clouds were not many, great swaths of white covered large parts of the expanse, casting city-sized shadows upon the land below. The cool morning and the prospect of soon finding their way out of the Lost Hylls raised the mood of the company a great deal. Zinder even ceased to grumble about the marmot's ramblings. They pressed on with Bur-gan-dor far more alert after his night of sleep. He only wandered off every hour or so.

They made good time until late that morning when, with the sun still in its ascendancy, the valley they walked along delved into a shadowed ravine. So deep it was that it temporarily blotted out the sun. The steep V-shape of the terrain made it difficult to leave the valley except from the north or south. They were still a good distance from the end of it when Bur-gan-dor abruptly stopped speaking.

"What is it?" Zinder whispered to the others, as if Bur-gan-dor had gone to sleep and he feared waking the marmot so that it might start talking again. "Has the little fellow finally talked himself out?"

To Zinder's disappointment, the marmot did not stay silent for long.

Nurien translated Bur-gan-dor's latest round of chatter. *"He's grown quite melancholy all of a sudden. He says that he hasn't had time to tell us all the things he'd hoped to say. He said, 'I wish I could go with you all the way to the end of the world, or wherever it is that you're headed. But my family will be wondering about me, wondering where I've wandered off to. At least I think they'll be missing me. The last time I wandered off for three days and no one gave me so much as a 'hello' when I returned."*

"In the same way that your family needs you," Kion said, "our people need us, too. But I don't think we should part ways just yet. You promised to lead us to the ravine which led out of these hills. Is this the one you meant? Have we finally reached the edge of this land?"

Nurien relayed his answer. *"No, but neither is it far. He says, 'There is a hidden crevice just ahead. Once you walk through it to the other side, the valley widens and will take you all the way to the edge of the hills. Only I do wish you would stay a little longer so that I could tell you about the great rain we had when I was young. It flooded the burrow and washed the whole family out into a rocky basin like straw in the wind.'"*

Kithian addressed the marmot once again. *"Bur-gan-dor, you have been of great service to us and we would gladly repay you by staying longer if we could. But need drives us on. You have a great love for stories, which is rare among beasts, so one word of encouragement I can offer you is that you will be remembered in the stories of men for what you have done."*

Bur-gan-dor shivered all over and hung his head low. *"But I am not worthy,"* he said through chirps and squeaks. He had said that phrase so often that Tiryn understood it without needing a translation. This was quickly followed by, *"for I am but a simple marmot,"* another of his oft-used phrases. He went on after that, but no one related those words and Kion soon cut him off.

"It is time now for us to leave, Bur-gan-dor. Please show us this hidden crevice you spoke of."

Chittering as he went, the marmot waddled on ahead with a great heaviness to his gait. Reluctant though he was, Bur-gan-dor proved faithful as always. He led them out of the ravine into a tumbledown fall of rocks. Kion had great difficulty traversing it and in the end was forced to stop.

"It's too steep, Bur-gan-dor, and too uneven. I can't push my gatherings any farther."

The marmot scurried back, chirping something anxious and sniffing at the cart.

"Very well," Kion said. "It looks like the two of you will have to help me. Bur-gan-dor says that if we can just get the cart over this large rock there is a hollow on the other side, which leads out of the hills."

Between the three of them they tried to raise up the cart, but it was simply too heavy. In the end, they had to empty it and pass the items over the rock by hand. Tiryn went first and dropped down into the hollow on the other side. Kion passed the items up to Zinder on top of the rock who then lowered them down. Tiryn climbed back to them once they'd gotten all their baggage over. Together with a great heaving push they got the cart over as well.

On the other side sat the hollow Bur-gan-dor had told them about. It cut straight through the hill with only a few slivers of light creeping in from high above. Tiryn unsheathed Rimewinter and slotted it beneath the straps across her chest to help them see.

They finished reloading the cart and Bur-gan-dor climbed nimbly down into the hollow to see them off.

"He says he'll tell his family all about us," Nurien said. *"They'll be glad to hear his stories for once—he hopes. He's not sure because, 'of course I'm only a simple marmot,' as he says."*

"I'm sure they'll appreciate your stories," Kion said. "And we thank you for showing us the way, Bur-gan-dor. You have saved us a great deal of time and we are in your debt."

"Yes," Zinder said, his expression softening for once toward the beast. "Tell the fellow he's got a fine nose for pathfinding. I am sorry that I complained so much about his noisiness. I'm sure he can't help it."

"And tell him from me that I think he's a dear little animal and that if we ever meet again I hope to be able to understand his stories better," Tiryn said.

"My white-haired friend says you have excellent pathfinding skills," Kion told the marmot. "And my sister will be learning the beast speech soon and would enjoy listening to more of your stories if we ever meet again."

"May your days be many and full," Kithian said.

"Send our greetings to your family," Nurien said.

"Oh, I will, I will," Bur-gan-dor said and Nurien conveyed his reply. *"You are the best humans a marmot could hope to meet. I doubt I'll ever meet any better. Then again, as you're the first I've ever met, perhaps I may never get the chance to find out. But if I do, I'm sure they won't be any better than you. You listened to my stories, and that is all a simple marmot like myself could ever ask."*

Tiryn reached out and touched his warm feathery fur. A tenderness came over his face and Tiryn took it for a smile. As they headed away from Bur-gan-dor, for once the marmot stayed silent, standing vigilant among the rocks until they could see him no more.

A short time after, they emerged from the long hollow out into a green valley with the faintest trickle of a stream running through it. Though more hills awaited to the south, the way was more even and the slopes less severe than the land from whence they'd come.

Tiryn glanced back at the opening one last time, imagining the furry little marmot with the yellow speckled fur at the other end waddling back home. He may have been a bit odd, but he had unknowingly taught Tiryn many things. And she found herself missing his chatter, and not as content with the quiet as she might have been, as they turned and made their way south through the last remnants of the Lost Hylls.

Chapter 9

FLAWED SIGHT

Tiryn gasped for breath. Her heart pounded a blistering rhythm. Her eyes flung open. Another dream. This time, she had no difficulty remembering it. Indeed, like all of her visions, she could not forget it.

"Nurien—I need to talk," she said in a whisper. She did not want to wake the others and no matter how quietly she spoke, Nurien would be able to hear. She grabbed hold of the dagger. The leather handle's cool touch helped restore her frayed wits. The hardest part about visions was that they made so little sense. They were jumbled impressions, disconnected from anything real. It was as though someone else's thoughts invaded her mind. But Nurien would know how to make sense of it.

"You remember this time," Nurien said, her voice as still as the unmoving night. *"Tell me what you saw."*

"It—It was about the boy we found in the stables—the first one. He was drowning. A thick arm reached out to grab him and pull him into a boat, but I didn't see whether or not he was saved. I don't think so, because then I saw him in bed, his eyes blank and lifeless, the same way he was when we found him at Dunach."

"Was his skin as rotted and disfigured as it was there?"

"No, that's why I think he must have drowned. And his lips —I can't forget his lips, they were some terrible dark shade of green. But there was something else. There was a mortar and pestle underneath the bed. It was made of onyx. Inside the mortar were thorns—sharp and new and green. I'm not sure what any of that had to do with the boy. A mortar and pestle are used by healers to prepare herbs. Perhaps someone had wanted to save him by finding a cure. But if he drowned, no herb or remedy could save him from that. So I'm not sure what that had to do with the rest of the dream."

"Sometimes visions come in shattered pieces. Parts or all of them might be things to come or things which have already been. Sometimes they are even of different events in different times and places fused together into a single vision."

"Do you know which one this was? Was it the past or the future?"

"It also could have just been a dream."

Tiryn unsheathed her blade. She couldn't say why, but it seemed more natural to address her glaive this way. Nurien had no face, but Tiryn treated the large gem in the pommel as if it were Rimewinter's eye.

"I don't think so. It feels more like the other visions, more certain and more real than a dream."

"Then we will treat it as such. This is encouraging. If you can tell the difference between a dream and a vision, that is the first step in developing your Sight."

"Everything is so hard to understand. How can you tell whether a vision is from the past or the future?"

"It comes from experience and reason. Mostly reason, though. This dream, for instance, is not likely to have been about the past for the boy certainly did not die from drowning. Unless of course the vision is not about the boy at all, but about someone else who drowned. The color on the lips is important, though. Such a striking detail must not be overlooked. It may be the key to the whole vision."

"But why have visions at all if there's no way of knowing what they mean?"

"We are but vessels. Our Sight is blurred and bent. There is only One who sees things as they truly are."

"I thought your visions always came true. Isn't it one of your gifts?"

"The gifts of a glaive are more art than precision, more principle than perfection. Even my visions fail at times or, more likely, I fail to read them properly."

"You are far too humble in this, Nurien," Kithian said. The sound of his voice sent a twitch through Tiryn's arm. She had not known he was awake. But then again of course he would be. Glaives never slept. Why would they need to? They were immortal with bodies of metal. They never wore out or showed signs of age. *"If not for your vision, we never would have come through the War of the Shattering."*

"Yes, but after my failure at Tinesplitter Isle, I question whether or not I am fit to use my gift again. I know it is wrong to question the Mastersmith's wisdom in this way—for he it was who gave the gift— and yet the doubts remain," Nurien said.

"That was a grave error, but when we stumble, what matters most is the next step we take, not the stumbling. And we must always be ready to help those who stumble find the path again."

"And that is what makes you a true friend."

Tiryn waited for her chance to speak. She preferred not to interrupt when others were speaking, which was why she was so quiet most of the time. It was not that she did not have things to say, but that she could never find the right moment to say them.

"So you think the vision is about someone else, then? Someone in danger of drowning?"

"Perhaps. Remember what I told you before. Until a vision comes a second time, it is far from certain. We must wait and see if it comes again. If it does, the second vision may give us new insights that the first vision lacked."

By now Tiryn's heart had almost settled into a regular rhythm. Though the vision was no more clear than when she first awoke, the simple act of telling Nurien had gone a long way to relieving the weight of uncertainty.

"I wish it wasn't that way. I wish things would be clear from the beginning."

"A Sight that is clear and deep and sees the truth from the beginning is much to be desired. But alas, in this shattered world, we must see with the vision we are given, and not lament the vision we lack. For discontentment mars all that it touches."

"Thank you, Nurien. And you, too, Kithian. Thank you for listening."

"That is one thing we will always do. We will always listen. And now, if possible, you should get some sleep. Another long day of travel awaits," Nurien said.

Tiryn returned the dagger to its sheath and placed it atop her pack. Though she closed her eyes at once, sleep was a long time coming. As she so often did, she clasped the driftwood necklace in her hand. The song of the Frin children echoed in her mind, bringing her a settled peace. And when at last she returned to sleep, the dark dreams failed to come.

By midday, they had left the Lost Hylls behind. Coming out to the south, they did not pass through Sicklewood as they had on the previous journey. Nor did they venture into the Dunshave east of the forest. Instead they traveled through a land of thick, clumped grass and groves of short trees, mostly hawthorns and hazelwoods. The lemon-tipped grass of the plains presented few rocks or steep slopes, but the land otherwise reminded Tiryn of the Wetherbone Tors surrounding Furrow. Goats, rabbits, deer, and all manner of birds breathed life into the land once again. The sight of these familiar creatures and such pleasant views quieted her worries, and thoughts of war and Vayd and Shadowriven faded for a time.

On the second day after leaving the Hylls, Nurien said that she no longer sensed the presence of the strange hunters following them. It looked as if they would reach Windle safely.

When the air broke clear that morning, great mountains soared, majestic and peerless, over the plains below. Though often mantled in clouds, bone-colored arms of stone thrust upward from the plains meeting as tributaries in some skyward river, capped in crowns of dappled light. Never had Tiryn or Kion seen such heights before and their eyes were ever drawn to them as they ventured south. Their path lay not in that direction, but parallel to it, and so the mountains could only entice them from afar.

"The northern spur of the Clarion Toths," Zinder said. "If you think those are tall, you should see the Clarions in their fullness. They're so enormous it's a wonder the Four Wards can hold them."

"I cannot imagine anything more glorious," Tiryn said.

"Like a wall at the edge of the world," Kion said.

They walked long in awe under the shadow of those great torrents of stone. Even Zinder, who had seen the Clarions at even greater heights, kept silent. The vastness of the peaks filled their thoughts all the while they wandered through that wide empty country. But by the third day, the mountains receded back into the mist and Tiryn was left with only their memory and a quick sketch she had made of them in her journal.

They now came upon the first ponds and fingered lakes of that land. A fertile smell danced upon the breeze. Wildlife abounded. Ducks, geese, sparrows, robins, thrushes, and many new birds Tiryn had never seen flitted merrily about. Beavers, toads, lizards, and snakes nestled in the rushes or upon the rocks. Sadly, the creatures disappeared at the company's approach and so they had no chance to speak with any of them.

Though the way remained pathless, it was easy and light, so much so that Tiryn and Zinder took turns at pulling the cart to give Kion's blistered hands some relief.

By the fourth day, the fourteenth of Sabrand, the first herds of cattle appeared. Most had deep reddish coats, some speckled with white. A few farmers in Furrow kept milk cows, but Tiryn had never seen actual herds before. One or two herders watched over each group of animals. The herders kept their distance from the travelers, though, and only a few bothered to return Zinder's enthusiastic waves and none replied when he called out to them.

"A dour lot, these cattle herders," he said. But it must have seemed a strange thing to see two young Inrisians and a nyn pulling a cart through their pastures. However, one herder, who only had four cattle, grazed her beasts in a small field which lay directly in their path and so they ventured to approach her and see if they might learn any news. The girl looked to be around Tiryn's age with burlap-brown hair tied in a loose braid. The weathered frock she wore was light enough to endure the summer sun without adding to its heat.

"Greetings, lass," Zinder said, doffing his hunter-green cap. He was the most skilled at speech and proper manners, having traveled over most of Inris vending his wares before the war began. If anyone could warm a stranger's heart it would be him.

"Well met," the girl said. Her tone was friendly enough, though not overly so. The stout black dog at her side was less friendly, though, barking low and deep. "Quiet, Nipper," she said. Those words, followed by a quick prod to the animal's flank with her walking stick, ended the creature's racket.

"Pardon us for bothering you, but you don't by chance have any news of the war?" Zinder said. "We've been far from well-traveled roads for some time and are anxious to learn how things fare."

The girl's eyes went from the dagger Tiryn wore across her chest to the sword that sat atop their baggage.

"You go armed, and yet you're not bandits or you'd have had your way by now."

"We mean no harm to you. Is Windle still safe?" Kion said.

A distance entered her voice. "I hope so. My father and brother both went off to defend it. The swordswain there is marshaling what men he can. I'm left to tend the cattle alone. Rumors come from many places. They say maybe Quelling has fallen by now. Some say maybe even Seabrim was attacked, but who really knows?"

"Do you know the name of the swordswain at Windle?" Kion said. Tiryn hoped she would say "Roardin," the swordswain who had helped them escape Fennigar and who had once served under Strom Glyre.

"His name is Forglen. Word is that he's a bit too full of himself, but he's all we've got. It's not like Windle is an important place. It's just a few farmers and workmen. Nothing much to sniff at."

"Oh, I'd say there's plenty to sniff at out here," Zinder said, wrinkling his nose at several large cow dollops nearby. "But as for this Forglen, I'm sure he'll do what's best for Windle."

"You're headed that way, then?" she said. "You're going to offer your sword to his service, aren't you?"

"Yes. If he'll have it."

"It's good to know that my father and brother will have more help. I only hope it is enough." She locked her mouth tight and with it any further words.

Tiryn caught a reflection of her own pain and doubt upon the girl's face. She did not know which was worse, riding off to fight, or waiting for the terrible news to come back that those who had left would never return.

"May your father and brother be back with you in these fields before long," Zinder said. And with a tip of his cap, he and the others thanked her and said their good-byes.

They wandered on through the open fields of thick grass, passing by more cattle, but they did not speak to any of the other herdsmen. Twice they saw shepherds with flocks of sheep, but they were too far off to seek out. The sight of sheep brought back more memories of home and the life they once knew. But that was all they were, memories. Furrow was gone and Kion and Tiryn would never be shepherds again.

The cattle herds grew larger and more frequent as the miles wore on. Toward the middle of the day, Zinder counted a herd one shy of forty. That was the last one they saw before they picked up a beaten-down little dirt road. Not long after, the first of many farm houses sprang up on either side. Constructed of the same wattle and daub typical of Furrow's cottages, it once again brought back bittersweet reminders of home, though these were painted brown and a few others a muddy red, and back home most all the cottages were white or gray.

At last, the town of Windle came into view after rounding a sharp bend. It rested neatly in a small valley bathed in the amber light of the late afternoon sun. A lattice of dirt roads connected the low buildings which made up the town. Most shared the simple style of the farm cottages, though the roofs here were not thatched, but covered instead with clay shingles. One building rose above the rest, far larger and grander than anything else within the town.

It had been built from redstone, a dark, maroon rock similar in strength and feel to that of limestone. It stood four stories tall with square towers on each corner which climbed another two stories higher. Despite its size, the pointed clay shingle roofs, fluted columns, and other ornamental flourishes showed that it was not meant for defense. The oaken wall surrounding Windle, made up of hundreds upon thousands of recently felled trees, offered the only real protection for the town against its enemies.

"That's the courthouse, known as Ruffand House," Zinder said. "Some noble or other named Ruffand had it built for the margrave centuries ago so he could have a place to stay when he held court out in Casting Limmring."

"It's a marvel. No mistake about that," Kion said.

"It looks like a giant castle made of clay, but the loveliest shade of red clay that there ever could be," Tiryn said. "I will have to make a sketch of it."

They passed through the western gate where a handful of soldiers occupied themselves in a game of chance. They paid no attention to those coming and going through the gate, transfixed by the bone dice they rolled in the dirt.

"Well that's something new," Zinder said. They'd been stopped at the gates of every other town they'd visited.

"Yes, a welcome change. Let's see if they'll tell us where to find the swordswain." Walking up to them, Kion gave the traditional cross-armed salute, but only one soldier bothered to look up. He barely gave Kion a glance before returning to the game. "Pardon me—I was wondering if you—"

"Pound the dirt, boy," the soldier said with a sneer. "Can't you see we're busy?"

"That's right." Another slapped the fellow on the arm. "Busy guarding the gate!" The two shared a scornful laugh and returned to their dice.

Kion scowled, and Zinder turned that unpleasant shade of red which signified a dramatic storm was bubbling upon his normally jovial lips. A timely hand on the shoulder from Kion quelled the storm before it could break.

"No need to waste words on folk like this," Kion said. "We'll find the swordswain some other way."

Zinder took off his hat and Tiryn feared the storm might come after all, but with a huff, he shoved it back into place and stamped off.

"If these are the sorts of snagjaggers you'll be fighting with, you might be better off starting your own army," he said. "Let's hope this Forglen is a different sort. I'm guessing they'll know how to find him in the courthouse. At the very least they're sure to have better manners there."

"You were wise to walk away," Kithian said.

"I agree with Zinder, though," Nurien said. *"If those men represent the quality of soldiers in defense of Warding, our hopes in this war are more grim than I feared."*

"There are always true-hearted men to be found in any land, though it may take longer to discover them in some more than others."

Hastening from the gate, they entered into the town. An odd quiet reigned over the streets considering how many houses and buildings ran alongside them. The only significant noise came a few streets later when they passed a long wooden building which sprawled the length of an entire block. The low structure was mostly rectangular, but in a few places it jutted out in other directions as if it had been added on to over the years. Several people worked outside, and several trundled in and out with armfuls of animal skins in various stages of the curing process. Sounds of splashing, squelching, and the general clamor of labor spilled out into the nearby street. A few laborers hung skins out to dry upon slats or lines of wire strung between poles. Others mashed the skins in large vats. Smoke whispered out from two chimneys on either end of the oaken structure.

"Ah, yes, the tannery," Zinder said. "That scabbard I made for you back in Charring—the one you tossed aside like it was nothing when you battled those dreadwulfs—was of Windle-work leather. Thankfully, the leather I had didn't smell this bad or I'd never have finished it." For once, Zinder was not over-stating things. The pungent odor of rot and stagnation assaulted Tiryn's senses.

"I still prefer it to the smell of fish," Kion said, fanning under his nose. "But only just."

They did not fully escape the stench until they arrived at the rather humble square in the center of town. It had a stone foun-tain with four life-sized bulls pointing in each of the cardinal directions, but no water spouted from it and the stonework was dry and crusted over. Paved paths ran around and through the square, but on the whole it was smaller than the Commons in Furrow.

They passed the forlorn fountain and approached the court-house on the opposite side of the square. Though its large oak doors stood open, two soldiers in green tabards stopped them once they got close.

"What business have you at Ruffand House?" one of them said.

"We seek Swordswain Forglen. Is he presently inside?" Zinder said.

"He's inside, all right, but no longer receiving visitors at this hour," the older of the two said.

"He only sees commoners for one hour at noon," the other said. "He's got far too many important things to attend to than to deal with the rabble."

Zinder's eyes flared. "We are not rabble, young fellow. Have you heard of the Sword of the North? Well, this is him. Write it down and tell your children's children in the years to come. He's here to pledge his service to the forces of Warding. He's come to end the war!"

The younger soldier snickered. "Laying it on a bit thick, are we? Frankly, I don't care if he's the cousin of the fane. No one's allowed inside except on official business or during the Hour of Visitation. Swordswain Forglen's orders. If you want to fight for the army, go sign up at the barracks. It's over on Manifest Lane, three blocks to the west."

"But we've come from Dunach," Kion said. "I have to speak to the swordswain himself. The fortress has been sacked and now lies abandoned. We have to tell him what we saw."

"Ah, first you're the Sword of the North and now you're a messenger from Dunach." The young soldier gave a mangled grunt. "Where's your uniform, then? And what's the password? You know we can't just accept messages from any country sod that wanders in from the fields unless we know him already or he gives the password."

"The password? The password?!" Zinder said. "We're here with important news of the war and you won't listen to us unless we have the password? How about 'balderdash'? That's the only password that seems to fit in light of this nonsense."

"Watch your tongue, nyn. I don't make the rules. If you don't like them I can offer you the chance to spend a night in the stocks and see if you come to respect them more fully."

The older fellow nudged his companion. "It's all right. Listen, as he said, we don't make the rules. You'll just have to come back tomorrow. I can write you down on the list, though. You'll be first in line. Not many folk bother to petition the swordswain these days."

Kion hesitated. This was not the reception they had hoped for. He had been received as a hero in Fennigar and Dunach. But Windle had its own way of working, apparently. Then again, these were only glinthelms, the lowest rank of soldier in the Warding army. The swordswain might see things differently, the way Roardin and Aonar had.

"Well, boy?" said the young soldier, though he could not have been more than two or three years older than Kion. "Out with it. Have you a name? Or shall I put down Sword of the North?" He let out a scoffing grunt.

Kion gave him an unwavering stare. "My name is Kion Bray. My friends and I will return to see the swordswain tomorrow at noon. Please note my name on the list."

The other soldier wrote down something and his companion waved them angrily away.

Kion swiveled the cart around and the three of them marched from the courthouse, its maroon stonework set ablaze by the setting sun.

"The swordswain will treat you differently," Tiryn said, hooking her arm in his.

"I am not so sure," Nurien said. *"It bodes ill that these soldiers are no better than the others. You shall know a leader by the quality of those who serve him."*

The warning in her voice rang out as clear as the tolling bells which sounded throughout the town, heralding the coming of dusk. They had only arrived a short time ago, but things did not look promising. Tiryn tried to tell herself that it would be different tomorrow despite what Nurien said. But telling yourself something and believing it are two very different things.

Chapter 10

A FEAST OF CRUMBS

The Red Ox Inn had seen better days. The second floor was entirely closed due to leaks in the roof. The smell of burnt bread pervaded the air of the common room and did little to help the appetite (though it seemed to have no adverse effect on Zinder's). Several of the chairs were cracked and in need of repair. Zinder's had two legs shorter than the others (which did have an adverse effect). One of the windows had been patched with glue and a metal plate, but it did not fully cover the hole and flapped in the wind. None of the half-dozen patrons looked glad to be there. Even the fire in the hearth lacked cheer, sputtering as though it longed to suffocate from despair at having to inhabit such a downtrodden establishment.

How entirely different from the last inn they had lodged at—the only other one Tiryn had ever visited—the Grizzly Griddle. There she had found lively conversation, a roaring fire, and the common room had rung with Baradoc's fiddle and the voices of patrons raised in song. But the present atmosphere was just as well. For in the same way that the dark is desired by eyes heavy with sleep, silence now suited her ears better than music and cheer. Such things belonged to the past. Her heart could no longer bear such merry surroundings. And so, in an awful way, the sullen mood of the room was perfectly fine.

As drab as the inside was, vibrant hedges, thick with thorns, surrounded the outside. These thornbristle bushes had the sharpest thorns in the Four Wards so it seemed odd and not a little dangerous to find them here. When Zinder asked the proprietor, a sallow-faced man named Mr. Bumpus, with two tufts of hair sprouting out near the tops of his ears, the reason for the bushes, his head bounced in a knowing way.

"Ah, it keeps the vermin away, you see. Surprising, isn't it? A traveling fellow came through and told me about it a few years ago. Rats, worms, and lizards, especially. They can't abide thorn-bristles at all. We had terrible infestations before we planted them."

"How interesting. Well, it's comforting to know we won't have to worry about any infestations, then," Zinder said.

When Mr. Bumpus brought them their meal he apologized profusely for the burned bread. "My cook left last week. I'm afraid the new one is not quite up to standard. He fell asleep while this batch was in the oven and that was the last of the dough. I'm terribly sorry."

Tiryn took her slice of squared charcoal as politely as she could. There were a few spots in the middle that were not entirely black which looked salvageable. Zinder was crestfallen, but he took it in stride.

"At least the soup turned out," he said. "I'm sure if we dip our bread into it we won't notice the burned taste…much."

"Yes, thank you, Mr. Bumpus. I'm sure we'll be fine," Kion said. Neither he nor Tiryn were used to staying in inns so they could hardly complain if this one was not the finest establishment in the Four Wards. At least they did not have to spend the night on the rough hard ground.

"We're sorry to hear about your problems with the cook," Zinder said.

Bumpus's head drooped. "Such troubles are to be expected I'm afraid. Half the town's fled to Rippling. The same thing happened in the last war. Whenever times get tough, the people go packing."

"Is there fear the town will soon be attacked?" Kion said.

"Nothing more likely. It's only a matter of time. We got word yesterday that Quelling has fallen. The haukmarn and the Noathryn are said to be marching for Jabble now. Once it falls they will descend upon Windle, sure as the leaves fall from the trees," Mr. Bumpus said, wringing his apron.

"Horn toads, it's worse than we thought," Zinder said.

"We may be too late," Kion said.

Tiryn looked into the face of poor Mr. Bumpus, with his sorry little inn and nothing but the prospect of even greater hardship before him. She read there the same fears tormenting her own heart. And yet, a tenacity survived somewhere behind those uncertain eyes.

"If Windle is soon to be overrun, why have you not fled with the others?" she said.

"Where else can I go? I can't pick up my livelihood and pack it on my back like other folk. This inn is all I have. I'll defend it with my kitchen knives if I have to."

"You're a brave man, Mr. Bumpus," Kion said. "I hope it doesn't come to that."

"You've got the new wall they put up around the town," Zinder said. "Surely they'll have the defenses in order by the time the haukmarn come. Windle won't go down without a fight."

"And yet still it will go down," Mr. Bumpus said.

"The Warding forces may yet prevail. I, for one, hope to be among those defending it," Kion said. "I've come to pledge my service to Swordswain Forglen and the Warding army."

The innkeeper regarded Kion as if he had just told a bad joke. "Well, you look to have the makings of a strong young soldier, but I'm sorry you'll have to serve under someone of his ilk. The best thing to be said of Forglen is that he hasn't fled yet. He cares too much about his reputation for that. None of his men care for him, though, as far as I can tell. Because he doesn't care a nick about them."

One of the other patrons called Bumpus over and so he left them to themselves.

Kion's eyes darkened. "What do you think, Kithian? It sounds as if what Nurien said about men reflecting their leaders might be true. This Forglen may be no better than the soldiers at the gates and the courthouse. Should I still seek him out?"

"We must go wherever the battle is fought. If Quelling has fallen then the east is closed to us. It is not certain we would reach Jabble before the enemy, though we set out this very hour. Windle seems to be most in need at this moment. So here is where we must make our stand. You should only ever flee a battle if it will help you win the next one. And as of yet, it is not clear that fleeing Windle will help the cause of Warding."

"Wise words and true," Nurien said. *"But if this swordswain shows himself unfit to lead, we may have to find some other way to oppose the haukmarn."*

"I hope it doesn't come to that," Kion said. "I can't fight the whole army on my own."

"It's looking like rain no matter what color the cloud," Zinder said. "But the sword's right. There's no use worrying about burnt bread when that's what's on the table. Worry is the enemy of a good meal. Ruins the digestion. We'll sort things out tomorrow. For now, we've got food that needs attending to and I, for one, intend to do my best to be attentive."

Zinder winced and grimaced with every bite, but forced the bread down as though his life depended on it, drenching each piece in mounds of the sickly green pea soup.

"This is even harder than those door stops you make," Zinder told Kion.

"They must have left it in the oven for half a day." Kion tried following Zinder's example, dipping his own bread in the watery murk, but gave up after three bites.

Tiryn scraped off the least burned bits into her soup. She got enough for a fine dusting, but that was all. She didn't bother with the bread and ate just enough of the soup to take the edge off her hunger. After forcing down his own portion, Zinder finished off the rest of Kion's and Tiryn's.

"Can't let it go to waste," he said.

"Your stomach must be made of cast iron," Kion said.

"Well, I am a blacksmith." Zinder tore off another hunk of charcoal and sent ashen flakes spraying into his soup. "Perhaps my insides are made of metal. That would explain how I survived being gobbled up by that dreadwulf, wouldn't it?"

"Ah, no wonder you're so fearless in battle, then," Kion said. "You're invulnerable."

"Exactly. Who needs armor when you've got skin of iron?" Zinder laughed at his own jest.

Retiring to one of the two rooms they'd rented in the back of the inn, Tiryn found the window entirely overgrown with thorn-bristles. Several wicked looking spikes poked right into the window panes. So thoroughly did the bushes smother the view, there may as well have not been a window there at all.

She could see why the rats and other vermin would be kept at bay. If only they were fighting a war against rats and not haukmarn, perhaps the inn would remain standing

Poor Mr. Bumpus. And poor Windle if the swordswain turned out to be as awful as the innkeeper seemed to think.

The swordswain saw them at noon. A pair of glinthelms ushered Kion, Tiryn, and Zinder into a spacious room with high ceilings and tall, metal-framed windows with glass tinted a faint rose gold. The dark wood paneling along the walls was replete with floral designs and graceful, vine-like patterns. Chairs rested behind long tables displaying carvings matching those used upon the paneling. Six rows of tables filled the main part of the chamber, the chairs all facing the same direction to form a gallery. A short wooden railing with a small gate separated the gallery from the other side of the room. Beyond the railing, two smaller tables and several more chairs looked up at a colossal desk made all the more imposing by the stairs leading up to it on either side. The desk had yet more carvings, as elegant and well-preserved as the rest of the room, though even more ornate. A giant bull carved in relief on the front was framed by wooden garlands rimming the edges.

Two more glinthelms—wearing burnished mail beneath their emerald tabards—stood rigidly before the desk. Kion and the others arrived and were instructed to sit down at one of the tables closest to the desk.

Entrenched behind the looming furniture fortress, and surveying them from the heights, Swordswain Forglen watched their approach with dark, glittering eyes. Though his emerald tabard had the double yellow bars of a swordswain ascendant on the shoulder, he wore no armor and his portly face and salty gray beard gave the impression more of a baker than of a soldier.

Tiryn, who had never been in a courtroom before, knew instinctively that this was what it was. And Kion was about to be judged.

One of the two soldiers at the foot of the stairs read from a scroll in a booming voice. "First petition of the day for his excellency, Swordswain Forglen, on this the fifteenth day of Sabrand in the year 838 of the Shattered Age."

"Thank you, glinthelm," Forglen said. Amusement played in his eyes and in his voice, which had a sing-song rhythm to it, as though he were half humming and half talking. "State the name, please, as well as a summary of the petition," he said without looking at anyone in particular.

"The supplication comes from Kion Bray, lately of Furrow. He comes with news from Dunach," the glinthelm said.

Forglen made a puzzled grimace. The pleasantness in his voice disappeared. "News? You brought me over here amidst all my many responsibilities for a bit of news? What could a commoner possibly tell me about Dunach that I do not already know?"

The glinthelm stared at the back wall. He had not met the gaze of the swordswain since he'd entered. Neither had any of the other guards. Forglen gave them a dismissive wave.

"Wait, is that a nyn I see? Well, this at least is something of interest." Forglen held such a lofty perch it was a wonder he even noticed Zinder at all, but perhaps Zinder's burnt-orange hat with the half white, half-black feather cocked at an artful angle had something to do with it. "Are you this Kion Bray whom the petition refers to?"

Zinder popped up from behind the table. "Oh, no, no, no, that's the lad to my right. I am merely his guardian. Though, I, too, was with him at Dunach."

Forglen unleashed a cavernous yawn. "Ah, I see. If his name is on the petition, he ought to be the one to speak. Very well, young man. You have the floor."

Kion rose, unfamiliar with the formal air permeating the chamber and daunted by the task of addressing someone bulwarked behind such an imposing barricade.

"*Do not concern yourself over this man's station and rank. The truth has a weight of its own.*" Kithian's voice came to the sword-speakers even clearer than the swordswain's. Though they had been asked to leave their weapons outside, Kion and Tiryn could still sense Truesilver and Rimewinter's presence, for walls and doors meant nothing to the bond between a swordspeaker and his glaive.

Kion gave a cross-armed salute. "Swordswain Forglen, I have come from Dunach. There I pledged to serve Varlance Aonar and was returning to make good on that promise. But the fortress…" His words stalled. How to speak of that tragedy? The mangled gates. The empty halls and rooms. The festering corpses in the stables. The shallow graves they'd dug beyond the fortress walls. No words could capture the horror and hollowness they had encountered there.

"Yes?" Forglen said, thrumming his fingers upon the desk. Deep notes sounded through the wood.

"It is lost."

"Lost? Our scouts have sighted no movements to the west."

"They are all dead or captured. Every last soldier. It was the work of Vayd Mokán. He has gathered a new army, one we cannot track and have yet to see." He gave a sideways glance at Zinder. "We do not know where it came from, or what manner of soldiers march within its ranks, but I have come to help you fight it, along with the rest of the haukmarn army."

"So Vayd has a new army, does he?" Forglen's expression was half curious, half incredulous.

"Yes, my lord."

"I suppose that's possible. There've been no sightings of him since the attack on Fennigar. But if you haven't seen this new army, then how do you know he travels with it?"

"We found an entry in one of the record books." Kion turned and motioned for Tiryn to bring forth Dengril's book from her bag. She handed it to one of the soldiers who passed it up to Forglen.

The swordswain muttered as he thumbed through the pages. "The fortress is taken…came in the middle of the night…dark beasts…and what? A large band of nyn? What's this? I thought you said you didn't know what sort of army he led?"

"Yes, well, it doesn't make much sense. Nyn are few and far between in these lands. And the few here are craftsmen and tradesmen like my friend. The attack came at night, after all, so we think that the account must be mistaken at that point."

Forglen studied Zinder suspiciously. "It would be highly unusual. I've never heard of the nyn attacking anything in the history of the Four Wards, but it makes me wonder if anything in this account is to be believed or not."

"I can assure you that the fortress was empty when we found it. We only found the remains of three dead boys in the stable. The rest had been swept clean."

"Bah! What's that you say? Would you have me believe that Vayd captured the fortress and left it abandoned?" Forglen's jowls inflated as his voice rose. The two glinthelms below his desk broke off their regimented stares to glance his way.

"Remember, truth needs no argument," Kithian said.

"I don't know why he didn't take it over. Perhaps he did not have a large enough force to man the walls."

Zinder fidgeted in his chair, only just holding his tongue.

"If he had enough to take the fortress, he had enough to man the walls. Gah! This has been a monumental waste of my time." He tossed the record book carelessly to one of the glinthelms who only just caught it before it hit the floor. "I shall send a scout to verify whether or not your words are true—I hope I don't regret it. We've got plenty of empty cells awaiting those who lie to the leaders of the Warding army." He fixed Kion with his small-eyed stare. The very smallness of it made it all the more intense. "As for your request to serve, it is granted. These glinthelms will escort you to the barracks and see that you are issued a weapon. I hope to find you ready when the haukmarn come."

Zinder waved his arm vigorously, his ears piping hot. "Pardon me, my lord, but Kion here is no common soldier to be sent off to bunk with the rest of the men. Varlance Aonar promised him the rank of swordswain, you see."

"Oh, swordswain is it? You don't say? How lucky for him."

"Varlance Aonar did promise me that, yes, but I'm happy to serve wherever and however I am needed."

"Kion, don't say that. You're too fine a warrior to be wasted in the common ranks. Make him a wardmark at least," Zinder said. "He needs none of your common weapons, either. He wields Truesilver, the flaming sword. It's true! The Sword of the North now stands before you!"

Forglen leaned back in his chair and let out a gargling sort of laugh. The sound of it echoed through the chamber, cruel in tone and harsh to the ears.

"You're saying that this boy is the Sword of the North? The one who bested Vayd at Charring? Ha! I'd sooner believe he's

Strom Glyre risen from the dead. Glinthelms, you have your orders. See the boy to the barracks—if he's not too proud to fight with the common soldiers and earn his bars like any other. Honestly, these petitions grow more tiresome by the day." He let out another tremendous yawn.

Forglen rose and the two glinthelms made their way toward Kion. Out from behind the desk, the swordswain looked to be barely as tall as Tiryn and tremendously round in the middle. Other than his tabard and the metal-hilted dagger he wore on his waist, no one would have mistaken him for a warrior. Kion gave a downhearted sigh, wavering between speaking his mind and letting the soldiers lead him away.

"Don't believe us, then?" Zinder sprang to his feet and bounded to the entrance before the other soldiers reached the railing. He flung open the doors, giving the guards there a start. "Show them, Kion. Show them you're no common swordsman. Show them what a swordspeaker can do!"

Kion cast a doubtful look at the open doors. Truesilver and Rimewinter lay upon a table across the hall. "Should I show them, Kithian?" Though he spoke softly, the courtroom had a way of carrying his voice.

"Kithian? Do you have some friend out in the hall who wants to join the army as well?" Forglen said, chuckling to himself as if there had been some trace of humor in his words.

"The truth does not always come through words."

Tiryn rose in anticipation.

Kion extended his arm. "Truesilver, to me!"

Truesilver shot from its scabbard and flew through the air, whipping past Zinder's head with such force it nearly blew off his hat.

The blade burst into crimson flame the moment it touched Kion's hand. Blood red reflections bathed the courtroom walls in a primal light. Tiryn had to take a step away because of the heat. It was like standing next to a blazing bonfire.

"I am the Sword of the North."

Swordswain Forglen stiffened, his expression showing first disbelief, then panic, and finally passing into cold calculation. Whatever plans he had for Windle's defense, from his hardened glare, it did not appear as though he was anxious for a warrior with a flaming sword to be a part of them.

Chapter 11

MESSENGER

Swordswain Forglen ushered Kion down a long dark hallway and into his private chambers. Zinder and Tiryn had been ordered to wait in the courtroom along with Truesilver. Forglen claimed that the sword "might burn the whole courthouse down," to which Zinder replied, "If you don't have Kion fighting for you, the haukmarn will burn a good deal more!" Despite his protest, the sword stayed where it was, but it remained close enough for Kion to sense its presence and hear Kithian's voice.

The swordswain's chamber was far smaller and more modest than the courtroom. His desk was one-quarter the size and lacked the bull carved into the front.

A vague amusement returned to Forglen's eyes once the two of them were alone. Seeing Truesilver set aflame had troubled him. A restlessness had set in. But now that he had separated Kion from the sword, his self-assurance returned.

"That was quite the display." Forglen gestured for Kion to take one of the two chairs before his desk as he eased himself into the padded one behind it. "But you really should be more careful with a weapon like that. You might take someone's head off the next time you send it flying across the room."

"Truesilver would never hurt anyone unless he was an enemy," Kion said. He meant no threat by the words, but saw from the swordswain's reaction that he took it as such. Some people see enemies even in those who would be their friend. Kion would need to choose his words more carefully.

"Do you really expect me to believe that a flying, flaming sword would not endanger my men?"

"With respect, Swordswain, Truesilver is not just a sword. I can hear its voice and it is wise and good. And I can assure you that it is no danger to you or your men."

Forglen's face contorted in a sudden fit. "You think me a fool, boy? A sword cannot speak. Flying and fire are strange enough, now you would have me believe that it talks?"

"I know it's hard to believe, but it's the truth."

"Then have it say something. Let me hear its voice."

"I'm sorry, but I can't. Only a swordspeaker can hear it."

Forglen rolled his eyes. "Oh, of course. You've been chosen, then. You're someone special. Well, let me tell you what I think. I think you might have gone mad. Have you ever considered that?" He stared Kion down with needling eyes.

"Perhaps it was not wise to have told him that I can speak. Many struggle to understand things outside of their own experience," Kithian said from the hallway, for through Kion, he could also hear what was spoken in the room.

Kion was at a loss as to what to say. This was not going at all as he'd planned.

"I have not gone mad, Swordswain. If you allow me to fight in the Warding army you will see that Truesilver and I have only come to help."

Forglen crossed his arms, self-satisfied, brooding on something clever that had just occurred to him.

"I'm sure you have good intentions." Forglen scratched his great jowls, teasing out his thoughts. "I'll tell you what. I will give you a chance to prove yourself. Perhaps I'm half mad myself for doing so, but then again genius is just madness turned right side up."

"Thank you, Swordswain. I promise that you will not regret your decision."

"Oh, I never regret anything. It's a sign of weakness. But now, listen closely. You must get one thing very clear. I am the swordswain here. Me. Not you or anyone else. And in time of war, my word is law. Is that perfectly clear?"

"Yes, Swordswain. I only wish to stop Vayd and drive the haukmarn from our lands. I have no wish to supplant you or anyone else."

Forglen's expression grew all the more smug. "You know, I could use my authority to take the sword myself. It might go a long way to getting these fools beneath me to show some proper respect. And then I would be the new Sword of the North."

The threat meant little to Kion. All it did was evoke pity for this small-minded man. "It won't work. The sword will only make fire when in my hands."

"Ah, of course. I suspected as much. But you need not worry. Fortunately for you, I do not intend to test your word on that. Before we go any farther, though, let me ask you this, do you truly wish to serve under me? Be honest. Do not think that I am unaware of what they say about me in the town and among the ranks."

"I..." Kion fought to find the right words. He had read in Strom's journals of men who treated him with disdain before he rose to the rank of bladewarden. They had resented him and used their power to keep him in place, often assigning him the most menial and thankless of tasks. Would this same thing happen to Kion?

Forglen certainly seemed nothing like Strom or the other leaders Kion had encountered. Aonar and Roardin had eagerly sought out his help. But Forglen seemed more intent on asserting his power over others. That was not the mark of a leader of men and Kion had no desire to serve under someone like that. Yet, in the midst of a war, a soldier could not choose his leaders. He had to fight where he was called and under whom he was called. What choice did he have but to submit to the swordswain's leadership? He could not abandon Windle in its hour of need.

"All I know is that the fane and the margrave have put you

over the defense of this town. And if you will have me, I will serve you as best I can."

"You always say the right thing, don't you?" Forglen mocked him with his eyes. Kion had seen that look before. He knew a bully when he met one. He'd faced plenty back in Furrow.

"Not always, but I try. My parents are dead, you see. One way that I can honor them is by striving to do what is right and good. And I have wise friends who have taught me as well."

Forglen regarded Kion shrewdly, contemplating his next words carefully. "Very well. I accept your service. I cannot make you a swordswain, even if I wanted to, for I lack the authority, but I think I see how you might best be used in this war. Will you pledge yourself to serve the Warding forces under me and to obey my commands?"

Kion felt the weight of those words. If he thought there was some other way to protect this land and its people he would have chosen it. But Kithian was right. Fleeing the battle would gain nothing. He had to fight where his sword was needed most. And if that meant following Forglen, so be it.

"I will serve you and the Four Wards with all that is in me."

"It is the right choice. Better the hard right than the easy wrong," Kithian said. It was true. But then why did Kion feel so unsettled? Almost the moment he said the words, a shiver of doubt ran through him. The self-satisfied look in Forglen's eyes had a great deal to do with it.

"Very good. Glinthelm!"

The soldier outside the chamber entered and saluted.

"Yes, my lord?"

"Have a tabard brought into the courtroom. I wish to accept this young man's service in the official manner. It is not every day we receive the services of such a renowned warrior into our ranks." Forglen's tone came across as less than genuine and the glinthelm hesitated before nodding and heading back out the door.

"Come." Forglen motioned toward Kion. "I don't often

bother with presenting the colors to new soldiers these days, but in your case I shall make an exception." He shook his head as he left, muttering, "talking sword," and smiling to himself. Kion followed him back into the courtroom. Both Zinder and Tiryn sat up, watching his every step.

"I apologize for keeping you waiting," Forglen said, the pleasantness in his voice as new as it was unnatural. "I believe we have resolved our misunderstandings. I see now, master nyn, that Kion is no ordinary warrior. Please join us in the courtroom for the bestowing of the tabard. It is a short ceremony that we perform to welcome new soldiers into our ranks."

"Well…" Zinder raised an eyebrow. "I'm glad you came around. He's the best hope the Four Wards have for ending this war."

"You're sure this is what you need to do, Kion?" Tiryn said, her voice strained.

Kion hesitated, his doubts resurfacing. "It is the right choice," he said, as much to himself as to her.

"All right, let's begin, then. This won't take long," Forglen said.

Tiryn and Zinder took their places on the first row of the gallery. Kion, Forglen, and three glinthelms moved to stand below the great desk with its giant bull looming over them. One of the soldiers carried the white banner of Verisward trimmed in gold with a gold diamond set in the field. Another soldier bore the folded emerald tabard worn by those serving Inris. A third stood with a cross-armed salute opposite the banner.

"I call to attention all people of the Four Wards," Forglen said, raising his arms in a flourish and raising his voice as if addressing a great crowd. "In times of danger, with our lands no longer safe, it falls upon the men of the Four Wards to defend them, giving all that their people require, even to the spilling of their own blood. As the representative of the fane, defender of Verisward, and his bosom ally, the mighty margrave of Inrisward, upon whose lands we now stand, I hereby accept the service of Kion Bray of Furrow into the hosts of the Four Wards." He nodded to the glinthelm with the folded tabard. "The presentation of the colors."

The soldier unfurled the simple tabard and draped it over Kion's shoulders. The only embellishment in the emerald cloth was the red bar stitched into the shoulder. The tabard landed far more heavily than the mere weight of the fabric could account for.

Kion had done it. He had finally fulfilled his promise to Aonar and Roardin. He had joined the Warding army. Though the circumstances were not what he had hoped, he could not help but think that his father and mother would have been proud.

Forglen drew forth the dagger at his belt, touching it to Kion's left shoulder, then the top of his head, then his right shoulder, and then his chest, each touch corresponding to the name of one of the Four Wards as he spoke the ancient words:

Veris, Koris, Inris, Bey
As in light of dawn's first ray
So shall it be again one day

Though spoken in a rote manner, for a brief moment after the swordswain finished, Kion was swept up into a rush of glory. It was as if he stepped outside of time and looked down upon the history of the world as an outside observer, as if he were not bound up in the story himself. He saw the Four Lords and the Four Ladies walking, as it were, out of a fine gray mist to sit upon their thrones. He saw ten thousand suns rise and fall upon the land while those rulers stood watch over it, shepherding it, tending to its needs, cultivating the land until it shone forth, full and bountiful and undefiled. All these images came to him from the simple repetition of words he had heard countless times before.

But this time the words spoke to him in a new way and he

found that he heard them as though for the first time. And he marveled that he had never understood them before. This was the true reason he had been given his glaive, not just to drive back the haukmarn and win this war, but to restore what had been shattered, to recover what had been lost, to reforge this broken world into what it had been meant to be from the start, to see the Four Wards as they were meant to be: united, secure, bountiful, in the fullness of their glory. All of this came to him in a moment and then the moment shattered as Forglen's voice broke in.

"Welcome to the Warding host, Glinthelm Bray." Forglen gave him a satisfied nod. For a moment Kion wondered if the gesture was not genuine and that this might turn out for the better after all. "You may or may not have heard that Quelling has fallen. No doubt Jabble will come next and if it falls, the enemy will march on Windle. As great as that sword is, it cannot win the war alone. Our greatest need is want of men. If Windle is to withstand the attack, we must swell our ranks three to four times what they are now. With that in mind, I am assigning you to the role of messenger. As a messenger, your first task will be to send for aid from the fortress of Bramble Eyre."

Kion stared at the swordswain as though he had just awoken from a dream. Forglen could not have shocked him more had he struck him with the dagger in his hand. "Go to Bramble Eyre? But I thought I was going to fight, to help defend Windle."

"We need more men or we cannot win, not if we had a dozen flaming swords."

Kion went rigid. Once again, this was not what he had expected, but words failed him.

"Your orders are clear. Are they not?"

Tiryn's face mirrored his own, full of confusion and doubt. Zinder was up on his feet, hat in hand. He, at least, had no difficulty finding words to say.

"Horn toads! This is preposterous. You've got the Sword of the North ready to fight for you. Have you lost your senses?"

But the hardness in Forglen's eyes was not that of a madman. If Forglen had been part of the defense of Quelling or Charring or some larger town, he would have been subject to the orders of a varlance or a highgild, but in Windle, as he had said, his word was law. And if he was ordering Kion to journey to the south, however futile that order seemed, Kion was duty-bound to obey.

"You will kindly restrain yourself, master nyn, while in my courtroom, or I shall have you removed." Forglen emphasized his words by pointing his dagger toward Zinder, who fumed all the more, but bit back his response. "Now, Glinthelm Bray, I have heard rumors that the fane's men will arrive soon from the south. If so, they will certainly pass through the Eyre. With that in mind, I will entrust you with a petition for the fane to send what forces he can to Windle. The petition may not come in time, but if Jabble holds out, we may have a chance. You are to deliver my petition to Namril Grundstaff, Lord of Bramble Eyre. After you deliver the message, you shall place yourself under his command. You leave within the hour. Is that clear?"

A messenger. He had lost Vayd's trail and now he was to be sent as far from where the battle raged as possible. When would he have a chance to face him again? Forglen may have been correct in saying that they could not win the war without more men, but if Vayd was defeated, the haukmarn would withdraw that very day. And it only took one sword to accomplish that. But looking into Forglen's eyes, he could tell that any arguments would be a waste of breath.

"Am I to be issued a horse?" Kion thought of Endrith and his horse Drowen. He had been sent to Quelling the last Kion knew. Had he taken part in the battle there? How strange that Kion was now forced to follow the same path as his friend.

"No. Unfortunately, we have none to spare. We have few enough as it is and we need every last one for our scouts and the defense of Windle. And there are no more to be bought since half the town has fled, taking what few horses they had with them. We will just have to hope that Jabble holds out until your message is delivered. It is a small chance, but one worth taking."

Kion remained unconvinced. If men were so needed, why would he not be given a horse? Or why not send some other soldier and allow him to stay and fight? He suspected it was all invented just to send him as far away as possible, but he did not know for certain. For who can truly say what goes on in the mind of another? Yet whether because he had mentioned Kithian's voice and he thought Kion mad, or from fear or jealousy of his blade, or because Forglen really did believe more soldiers were the only hope of defending the town, the orders were clear. He was being sent south and there was not a thing he could do about it. In his journal, Strom recorded many such orders he disagreed with, but he fulfilled them all the same. Such was the call of a soldier, to fight where he was told and to win where he fought.

Forglen sheathed his dagger and nodded to the other glinthelms. "Very well. I believe that concludes the ceremony. I'll have the petition sent down to you. You shall await it in the foyer."

Forglen tromped from the room, his gait heavy and graceless. Kion, Tiryn, and Zinder watched him go, still stunned by what had just happened.

"Are we going to stand for this?" Zinder said at last. "Do you intend to let that petty little scoomdigger keep you out of the war? What if Vayd leads the attack on Windle? We'll be missing our chance to stick a sword in his big gray gut and send him into oblivion."

"I don't see that I have a choice," Kion said. "I pledged to serve him and he has the authority to send me wherever he wishes."

"As long as the orders are not evil, a soldier must do his best to obey them," Kithian said. They were not the words Kion wanted to hear, but as always, Kithian spoke the truth.

"Do not lose heart, swordspeaker," Nurien said, her voice more

tender than usual. *"It often turns out that the unwanted road leads to where we most need to go."*

"If the fane's men are at Bramble Eyre, you may do more good there than here." Tiryn cast a hopeful gaze up at her brother.

"Indeed, I sense that we may find unexpected allies there," Nurien said.

"Well, it looks like there's nothing for it. A blacksmith should never argue against a blade, especially a talking one." Zinder patted Kion on the arm. "Welcome to the Warding army, lad."

Kion walked out into the hall where he and Tiryn gathered their glaives. So they were off to Bramble Eyre, horseless and dismayed. Such was Kion's first day as a soldier in the Warding army.

The stirring scent of fresh bread wafted from a bakery somewhere down one of the streets. An old man sat by the desiccated fountain of the square, peeling an apple and letting the rind fall to the pavement. Two children chased after a tiny lizard as it scurried for cover beneath a pile of crates outside a leatherworking shop. A man and a woman haggled loudly in front of a cart over the price of a bag of turnips. All around, life went on as though war and death and calamity did not threaten this place, as if its doom were not even now marching toward it.

Within a month all of this might be gone. Three hundred men and some wooden walls would not be enough to resist the haukmar attack. The town would be overrun and the lives of its people lost or forever changed. All because of one man's fears. Because he saw Kion's sword as a threat and not a gift.

Kion could defy Forglen's orders. He could stay and find a way to fight the haukmarn when they came. But he had tried defiance in Whitewind. And he had nearly paid for it with his life. No, he would not repay foolishness with dishonor. His path lay to the south. Perhaps he could reach Bramble Eyre in time for the reinforcements to come. Or perhaps the journey would offer them some other chance to strike at Vayd and the haukmarn. Perhaps as Nurien said, the unwanted road would turn out to be the path where he was needed most.

"Perhaps we should not have shown the swordswain my fire," Kithian said to Kion as they walked back through the square to the Red Ox.

"Perhaps," Kion said. "But I think it was telling him that you could talk that made him want to get rid of me more than anything. The fire at least is something people can see with their own eyes. As you said, it's hard for people to accept that a sword can speak when they can't hear the voice themselves."

"It may be wise not to speak of that to others," Nurien said.

"I agree," Tiryn said. "We don't want to attract unwanted attention. And we certainly don't want people thinking we've gone mad."

"Yes, only I can think that," Zinder said with a chuckle.

"Well, but we're only half as mad as you," Kion said, ribbing him.

"Ah, but what is it you said Forglen told you? 'Genius is only madness turned right side up?' Guilty as charged!"

"I believe Nurien is right. We should keep our true nature a secret going forward. Unless need or wisdom dictate otherwise."

"I only wish that everyone could hear your voices. That would make things easier," Kion said. "Why did the Master-smith only give this gift to a few?"

"A better question would be: why did he give it to anyone?" Kithian said. *"For if it were given to more, then why not to all? But a gift compelled is no longer a gift. No, the Master is free to impart his gifts upon whom he will."*

"And you must not forget one thing more," Nurien said. *"That with the power to hear comes the responsibility to heed. Many might suppose they should want to hear our voices who would not give proper weight to our words, or worse, might twist them to mean something*

else. For it is one thing to be heard and quite another to be listened to. It is the bond between glaive and swordspeaker that allows you to understand our words almost before we speak them. That bond is not easily or lightly bestowed. It is a mystery far greater than our speech itself and one which not even the glaives fully understand."

After Kion finished sharing Nurien's and Kithian's words, the company fell silent. It was true that though the words of the glaives could be repeated, the quality of their immortal, quickening voices could not. To hear them was to come alive all over again, indeed to feel that one had only ever lived in a kind of half-light before the arrival of the sun in all its fullness. Not even Zinder, Kion's closest friend in all the world, could truly understand all that the bond between him and Kithian meant.

Yet it was enough that they did speak. For though others could not hear those voices, and might not fully understand them even if they could, Kion and Tiryn did. And through them, the wisdom of the glaives once more spoke to the world of men.

Chapter 12

DISHONORABLE MEN

Before leaving they inquired to see if anyone would sell them a mule, but the best price they found was five times what one would have normally cost. And so, amidst Zinder's grumblings about the outlandishness of prices brought on by the war, Kion found himself once again at his old place in front of the cart. The journey across Noath, and especially the Lost Hylls, had loosened the wheels and one of the boards was badly cracked. Zinder had done his best to repair them, but the board and both of the wheel fittings would need replacing before they reached Bramble Eyre.

"It pains me to watch you toiling away mile after mile with that thing," Zinder said as they discussed the state of the cart. "Oh, my dear Crusty. Why did I abandon you?" he added, forgetting, of course, that his beloved mule would have suffered the same fate as the other animals in Whitewind had he gone there with them.

"You said that Tiller is along this road and it's a farming village, isn't it?" Tiryn said. "There's bound to be someone there who will sell us a mule."

"Yes, yes, quite true." Zinder's eyes sparked with a fresh idea. "I may know someone who won't gouge us like these Windle swindlers. I did a good deal of work for a farmer there some years ago. He may have a beast he'd be willing to sell us for an honest price."

That was something to hope for over the long miles ahead. Another thing to lift Kion's spirits as they headed out came in the form of the gloves now covering his hands. Zinder had purchased them for three silver nicks—an awful price—but Kion was glad he'd spent the coin. His blisters had begun to heal and the gloves would hopefully prevent him from getting new ones.

Kion buried his newly acquired tabard inside the baggage. In the summer heat it would only make the journey that much more miserable and despite the ceremony with Forglen, he did not feel like a soldier of Warding. He had expected to be introduced to other soldiers, to be trained in tactics, to listen to battle plans, perhaps even hear a stirring speech that would inspire him and his fellows to rush out and win the day. But there had been none of that, and now he was heading away from the war and not to it. During his search for his mother, Kion had twice turned away requests to fight for the Four Wards. Now that he was ready, he was sent on a fool's errand to the most remote outpost of Inris in the middle of the great Fathomwood Forest.

On the road they passed through the early summer green of rye, oat, and barley fields. Some had been left unsown for pasture and small herds grazed idly, the cattle unconcerned by thoughts of war and invasion, content from the glow of the sun and the crunch of good moist grass between their large, dark lips. The herdsmen, as before, watched the company's progress warily, keeping protective watch over their animals.

They made camp that day on the edge of a cattle field. The next morning Zinder claimed one of the bulls had wandered over with its herd to investigate him during the night.

"I had to hoot and carry on and flap my arms like a chicken until they wandered off. It's a wonder you slept through it. Needless to say, I got less than three winks of sleep, if that."

"It sounds like we are in your debt, then," Kion said. "There you were fighting off the ravening hordes and the two of us sleeping blissfully away and none the wiser."

"Thank you, Zinder. I did sleep unusually well last night," Tiryn said with a grin.

"Well, at least one of you values my eternal vigilance. Don't blame me if I start nodding off along the way. That's all I have to say."

"If you need to catch up on your sleep, don't hesitate to throw yourself in with the rest of the baggage," Kion said, the spark in his eye matching Zinder's.

"We'll see how you feel when I take you up on it!"

But of course Zinder never would. Even if he started falling asleep on his feet like the marmot, he would never descend to be carried along in a cart. He had far too much dignity for that. And he would not do anything to add to Kion's burdens.

"The cattle were not the only troublesome thing that came in the night. The shadows have picked up our trail again," Nurien said. Tiryn's smile dissolved into a tight-lipped frown.

"We must be vigilant, then. Whatever they are, they have not chosen to assault us yet. Perhaps they are only spies, meant to inform Malix of our movements," Kithian said.

"A craven enemy is not one that I fear," Kion said.

"There are more ways to be defeated than by open attack," Nurien said. *"As Kithian says, we must be ever watchful."*

It was one thing to be pursued by haukmarn or even dreadwulfs. Those at least Kion knew and could fight if it came to it. But how to prepare to face an enemy they had never seen?

The field they slept in that night was the last cattle field they saw. The pastures and farms dwindled away with the dawn and they walked that morning through a much wilder country. Thick clumps of broom grass, like the kind that grew in Noath, sprouted alongside the road. Stands of maple and birch grew there as well, offering welcome shade. Game abounded in the form of leaping deer, plump grouse, and darting rabbits, but their provisions were still ample so they did not bother hunting for now.

In an open stretch of road, where the sun hammered down, they came upon a forlorn and gruesome sight. They had anticipated some form of carnage when they spotted several vultures winging their way south, but they had not expected to see such a large carcass beside the road. It belonged to a dead horse. Scavenger birds of all sorts swirled about it. But the air of rot was not as sickening as it had been in the stables and judging by how much flesh remained it could not have lain there for more than a day.

"What a terrible thing," Tiryn said. "Was it a wild horse, do you think?" No tack was visible upon the beast.

"No," Zinder said. "The coat has been too well cared for. Most likely a draft horse that escaped from one of the farms."

"Fire and ice, that's an awful waste of a fine animal," Kion said, rubbing his aching arms.

"Could you hear what those vultures and crows were saying before they left, Nurien?" Tiryn said. "With some of the birds earlier this morning I thought I could make out a few words in their song, but those creatures seemed to make nothing more than squawks and screeches."

"So it is with most of the beasts that prey upon others. They have forsaken the beast tongue and hear only the voices of their own kind," Nurien said.

Putting the dead horse behind them, in distance though not in thought, they toiled onward until about midday when they encountered a pleasant little clearing beside the road, surrounded on three sides by a wall of ash trees, low in height, but abounding in thick leaves, making them look more like giant bushes than actual trees. The trampled dirt and the remains of many campfires showed that travelers frequented this place, some quite recently. In the center of the clearing a well invited them to slake their thirst. Its dull gray stones piled up to a height just over Zinder's head. A weathered bucket and rope allowed them to take their fill and replenish their waterskins. The water had a trace of bitterness to it, but its coolness had a salutary effect upon their parched throats.

"We ought to be about halfway to Tiller by now," Zinder said.

"Tell us about this farmer friend of yours," Kion said,

splashing his neck with water from the well and relishing the cool streams that trickled down his back.

Zinder cocked his head with an eye toward the sky, casting his mind back through the years. "He is a kindly sort, generous to a fault, simple. He was not married when I knew him and he was already old then, so I imagine he has remained without a wife. But if he's still living, he may not only sell us a mule, but he might offer us a place to stay. Tiller is too small to support an inn."

"What's his name?" Tiryn said.

"Marlund. Marlund Pander. But don't hold it against him. He's as hard-working and good-natured as they come."

"I hope he's not the sort of farmer who doesn't like shepherds," Kion said. "Until I met Endrith I didn't think that sort existed."

"Yes, it's shameful the way they treated you in Furrow. I think it was mostly owing to that rotten Shaw family. If they hadn't been so full of coin and so full of themselves, things might have been different. Whenever men get to thinking they're better than someone else just because they've got more, ill deeds ensue."

"Well, let's hope Farmer Marlund remains just as you say," Kion said. "We must push on for Tiller now."

"Hold. Did you notice that dark shadow within the trees?" Nurien said, her question as chilling as it was unexpected.

"Kion's right, we must—" Zinder said, but stopped when Tiryn shared Nurien's warning.

"No, but I see it now. It's rather large isn't it?" Kithian said.

"And there is something else. The birds. Have you noticed the utter absence of their chatter?" Nurien said.

"Kion, perhaps we should see what is behind that shape," Kithian said.

Kion informed Zinder in a low whisper of their plans. He drew forth Truesilver and Tiryn unsheathed Rimewinter and the three of them ventured toward the back of the clearing where what looked like a great curtain of leaves hung shrouded in shadows. The closer they got, the deeper the shadows grew.

Nurien's voice halted them before they reached the edge of the trees.

"We are being watched," she said.

"By who?" Tiryn said, barely voicing the words.

"Is it the shadow hunter?" Kion's eyes darted from tree to tree.

"I see them," Kithian said. *"There are eight of them within my sight, all armed with—"*

"Get down!" Nurien's cry cut him off. Tiryn was the first to hit the dirt, followed by Zinder whose exceptional nynnian senses perceived the three whizzing arrows the moment they let fly. Kion was the last to drop, but by some special mercy the arrow aimed for his heart zinged off the flat of his upheld blade and he half-wondered if Truesilver hadn't moved to block it of its own accord.

Low curses betrayed the presence of the bowmen, but before they could nock another round of arrows Kion was back on his feet.

"Glaivefire." He swung his blade forward to launch the newly born flames toward the closest tree.

"Nurien, help us," Tiryn shouted.

Flames erupted along the trunk of the tree and spread among its branches. Another volley of arrows came flying. A fan of ice shot from Rimewinter's hilt and met them in the air—knocking them away in a sequence of splintering bursts—all but one. That one went straight for Zinder, who had sprinted back to the cart for his crossbow, but he gave a well-timed hop and the arrow skipped beneath his feet.

"Into the trees," Kithian said. *"We cannot trust Rimewinter to stop every arrow. We must flush them out."*

"Tiryn, go back with Zinder and use the cart for cover," Kion said and launched into the woods. He flourished his sword before him and the flames billowed into a ruby wall of death, shielding him from further attack. He plunged into the inferno, driving the fire before him with arcing strokes. Though the glaivefire ignited all that it touched, Kion felt none of its heat, protected by the blade that he carried. Shrieks and cries echoed through the woods. They were the voices of men, and not haukmarn.

"Curses!" "Get out!" "Fall back!" they shouted as they abandoned their hiding places and fled into the woods.

"Can you see them, Kithian?"

"They have passed beyond my glaivesight, but I can hear them crashing through the trees. They will not soon return. We should hasten back to the others."

Tiryn screamed and Kion's heart turned to water. He turned and ran back through the blaze.

"Nurien, you did it!" Tiryn's voice rose in wonder and relief.

"No, we did it—together," Nurien said.

Kion burst through the flames and into the clearing.

Two men lay on the ground, halfway between the trees and the cart, their limbs and torsos encased in glittering blue ice that shone blindingly in the sun. Only their heads and feet remained exposed to the open air. Both cursed their ill fortune and cried out beasts caught in a trap. A short sword lay on the ground beside each of them.

"Please! Let us go!" one of them said.

"Don't ensorcel us! We were only doing what we were told!" said the other.

Both men sported ragged beards and ragged hoods. They had the look of desperate men, of scoundrels and cheats, the sort who lived in the wilds and earned their keep at the expense of the innocent and the weak. Such men were common enough before the war, but it was a wretched man indeed who would ravage his own countrymen rather than the enemies within his borders.

"That's right, you filch-mongers, blather on, beg for mercy," Zinder said, coming out from behind the cart with his repeating crossbow in hand. He kept it trained on the captives. "You're perfectly brave when you're shooting at two children and a nyn, snug and unseen in your little forest hideaway. Not so confident when you're up to your teeth in ice, are you?" He stamped toward them, mad as a hornet, his face flushed with the full range of reds.

"After we knocked down all their arrows, four of them charged from the woods. Rimewinter pinned the first two and the others fled," Tiryn said. She stayed beside the cart, still breathing hard from the narrow escape. She had defeated a far more fearsome foe in the snowwinder on Tinesplitter Isle, but she was still unaccustomed to battle.

Kion quenched his blade, not wanting to melt away the ice which held the men fast. The billowing wall behind him fell away too. He cast a glance back at the trees, but no more arrows came, nor could he see any sign that the other attackers would return to rescue their companions.

"Please, please, we didn't want to shoot," said the older of the two men. He had a small scar across the bridge of his nose and his teeth were so crooked it was a wonder they didn't fall out.

"He tells the truth. We weren't going to attack until you came toward our hiding places. Then we had no choice," said the younger of the two, a man with a small nose and mouth, and an even smaller amount of courage in his eyes.

"As if we would ever trust the word of cut-thieves the likes of you!" Zinder said.

"We'll see if he's telling the truth or not," Kion said.

"*Yes, we shall see. But his is a crafty mind,*" Kithian said. Though he could usually sense the truth of any words spoken in his hearing, with those accustomed to clever speech or devious ways, Kithian needed Kion's touch.

Kion knelt beside the younger bandit, who lay frozen on his side. He kept Truesilver in his right hand, but with his left he reached down and touched the back of the man's head. The bandit wiggled about to avoid Kion's grip, forcing him to grab hold of the man's hair.

"Don't kill me! Don't chop off my head! I'm too young to die!" The fellow moaned and wailed for all he was worth, filthy tears pouring down his face.

"I'm not going to kill you. Unlike you, I do not attack defenseless people. But I can tell the truth spoken by those I touch. So you will hold still while I question you unless you want your hair pulled out."

"It's just like I thought, they're both sorcerers! One of fire, the other of ice!" the older bandit said, his head quivering both from fear and the terrible chill of the icy encasement.

"I'll tell you anything—anything," said the younger one. "Just don't kill me. Please!"

"I already told you, I have no intention of harming you in any way. But I warn you. I will know if you are lying and it will not go well for you if you do."

"You should thank your wandering sparks my friend's the one asking the questions and not me," Zinder said. "I don't deal as kindly with scoundrels."

Tiryn came forward cautiously, a mixed look on her face, part pity and part dismay. Kion allowed the man a few moments to calm down. Like the other one, though, he could not keep from shivering.

"Tell us why you were hiding in the trees," Kion said. Behind him, a tower of smoke poured up from the woods.

The bandit grimaced, fearing his answer might change Kion's promise not to kill him, but fearing even more what might happen if he told a lie.

"We were lying in wait to waylay travelers," he said. His eyes flicked to Kion's magnificent sword, with its golden hilt and spectacular citrines, dancing with motes of amber light. In the reflection of that light his face softened and he looked less a rascal. The fear in his eyes gave way to shame.

"By waylay, you mean rob and kill?" Zinder said.

"Well…I…yes, if you have to put it direct. But we only attack the rich. We leave the poorer travelers to themselves." The words came out hollow. The man was not proud of the life he lived.

"And we looked to be on the poorer side of things," Kion said. "That's why you didn't attack us at first, I take it?"

"…That's the gist of it."

"He speaks the truth," Kithian said.

"What he's actually saying is that he and his band of snagjaggers don't bother with poor people because it's not worth the trouble," Zinder said, sneering in disgust.

"How many are there in your band?" Kion said.

"I'm not that good with numbers," the bandit said.

The older bandit piped up before Kion or Zinder could press him on it. "Two dozen, plus the warder and his second."

"The warder? So you're a mercenary band? Or were before you fell to thieving?" Kion said. Warders led mercenary bands all across the Wards, though they were more common in Verisward to the south. Many had fought for the Warding army during the last war, the War of the Claws.

"You've struck it," the young bandit said. "We'd fallen on hard times. The margrave wouldn't pay, even after the war broke out, so we took to this unhappy life. We didn't want to. We were honorable men once, by the forgelight we were."

"Hmph. Honorable men don't lose their honor when it becomes hard to keep," Zinder said.

"And your friend told the truth about the size of your band?" Kion said.

"I was being honest when I said I'm no good with numbers, but that sounds about right."

"Ask him what lies behind the curtain of leaves. Though we could find out easily enough ourselves, I imagine it has something to do with their business in this clearing," Nurien said.

"Tell me," Kion said. "What lies behind that curtain of leaves in the forest?"

The bandit hesitated, his lips tensing. When he spoke, his voice was low and crestfallen. "A carriage."

"It belonged to some of the innocents you robbed?"

"Yes, sad to say."

"Where are they now?"

The young man looked away. His shivers grew more violent. "Dead."

A threatening rumble sounded in Zinder's throat. "Gutter-scum," he muttered under his breath. Tiryn gave a shudder.

Kion's throat went dry. He'd never met such worthless men. "Do you kill everyone you rob? Is that how it is?"

The young bandit was silent, but the older one spoke in his place. "We make no defense for our actions. That's the way of the wilds. If you mean to do justice, spare the boy, at least. I've lived to see enough misery, but he's got days yet ahead to maybe see some light."

"No one more will die here today," Kion said. "Though I don't doubt that you deserve it, justice is not mine to give. We will take you to Tiller. The fielder there can have his way with you."

"But he'll hang us, he will, if you tell him about the carriage," the older man said.

"And we didn't kill them. Honest we didn't," the young man said. "There's others in the band that do that sort of work."

"Tell that to the fielder and see how you fare," Zinder said.

"You'll have to face whatever punishment the fielder gives you," Kion said. "I cannot promise you will live, but you will face justice. And you can go frozen or unfrozen, it makes no difference to me."

Neither man looked at all pleased with Kion's pronouncement, but hearing the hardness in his voice and shivering more by the moment, they mounted no further protest.

"He can't prove we killed anyone," the old man said. "I suppose we'll just have to take what's coming to us. I knew this day would come sooner or later."

"Good. Zinder, get the rope. Tiryn, go ahead and break the older man's ice." Kion rose and Tiryn drew near. "What are your names?"

"I'm Jalik. And that's Renin," the young bandit said.

"Well, Jalik and Renin, my name is Kion. This is my sister Tiryn, and our friend over there is Zinder. It looks like you'll be traveling with us for a time. You've seen what her dagger and my sword can do, so I trust you won't try anything foolish."

"We know when we're beat," Renin said.

But before Tiryn could free him from the ice, a rustling of leaves sounded from the forest. Kion tensed, fearing the other bandits had returned. Instead, a tall girl ventured out from behind the mysterious curtain of leaves. She had eyes the color of spring grass. Her dark hair was pinned up in a bun and she wore a plain brown dress, but the bun was frayed and her dress disheveled and stained with sweat. She approached with great care, her steps wearied by some unseen burden. Her eyes and cheeks glistened red from recent tears.

"Hullo there," Zinder said cautiously, as if he might frighten her back into the woods. "Are you all right?"

The girl nodded and drew an unsteady breath. "Dalia Unwith, at your service." She made a graceful curtsy which seemed out of place with her appearance and the smoking trees behind her.

"Greetings, Dalia," Kion said. Some mystery followed this girl, one bound up in pain and sorrow. "How did you come through the woods?"

Her young frame stiffened. "I was hiding in a carriage in a secret compartment. Those bandits killed my masters and the guards who protected us," Dalia said. Her manner of speech was as humble as her dress, her words direct and plain, though weighed with grief and regret.

Zinder let out a low growl and squeezed his crossbow trigger dangerously tight. "Gutterscum," he muttered.

A flash of rage shot through Kion. He already knew that

these bandits were murderers as well as thieves, but putting a face to their crimes enflamed him to the point that he went and sheathed his sword, lest he do something rash.

Tiryn strode past Kion and the bandits let out a teeth-chattering groan as she left them encased in ice. She rarely took the initiative with strangers, but Dalia was close to her age and in clear need of comfort.

"Come, Dalia," Tiryn said, guiding her toward the cart with a gentle hand. "Tell us your story."

Chapter 13

OF GRIEF AND MEMORY

Dalia kept her eyes to the ground and her voice scarcely rose above the rustle of the wind through the trees, but Kion did not miss a single word. For she spoke with a quiet suffering which commanded attention.

"Master Odwin and his wife were always good to me," she began. "I've only been with them a year, but Mistress Odwin was like a second mother. My own died when I was very young. The Odwins were both getting on in years and rarely traveled. But when he was young Master Odwin made a handsome fortune as a jeweler and still kept many pieces of finery from those days. For my birthday, Mistress Odwin gave me this." She held out her right hand to show the tiny emerald embedded into a golden ring fashioned as a wreath. Small as it was, for a servant girl it must have been worth half a year's wages.

"It's lovely. She must have been a very kind woman," Tiryn said.

"Oh, she was. So very, very kind."

"And they were with you in the carriage when the bandits attacked?" Kion said.

"Yes, and the guards, Ferig and Girdo. They had worked for the Odwins for many years and so I'm afraid were past their prime, but they fought bravely." Shaken though she was, and on the verge of tears, Dalia had no difficulty finding words. She showed herself to have a bright mind and clear speech.

"They gave their lives protecting their friends. There can be no greater sacrifice," Zinder said, marking the two bandits with a cold glare. They avoided his gaze, instead fixing on Dalia as if she were a specter sent to haunt them for their evil deeds.

"I'm sorry about your masters and their guards." Kion had half a mind to leave the two bandits there to shiver to death, but he'd almost died from the cold himself and would not wish that fate even on a haukmar. Still, it wouldn't hurt them to suffer a little longer in the cold while Dalia finished her tale.

Dalia hesitated, breathing deeply to gather herself.

"You don't have to tell us any more, Dalia, if you do not wish to," Tiryn said.

"No, it's fine." Dalia gave a dutiful nod, as if she needed to continue the story for her own inner reasons. "Ferig and Girdo held the bandits off until Mistress Odwin could get me inside the hidden compartment below the floorboards. I begged her to let me suffer her fate, but she ordered me inside. The space was not really meant for a person, but I was just limber enough to fit. That was her last kindness to me, to spare my life." Here she bowed her head and struggled so mightily Kion doubted whether she would go on, but somehow she found the strength.

"After that, I listened to the horrible attack unfold. I heard the screams and it was all I could do not to scream myself." Her eyes hollowed, growing gaunt from the memory. "But at last they finished with their butchery and ransacking of the carriage. I hoped they would leave so I could escape, but they dragged the carriage into the woods and took up hiding places around it. I was trapped with no way out until I heard more sounds of battle. But this time the bandits fled. I waited until I was sure that they were gone. I had a hard time getting out, but once I did I heard your voices. That's when you saw me coming out of the woods."

Tiryn wrapped an arm around her and said softly in her ear, "That must have been terrifying. But I'm glad you lived."

"Yes, m'lady. It's a mercy to be sure, though in truth I would have rather been beside my mistress. It was very hard to hear her cries." Though she staved off her tears, Kion did not miss the strain in her voice. Dalia stopped, then, and was unable to say more. Watching her wrestle with the same pangs of grief which gripped his own heart brought a strange sense of comfort. Dalia had not lost her mother, but Mrs. Odwin had been something like that to her. And yet outwardly at least, and perhaps inwardly as well, she bore the loss with surprising strength. It was not that the sadness was not there, but that she refused to let it master her.

"Dalia, you said your mother is gone? What of your father? Do you have other family?" Tiryn said.

Dalia's voice quickened. "My father and two younger brothers live in Rippling. Now that the Odwins are gone, I will go to them."

"Rippling, you say?" Zinder said. "Why, that's right along our way."

"We should very much enjoy sharing your company," Tiryn said.

"Indeed," Kion said.

"I would be in your debt." Dalia gave Tiryn's hands a tight squeeze.

Tiryn embraced her again. "Don't worry, you'll be safe with us."

By now, the bandits' teeth were chattering like woodpeckers and though the sun sweltered hot as ever, Rimewinter's deep blue ice showed no sign of melting. The men's lips would soon be the same shade of blue as the ice.

"It's time we bound these two up," Kion said.

"If we gave them what they deserved, we'd roll them all the way to Tiller," Zinder said.

Tiryn pointed Rimewinter's tip toward the ice holding Renin, causing it to shatter into large chunks. Zinder kept his crossbow pointed at the bandit and Kion tightened his grip on Truesilver, but all the man did was shake off the ice and rub his reddened arms.

"Th-thank you," Renin said. "Another m-minute and my l-l-lips would have f-f-frozen shut."

Zinder bound his hands while Kion stood ready should the thief try anything foolish. Zinder also tied a cord between Renin's feet so that if he did attempt to run he could not break away at full stride. After he finished binding Renin, Tiryn broke Jalik's ice and Zinder bound him as well.

"There we are," Zinder said, wiping his hands in satisfaction. "Enjoy your new bonds. Any mischief and it's back to the icebox."

The bandits gave him dark looks. Kion doubted they would go easily to meet their fate. Traveling with two thieves in tow would make the journey all the more dangerous. But there was no way around it. Best to get moving and get it over with. The sooner they reached Tiller, the sooner they could be rid of them.

"I wonder what they'll do to them in Tiller." Dalia glanced at them, her eyes full of trouble and doubt.

"Will you be all right traveling with them after what they did to your masters?" Kion said.

"I can't change what's been done, however much I may grieve for that which was. And the open road is no place for a girl alone. I trust that I'll be safe in your company, m'lord." Dalia gave a half curtsy. Once more, Kion marveled at her resilient spirit.

"Please, call me Kion. We're commoners just like you."

"Oh, truly? With a sword like yours, I assumed you must be a noble or at least a merchant's son. How did you come by such a blade?"

"It's quite a long story. Why don't I tell it to you as we go along the road?"

"Yes, yes of course," Dalia said with the relief of one who has just come out of a terrible storm to a roaring fire. "A good story is always welcome, but especially on a day like today."

The unexpected and unwelcome addition of the two bandits slowed their progress considerably. Jalik and Renin, who spoke hardly a word during the long miles that followed, could only go so fast with ropes tied around their ankles. Beyond that, they dragged their feet and walked even slower than they might have. They were in no hurry to make the acquaintance of Tiller's fielder. At one point Zinder picked up a stick and began prodding them to move faster. That helped, but the bandits' scowls deepened with each passing mile.

Dalia more than made up for the bandits, though, for she seemed ill at ease with silence. It was not that she had to be the one talking, but that a conversation of some sort ought to be the natural state of things when in the company of others. She had many questions and soon drew out of them as much as they would tell her of their adventures thus far. She did not doubt a word they told her, fantastic and wild as the glaives and their gifts must have seemed. The only thing Kion failed to speak of were Kithian's and Nurien's voices, for there was no need to share that secret and the bandits were listening as well. They already thought of him and Tiryn as sorcerers. There was no need to make them think, like Forglen, that they were mad as well.

Everyone took to Dalia from the start. Zinder was happy to have someone so talkative and Tiryn found Dalia's soft, respectful manner endearing. Kion listened as best he could, but was too weary from pulling the cart and too worried about the bandits to engage in much conversation. He expected them to bolt or attack at any moment and often glanced back to where Truesilver lay atop the cart, ready to call to his hand should his fears come true. Though he did not speak to either glaive during the journey, that did not mean that they did not speak to him.

"You handled the bandits well," Kithian said soon after they left the clearing. *"Though it is right that we deliver them to the magistrate, they may do something along the road or come nightfall. But do*

not fear. Nurien and I will be vigilant. We will not let them escape without warning you the moment they make the attempt."

"Perhaps even before it happens," Nurien said. *"But I do not think that they will flee. For though they are ill-contented with their fate, they fear the ice and fire they saw in the clearing as much as they fear justice in Tiller."*

"It saddens me to see what the Four Wards have come to if bandits roam so freely upon its roads. Such lawlessness was rare in times past. The only fear men had then came from the dim-touched that survived the war. And most of them were hunted down in the years after it ended."

Kithian and Nurien spoke, then, of some of the dim-touched creatures that fought in the War of the Glaives. They spoke of the cinderswallows, bat-like creatures with a thirst for blood and hot places; the nictmain, large horse-like beasts with twin horns, fearsome in the charge and hideous to behold; the hilgorn, masses of dirt and rubble, slow to move yet with skin harder than any armor; the drakyn, lesser cousins of dragons, cunning and with poison tails; and worst of all, the great dragons themselves with their breath of smoke and fire, first of all the dim-touched and most dreaded among those within the enemy's ranks.

"Malix will continue to call all such creatures to himself that survived and multiplied down through the years," Kithian said.

After that the two glaives grew silent, as was their wont, brooding upon their immortal thoughts until several miles had gone by and the sun had slid halfway down the sky. Then Kithian spoke again, responding to something Dalia told them of how she had warned her masters not to make the trip with only two guards.

"We'd heard rumors of bandit attacks on the road to Rippling," Dalia said. "But it was not something that we knew of for certain. Still, we ought to have taken heed. For Swordswain Forglen, it is said, no longer sends men to guard the road or to protect the Midway Well."

"When men fail to lead, the people suffer," Kithian remarked.

"Master Odwin had wanted to press on through the night and save half a day's travel, and in so doing perhaps give less opportunity to any ruffians," Dalia said, "but one of the horses took ill on the way and had to be left to die. The horses were past their day, you see, but my goodhearted master would not leave them behind, for, like his guards, they had served him for many years. But a single worn down horse could not go a day and a half pulling that large carriage without stopping, so we were forced to camp at the well."

"Poor fellow, your master," Zinder said. "He suffered for his kindness."

"Kindness is worth suffering for," Tiryn said. "Even so, I wish it had gone otherwise for Master Odwin and the others."

"So do I," Dalia said. "Though now that they are gone I have decided to take comfort in the good things they did for me, and in the privilege of knowing and enjoying their kindness, if only for a season. That seems a better choice than dwelling on the sorrow of their deaths."

She went on to speak of all the things her master had done, of how generous he was, and how well-spoken, of his sharp mind, and how well-liked he was among the people of Windle. Dalia had equal praise for Mistress Odwin. They had passed hours together sewing and speaking of her younger days. She had been born into a wealthy family, her father owning mines in the Hemming Hylls. In her younger days, she had been quite the talk at the dances and festivals held across Inris and had visited every town in the north, from Seabrim to Rippling. But Master Odwin was more thoughtful and generous than all the others who sought her hand and so won her heart.

As Dalia went on reminiscing about her fallen masters, Kion could not help but recall all the many admirable qualities of his mother. How kind and gentle and good she had been, and not just to him and Tiryn. Like the Odwins, she had been kind to all, even those who called his father a coward or mocked his family as uncouth shepherds, little better than the animals they tended. And yet unlike Dalia, who chose to draw strength from the memory of her masters' goodness, he saw it only as a lack, an absence, a loss. He saw himself as robbed of a treasure, one that he could never recover.

Through Dalia's memories, the treasure of her time with the Odwins was not wholly lost, but lived on in her. Perhaps instead of putting his mother out of his thoughts as he so often did, he should, like Dalia, take comfort in his memories. But could he? Would his heart allow him to see past his grief to the goodness that had been? Could thankfulness triumph over sorrow in the end? He was not sure. But oh, how he hoped that it could.

Chapter 14

RING OF FIRE

In a shadowy glen, just off the road, sat a crumpled, disheveled figure at the base of a wrinkled old oak. Truesilver lay propped against the tree beside him, the glow from its blade gone dark for the near full moon provided more than enough light to keep watch over the sleeping camp. Yet still, with so many nearby bushes and trees, dark patches abounded and Kion's eyes made a circuit, passing from shadow to shadow, searching for any sign of trouble.

Still he missed it when it came.

An arrow let fly, coursing through the darkness and striking square in the middle of the figure's exposed chest. The darkness came alive as a dozen men in ebony leather stormed the clearing. Jalik and Renin leapt to their feet, clued in by certain night sounds that Kion had failed to recognize. The leader of the bandits, a man with an angular face and a bristly gray beard, stormed into the clearing with a hearty cry of "Fellswords to victory!" He cared not whom he awoke, for the camp was surrounded and overrun. The Fellsword bandits had swept in and freed their men. All that remained was to slay the sleeping figures where they lay, loot their bodies, and stride off into the night.

Only they had not won. Not at all.

Kion leapt up from his dark hiding place, several trees away from where the arrow had pierced his stuffed clothing.

"Truesilver, to me." The sword flickered and its handle sprang into his gauntleted hand with a loud clink. "Glaivefire."

He swept Truesilver along the ground behind him. In a dazzling flash, the flames licked up the circle of oil surrounding the clearing. A costly ploy to spend three full flasks, but it was worth it. Before the bandits could take two steps, the camp was ringed in a menacing ten foot wall of crimson flame.

Tiryn, acting upon this signal, drew forth her glimmering dagger. The bandits trapped inside the flames cried out in confusion and dismay, darting this way and that, hunting for a way out of the inferno while Tiryn spoke into the chaos. "Glaivefrost."

Frozen blue balls struck the men in the chests and legs. Only three of the missiles failed to find their mark. Though the balls were small, the ice webbed out from the point of impact, rapidly spreading across the rest of their bodies. Jalik and Renin were the first to drop, with Jalik crying out, "Not again!"

One of the bandits who managed to avoid the icy barrage went after Dalia, who, along with Zinder, had jumped up from her hiding place. But before he could bring his raised sword down and end her young life, Zinder landed two bolts into the back of his legs. His third shot skidded off the leather covering the man's torso, but the first two were enough. The man crashed to the ground with a scream, dropping his blade and clutching at his legs.

The bandit leader, though already succumbing to the ice enveloping his frame, staggered toward Tiryn and swung his sword in a murderous arc. But his arm froze in midair, poised above his head, turning him into an icy statue.

"Warder, are you all right?" a man outside the ring of fire cried.

"What should we do?" cried another.

"We dare not shoot into the fire for fear of striking our own," said yet another.

The bandit leader, whose head and feet remained uncovered, shouted back to them. "It's sorcery, men, black sorcery! I should have believed you. Fly to safety. We are lost!" His face hardened, resigned to his doom, but his voice rang with a commanding air. The bandit had a nobility about him, wicked and fallen though he was. For he would save his men, though he himself was lost. For the first time, Kion caught a glimpse that perhaps these bandits were not as cutthroat as he had supposed. Perhaps, as Jalik and Renin had claimed, they had at least been honorable men once. But was any of that honor still left?

"Hold, mercenaries!" Kion shouted over the din of confusion. "If you would save your warder, hear my words."

"Don't listen to him," shouted one of the other bandits, who lay on his back inside a barrel of blue ice. "His voice will bewitch you and make you cast yourselves into the fire."

"I am no sorcerer," Kion said. "Flee if you wish, but if you fail to listen to what I have to say, you will be abandoning your leader."

The leader's grim face lost some of its edge. "You may act like a sorcerer, but you talk like a man. What game are you up to? You've beaten us clean and simple. Do your worst if you will. By the sparklight, we would have treated you no better if things had gone the other way."

No sounds of flight came from beyond the circle of fire. They refused to abandon their leader after all, even when beaten.

In the ensuing silence, Dalia stared in amazement at the blue ice and red fire. Though they had told her of their plans and of the weapons' gifts it was another thing altogether to see them with her own eyes. Kion stepped in front of her and Tiryn, where he could address the bandit leader face-to-face.

"We know what you did with the merchant in the carriage and to those who traveled with him," Kion said. "You prey upon your fellow countrymen while honest men fall daily to the haukmar axes. For the slaughter of innocents you deserve the gallows. And yet you came to the rescue of Renin and Jalik, which shows that you still have some trace of dignity amongst you. Tiller is not far from here. Tell me why I should not bind you all and send for the fielder to see justice done?"

The leader's face went slack. He stared expressionless into the fire. Its flickering reflections only deepened the sorrowed and embittered lines stamped upon his face. The wild defiance that had blazed in his eyes withered away. A broken and defeated man stood before them encased in ice, sword upraised, frozen in the midst of the latest in a long train of violent and shameful acts.

"You should turn us in," he said. "It is as you say. We deserve the gallows. In truth, I would welcome such a fate."

The words were met by shocked silence among his men, yet none spoke against him.

Kion had no idea how to reply. He did not know what he had expected when he called out to these men, but it was not that. That faint spark of honor he had seen when the bandit leader first told his men to flee was brighter than he had supposed. How had they come to fall into such disgrace?

"You are not common bandits," Kion said. "I can see that by the way you are armed and armored. And your men call you warder. You were mercenaries once. You fought to defend the innocent, not to ravage them."

"If my ears heard right," Zinder said, "these are the Fellswords, one of the greatest companies to fight for Warding since the last war. Though I'd rather not believe it, since that would tarnish all the worthy deeds those men are said to have done."

"Is this true?" Kion said. "Were you a great company once?"

"Yes. The greatest in all of Inris by the estimation of some," the bandit leader said.

"What led you to take up a life of thievery in the wilds? Are a few gold rounds really worth more than the lives of innocents?"

"The answer to that is simple. What drives any man to impose his will upon others? Pride. The margrave's officials refused to pay us what we were worth. My men are the best company north of the Savron Toths, veterans of over forty battles, and they spit in our faces. The only thing they offered was food and shelter as payment. After all our years of honest service, spilling our blood against the haukmarn on the border, keeping the people of Inris safe, that was how they repaid us. It was too much, so I vowed to become an enemy of the margrave from that day forward.

"You may think of us as wretched monsters for what we've done, and you would not be wrong. But murderers suffer the penalty for their crimes whether or not they are caught. It's not like killing on the battlefield. Gruesome as that is, a man can sleep at night if he knows his cause was just and that he saved the fellows fighting alongside him. We have earned far and above what any army could have paid us these past few months, but there are wages of another kind that each man must pay. Every coin we stole is stained with blood and I for one can bear it no more. Take us to the fielder or slay us where we stand. Either way, our ill-fated journey ends here."

Again, silence reigned over the camp, interrupted only by the crack and snap of the branches above the wall of flames.

"The man is not lying," Kithian said. *"He feels a sense of relief now that he has finally been defeated. For to live by lies is a wearisome thing to those who once knew the truth."*

"He has come to see his folly, as surely as though looking into a mirror," Nurien said. *"Would it be possible, Kithian, to give this man and his men a second chance?"*

"I am as ready to forgive as any, but forgiveness cannot cover the debt these men have earned for the innocent lives taken by their hands." Though his voice was as strong and firm as ever, Kithian took no joy in his words.

"Very well," Nurien said dutifully.

Tiryn stepped forward and placed a hand on Kion's shoulder. "What if we let Dalia decide their fate?"

Tiryn's question took Kion by complete surprise. "What do you mean?"

"She is the one they have wronged. Would she not be in a better position to determine their fate even than a fielder?"

Zinder approached with a simmering scowl. "But what about all the others they've killed and robbed? Would that be justice for them?"

Tiryn turned to Dalia, who was as confused as Kion by this sudden turn. "We cannot know all that they have done in the past, but I say we let Dalia speak for those people as well," Tiryn said. "There is no one better to pass judgment."

Kion saw what Tiryn was doing. She was hoping that Dalia would set the men free. Like Nurien, she wanted to give these men a second chance.

"Would it not be right for her to do so?" Nurien said. *"Should not the wronged have the right to demand restitution from the one who has done the wrong?"*

"That is, I suppose, the intent of justice," Kithian said.

"What do you say, Dalia? Will you pass judgment on these men?" Kion said, still unsure if this was the proper choice, but willing to see what might come of this.

Dalia opened her mouth to speak, but for once, no words came. Her eyes went from one bandit to the next, each one trapped in a glistening prison of ice. Emotions and memories played out their inner dance behind the mask of her face.

"But I'm just a servant girl," she said. "How can someone like me decide the fate of others?"

"The fact that you do not wish to give out justice may be the most important reason why you should," Tiryn said.

Dalia choked back a sob. Tears shone in the firelight, brimming at the corners of her eyes. Her inner battle raged on for several moments until at last she gained a hard-fought peace.

"Very well. I will do it for the Odwins, and for Ferig and Girdo," Dalia said. She moved reluctantly to stand before the bandit leader.

"So you were in the carriage as well?" the man said.

"Yes, and I had to listen while your men killed the people I loved. The Odwins were their names. Padroff and Telanna Odwin. And their guards were Ferig and Girdo. They were as dear to me as my own family. Good, kind, honest people, who did not mean anyone any harm." The tears trickled out of her eyes.

"I am truly sorry," the bandit said. Tears fell from his own eyes as well. "What a wretched path I have chosen."

"I agree with what Kion said. Your crimes deserve death." A coolness swept over Dalia and her voice grew strong. The bandit nodded in quiet surrender, having expected nothing less.

"But I cannot bring myself to consign you to such a fate," Dalia continued. "Nor do I think the Odwins would demand your death if they were in my place. For if they taught me anything it is that mercy is stronger than hate. Perhaps there are some who do indeed deserve death and for whom all hope is lost. But I cannot bring myself to ignore hope, not when I see how the burden of your deeds weighs upon you.

"So to you and to your men I say this: I forgive you. In the name of my dear sweet master and mistress I release you from the punishment you deserve and I offer you instead another path." Dalia clutched at her skirts and wavered, but only for a moment. "You are soldiers it would seem, or once were. Fine ones by the sound of it. And Kion has told me that a battle is coming to Windle and that there is a great want of men to fight it. So if you would atone for your crimes and submit yourself to the will of a simple servant girl, I...I would order you to fight, to swallow your pride and fight as the common soldiers do, even if those in command give you nothing more than food and shelter in return." Dalia gathered herself up to her full height and took in a long, deep breath before finishing. "And that is all I have to say. I hope the Odwins would be pleased. And I hope, I dearly hope, that in this way some good may come from their deaths."

The bandit chief's face was awash with tears. His mouth trembled not from the cold, but from the wave of emotions coursing through him. The tears cleansed his face, softening the hard lines and muting the scars and a youthful light shone once more in his eyes.

"If that be your will," the bandit said. "Then we will fight in your honor and for that of your masters and all those we have wronged." He steadied himself, blinking away the tears. "And thank you," he said. "For giving an old man his life back. You have saved us in more ways than one."

"He means what he says," Kithian said. *"Dalia has won a great victory this day by her words and by the mercy behind them."*

"It is no small thing for a heart to turn from the path of destruction to the path of life," Nurien said.

Tiryn nodded and took hold of Dalia's hand. Together they shared a tearful look of wonder and amazement, Dalia as surprised as anyone by what had just come to pass.

It was not the way justice was usually rendered in Inris, yet on a country road, away from any settlements, and in the midst of a war, perhaps it was not wrong for justice to take on a different shape. And when all was said and done, Kion was sure that justice had indeed been done.

Chapter 15

CONTEST OF MANNERS

Tiryn nodded slowly as the last of the bandits marched away north.

"I knew the moment I asked that you would make the right choice, Dalia," she said. "Still, it's one thing to think something's going to happen and quite another to see it come to pass."

"*Uncertainty is foresight's shadow. It is a tension that never becomes easy to abide,*" Nurien said.

"I'm not entirely sure I did make the right choice," Dalia said. "Men of that sort are not known for keeping their word."

"These will," Kion said.

"I wish I had your confidence," Dalia said.

"Trust me. They will keep their promise."

"If so, let's hope that Forglen lets them fight," Zinder said. "As renowned as the Fellswords are, he might be afraid that they will outshine him, the way he was afraid of Kion. It's an awful shame when men put themselves and their reputation before the lives of their people. I'd like to give a good knock in the head to whoever entrusted him with the defense of Windle."

"Well, it's one thing to dismiss a single soldier," Kion said. "It will be much harder for him to turn away a whole group of them. And Forglen at least seemed honest about Windle's need of men. So maybe it will turn out for the better. Forglen may have lost one sword, but he gained twenty. And that would not have happened if I had stayed."

"Ah, lad, that's where you're mistaken. You're worth five mercenary bands, though I know you're too humble to say it."

"*It is true,*" Kithian said. "*But we need not dwell on what we cannot change. Let us hope the Fellswords make their mark.*"

"*Much good will come of what happened here today, of that I can assure you,*" Nurien said.

The preparations and planning for the bandit attack had robbed them of most of their sleep. So rather than setting out at first light as usual, they caught some much needed rest and did not set out until late into the morning.

A soft rain sprinkled the road as they trekked once more southward. It was the kind of rain that left you more refreshed than damp and it kept the strength-sapping heat at bay, at least for a time.

Winning over the bandits had lightened everyone's hearts, none more than Tiryn's. The thought that they had turned those men from their crooked path gave her renewed hope for the war. Perhaps Inris was not destined to fall as it so often seemed. Perhaps the people of the Four Wards would band together and drive the haukmarn from their lands in the end. For a time, such thoughts so comforted her that even the loss of her mother faded to a dull ache. Dalia's company helped as well. Tiryn had admired her strength and resilience even before the affair with the bandits. But seeing her so courageously set aside her own grief and pain and show mercy upon those who had murdered those dear to her had raised Dalia even higher in Tiryn's estimation.

As they talked, Dalia spoke of her former masters so vividly it was almost as if they were still alive. She painted Tiryn a picture of her life with the Odwins that was so real Tiryn could almost see their home and smell what was cooking on the stove. Of all her many chores—cooking, cleaning, sewing, fetching things from the market, nursing her masters when they were sick—Dalia's favorite by far was cooking.

"It was a privilege to cook for them," she said. "They were

not particular at all in what they ate and their kitchen had the finest foodstuffs, pots, and crockery you could imagine. It hardly seemed like work at all. They even let me eat with them! Can you imagine? And the smells—oh, the smells. Fresh baked herb bread was my favorite, but cherry pie and sweet potato soup were not far behind."

Though Tiryn posed many questions about Dalia's life with the Odwins and before that with her family in Rippling, Dalia asked as many as she answered. Though they'd told her all about their journey from Furrow to Charring to Noath and back, Dalia always wanted to know more, especially about the glaives and their history. The more Tiryn shared, the more enthusiasm and curiosity Dalia showed. And so the time passed quickly by.

The company pressed on toward Tiller. Moss coated the rocks beside the road, making it feel as though they walked through an old riverbed. Several ponds and small lakes could be seen down the side paths to the east and west.

"This is called the Egramoor," Dalia informed them.

The sun showed them mercy down this stretch. Cool gentle airs caressed the moors. They passed through shaded vales and along smooth paths. The voices of birds flitted past upon the wind and Tiryn caught snatches from their song. *"Wonder of wonders,"* and *"Swift the air,"* and many times came the phrase *"Honor the Master of the Day."*

Sadly, it did not last. The songs gave way to isolated chirps and the sun soon conspired to scatter the clouds and bring its heat once more to bear upon the company. The mossy land gave way to farms and herds. Waxy shoots of wheat bristled against the breeze, green and supple. An occasional plot of barley or leafy cabbage wove itself into the gently undulating tapestry. Wild patches persisted as well, bursting forth like a verdant rash wherever the cultivated fields receded. Blackberry and raspberry bushes sometimes broke into the thick growth, but there were too many tangles of vines and weeds to justify any dalliance from the path. They only plucked the few berries which grew along the edge of the road from bushes that had not yet been picked over. By now the breeze had spent itself and though Rimewinter kept Tiryn cool as always, the others dragged their feet, Kion most of all, dogged as ever by the loaded cart.

But they did not have to endure the road much longer. Shortly before midday they topped a mild rise and got their first glimpse of the little town of Tiller. Some three dozen houses lay clustered around a thin ribbon of dirt road. A single intersection in the form of a roundabout shone in the center with a colorful burst of planted flowers. The intersecting road ran only a short distance on either side. The small, white-washed houses had the thatched roofs typical of Inris. The only building of note was a two-storied, timber-framed structure with a severe roof and a thin tower atop it. As they made their way into the shallow valley, they discovered that it was a bell tower, for its noontide notes tolled out across the land, long deep peals that harkened to all who heard them. "Life goes on, on, on," they seemed to say. "The day is long, long, long. And filled with song, song, song." The notes brought a perilous ache to Tiryn's heart which did not wholly fade until long after the bells went silent. How hollow life had grown in the absence of music, yet even so she despaired of ever singing again and welcomed the return to conversation when the last peals faded.

Before they reached Tiller, they passed more farms. Most occupied no more than a handful of acres. Cattle, sheep, and pigs wandered inside their pens or fenced-in fields. The fences were worn down in many places, but the animals remained, content to graze within their allotted boundaries.

A quarter mile from the edge of the village, they stopped at one of the farms. It had an old wooden barn that leaned to one side. From behind it rose the scattered clucking of chickens, but the coop was not visible from the path. Bales of hay sat out in neat, checkered rows in one of the fields. Another field had a green carpet of wheat that ran up and over a gentle hill. The farmhouse rested atop a sudden swell of land, looking out across the fields, a vigilant guardian over the pastoral scene. The house was a quarter the size of the barn and also made of wood, unusual among Inrisian dwellings. Like the rest of the village, it had been white-washed, though the paint had faded considerably.

A short, precipitous set of stairs cut into the hill upon which the house sat, with almond-shaped stones leading up to the front door. Four goats wandered about the hill, doing their best to rob the ground of every last shoot of grass and, judging by the baldness of the rise, succeeding quite well. Kithian hailed the goats and the tone of their reply was respectful enough, but neither Kithian nor Nurien relayed their response and the goats soon went back to eating, their chief concern.

"This is the place," Zinder said. "Except for the paint, it hasn't changed one sliver since I saw it last."

They ambled down the dirt path. Three stout oaks lined the way, each one taller than the one before.

"We've reached the home of Marlund Pander at last. If memory serves, both of his parents had just died the last time I was here and he was in desperate need of help repairing several of his tools. I ended up having to make him a brand new plow. The old one had been struck by lightning if you can believe it. Rotten luck, that. But broken things and want of new ones are what keep a smith in business."

While the others waited at the base of the hill, Zinder bounced spryly up the steps and unleashed a flurry of knocks upon the front door. No answer came so he knocked again. After another silence, he raised his hand for a third round when a voice shouted from inside the barn. The words were impossible to make out, but the tone implied some form of salutation.

Zinder rejoined them and together they went to investigate. Before they arrived, one of the two smaller side doors opened and a large, ungainly man strode out of the barn to meet them. He tottered so badly when he walked that at first Tiryn wondered if he wasn't hurt. But it turned out that this was just the way he got about. He had dark button eyes and a reddish-gray swirl of hair, which appeared to be comprised solely of a handful of remaining strands wrapped around his shiny pate in a way reminiscent of a cinnamon roll. Sweat glistened on his cheeks and on top of his forehead like sprinkled sugar. Bits of hay and chaff stuck to his tattered pants and shirt, both stained with every variation of brown and black.

"Hullo, old friend! Zinder Hamryn at your service. Do you remember me?"

The farmer's eyes flashed, but his words took their sweet time in coming. "Zinder Hamryn…Why, of course I remember you. That plow you made me is sitting behind us in the barn back there. Pretty near the finest implement this side of Rippling. I've had offers to buy it for twice what I paid you. But no sir, I wouldn't part with old Lancer for all the wheat in Casting Limmring. How are you, old fellow?"

"Ah, dear old Marlund. You're just as warmhearted as I remembered. You may have lost a few hairs, but you've lost none of your good manners."

"Likewise, likewise, I'm sure, Master Hamryn. So what brings you back to these parts?"

"I'm afraid I've come to ask of you a favor. You see, my friends and I are in need of shelter for the night. There's nothing in Tiller, of course, and we were hoping to enjoy a night away from the elements."

"A night of rest, you say? Away from the elements? Well, sure. I'd be delighted to offer you a place. But have your manners slipped so much over the years that you've forgotten to introduce me to your friends?"

"Oh, horn toads! So I have!"

Zinder hastily introduced the others.

Kion gave Marlund a tentative handshake. Though he was Zinder's friend, Kion still looked uneasy around him. He found it hard to trust a farmer. Tiryn, who hadn't had to deal as much as Kion with the farmers in Furrow, thought Marlund a perfectly pleasant sort and gave a deft curtsy.

"At your service," Dalia said, giving her own bow.

Marlund's cheeks ripened. "Pleased to meet the lot of you." He paused and looked up at his house, drawing a long deep breath as if he'd just woken up from a nap. "Forgive me, it's been so long since I had any folk out this way. I'm sure I can't offer you the hospitality you deserve. I'd let you all stay in the house, but it's more of a mess than the barn, if you can believe that. I suppose it's what comes from twenty years of living alone. If I'd known you were coming—"

"The barn is perfectly fine," Zinder said. "We've slept in far worse places."

"Yes, well, it does get rather toasty in there, but it will keep the wind and the rain off you, should it come."

"Of course, and we'll be happy to compensate you," Zinder said.

"Compensate? Oh, no you won't. You'll not pay one silver nick. The pleasure of your company and a little news of the war, that's all an old farmer needs. I get precious little of either out this way."

The two went back and forth several times over the issue. Old Marlund, kind as he was, was hard as steel when it came to his principles, and seeing that it was his farm, he held fast to his way of doing things.

"Fine. Fair enough," Zinder said at last, but he could not resist one last attempt. "But at least let me fix something for you. I've gone far too long without doing any real smithing or tinkering."

"Only if you let me pay you a proper wage. Your services are worth far more than a night in a barn."

"Very well, I yield, I yield!" Zinder said, throwing up his hands.

A gust of wind blew past the barn just then, unraveling Marlund's swirl of hair and turning it into a threadbare banner.

The farmer wrangled it in and fixed it without batting an eye. He kept his hand on top of his head after that.

"You know, Marlund, you really ought to consider a hat," Zinder said. "I don't believe any of mine would fit you, but perhaps with a few alterations—"

"Enough with the gifts, my friend." Marlund's face drooped into a frown. It was the first sign of displeasure he'd shown, but there was no malice in it, only a kind of country firmness. "You are the guests and I am the host. Allow me to offer you such meager hospitality as I can. Even a crusty old farmer has to do his best."

Zinder shrugged and grinned and followed Marlund into the barn. That was always the way with Zinder, he never liked to be outdone when it came to manners, but in the person of Marlund Pander he had met his match—at least for now.

Chapter 16

SNOW GLAZE

A place was made for Tiryn and Dalia to stay in the loft while Kion and Zinder would sleep on the ground floor. There was more than enough hay, but it was baking hot, especially up above. They only spent enough time in the barn for Marlund to show them their quarters and deposit their belongings. The most interesting thing Tiryn spotted before she left was the plow. Whether from Zinder's skill or Marlund's fastidious care—probably both—it hardly looked more than a year or two old. The blade glistened with an oily sheen. The handles, braces, and central beam had the damp appearance of a fresh coat of varnish. The yoke and harness, which hung on a nearby wall, were untarnished as well.

Back outside, Marlund and Zinder wandered off to a little shed behind the barn to see about the repair of some of Marlund's tools. Kion ventured under the shade to practice his forms. Chances for sword-work had been few ever since they'd left Whitewind. Usually he was too exhausted from the day's journey to bother. But today, after only having to endure a half day's journey, he was anxious to get in a bit of practice. As Kithian instructed him and commented on his movements, Tiryn and Dalia sat down under the shade of another tree to observe.

Kion's grace and art were a pleasure to behold. In many ways, it was simply another form of dance. The fact that Kion moved so naturally and easily came as no small surprise since he had no skill whatsoever when it came to actual dancing.

Dalia seemed unusually interested in the sword-work. And

for the first time since they'd met, she remained silent. At first, Tiryn barely noticed the change, enjoying the rush of wind through the upper boughs of the trees, which gave the sound of distant crowds roaring at a fair. She soaked in the sunlight and shadows dancing upon her face. The farm had a slumbering quality to it and Tiryn might have happily dozed off, had it not been for Dalia's odd behavior. Something was not quite right about it. After they'd finished taking their fill of water and several minutes had gone by without a word between them a terrible thought snuck into Tiryn's mind.

"Dalia, forgive me for being direct, but the way you're looking at my brother…is it…are you…*interested* in him?"

Dalia tore her eyes away. Kion had not glanced their way once, fully consumed by his forms and with his back to them more often than not.

"Hmm? Oh, sorry. Did you say something?" Dalia said.

"The way you're looking at Kion. Are you…?" Tiryn said in a whisper.

Dalia chuckled in a strained fashion. "Oh, no, Tiryn. I was just thinking about the battle with the ruffians and the way the fire gleamed and the ice glistened. It's all so very much for a simple servant girl like me," Dalia said, but the tenseness in her voice betrayed her.

Tiryn sounded her with a steady look, but Dalia would not meet her gaze.

"I will never forget it," Dalia went on. "It's such a strange thing how our paths crossed the way they did. If you had not come, I might still be trapped inside that carriage, or discovered by the bandits, or far worse." Dalia's tone was as earnest as ever, but she was not telling the whole truth. Perhaps being rescued and then seeing Kion stand up to those ruffians had swept her up into some sort of feeling toward him. Tiryn could not be sure, as such things were beyond her. She'd never had anything more than a few childish fascinations with boys and those had passed within a four-mark or two. But if Dalia did have feelings for

Kion, she was not ready to admit them, and that was just as well. Better not to press her on it and hope that they would just go away.

"I'm glad we found you, too," Tiryn said.

Dalia's gaze turned distant again. "My father always said to me, 'Dalia, your heart goes out too quickly. Be mindful where you send it.'" She gave Tiryn the kindest smile, resigned, but not without hope. In it, Tiryn saw the face of someone who accepted her lot in life and yet did not begrudge it. Dalia was a pretty girl. No doubt most boys would welcome her attention. But Kion had no time for such things and such pursuits would only bring sorrow. "You'll meet him, you know, my father. He's a good man, and for a commoner, well-esteemed. Most of the town watch knows and respects him."

"How wonderful. I'm sure I will like him very much." Tiryn eased against the oak, grateful the conversation had turned in another direction and that she'd wrested Dalia's attention away from her brother.

"He's a rat-catcher. Not just any rat-catcher—the Chief Rat-Catcher of Rippling."

Tiryn leaned forward. "Truly? I didn't know Rippling was large enough to have its own rat-catchers."

"It's grown quite a bit since the last war. They say it's almost as big as Charring now. I haven't been back in more than a year. I'm anxious to see how it's changed."

"The world so often changes while we're not looking, doesn't it?"

"Yes. Not all change is for the better, though. The year before I left, a new daysman was appointed, after the old one died. Daysman Blovius Shrool. He's terribly strict. Puts people in the stocks almost every other four-mark. And he cut the rat-catcher's pay in half. That's why I had to leave and enter the Odwins' service."

"You send money to your father, then?"

"Yes, all of it. Now that I'm coming home, I'll try to look for another appointment, but it will be hard to find one with the war."

Tiryn tugged on the end of one of her braids, thinking. "Perhaps you can earn something by helping out the soldiers. You like to cook and you know how to sew and many other things besides."

"I hadn't thought of that. You're so clever, Tiryn, and it's thoughtful of you to say. Zinder told me that you're quite a good cook yourself. He said that you make an especially good potato soup."

Tiryn's heart clenched. That was Mother's specialty. She fought through the stab of memory. It took a great mustering of will to hold back the tears. In the silence, Dalia placed a hand on Tiryn's arm, and that gentle touch told her that Dalia knew and understood her struggles, though no words passed between them.

"I do my best," Tiryn said, at last taking a breath.

"Zinder also said that your dagger can make ice cream," Dalia said. "Is that true? I've never had ice cream before."

Somehow a chuckle wrestled its way into Tiryn's throat and in a moment, the storm had passed, swept away in the absurdity of Zinder's claim.

"You can't take half the things Zinder says seriously. I wish it were so, but even if it was, using such a storied and ancient weapon as Rimewinter for making sweets would be rather undignified, I think."

"Why do you think that?" Nurien said. *"If it will serve my glaive-bond or our common cause, no task is beneath me. Did I not make ice to cool your friends along the road?"*

Tiryn suffered the awkwardness that comes from hearing a voice that others around you cannot.

She and Kion had only eaten ice cream once at the Seven Fires Festival. Aunt Lizet had sent some extra coin that year, the year after Father died. Tiryn had been very young, but she could still remember the taste to this day: sweet and fullsome, with the softness of butter and as fresh as a crystal blue sky. It was a pleasure so rich, it almost felt too good to be real.

"Oh, Tiryn, we should make some!" Dalia's eyes shone bright.

"To be clear, I cannot make ice cream. That would require milk. I can only make things made from water. But I could provide you with enough crushed ice to make snow glaze."

"Snow glaze?" Tiryn said, forgetting that Dalia was there.

"What?" Dalia said.

"Oh, it's just that Rimewinter can't make actual ice cream. Only…snow glaze." Whatever that was.

"It is a dessert eaten along the southern coast of Verisward. In the north it only gets hot in the summer, but there the sun blazes all year long. Snow glaze is made from a ball of crushed ice with some fruit juice and honey poured over the top to make it sweet. You still have some of the raspberries you picked along the road. We could make a few glazes from that."

It sounded delicious to be sure, but Tiryn still resisted. It didn't seem right to use her glaive for something so trivial. Still, she didn't want to simply reject Nurien's kind offer and it would be a delight to the others as well.

"I've never heard of snow glaze, but it sounds delicious," Dalia said. "How do you make it?"

"With a ball of ice dipped in fruit juice and honey and served in…"

"Typically inside a baked cone of hardened sweetbread, though any bread or even a bowl will do. If you can borrow a few things from Farmer Marlund, you could probably make the cones as well."

Tiryn conveyed Nurien's words as if they were her own.

Dalia clasped her hands together, beside herself with excitement. "Baking sweetbread? Ice dipped in honey and fruit juice? Oh, Tiryn, we have to try. It's the closest thing to ice cream I'll probably ever taste."

"Well, Dalia, I don't know. We don't have any flour or honey or the other things we'd need. Perhaps once we reach Rippling—"

"Now, Tiryn, you're the one who's been roving all across Inris, aren't you? Where's your sense of adventure?"

"She's right, you know. There's nothing wrong with trying something new. We have the whole afternoon before us for once. It might go a long way toward lightening everyone's spirits, not least of all your own."

"But I—"

Dalia gave Tiryn's knee a quick tap. "Now, every farmer, even those that live alone, has to have a hearth, if not an oven, as well as flour and salt and the other things we'll need for the bread. And of course we already have the raspberries. The only thing we might be missing is the honey." She popped up and pulled Tiryn with her. "Let's go find out!"

"But Farmer Marlund said his house was a mess. He wouldn't want us poking around uninvited. He'd probably faint from embarrassment if he found out." Tiryn might too.

"Then he doesn't have to know. At least not until after we've made the glaze. And once he tastes it, I'm sure all will be forgiven. Oh, Tiryn, honestly, you do worry too much. I used to surprise the Odwins all the time with things like this and they adored it."

"But we can't take his flour and things without permission." It was Tiryn's last defense, but she knew Dalia would swat it away, just as she had the rest of her excuses.

"It's not stealing if you use someone else's kitchen to make a treat for them. And Farmer Marlund is the sort of person who's especially keen on hospitality—most country folk are. Now, come, no more excuses. Let's have our own little adventure while we can."

As Dalia dragged her back up the path toward the house, Kion stopped his forms for the first time. His dark hair was shot through with sweat and clung to his neck and the sides of his face.

"What are you two up to?" he said, breathing heavily.

"I'm being kidnapped, Kion," Tiryn said as Dalia forced her along. "Save me."

But he only gave her a curious look. "And here I thought we'd sent the last of the bandits packing. Well, just don't torture her too much, Dalia," he said. "And let me know the terms of the ransom as soon as you can."

"Oh, I'll take good care of her, don't worry. But please do make sure no one comes up to the house until we're done. We don't want anyone spoiling our surprise!" Dalia's eyes lit up even brighter when she looked at Kion, but Tiryn told herself that it was only just the thrill of sneaking into the farmer's kitchen and the adventure of the snow glaze.

"As you wish, Lady Bandit," Kion called after them. "Your secret's safe with me."

Dalia blushed, and Tiryn felt her own cheeks flush as well, but for a far different reason. But there was no time to stew over what might become of such foolishness. Those worries were swept away by the present mischief as she staggered up the hill behind Dalia, her uneasy partner in culinary crime.

Zinder licked the last bit of sticky, glistening ice from his fingers with unabashed relish. "I told you the blade could make ice cream! What a delight!"

"Not quite. But it is just the thing for a summer's day," Kion said. He was nibbling away at the sweetbread cone in his hand, sitting in the shade among the others.

Tiryn, Dalia, and Farmer Marlund had their glazes in various stages of consumption, but none could match Zinder's voracity when it came to the serious business of eating. Tiryn could hardly believe how well the glazes had turned out. Dripping with raspberry juice and honey, the balls of ice had turned a pleasant shade of purple. The sweet mounds crowning the golden crusted cones looked like something out of a dream. And they tasted like it, too.

As expected, Farmer Marlund had turned beet red when he found out that Dalia and Tiryn had been busying themselves inside his house. And Tiryn could see why. Every room was packed to the rafters with useless, broken-down knickknacks that weren't worth a lump of clay. The house was so overrun with rubbish, it reminded Tiryn of the dragon hoards from fables. A hoard it certainly was, only the hoard of a dragon with no eye for anything of value. It seemed hard to fathom that the person with the pristine plow and the person who lived in the house were one and the same. But Marlund got over his embarrassment once he tasted the glaze and he harbored no ill-will toward the girls.

"You're not mad?" Dalia said after they'd all had their first taste.

"How could I be?" Marlund said. "This is the tastiest thing to come out of my kitchen since my mother was alive. I'm only sorry you had to wade through my disaster to make it."

"I am surprised you let Dalia put you up to this, Tiryn," Kion said. "You're not usually one for breaking rules."

"It certainly wasn't my idea." Tiryn gave a meaningful look toward her dagger and Kion understood. Dalia was too distracted looking at Kion to notice.

"Are you glad that you listened?" Nurien said.

"Seeing the looks on everyone's faces, especially Zinder's, when they took their first taste, was worth the terrible fit of nerves I had to suffer through, though." Tiryn tried to answer Nurien's question without making it obvious. What she didn't say was that it had also reminded her of her times with Mother in the kitchen, and that had been the best thing of all. But she wasn't strong enough to speak of that now.

"And now that we've found our way around the kitchen, I propose that you let Tiryn and I cook dinner this evening—and breakfast before we leave in the morning." Dalia wiped away a dark dribble of melted raspberry ice from the edge of her mouth. Tiryn gave a little grimace. How forward that girl was! Had they not mortified poor Farmer Marlund enough?

"Well, I…" Marlund began.

"Come now, Marlund." Zinder jumped in, not about to let the prospect of a good meal pass him by. "You said it yourself. You haven't eaten anything this good since your mother was here. And you do want to show the best hospitality to your guests, don't you?"

This time it was Marlund who had to yield for Zinder had used his own kindness and good manners against him. "Oh, horsefiddle, I suppose they have braved the kitchen once and didn't die. All right, I'll consent—for the sake of hospitality." The delight in his eyes as he took another lick of his snow glaze showed that he, like Zinder, prized a good meal above a little embarrassment.

And so that evening they dined on carrot chowder, honey rolls, grilled bluemouthed kipper, and roasted mushrooms. The food was arrayed across a tattered brown blanket under the twinkling sparklight, the dazzling streaks painting the night sky with their wandering brilliance.

Zinder and Dalia did most of the talking. They spoke of life in Rippling and Windle and the lands of Casting Limmring, of the war and the haukmarn conquests of Grettling, Fennigar, and Roving, and of the current siege at Quelling. When the conversation turned to Charring and Kion's battle with Vayd, Dalia hung on Zinder's every word. Though she had heard most of it the day before, no one would have known. The tale had lost none of its fascination. Whenever Zinder told of Kion's battles with the haukmarn or the dreadwulfs, or any of his other deeds, she sat in rapt silence, her expression one of awe, her eyes drawn frequently to the hero of the battle himself.

Thankfully, Kion seemed not to notice. He was too worn out from the sword-work. Perhaps Dalia's interest in him was wholly innocent, more of an admiration for his feats in battle than anything serious. Given enough time, though, it might turn into something more, but since they would part ways in Rippling, it would surely never have the chance to blossom into anything deeper.

Marlund could hardly believe half of what Zinder said. Haukmarn and Noathryn invaders were one thing, and he'd heard a few rumors about them, but battles with dim-touched creatures and the gifts of the ancient glaives were too much for the simple farmer to fathom. Not until Kion briefly lit up Truesilver's blade did his doubts finally give way. After that, "there may be some hope," was the refrain he repeated over and over again. Marlund had not fought in the last war, for his father had taken ill and he could not leave the farm. Yet he had a fighting spirit. He deeply regretted missing the war. He was too old now to be of much use with a sword, but he had been bringing bales of hay into Tiller once an eight-mark to supply the soldiers' horses in Windle and Rippling.

"If there's any way I can help with the war I will," he said. "I don't want to see my dear fields—or our people—trampled by those vile brutes."

"That's the spirit," Zinder said. "Everyone will be called upon to make some sacrifice before it's all over."

"Is there anything I can do to aid you, Kion?" Marlund said.

Seeing the farmer's earnestness, and the way he had welcomed Kion and the others onto his farm, by now Kion had warmed to the old farmer. He was nothing like the ones from Furrow.

"That's kind of you to offer, but giving us food and shelter for a night is more than enough. You've helped us a great deal already."

But Marlund had the old country stubbornness about him and refused to leave it at that.

"How about the cart you've been hauling halfway across Inris? Surely that must be slowing you down. You'd get to

Bramble Eyre a lot swifter if you had horses. Horses I have not, but I do have a mule. Tapper's his name. He's a fine animal."

"Oh, no, sir, we couldn't take him," Kion said. The others gathered around and raised their voices as one in protest. Though they had talked previously of purchasing a mule from Marlund, that was before they found out that Tapper was his only draft animal. Taking the beast away would cripple his livelihood.

"Don't you see?" Marlund said. "When they come through Tiller, I don't intend to flee. I intend to stay and fight."

"You would only be throwing your life away if you did," Zinder said, jumping up and shaking his spoon.

"But this farm is my life. My family has owned it for four generations. If they take my land, they've as good as killed me." Marlund looked from the house to the barn, his lips pressed tight. Everyone had stopped eating. A soft breeze whispered among the trees. "I'm too old and tired to run. No, here is where I mean to stay until the end."

"Oh, dear. I can see there's no dissuading you. But that doesn't mean we have to take your mule."

Marlund grabbed Zinder, sitting next to him, by both arms. "Oh, but you must, you must. He's served me faithfully for nigh on ten years. He's a fine beast. If you leave him here, he'll only join me in my fate."

"But your work, how will you continue to farm your land without your mule?" Tiryn said, moved by the farmer's resolve. She still hoped he wouldn't stay and fight, but she could not help but admire his courage.

"The plowing's already done so I mostly use Tapper for trips into town or hauling loads around the farm. But I won't be doing any of those ever again if the haukmarn come, and if they don't, I can always buy a new mule next spring. It seems more likely, though, that the enemy will be here before I ever bring the wheat to harvest if all that you've said is true. You must take him, to keep him from becoming mere spoils of war."

"I believe they will give me a horse once I reach Bramble Eyre," Kion said. "I can bear the cart for a few more days."

"You may be able to bear it, but it will slow you down. What if you don't reach the fortress in time? This will help you, Kion. It's my way of aiding Warding in the war. You simply must let me do this."

"To be honest, I'm not sure how important my message really is. If it was urgent Forglen would have given me a horse."

"He was flat-out jealous of you, that's what it was," Zinder said.

Marlund set his plate on the grass and rose to his feet. He paced back and forth between two of the oaks, his plain but honest mind churning, his big boots clumping and clodding over the ground. Whatever words he sought were a long time coming, but in the end they came.

"No. Forgive me for being so forward, but you're wrong," Marlund said, getting worked up. "Forglen may have sent you on a fool's errand as he sees it, but he's not the one in charge, not ultimately. You've got a destiny to fulfill and wherever it takes you, that's where you were meant to go. You may not see all the details at the moment, but you need to get to that fortress just as fast as ever you can. Don't ask me how I know, I just do. Farmers know things others don't. And it's no use questioning it. Everything happens for a purpose, even when we don't know what that purpose is. I know you were meant to have my mule and my cart and there's not a thing you can say that will convince me otherwise. You're going to win this war for us, and I'm going to help you, even if it's just in this small way. Is that clear?"

Marlund proved as stubborn as any mule. Oh, they tried for another half an hour to change his mind, but his back would not bend no matter how they loaded it with reasons and refusals of their own. In the end, the farmer's iron will bested them all. When it came to standing on principle and insistence on any matters touching his honor, generosity, kindness, or manners,

Tiryn had never known Zinder to suffer defeat, and now he'd been outdone by the farmer twice in one day.

"Well, horn toads," Zinder said, giving in at last. "I don't believe we have a choice after all. When someone's dead set on giving you something, there's nothing you can do to stop it."

"Good. Now you're finally talking some sense." Farmer Marlund nodded in satisfaction.

Tiryn had to admire his stubborn kindness. Such a firm, honest, grounded fellow. You didn't come across his kind everyday, but such people made the world go on through all its travails and troubles. Perhaps it was only a small effort in a very large war, but then again, what were great deeds but the sum of many smaller ones?

Chapter 17

THE FURLS

The company rose early the next day, to hopefully set out just after dawn. Dalia rose even before the others, not bothering to rouse Tiryn, and snuck back into Marlund's kitchen to prepare a breakfast as lavish as the dinner the night before. She made fried potatoes and bacon, flaky muffins served with butter and honey, and a cheese-covered dish of mashed potatoes and spinach so delicious it almost ate itself. And she managed all this without waking Marlund, who snored away louder than a dragon in the next room.

The aroma of breakfast came to Tiryn before she awoke, adding savor to her dreams and pulling her out of them on a feathery breeze of scented delights.

"You slept well," Nurien said.

Tiryn stretched through a yawn. Nurien was right. She had not felt so rested since they left Whitewind. "Yes, I will miss this place," Tiryn said.

"The shadows seem to have withdrawn while we were here. Perhaps they will return again, but for now we are safe."

The pursuing shadows had not even entered Tiryn's thoughts while in this place. And even now the thought that they might return seemed more distant than the war itself.

Dalia's voice drifted up to the loft, along with the tongue-tingling smell of fried potato wedges fresh from the griddle.

"Shoo, shoo. Not for you," Dalia said.

Tiryn threw off her blanket, grabbed Rimewinter, and climbed down the ladder to see what was happening.

Dalia had a stick in her hands and ran about, chasing off the goats, but one always managed to scamper past and make its way back to the heaping plate of potato wedges resting on a tattered blanket.

"Good morning, Dalia. My, you've been busy. Why didn't you tell me you were cooking? I would have helped you."

"Well, it'll all be for naught if these goats have their way. Tiryn—please—would you guard the food while I bring the rest of it down?"

"Of course." She dashed in front of an over-eager goat just in time. "I thought goats only liked grass and roots."

"Not this bunch. They'll chew the hem off your dress if you let them. Here's my stick." Dalia tossed her the stick and bounded off back toward the house. Tiryn failed to catch it and it landed in the midst of the goats. But that was fine. She didn't need a stick anyway.

"Nurien, do you care to have a word with them?"

"I'd be happy to. Now pay attention and see if you can pick up some of the words you've been learning," Nurien said and then addressed the goats. *"Greetings, Family Nak. I'm afraid you'll have to refrain from helping yourselves to this food. It's meant for your master and his friends."*

The goats cried and squealed and did not back away as Tiryn had expected.

"They claim that their stomachs are tight with hunger, which is of course nonsense. They are some of the fattest goats you'll ever see, but they're never satisfied. The fatter they get the more they want," Nurien said. *"Now listen here, my glaivebond and the rest of our companions are about the Mastersmith's business. I speak in his name and you would do well to heed my words."*

The goats whined some more, but eventually withdrew, dragging their hooves as if going off to die and not to another patch of green juicy grass just up the path. Tiryn caught the words "understand," "service," and "poor little goats," among their bleating but she did not once hear the word for "sorry," or anything that sounded remotely like an apology. All animals were not as helpful and as well-mannered as Scriff and Bur-gan-dor, it seemed.

Tiryn did not trust the goats to keep their word and so she remained to keep watch over the food while Dalia brought down tray after tray. A bright-eyed Farmer Marlund came with her on her last trip, carrying the green potatoes and a pitcher of water, while Dalia brought the muffins, butter, and honey. Tiryn went into the barn to wake Kion and Zinder.

"If war must come, we might as well go on feasting and being merry until it does," Marlund said.

"Hear, hear! Three cheers for the Mistress of Breakfast!" Zinder said.

"Yes, thank you once again, Dalia," Kion said. "We shall enjoy it while we can, though if we want to reach Rippling by tomorrow evening we'll have to set off soon."

"Oh, dear," Zinder said with exaggerated dismay. "Now that you're a soldier all you do is give orders. Be mindful you don't push us too hard or you might have mutiny on your hands, Glinthelm."

Despite Kion's wishes, they tarried overlong at the meal, but the richness of the food warranted the delay. Though Kion finished first and excused himself to the barn to ready the tack and harness and prepare their new mule, he didn't chastise the others for lingering at the meal; he himself had gone for seconds, after all.

"*Greetings, Tam-del-wir,*" Kithian said from inside the barn, in answer to the mule's braying.

Kion said something in reply which Tiryn could not make out and from then on the mule and Kion alternated in what sounded like a pleasant exchange. Hopefully, Tapper would prove as talkative as Bur-gan-dor so that she could make further strides with the beast speech.

Dalia and Tiryn got up next, hurrying off to clean the dishes and pack the bedrolls into the cart. Zinder was the last to go, though not from any desire to shirk his duties. He was the hardest worker of them all, but when it came to meals, especially ones like these, all other considerations melted away until he was finished.

Once all was packed away, Marlund led Tapper out of the barn. The russet mule was a little undersized when it came to height, but made up for it in girth. Like the goats, Tapper had led a fine life when it came to diet. He would certainly not eat as well on the long road to Bramble Eyre. It was clear right from the first where he'd gotten his name, for he had the habit of tapping his right front foot in an irregular rhythm.

"Does he always do that?" Zinder said.

"Only when he's not moving." Marlund said. "He doesn't like to sit still. I imagine he and Kion will get along well." He gave the mule a good-natured slap on the back.

"Yes, perhaps Tapper and I will just head off now and the rest of you can catch up," Kion said.

The mule gave a high-pitched whinny and a much deeper bray.

"He says that he hopes to honor his master by serving you just as faithfully," Nurien said.

Tiryn came over to scratch his neck. "We're glad to have you, Tapper."

Nurien conveyed Tiryn's message and for once Tiryn found that she understood most of the reply.

"Yes, yes, up, up. Ready to serve. Just point me in the direction you need to go," was how she heard it, and Nurien confirmed later that she'd more or less gotten it right, only that the "up, up," part had been "step, step."

"Well, old friend, I'm glad our paths met once again." Zinder gave Marlund's hand a rigorous shake once he'd climbed atop the cart. It was four times the size of their old cart and loaded not only with the glaives and the supplies they had brought from Whitewind, but Marlund had added more oil, oat cakes, and parcels of dried meat. "You've given us far more than we could have ever hoped. I'd promise to name my firstborn after you, but alas, I'm not destined for the married life. And yet somehow I ended up with two children to care for despite my failures in love."

"Well, we have that in common," Marlund said, fixing his unruly strands of hair after the morning breeze had ruffled them out of place. "Take care of these youngsters, Zinder. You may be pretty near the finest blacksmith I've ever met, but I can tell you're an even finer friend to these children—children, why they're practically grown, aren't they? And wandering all about the Wards with enchanted weapons and such things the likes of which I never thought I'd live to see. I can't say how they'll stop the haukmarn exactly, but I know in my bones they will win this war for us."

"Good-bye, Mr. Pander," Dalia said. "And thank you for the use of your kitchen."

"Yes, thank you for everything," Tiryn said. "You're a dear friend." She wanted to plead with him one last time not to stay and defend his farm, but knew that her warnings would only go unheeded.

Kion leaned forward and offered Marlund his hand. "I hope war does not come to this place. You may not ever fight in the Warding ranks, but you're as true as any soldier that ever dressed for battle. Thank you for all your kindness."

"If I could give you more, I would," Marlund said.

"It is more than enough," Kion said, and stepped up into the cart.

Zinder gave a flick of the reins and a whistle and the cart rolled past the house and onto the main road at the end of the path.

"Take care of Tapper," Marlund called out after them, his voice fading already among the fields. "And bring us victory!"

They all waved one last time and then joined the road that would lead them on to Tiller and beyond. Marlund remained atop the little hill where his house sat in the dimness of the early morning, watching them go until a dip in the road took him finally from view, but the image stayed in Tiryn's mind long after. It comforted her to imagine he'd still be there, standing tall and proud until the day they returned. Such a fancy would never come true, but she could not bear to think of it any other way.

They rolled past the last few angular houses, leaving Tiller behind and casting themselves once more out into the wide open country. Gentle sunlight warmed a few lonely farms, but soon the land returned to grass, brambles, and small groves of oak. In order to make up for the delayed start, they stopped only briefly for lunch and then mostly for Tapper's sake. They ate the better part of their meal once the cart started out again.

Masses of clouds loomed swollen and gray, but though they never let fall more than a handful of droplets they did tame the summer heat. By the time the sun began its retreat over the western horizon, the farms had faded and its muted glow shone over long rounded hills covered in broken rock and sprinkled with vibrant lichen.

"The hills look like rolled-up scrolls," Tiryn said.

"They're called the Furls," Dalia said. "There's not much game out here or even many growing things, but they are quite lovely, aren't they? Beyond them are the Clarion Toths. Sometimes you can see them on a clear day."

"Yes, they do look like scrolls," Kion said, eyeing Zinder with an amused air. "This would be an excellent place for your friend the Scribe to dwell. If we stumble across him, do you plan on paying him a visit?"

"The Scribe!" Zinder's cry startled the whole cart. In a nearby grove, birds scattered from their trees. "He's no friend of mine, I can tell you that—the farthest thing from it. Why did you have to go and bring him up? It was a perfectly fine day."

"The Scribe?" Dalia said. "Who is that?"

"Oh, just some character Zinder made up for a little side story he's been writing in his head," Kion said, grinning at Zinder's pink nose and the pitch of his voice as he unleashed his vehement reply.

"Made up! Made up? You've seen his signature on that fragment we have from *The Lay of the Glaives*. Are made up characters capable of manifesting themselves through pen and ink?"

"If you ever write about them in a book they are."

"Ah, clever, clever. You know what I meant."

Kion related Zinder's supposed run-ins with the mysterious, unnamed Scribe to Dalia. This unknown person had supposedly sent them to Roving where Kion found Truesilver and later he'd led Zinder on a wild chase through the streets of Fennigar. The one good thing Zinder had to say about him was that he'd provided them with two fragments of a long poem entitled *The Lay of the Glaives*.

"The Lay records events which took place long ago," Zinder said. "And since we're wrapped up in the affairs of the glaives ourselves, I can't help but wish that we could get our hands upon the rest of the poem."

"Do you know anything about the *Lay*, Nurien?" Tiryn said in a whisper that only her glaive could hear.

"No. It must have been written after I went dormant."

"It tells of the events of the Shattering and the War of the Glaives," Kithian said. *"It was written by Selas Brindel—a renowned bard whom some called a seer—as a remembrance of the events surrounding that terrible war."*

Zinder's eyes popped when Kion told him what Kithian had said. "Selas the Golden Tongued? Why, his works were all thought to be lost. The authorship of the *Lay* has never been given anywhere I have read. Is he—are you certain?"

"Yes, of course," Kithian said. *"I can still recall the day it was first played in the great dome of Gilding."*

Kion repeated the words, doing his best to make it seem to Dalia as if they were his own.

"So, he was a musician," Tiryn said. "There was music, then, that went with the *Lay*."

"*Yes, and high and beautiful the notes rang within Selashar's Dome.*"

"Wait, Selas—Selashar?" Zinder said, leaning against the back of his seat, thunderstruck. "Shar's dome! Was the great dome named after him as well?"

"*It was Selashar who designed it. He had other skills besides poetry and music,*" Nurien said.

"Shar's dome…" Zinder stared off with the eyes of his mind at the great dome he had seen long ago. It had always been his dream to return to it, greatest of all the ancient wonders of old.

"So others knew of the glaives back then," Kion said.

"*Yes, our fame endured long after the war ended, but those generations are long gone. And history turns to rumor if its gardens are left untended,*" Kithian said.

"And what about those other weapons you carry with you?" Dalia said, giving both Kion and Tiryn puzzled looks at their frequent pauses. "Are they glaives as well?"

"You're very perceptive," Kion said. "How did you know?"

Dalia's face glowed in the light of Kion's compliment and that uncomfortable sensation stirred again in Tiryn's stomach.

"Well, they look so old for one thing," Dalia said. "And I couldn't think why else you'd bother carrying such weapons with you all these miles."

"Yes, we found those weapons on Tinesplitter Isle when we found Rimewinter," Tiryn said, eager for once to insert herself into a conversation and deflect some of Dalia's attention away from Kion.

"Will there be more swordspeakers, then?" Dalia said, her eyes returning to Kion after only the briefest glance Tiryn's way.

"We don't know," Kion said. "But we're going to keep them in case we find one."

"And how are the swordspeakers chosen?" Dalia leaned against the edge of the cart, one hand under her chin. She looked positively silly, staring at Kion the way she did. Oh, bother, were such things going to become commonplace now that Kion and Tiryn were older?

"Only the Mastersmith knows. He's the one who created the glaives," Kion said, utterly oblivious to Dalia's odd behavior.

"I was the last person in the Four Wards I thought would ever become a swordspeaker," Tiryn put in.

"I don't suppose there have ever been any nynnian swordspeakers?" Zinder said.

"No, no nyn can ever be granted that honor, not after their betrayal of the Four Wards during the War of the Glaives," Kithian said.

"I'm afraid not," Kion said, not bothering to repeat the troubling part about the betrayal.

"The nyn served Talinyon and Malix in the War of the Glaives, though afterwards they repented," Kithian said.

"I wondered at that," Nurien said. *"I have no ill-will toward Zinder, but his presence among you has always been a mystery to me. I had thought Malix corrupted them all."*

Tiryn could hardly believe what the glaives were saying. The nyn had been corrupted? How could that be so? Zinder was the kindest and best friend they had in all the world. But did the rest of his kindred share his disposition? Was there some truth perhaps to Dengril's account from the fall of Dunach?

"It seems that what the Frindalians said was true; the nyn were on the side of the enemy in the past," Kion said.

"We were deceived, blast it!" Zinder said. "Or so the tales say. But that was so long ago, who can tell the truth of it? The important thing is that that was then and this is now. My people are decent, honorable folk now, though a few of them can be a little cantankerous and foolish—just like anyone. There's good and evil no matter where you go. But we learned our lesson and put all that behind us."

"That's true," Tiryn said. "No one should be held responsible for the deeds of their ancestors."

"You're the first nyn I've ever met," Dalia said. "But if you're any indication, I'd say the nyn are every bit as trustworthy and honorable as you say."

"Much can change in eight hundred years," Nurien said.

"To be in the world is to know change," Kithian said. *"Therein lies our greatest danger, and also our greatest hope. For it may change for the worse or for the better."*

Looking at Dalia, and the way she looked at Kion, Tiryn couldn't help but think things were changing for the worse.

Chapter 18

WHERE FIRES BURN COLD

They camped that night by a little stream called Broken Brook, along with two other sets of travelers bound for Rippling. One, a potter and his family, hailed from Windle. The other, an older couple, had come from their farm at the base of the Furls. Tiryn made a little sketch of them in her journal as Kion and the others spoke with them concerning their travels and the war. The potter was friendly enough, though his wife had a sour air about her. Their three children were curious about the other travelers, as children naturally would be, but their mother kept a tight rein upon them and scolded them whenever they spoke up. The old farming couple said not a word, but kept as far away from the others as possible.

The potter had no news to offer beyond what they already knew, but was eager to listen to Zinder's tales of the Sword of the North and his battles against Vayd Mokán and the haukmarn army. Zinder failed to mention that the Sword of the North was the young man sitting across from them at the campfire and the potter was too simple to discern the truth.

Listening to Zinder's stories brought back Tiryn's old worries about the war. Though Kion would not go into battle anytime soon, Vayd was still out there, and Shadowriven with him. Was he back leading the haukmarn now? Or was he devastating some other village like Whitewind? Of all the troubling aspects of this war, Vayd was the most enigmatic. Tiryn had never actually seen him, which only added to the mystery. What drove him and the rest of the haukmarn to attack Inris relentlessly year after year? Was it the desire for better lands? Greed? Vengeance for some past wrong? And how did Shadowriven play into all of this? Understanding the enemy was the first step in defeating him. And until they did they had as much hope of stopping a raging storm as she did the deadly ravages of Vayd Mokán.

The next morning, the company set out before either the potter's family or the farmers. Tapper was already tapping his foot well before dawn and ready to go the moment they put him back in the harness.

"You and Crusty would have been fast friends," Zinder said, catching himself in a wistful sigh.

The road drew closer to the Furls as it ventured south. Early that morning, when the light was yet new, for the second time on their journey the great heights of the Clarion Toths rose beyond the hills, mostly shrouded in mist, but jagged and imposing wherever the peaks broke through. The soaring mountains lingered for about an hour before the haze enveloped them completely, but the Furls grew ever larger and closer.

They passed three more groups of travelers that day, another large family with a mule and cart of their own, another farming couple with a small child and much younger than the farmers they'd met at Broken Brook, and a lone trapper dragging a large bag of furs behind him. They spoke briefly to each as they passed them by, but their stories were all the same. War was coming, and Rippling was the safest place in Casting Limmring. The trapper did add that he might attempt to secure passage aboard a boat to Madrigal along the Merriling River, provided his furs could fetch a high enough price.

They drove Tapper hard, stopping only at need, and taking their meals for the most part in the cart. The closer they got to Rippling, the rougher the road became. Deep ruts and exposed rocks made the last few miles a trying affair. The cart bounced and wriggled this way and that, tottering unevenly as Zinder and Tapper did their best to navigate the mangled path. Matters only worsened when Rippling came into view. For dozens of carts and mules and weary travelers crowded the last two miles of the road. The whole countryside seemed to have emptied into the valley to descend upon the town. This human river settled into two channels, both headed toward Rippling. No one was leaving. Every last traveler was hurrying to reach the gates before nightfall. Tapper joined this tattered stream behind another mule and cart and their pace slowed to that of a shuffling walk. There was no way around it, there were simply too many people on the road and no other way to arrive sooner unless they rudely pressed ahead of those who'd arrived before them.

From their vantage point on the outer rim of the valley one thing was clear: Rippling was a filthy town. Smoke drifted over large parts of it, giving it the appearance of a smoldering ruin. Except it wasn't a ruin. It was merely the fires of industry, the blacksmiths and smelters, the smoke houses and inns, and the trash heaps and barrel fires of people cooking in the streets. The central part of town had older, nicer looking homes, many of which had two stories. Those had timber frames, slate roofs, and abundant windows, though the smoke had stained most of them black, curbing their usefulness. A twenty foot stone wall fashioned of dark granite ringed the central district, which was about the size of Windle. Outside the weathered barrier, a sprawling mess of one-story shacks and poorly built houses expanded the town farther into the valley. These had been recently and hastily built and not at all made to last. Most of the smoke came from the outer district. Around this, a wooden wall similar to Windle's, though not entirely finished, marked the limits of the town. Altogether, these two districts were as large as Charring, if not slightly larger. The Merriling River formed the southern boundary of the town, glinting in the dusk and carrying its gray waters swiftly to the east.

"When I was six, gold was discovered in the Furls," Dalia said as the cart crawled toward the outer gate. Around them came the murmur of other conversations, mixed in with clopping hooves, shuffling shoes, and the jangle of tack and harness. "The Jeslan family swooped in and bought the land and opened a mine. Every year since then more and more folk, mostly miners, have found their way into the town. The Jeslans built most of the houses in Spiketown, which is what we call the outer district. The town center is known as Old Rippling."

"Doesn't the daysman do anything about the filth and the squalor?" Kion said. "Even from a distance, it looks as if half the houses in the outer district should be torn down."

"It's commonly believed that Blovius Shrool is in the pay of the Jeslans. He's done almost nothing for the town, but the margrave appoints the daysmen so there's little we can do."

"And where does your family live?" Kion said.

Dalia's voice brightened, partly from the mention of her family and partly because she had Kion's attention. "Just inside the boundaries of Old Rippling. We have a small house right up against the wall."

"Well, I'm anxious to meet them, though at this rate, the war might be over before we ever get inside," Zinder said.

They arrived at the gates three hours after dark. A dozen soldiers in emerald tabards stopped for questioning the various travelers attempting to pass through. The entry tax set Zinder back three silver squares—nearly a third of a gold round—but the soldiers were only enforcing the daysman's orders so it was useless to complain. Blovius had upped the normal fee, which traditionally had been levied only upon merchants, on account of "war preparations."

Kion donned his green tabard before they reached the gate and that at least kept Zinder from having to pay another full square. An unexpected pride welled up in Tiryn when she saw her brother give the soldiers a cross-armed salute. She had always dreaded his becoming a soldier, but it was the thought of losing him that she found so frightening. To see him in that masterful green, so elegant and dignified, filled her with a strange joy. He truly was meant to be a warrior.

The soldiers rattled on about various rules and laws the daysman had put in place, but Tiryn was too caught up with thoughts of what lay ahead for Kion to pay any attention. He responded to all that was said with thoughtfulness and respect. If only Mother and Father could have seen him now…The thought reopened old wounds and she gripped the edge of the cart to steady herself against the wrenching pull of sorrow.

"Your brother is turning into a man," Nurien said. *"And that both saddens you and brings you joy. Such is often the way of life. The gladness is inseparable from the sorrow and when one takes hold the other is swift to follow. Learning to endure the shifting nature of our moods is a battle we all have to fight, even glaives. But that which shakes you is what gives you strength."*

Tiryn let go of the cart and gripped her dagger instead. Nurien's words and presence gave her the strength she needed to endure the storm of sadness and fear until it passed. All Tiryn could recall after they left was that the soldiers had given Kion directions to the army's stable where Tapper and the cart could shelter for the night.

"They want you to stay at the barracks?" Dalia said, disappointment etched on her face.

"That's part of being a soldier," Kion said. "But we'll go to your home after I get Tapper stabled. I should have time for a short visit and I would like to meet your family."

"Yes, so do we all, and we'd like to enjoy some more of Dalia's fine cooking while we're at it, I hope," Zinder said, unashamedly inviting himself to dinner.

"My father wouldn't have it any other way. A meal is the least he could do for the people who rescued his daughter," Dalia said. Though her words addressed them all, her eyes reserved a special gleam for Kion.

"All right, then, let's be off. I'm anxious to put these gates behind us before those soldiers decide to fleece us for more. I don't mind sacrifices in a time of war, but some laws are just robbery by official decree," Zinder said now that they were out of earshot of the guards. "And a fat lot of good the tax is doing from what I can see. That outer wall looks like it would blow over if I sneezed."

"I agree. It's wrong to take advantage of people like this," Kion said. "They're coming to Rippling for protection and instead the daysman inflicts further burdens upon them."

"At least he's building a wall," Tiryn said, not wanting to think ill of someone she'd never met. "That's something, isn't it?"

"Well, with Fathomwood just across the river, I doubt the wall is setting him back much," Zinder said. "But I suppose it means he at least isn't planning on betraying his town into the hands of the haukmarn the way Ilk did at Charring."

Tapper brayed in protest as a wave of smoke blew over the cart. The greasy black cloud smelled of sewage and standing rain water. Husks of old vegetables, sawdust, and other debris covered the road.

"What did he say?" Tiryn whispered. She thought she knew, but wanted to be sure.

"He said that this is a place where the fires burn cold," Nurien said. *"That is a mule's way of saying that it is an ugly, undesirable place."*

An ugly, undesirable place. Yes, it turned out Tiryn had understood him after all. And she had to agree.

They left Tapper and the cart at the stable. The mule looked content with the bucket of oats he was given, but his tapping foot started up the moment they left his stall, as if he was already impatient to return to the road.

It was a quarter mile from the stables to the Unwith home. The house sat up against Old Rippling's wall on Knuckle Street. All of the houses that ran along the wall were roughly the same size and, in contrast to most of the others in the district, of a single story. The streets in that part of town were paved with cobblestones and relatively clean compared to the dirt roads of Spiketown. Unfortunately, since Spiketown began just over the wall, its putrid stench drifted in. But inside Dalia's tiny little home, with the flickering flames of the hearth and the joy on the faces of her father and brothers at Dalia's unexpected return, the outside world and its filth soon faded away. One family, at least, in Rippling grew a little more whole that night. Though the reunion of Dalia and her father and brothers could have made Tiryn and Kion miss their own parents all the more dearly, instead it brought them hope. Though they could never know the fullness of Dalia's bliss, that such joy yet lived on in the world was no small comfort. Grief may have darkened their hearts, but its power was not absolute. There was still light and goodness that endured, and the strong, tender bonds of family brought healing even to those who stood on the edge of their glow.

"Welcome, welcome, my friends. Welcome to our home, and thank you, thank you, thank you, for bringing our precious Dalia back to us," Mr. Unwith said. He stood only a little taller than his daughter. He had a hooked nose, but his eyes were the mirror of hers, green and glittering and all the more beautiful for the joy radiating within. His generous smile was missing a right front tooth, but that did nothing to mar the kindness of his face. He wore a plain tunic and trousers that had been patched several times over. The clothes ballooned over his twig-like frame, scarcely finding any purchase. For all that, his face bore the marks of vigor and health and his step, though a little hunched, was as spry as someone half his age.

Mr. Unwith's two sons stood a head taller than their father. One had short hair which stuck out at every conceivable angle. He introduced himself as Clev. The other brother had a more innocent face which marked him as the younger of the two. His hair came down to his chin and his name was Hiff.

After the introductions, they made their way from the living room to the kitchen to take some tea. Though clean and quaint and framed with a buttery brown wood, the kitchen scarcely had room to fit them all. Clev and Hiff stood while the rest took their places around the table. Then Dalia set about telling the tale of how the Odwins met their unfortunate end, and of her rescue by her newfound friends. Her eyes softened whenever she glanced at Kion or mentioned him, but Tiryn was too grateful for the tea and hospitality to be bothered by Dalia's looks. But for the first time Kion finally noticed the attention. His brow furrowed in confusion, as if he questioned whether or not he read her glances properly, though Tiryn didn't see how he could miss their meaning.

"So this is the Sword of the North we've been hearing about? And Tiryn is called the Maid of Ice. And the both of you are traveling with an honest-to-goodness nyn. You're the first one I've met since the last war, and the first I've ever welcomed into my home to be sure," Mr. Unwith said once the tale was finished.

"Yes, my people are a rare sight these days. A bit like diamonds," Zinder said with an impish creep of the eyebrow.

"If I had the money, I'd ask you to make me some better rat traps. The ones I have are fine enough, but they break far too often for my liking. But what of these blades you carry? How is it that they can fashion fire and ice out of nothing?"

Kion and Tiryn both unsheathed their weapons, to the Unwiths' great delight.

"Truesilver and Rimewinter," Mr. Unwith said. "I'm no smith or swordsman, but I've never seen such quality by the hand of any man."

"Are there more of these weapons?" Clev said.

"Those weapons we set down inside the door are also glaives," Kion said. "But they only awaken when in the presence of the one they are called to, so I'm afraid we can't just give them to anyone."

"But we will find the ones who need them," Tiryn said. The

moment she said it, she knew it to be more than just a wishful statement.

"*I sense it, too,*" Nurien said. The bond between them made it seem as though they shared the same thought at times, that it belonged neither to Tiryn nor Nurien but both of them together. Tiryn could not explain how this could be, but she found it deeply comforting, as though the mystery made it all the more precious, and that if she could somehow understand it, it would weaken the bond.

"Warding could sure use them in the war," Hiff said.

"You should have seen the way they stopped the bandits," Dalia said. "With weapons like these, the haukmarn's days are not long in the land." Her eyes rested on Kion once again. Tiryn stared at Dalia as hard as she could, silently willing her to leave her brother be, but she might as well have been invisible. Dalia's eyes never left him.

"Yes, it's true. If they saved you, dear Dalia, they can save us all," Mr. Unwith said.

After a moment of silence in which Dalia finally looked away, Mr. Unwith rose from the table. "Now, late though the hour may be, and humble as my kitchen is, I would be a poor host if I did not offer you a meal. Come, daughter, let us prepare something for our guests. I'll put some more logs on the fire."

"Of course, Papa. I know just what to make them—your favorite: radish stew."

"Sounds delightful!" Zinder fairly bounced with anticipation in his chair.

"Yes, well, the table of a rat-catcher is hardly worthy of all you've done for my Dalia, but her radish stew is the best in all of Inris."

"Oh, Papa, you're too kind."

"No, he's right," Clev said and Hiff echoed the sentiment.

"Well, I suppose things always come out better when cooking for those you love," Dalia said. Her gaze passed around the room, drawing warm smiles from her father and brothers before settling on Kion. This time his face turned red.

"Oh, dear," Tiryn thought. That was not a good sign. Kion never blushed at anything. He and Tiryn needed to have a talk. For she did not need the gift of foresight to see where this was going.

Chapter 19

RUMBLINGS IN THE DARK

Tiryn could not talk with Kion alone that night since he left for the barracks soon after dinner. He was worn ragged from the day's journey. They all were except Dalia. She stayed up talking with her father and brothers while Tiryn fell asleep in the room they were to share. Tiryn plunged into an uneasy slumber, hoping she did not dream of Kion and Dalia taking a stroll together along the banks of the Merriling. She did not dream of anything like that, though. She dreamed of something far worse.

In her dream, the drowning vision returned. Only this time, it was not the soldier from Dunach who went under. It was Kion. He slipped beneath the water while Tiryn stood on the forested banks of the lake, watching him go down, helpless to do anything about it. But Kion did not stay under for long. He rose in a great tumult mounted on the back of a terrible creature, its skin glistening as though coated in oil. An arrow-shaped head, lizard-like and menacing, crowned its long serpentine neck. Folded wings the size of rooftops nestled close to a body covered in supple, seamless scales. A dragon. There was no other name for it. And Kion was riding it.

Even in dreams, dragons are terrible things, and the reek and the presence of it bristled with peril and wrath.

"Kion, what's happening?" Tiryn cried out.

But he did not answer. Instead, he lifted higher and higher toward a large mass of billowing darkness. He drew forth Truesilver with a cry, but the blade had no fire and no crimson light gleamed from the metal.

"I am coming. And this time I will defeat you!" he shouted.

"Kion, wait! It's Tiryn! Come back and take me with you!" she shouted, but he had already flown far away. Her voice died upon the waters.

She ran toward the shore. If this was indeed a dream, perhaps she could find a dragon of her own and follow him. But her feet never touched the water. The ground shifted underneath her and cast her down. She tried to rise, but the mud and rocks buckled and her feet slipped out from under her. As she scrambled to her feet, the great billowing darkness loomed ever closer.

"Kion, help!" she called out.

But Kion was a small shape now against roiling clouds. He and the dragon vanished into the unending dark.

The world spun around her. Her vision blurred. Nothing held fast. All directions fused into one. Silt and stone poured down upon her. A wave of dirt swept over her. It swallowed her in an angry, vicious whirlwind of crushing rock. In the end, the terror was too much and she jolted upright, her eyes blinking furiously in the night.

But the shaking did not stop. The bed and the walls, the ceiling, and the floor, all rattled and creaked and shifted and bowed. Dalia lay in a hammock along the opposite wall, banging against the side like a passenger in the hold of a storm-tossed ship.

"Dalia, wake up!" Tiryn said. They had to get out of the house before it snapped apart and came crashing down around them. But Dalia did not stir.

Tiryn lurched out of bed, but the boards bulged and sent her sprawling against the door.

"What is happening?" Nurien said. The blade fell and bounced around the floor, a mad hornet looking for someone to sting. It flashed in the moonlight. Had she not sheathed it? Or had it fallen out? *"Call me to your hand before I hurt you or Dalia."*

Nurien's voice was the one firm thing in all the turbulence. It stilled Tiryn's thoughts long enough for her to see the danger.

"Rimewinter, to me," Tiryn said. The blade streaked toward Dalia's neck, but at the summons of Tiryn's voice it veered from its deadly course and into Tiryn's hand.

The moment the cool handle clapped into her palm, the shaking died. A few minor tremors followed in its wake, but as suddenly as it began, the quaking ended.

"Did you stop it somehow?" Tiryn said.

"I have no idea why it ended."

Dalia, unbelievably, remained fast asleep, wrapped safely in her hammock and blissfully unaware of what had happened.

"Whatever the reason, I'm glad it stopped." Tiryn got to her feet, rubbing her bruised knee and elbow. She was used to taking a tumble, clumsy as she was when it came to anything except dancing.

"I am surprised no one else stirred. Zinder and the Unwiths are all still asleep."

"Yes, that does seem hard to believe."

What had happened? Where did the vision end and the real world begin? The tremors were horrible, but now that they were over, the terror of her dream rushed back. She had to talk things out with Nurien, to discover just what had happened.

Though Dalia was clearly a sound sleeper, Tiryn did not wish to risk disturbing her. She slipped out the door without making a sound. Zinder, Clev, and Hiff slept away on the floor of the main room, the glow from the kitchen hearth lighting softly upon their unmoving frames. The kitchen door stood open, but the other bedroom door was shut. Mr. Unwith's snoring rumbled through the wood, the one disturbance in the now perfect peace of the house. It was the kind of noise that her dreams may have converted into a quake, but no, the floor had buckled and sent her tumbling. And Nurien had felt it too. The chairs and the table in the kitchen had shifted and one chair had even tipped over, further confirming that it could not have been a dream.

Tiryn eased the front door bolt from its fastenings, laying the thick wooden beam aside. She pried the door open, but this one creaked awfully. Zinder rolled over and mumbled something about "getting to the hattery," but did not wake. Tiryn squeezed through the crack and closed the door again, enduring another high-pitched creak.

Outside, the pavement shimmered from a recent rain, though it must have been a light one for few puddles remained. The houses on the opposite side of the street loomed over the Unwiths', all two stories tall and wider as well. A crescent moon cast a mantle of sleepy enchantment over the town. Lampposts lent their aid to the slender moon, shining misty light upon the pavement. Their iron housings mimicked the shape of rising waves, each lamp a miniature image of the sun setting down over frothing water. The only thing marring the tranquil scene was the stench drifting over the wall from Spike-town. Tiryn let her feet take her away from the cross street where the smell was strongest. She reached another intersection and followed it deeper into Old Rippling, all the while talking quietly with the naked glaive she wore strapped to her chest.

"I had another dream, Nurien. It was the same one I had in Sicklewood, of Kion leaving me. I've had it two times now. Does that mean it will happen?"

"*No, as long as a vision has not come a third time, it may be averted, or it may come in some other form.*" The pitch of Nurien's voice matched the softness of the moonlight. It was just what Tiryn needed to hear. "*Tell me exactly what you saw.*"

Tiryn related the dream, reliving the dread presence of the darkness and the panicked fear of seeing her brother ride off without her as the ground came down on top of her.

"*It is strange that you saw Kion riding on the back of a dragon. There were never many dragons even in the time of the Shattering, and most of those were killed during the war. And then there is the size of it. Judging by the way you described it, it sounds more like one of the drakyn. They are fearsome, yes, but without the power to speak and lesser in stature and in all other ways than a true dragon."*

"But dragons are evil, aren't they? If drakyn are like them, aren't they evil as well?"

Tiryn paused under a street lamp. Over on some distant street the sound of shuffling feet told her that she was not the only one wandering the town at this unseemly hour. Had others felt the same rumblings that shook the Unwiths' house and taken to the streets as well?

"Yes, dragons and drakyn are both dim-touched creatures, created by Malix and Talinyon's twisting of the Spark. We believe the dragons were created first, but they proved too independent and prideful for Malix's liking and that is why so few of them ever came into being and why he made the drakyn to take their place. But all of them are evil and bound in some way to the one who created them."

"But if they are evil, then why would Kion ride one?"

"That I cannot say. Let us hope your vision was marred when it comes to that detail. Rarely have I ever had a vision that came true exactly in the way it was given."

"I sometimes think that it would be better to have no visions at all than to have to guess what part of them is true and what is not."

"Rather than question the gifts we are given we must strive to use them as best we can. The only hope I can offer is that the clearest visions come when we are most disposed to accept them for what they are. It is when we resist and fight against them that the visions diverge from showing us the whole truth. Yet it is one thing to say this and quite another to submit to what we are shown. For many things are hard to see."

These were not the words Tiryn wanted to hear, but knowing that Nurien understood her fears made them easier to bear. And yet, as Nurien said, knowing that something was true and acting upon it were two different things. She doubted that she would ever be wholly at peace with this gift.

"Thank you, Nurien. I will try to accept them more."

She walked for a whole block in silence, pondering Nurien's words.

"I wonder if I will ever receive a vision about something good. They always seem to threaten awful things," she said at last.

"Learning to accept our fate, good or bad, is the key to understanding it. Remember when I told you that discontentment mars all that it touches? That is because the root of discontent is the unwillingness to see the world as it is."

"But is it wrong to want to change things for the better?"

"No, but only if you know what is truly better. Can you be sure that your desires are always for the best? Who can see the final end of a thing? And yet it is the way of this shattered world that each person always believes that what he does is for the best."

The old sadness returned to Nurien's voice, for the lesson of those words had come to her through bitter experience. The Longwinter and the imprisoning of Malix were born out of a desire to protect the Four Wards from a terrible evil, and yet others had suffered because of that decision, and in the end, it had all been for naught. Malix was loosed upon the world once more.

"You are right," Tiryn said. "I need to face the truth, whatever it may be. But that doesn't mean it will be easy."

"You will succeed where I failed."

"We will succeed together. I cannot do this without you."

"You are right. We will do this together."

The terror of the tremors and the trouble of her vision finally began to loosen their grip on her. Talking to Nurien had given her suffocated spirit a breath of much needed air. Walking out in the cool night beneath the street lamps had helped as well. But she had wandered long enough. It was best to head back to the Unwiths' now.

Tiryn stopped at an intersection. Had she gone four blocks or five since she left the house? She couldn't see the wall from where she was, but if she kept going in the same direction she would hit it eventually and from there could find her way back to Knuckle Street.

Before she could get her bearings, a stab of panic gripped her. If someone had pricked her in the neck the sensation could not have been any sharper. Someone was following her. Her eyes jumped from shadow to shadow in every direction. Whoever was following her was in one of those shadows, she was sure of it—or was she? She couldn't see anything definite. It might just be her imagination playing tricks on her. It often did that in the dark. Or had Nurien's hunters finally returned?

"Nurien, do you know the way back to the house?"

"Yes. You simply have to turn around and head back up—"

Nurien's reply was cut short when Tiryn's feet shot out from under her. She let out a feeble cry as, for the second time that evening, she found herself colliding with the ground.

"Are you all right?" Nurien said.

"I'm fine. Perfectly fine. And perfectly clumsy. I just stepped on a slick stone." She got up and moved away from the spot where she fell, rubbing her hip. Underneath the lamp some oil had mixed with the rain and of all places, Tiryn had planted her foot right in the middle of it. "Nurien, I just had the strangest thought—that I was being followed. I can't be certain, but a part of me wonders if it isn't those shadowy things that have been hunting us since Dunach."

"I don't sense any—wait, someone is coming this way. It's not the shadow hunters, though. It's the city watch. It would not be good for them to see you. Slip into that alley across the street."

From the same direction as the shuffling feet earlier came the hurried pounding of boots upon the pavement.

"But why should we—"

"There is no time. Hide—quickly—before they come."

Tiryn made a dash for the dark narrow street. She ducked into the shadows, but twenty paces in, the street ended in a high brick wall. Stacks of crates rose in front of it, some without lids and overflowing with wretched-smelling refuse.

"Oh, no. This won't work," Tiryn said.

"Do you think you could make it over?"

"I'm terrible at climbing," Tiryn said.

The pounding feet had reached the outside street. They sounded close.

"You have to go over if you don't want them to take you," Nurien said.

"Take me, but why would they—?"

"The curfew. They mentioned it at the town gates. Forgive me. In all the confusion of the quake I failed to consider the hour."

Curfew? Tiryn had no memory of that being mentioned at the gates. Then again, she had been so distracted that they might have listed off a dozen rules and she would have been none the wiser. She turned her back to the wall. Two figures loomed out of the darkness at the entrance to the alley.

"You there. You're not supposed to be out at this hour," one of them said. The voice was sharp and hostile.

"Curfew starts at midnight," the other said. "Daysman's orders."

Tiryn was in too much of a daze to make any coherent response. The knowledge that she was a common girl, far from home, in a very strange and dark city came crashing down upon her.

"Is that a dagger you've got there?" the first soldier said.

"Why are you armed? That's not allowed either."

"It'll be a double fine for you, miss. I hope you or your family has deep pockets," the soldier said with no small amount of satisfaction.

"I am sorry, glaivebond," Nurien said. *"I failed to protect you. Nor did I foresee this."*

Tiryn marshaled her courage and forced herself to think clearly. She wanted to reassure Nurien that she did not blame her. It was an honest mistake. Everything would all turn out all right in the end. Walking the streets could not be that much of a crime.

The two soldiers advanced, filling up the alley with their broad shoulders.

"Hand over the weapon and come with us," one of them said.

"War's too important to have folk causing mischief at night. That's why we're hauling you off to prison."

That last word stopped her breath for several heartbeats.

"Prison?"

Perhaps this was not going to turn out all right after all. And, oh dear, oh dear, what was Kion going to say?

Chapter 20

TRAPPING RATS

The Unwith home was silent as a mouse. Or perhaps a very quiet rat.

Kion stood just inside the front door, staring through Zinder and the Unwiths as though they were not there.

"I never should have agreed to stay in the barracks," Kion said. "I'm supposed to protect her. I let her out of my sight for one night…"

"You had no choice," Kithian said. *"You're a soldier now. You did what the wardmark told you. Do not worry. She could not have gone far."*

"We assumed—we hoped at least—that she had gone to find you," Zinder said. "Oh, bother, she must have crept out right over my pointy little nose. If only I had a longer one, she might have tripped and given herself away."

"Don't blame yourself. I didn't hear her leave either," Dalia said, her usual bright eyes dimmed. Gone were the strange looks she had given Kion the night before, but whatever that had been about did not matter in the wake of Tiryn's disappearance.

"Was it the quakes last night?" Kion said, his mind fumbling to make sense of his sister's disappearance and desperate for any hint of a trail.

"Quakes?" Mr. Unwith said. "What quakes?"

"Some soldiers at the barracks felt them," Kion said. "I didn't notice them either, and from the sounds of it, neither did you. But Tiryn's a light sleeper. She may have felt them and run outside for safety. No—that makes no sense. She would have warned the rest of you first."

"This gets odder by the minute," Zinder said. "Quakes? What's next? A volcano in the town square?"

"Well, it's no use standing here," Mr. Unwith said. He went to the corner where one worn hat and three tattered coats hung on a standing rack. He donned the hat and the smallest coat. "Come with me to the fielder's house. He will be able to help us. If we leave now, we may catch him before he heads to the courthouse."

Dalia and her brothers stayed behind while Kion and Zinder followed Mr. Unwith into the street. The lamps still glowed, for dawn had only just arrived. The three of them whisked across the pavement, Mr. Unwith surprising Kion with his speed and energy at his age and at this hour of the morning. Old half-timber houses sailed by as they plowed through the city in the half-gray dark.

The fielder's house sat near the center of Rippling. By the time they reached it, the sun had risen high enough that the lamps were no longer needed and lamplighters appeared with their brass snuffers on long poles to preserve the oil for another day.

They caught Fielder Rudfeld coming out of his door, which saved them the trouble of having to knock. He just barely passed Mr. Unwith in height, but his frame was far stouter. He regarded them with caution.

"Hello, Unwith," he said. "Your appearance at this hour cannot be good news. Has the stone-work in the south sewer come down again?"

"Oh, no, no, nothing like that, Fielder," Mr. Unwith said. "Someone's gone missing. This is Kion Bray, a soldier in the fane's army and his friend, Zinder Hamryn. It's Kion' sister who's gone missing."

"And this couldn't wait until I got to the courthouse?"

"Oh, no, I'm afraid not. These people rescued my daughter

from bandits, you see. I owe them her life and I know how busy you get once you arrive there. You'd want to schedule an appointment and fill out papers and make an official inquiry, so I thought I would catch you before all that got in the way."

"Old Unwith's as good at catching officials as he is rats. I can see that I won't know any peace until I've tracked this girl down. Come, walk with me and tell me what happened."

By the time they finished the ten-minute walk to the court-house, Fielder Rudfeld had a pretty fair hunch as to the mystery surrounding Tiryn's fate. Instead of entering the front of the stately old building, dressed out in a fresh coat of white paint and standing three stories tall, he took them around back to a squat building cringing in the courthouse's shadow.

A decidedly grave and lifeless fellow let them into the prison. Inside, grime-coated stonework formed a series of murky chambers and what little light penetrated the slitted windows was cheerless and drab. It festered with the worst kinds of odors, made all the more pungent by the stagnant air. The fielder went to the ledger hanging on the wall and read down the list. The paper was stuffed with names.

"She's not listed," he said. "Is this list up to date?"

"Ah, now that you mention it, no. It hasn't been updated with the list from the night watch," the jailer said. "I've only just cracked open my eyes. You can't expect everything to be in perfect order at seven o'clock in the morning." He retrieved another slip of paper from a drawer in his desk and handed it to the fielder.

"Here she is," the fielder said with a frown. "Tiryn Bray. Brought in for violating curfew and the possession of a weapon without the proper papers. It's just as I told you, Unwith, though I didn't figure on the weapon part. Old Blovius has been rounding them up like this for the last eight-mark. I'm afraid she won't be getting out anytime soon."

"Violating curfew?" Kion said. "Surely that's not a serious crime."

"Ah, well, with Blovius it's less about the crime and more about the fine. And the weapon part makes it worse. That's where the real problem comes in. She'll definitely have to be held until trial for that."

Kion took a step back. Trial? Fines? What did it all mean? And why had Tiryn gone out at night? The soldiers at the gates had told them about the curfew. Had she not listened?

"Scoomdiggers. It's the same in every town," Zinder said, his face tight as a drum. "The business of men in charge is to ruin the business of the ones who aren't. Scoomdiggers, the lot of them."

"I am afraid Zinder speaks the truth, at least as far as these men are concerned," Kithian said. *"The daysman appears only to be interested in what benefits himself. This fielder is not like him, though. He is forthright and just and therefore our best hope of helping Tiryn."*

"Thank you," Rudfeld said, nodding to the jailer.

"Don't we at least get to see her?" Kion said, staying back.

"Not until the afternoon. And only by appointment," the jailer said. "What time would you like me to put you down for? There's a long list of people waiting to see their loved ones, but...given the right set of circumstances..." He gave a meaningful look at Zinder's coin purse. "I might be able to arrange something."

"Whyyoulittle..." Zinder mumbled under his breath.

Rudfeld, inured to the corruption, didn't bat an eye. "That won't be necessary. Come, let's discuss the situation outside," he said.

The fielder accompanied them onto the little stone path which wrapped around the side of the prison.

"You saw that, didn't you, Fielder?" Zinder said, hot as coal fire. "Are you going to just let that sort of blatant pandering go unpunished?"

"I would if it were in my power, but the jailer is under Shrool's protection. I can only act where he allows," Rudfeld said. Zinder could only shake his head. "Now listen to me.

You're friends of Klesper Unwith and as annoyingly persistent as he can be when he gets an idea into that granite skull of his, he's the best rat-catcher Rippling has ever had, so I'm on your side— let's get that straight from the start. I can see that you're quite upset and I don't say that I blame you. But unless you have some noble blood or are willing to hand over large sums of money, I am afraid that I cannot be of much help, at least not until the trial, which should take place in five days, on the last Vairlin of Sabrand."

"Five days!" Kion said.

"I'd pay every last coin I had to get Tiryn free, but not to crooks and bandits," Zinder said. "It's unconscionable!"

Klesper raised a defiant hand. "You'll not pay one silver nick if I have anything to say about it. Fielder, there's a war going on. We can't be treating each other like this. This boy may look like any other soldier, but he's different, and his sister too. That weapon they found her with was no ordinary dagger. It's an ancient weapon, a weapon that froze twelve bandits in their place with darts of pure blue ice and Kion's sword circled them in a wall of red fire. He's the same boy who bested Vayd in Charring. He's the Sword of the North and his sister is called the Maid of Ice. And we've got to help them."

Fielder Rudfeld eyed Kion with fresh eyes. "Are you truly the Sword of the North? For all the tales I've heard of him, no one can ever agree on what he is supposed to look like."

"Yes, I fought Vayd at Charring. But I wouldn't have beaten him without my blade. Would you like to see it?"

At a nod from the fielder, Kion removed the baldric from his back and unsheathed Truesilver. The golden hilt and silvery blade amplified the morning light as though the sun had been waiting to reveal its full splendor. The reflections bathed the dingy outer walls of the prison in a resplendent glow. It was no longer a mean and ugly place, but rather something worthy of the fane's own palace.

"By the forgelight, that's something, isn't it?" Rudfeld said.

"My sister's dagger is of the same kind, fashioned by the Mastersmith himself."

"Well, I don't know who that is, but whoever he is, he's the finest smith I've ever heard of. No ordinary man could fashion something like that. Which makes it all the harder for me to have to tell you that there's nothing I can do until the trial. It's Daysman Shrool's decision, not mine, however much I should wish to help you."

"But I've been ordered to Bramble Eyre to see if they can send any soldiers to aid the war in the west. I can't wait five days until her trial."

"Much as it pains me to say it, I'm afraid you'll have to leave her behind, then. I'll make sure that no harm comes to her while she's here. Of that I can assure—"

"I won't leave my sister," Kion cut him off, but then caught himself. "I'm sorry. I know you're only trying to help. But I cannot leave her. She's the only family I have and I need her help to win this war."

"And what if this Daysman *Drool* decides against her in the trial? What then?" Zinder said. "Couldn't he keep her here as long as he wanted?"

"That is true. Blovius finds new reasons to keep people all the time, or he could even delay the trial on account of the war. The truth is, he's been wildly unpredictable ever since the war started."

"All the more reason to get Tiryn out now. There has to be a way," Kion said.

Klesper let out a triumphant exclamation, as if he'd just snagged the biggest rat of the day. "I have an idea!" He kneaded his hands together as he spoke, relishing in the unfolding of his plan. "Blovius is having a big banquet tonight for all the old families and the leaders of the army. He's had one every four-mark since the army came. My sons and I always have to work extra late and extra hard on these days to ensure that no rats ruin the festivities and make him look bad. With all the inrush of people it's growing harder and harder to do. For every new person ten new rats make it into the city along with them. You go to him, Fielder—I know he would never talk to me directly—and tell him that if Tiryn is not out of that prison by noon today that tonight he'll be dining with the rats!"

"Brilliant plan, Mr. Unwith!" Zinder snapped his fingers. "Take that, Daysman Drool."

"But, Klesper, your livelihood. Think of that. You have a family to feed. What if Shrool throws you out?" Rudfeld said.

"Even if he does, he'll never replace me by the time of the banquet. He'll have to call it off and look like a fool to all those important friends of his. And besides, no one wants to do my job. He'd have to pay someone else twice what he pays me and when it comes down to it, that's what will really pinch him the tightest. He can't stand parting with a single silver nick."

"Mr. Unwith, that's very kind of you, but we'll find some other way. I could never ask you to risk everything like that," Kion said. Mr. Unwith's courage and generosity moved him deeply, but he couldn't allow this man to suffer hardship for Tiryn's sake.

"You don't have to. I'm doing it anyway." Mr. Unwith gave Kion an unassailable look. "And it's not all that much of a risk, really. If war comes to Rippling, we'll all be out of work anyway."

"I don't like to admit it, but he's right," Rudfeld said. "It is probably the only way to free your sister before the trial, short of paying off both the jailer and the daysman to the tune of some fifty gold rounds."

"Scoomdiggers," Zinder said. "It's bold-faced robbery! But you know, in the end I would pay it, if that's what you decide."

"No, I can't ask you to pay that, though I know you would," Kion said. Then he added, as softly as he could, "Kithian, what do you say?"

"The road ahead is long and it would be unwise to spend so much of Zinder's coin on something so needless and unjust. Nor would I advise

you to wait five days. Every day is vital in this war. If there truly are forces awaiting orders in Bramble Eyre, five days might be the difference between victory and defeat."

"Who is Kithian?" Fielder Rudfeld asked in the silence that followed. Fire and ice, he'd heard Kion mention Kithian's name. Kion looked at Zinder and shrugged. There was no way around it but to tell the truth and the fielder seemed trustworthy enough.

"The sword can speak as well, but only Kion can hear it," Zinder said. "I know, it's not fair, but Kion doesn't have my rakish good looks so it evens out."

The fielder gave them a sour look, clearly unconvinced, but Zinder's manner made it come off like some private joke between them. Everyone shared a nervous laugh and then Kion said, "All right, then. I believe Mr. Unwith's plan gives us the best chance of getting Tiryn out. And if the daysman dismisses him, we will find a way to make it right."

"That settles it, then," Mr. Unwith said.

They departed back around toward the front of the courthouse.

"Well, Mr. Unwith," Zinder said, "it looks like you're about to catch the biggest rat of them all!"

DIFFERENT PATHS

The rest of the morning was spent in nervous pacing between the kitchen and the main room of the Unwith home. Dalia made and served pot after pot of clover tea. Clev and Hiff had to go off hunting rats and checking traps around the city—everywhere except near the daysman's mansion of course. Klesper stayed home with Kion and the others.

Zinder passed the time fixing a broken down clock that had belonged to Klesper's grandfather. That was his preferred way of dealing with worry—fixing things, doing something with his hands. The clock had been passed down as an heirloom, but only for sentimental reasons, as it had not told time since Klesper's grandfather was still living. Zinder had to fashion parts from spare wire, string, and bits of wood that Klesper scavenged for him, but he got it working. Once restored, a clever little wheel of dancing couples sprang out upon the hour from a window above the clock face and it played a chiming tune that Dalia recognized at once.

"Oh, Papa, you used to sing that to us when we were young, didn't you?"

Kion recognized the song as well. His own mother had sung it to him and Tiryn on many a night.

"Yes, it's been so long, I'm not sure that I remember the words," Mr Unwith said. He sat in his large rocking chair, its creaking keeping its own wooden time. "Do you remember them?"

"Yes, Papa. Shall I sing it for you now?"
"I should like that very much."

Oh, dear sweet times of glee
You sitting on my knee
To ride a bucking horse
Oh, fond, sweet company

Of laughter is no lack
You riding on my back
This rambling raucous trip
Up to the moon and back

So let us run and play
Along our merry way
Me holding fast your hand
Together all the day

I'll hold it 'til you're grown
And to the four winds flown
Yet don't forget these times
When you were all my own

The tune was lively and quick, and Dalia's voice light but sure. Yet for all that, everyone, including Dalia and Mr. Unwith, turned melancholy once it was finished. They gazed upon the clock, musing upon the words.

"When you were all my own." So much had changed since Mother last sang it to them. Like young birds, they had been thrust from their nest and forced to fly. But he and Tiryn had not so much flown to the Four Winds as been blown and tossed about to places they did not wish to go. And now, where had Tiryn flown? Where had the cruel winds of fate carried her?

The tea cups drained and the clock played its tune thrice more before a knock sounded upon the door.

Everyone rose to their feet.

"Yes, who calls?" Mr. Unwith said.

"Your old friend, Fielder Rudfeld."

Mr. Unwith flung wide the door.

"And I'm not alone."

Tiryn rushed in and threw herself into Kion's arms. They held each other for the longest time. The prison and the doubt and the war and the grief all faded away in the joyous wonder of that precious meeting. After that she swept Zinder off his feet, squeezing both laughter and tears from his twinkling nynnian eyes.

"Thank you, Mr. Unwith, oh thank you, thank you," Tiryn said, hugging him. She rushed over to Dalia and embraced her as well. "And thank you, Dalia. If we hadn't met you I would have been shut away in that prison for another five days at least, and maybe longer. Fielder Rudfeld told me that the jailer and the daysman would have raised the fine until they had our last silver nick. But the fielder proved a true and dear friend and his persistence—and Mr. Unwith's courage—won my freedom. Oh, I never knew rat-catchers could hold such sway over the rich and powerful."

Tiryn's lips spilled over with words of gratitude. A whole day's worth of talking poured out from her all at once; she who almost never had much to say out-talked them all that day. She smelled awful, but she looked wonderful—and happier than she'd been since Mother's death. And Rimewinter was strapped safely in its place across her chest.

"*Welcome back, Nurien. You passed the evening in an unusual manner,*" Kithian said, a settled pleasure in his voice.

"*Well, I do not foresee everything,*" Nurien said. "*It is good to be back.*"

"But, Tiryn, now that you're safe, you must tell us what in the Four Wards sent you out into the street at such an hour?" Kion said.

With her face aglow, partly from relief and partly from

chagrin, she explained all that had happened to her since the tremors and her unfortunate stroll through Old Rippling. She had more or less finished when the Unwiths' clock struck one and all paused to listen and watch the mechanical figures emerge and perform their dance.

"I know this song," Tiryn said.

But Dalia did not sing it this time. Nor did Tiryn. Though from the sobering of her expression, the words clearly played in her thoughts. They played in Kion's as well, but the last verse no longer troubled him as it had before.

For the bird had returned to her nest. Tiryn had flown back from the Four Winds at last.

Mr. Unwith emerged from his bedroom wearing his beaten old leather coat and stiff-brimmed hat, and with a sizable bag slung over one shoulder. In one hand he held a long pole with a spear head on one end and a net on the other. His big black boots went up to just below the knee.

"That's a fine hat you've got there," Zinder said.

"Well, it's practical. Keeps dripping water off me down in the sewers. I coat it with a special oil my father taught me how to make. Not the most comfortable thing, but I keep dry." He stopped at the door and gave each of them a heartfelt shake of the hand. "I wish I could see you to the ferry, but I have to keep my end of the bargain. Can't have rats crashing old Blovius's party. Except the ones on the guest list! Clev and Hiff will be sore they couldn't see you off. But Dalia will accompany you to the ferry, and I suppose that's fitting since she's the one who brought you here. I can't thank you enough for bringing her back to us."

"We owe you no small thanks as well for snatching Tiryn out of that awful prison," Kion said.

"Yes, it was a horrid place," Tiryn said. "Thank you again,

Mr. Unwith. You took a great risk standing up to the daysman the way you did."

"Shall I accompany you on your way to the mansion, my friend?" Fielder Rudfeld said.

The two men said their last good-byes and departed. Kion, Tiryn, and Zinder loaded a few last belongings into the cart and set off with Dalia for the docks.

Tapper's hoof had been going the whole time they said their good-byes. Now that they were finally underway, he let loose several whinnying cries.

"You're ready to use my services again?"

"We certainly are. It's a long road through the forest to where we have to go. Are you ready for the challenge?" Kion said, enjoying, as always, his newfound ability to converse in the beast speech.

"The longer the road, the stronger I get. See how broad and stout my back is? It was born to be loaded down. It is in serving that I find my greatest pleasure."

Dalia rode in the back with Tiryn. She was unusually quiet. It was the strained silence of longing to speak but failing to find the words. Kion sensed the same unease in Tiryn. Something was troubling them both, but neither could bring herself to say it. Kion did his best to overlook the tension, instead bantering with Zinder about which of the two hatteries in Rippling was better, and consoling him because they did not have time to visit either one.

Later, they passed by a smithy and Zinder peered in through the windows with a curious eye, wondering aloud when he would ever forge again.

They traveled on through the heart of Old Rippling. People packed the streets, hustling this way and that upon a thousand different errands, haggling with vendors over the dwindling scraps of food, hauling their worldly goods on carts, mules, or their own backs. Some sought lodging, others simply wandered in bewilderment, lost in a river of strangers. An air of press and panic made every voice more shrill, every word more urgent. The loveliness of the fine half-timber buildings of Old Rippling, with their flower-boxes full of marigolds, and their lead-paned lattice-work windows failed to stir a single soul. This was a town on the brink of war. All the beauty it had left was smothered by the growing din of fear and uncertainty.

They worked their way down overloaded streets, the burden of Tiryn and Dalia's silence growing heavier the longer they carried it. Eventually, even Kion and Zinder's conversation died away under the weight of those unspoken words. They were all waiting for something, though Kion knew not what it was.

The crowds thinned enough at last to get a view of the wide swath of weathered planking which spread out before them. The warped boards ran for several blocks along the river and ended in a long stone dike which ran the length of the pier. Some eight feet below the support wall, with stone ramps leading down, the gray Merriling River rumbled past the town, a long, slow churning born in the lofty heights of the Clarion Toths and wending its way across all of Inris. Beyond Rippling, the river cut through Fathomwood to Madrigal and from there issued forth at Seabrim into the frothing waters of the Diring Sea.

Of those who had come to Rippling of late, any who could afford it hired passage for the long trip to Madrigal, capital of Inris and the largest—and most well-protected—city of the North. A myriad of jutting platforms ran out into the river from the base of the dike wall. Many of the docks were empty, though in a few places vessels ranging in size from small rowboats to a long keelboat with a single sail loaded passengers and goods. In other places, shipwrights worked feverishly at building new ships. Their hammering and sawing contributed to the general racket along the docks. A handful of soldiers milled about, for the most part heedless of the hubbub around them, content to occupy themselves with idle chatter, present simply because they had been ordered to be there. Kion, who had taken to wearing his tabard while in Rippling, tried to catch their eye and at least salute them, but not once did any of them look his way.

The cart pulled up to the end of a wobbly wooden ramp on the far end of the docks. There, a single barge, manned by a single ferryman, sat bare and waiting for passengers. The rotund pilot had long, oar-like arms and the chest of a bull. He wasted no time in stepping onto the ramp to receive them. Zinder booked passage for a square and a half, at which he shook his head, but as the ferry did not look to have any other business, he could hardly fault the man for the steep price.

"Not many care to endure the eastern road these days," the ferryman said. "The river's much faster. But it takes no coin to travel on your own two feet. In a few more days they'll have no choice. The shipwrights can't make enough boats to carry everyone to Madrigal who would go."

"We're not headed for Madrigal," Kion said. "I am a messenger of the army, sent to seek aid from Bramble Eyre."

"Ah, Bramble Eyre. Well, let's hope they send help, then. We haven't heard anything coming from that way since before the war." The ferryman excused himself to get the cart and mule tied to a long rail which ran down the center of the barge, but he had said enough to sow yet more doubt about the wisdom of their journey. If there had been no news from Inris's southernmost fortress in almost two months did the fortress even still stand?

"Well, it looks like this is good-bye," Tiryn said, breaking her silence at last. With those words, a great dam broke and the well of unspoken words and emotion surged over Dalia. Her face flushed pink and her eyes grew moist. Fear and regret and hope and anguish all swirled together upon her lovely face.

"I wish that I could come with you," Dalia said, expelling her words in a desperate rush. "I know I don't have any skill in battle or any great knowledge in pathfinding to lead you through the forest. But I can cook and sew and wash, and…and I could polish your armor and weapons and…I…"

Kion took Dalia's hand in his. How firm and strong it was. It was a hand that had done much work. It burned with surprising warmth, bordering on feverish. Kion had never held the hand of a girl before. The farm girls all shunned him and the shepherd girls he had known had all been too young or too old to show him any interest. He did not know what to say, but he could not bear the silence and so forced himself to speak.

"Dalia, you may be the kindest person we've met on our journeys. I'm so grateful that we happened upon you in that clearing. The way you endured your masters' death, the death of those you held dear, gives me hope and courage in the face of my own grief. For that, and for your family's help in rescuing Tiryn from prison, and for inviting us into your home and all the hospitality you showed us, I thank you. But we cannot bring you down the road that we now travel. Too many dangers await and I would not put you in harm's way for all the treasure in the fane's coffers."

She gripped his hands all the tighter. "I can be brave. Take me with you and you will see."

"I know that you would be as brave as any of us. To face the men who killed your masters and grant them mercy the way you did showed the kind of strength that I could only wish for. To hold on to hatred and bitterness is the path of fear. But you chose to walk the path of love. For love is the opposite of fear.

"But as brave as you've proven yourself to be, I was given this sword to protect the people of Inris, not to lead them into peril. You must remember your father. He is a good, kind man, just like his daughter. He needs you, Dalia, far more than we do, and your brothers as well. If battle comes to Rippling, you must be at their side, whether to flee into the hills or to face the suffering of war together. They will need your strength and bravery in the coming days. You are family and when the world is falling down around us, that is when we need our family most. And so, I fear that this is good-bye."

Dalia struggled for breath, as though she'd just finished a race, and from the look in her eyes, it was a race she had lost. It hurt to see her suffer and struggle this way, but there was nothing Kion could do to ease the blow. Their roads lay clearly before them and they did not lie in the same direction. He let go of her hands. Then her first tears came.

Tiryn stepped in and embraced her. "Don't be sad, Dalia. Remember the snow glaze and the journey through the Furls and the Egramoor and all the good things we shared. You have been a true friend."

"I shall miss you, lass," Zinder said. "You'll think of me on the hour, won't you? Whenever you hear the clock strike?" He hugged her waist, a rare show of affection from the close-vested nyn.

Dalia staunched her tears. Her gaze lingered upon each of them, but longest upon Kion. In those glittering green eyes he read so many dashed hopes that it was almost too much to bear, but he did not look away. She deserved that much at least.

"I am sorry," she said. "I knew that I couldn't go before I asked. Not least of all because of my father and brothers. But sometimes I can't hold the words inside. It's a fault of mine. I had to say them, even if I knew it wasn't meant to be. Papa always tells me, 'Your heart goes out too quickly. Be mindful where you send it,' but I'm afraid I can't help myself." For all her sorrow, a growing peace settled upon her face. Her hopes may have been dashed, but she would not cling to the shards. That would only lead to further sorrow. As she had let go of the Odwins, so she would let go of Kion.

"You have nothing to apologize for," Kion said. "It takes courage to hope. Never be ashamed of that. Good-bye, Dalia. May you and your family hold on to each other in the days to come."

They turned and walked down the ramp, leaving Dalia on the docks. The ferry put out into the river, drifting away sluggishly, as if struggling to pull free of invisible bonds which held it to the shore. Dalia stayed until they were midway across the river, then quietly slipped away. She walked back through the crowded streets, back to the little house on Knuckle Street with the pleasant kitchen and the newly restored clock, there to wait the return of her father and brothers from purging Blovius's mansion of the horrid little creatures which threatened to ruin his feast and reputation.

"She cared for you," Tiryn said.

"Yes, that was very clear," Kithian said. *"There was no duplicity in her thoughts. She was one of the most honest people I have ever encountered."*

"Did you feel the same?" Tiryn said, nervously searching Kion's eyes.

"What does it matter? Nothing would ever come of it. My path is to war. I have no time for matters of the heart."

"I thought that is what you would say, but I wasn't sure. I am sorry for Dalia, though. She couldn't help her feelings any more than rain can keep from falling. But even though I didn't want her to feel the way she did about you, I'm glad she said what she did at the end."

"Yes, if only we could all be so honest and brave." Kion turned toward the smaller dock on the opposite bank. Not far beyond it lay the beginnings of Fathomwood, greatest of all forests in the Four Wards. To there Kion now tasked his thoughts. For to dwell upon what could not be was a path to nowhere. Dalia had taught him that. And a great deal more besides.

Chapter 22

DRENCH AND DRUDGERY

A quarter mile from the banks of the Merriling, the road plunged into a tapestry of trees that stretched from north to south as far as any of them, even Zinder, could see. The rounded crowns of bronzewood trees wove together in a covering so thick few rays of light penetrated to the forest floor. Their prickly leaves grew large and thick and waxy, the color of dark moss, though the scarcity of light made them even darker. But when the wind blew strong through their boughs, the underside of the leaves flashed a deep red, as if covered in dried blood. The name of the trees came not from the color of their wood, but from its temper. Many an axe had foundered and chipped while attempting to bite into these hardened trunks. And rare was the hand that could craft and mold such wood into anything useful. Thus, Fathomwood had remained largely untouched and had grown to be the largest wood in all the Four Wards.

The tree branches did not cover the road, though, and so they walked for the most part under the light of the sun.

"The hunters pursue us once again," Nurien said as night closed in upon the forest.

"I daresay the woods are dark enough for them to keep pace with us even during the day," Kithian said.

"At least the sun shines upon the road. They won't do anything to us in the light, will they?" Tiryn said.

"It is hard to say since we do not know the true nature of what hunts us, but the fact that they now move during the day bodes ill for us, I fear," Nurien said.

"Let them come," Kion said. "I am tired of being hunted like one of Unwith's rats. I would know once and for all what it is that pursues us." But from the looks on Tiryn's and Zinder's faces, neither of them shared his opinion.

They hunted long for a place to camp, traveling on for an hour into the dark until they came upon a fallen tree. It had pushed the underbrush back enough to carve out a small stretch of bare ground. All around it, though, the ground was choked with thornbristles and an over-abundance of dark, twisting vines.

"I've never seen such a tangled mess," Kion said.

"Well, at least these bushes will keep the vermin away," Zinder said.

"Yes, these are the same bushes that grew around the Red Ox Inn," Tiryn said.

"Klesper also had high praise for the thornbristle. He told me they were his secret weapon against the rats. They give off some sort of scent, he said. Rats and insects cannot abide it."

"I daresay even the birds and the beasts are averse to these woods," Kion said. "We've seen no more than a handful all day. If we're forced to hunt here, our prospects will not be promising."

"We should have sufficient provisions to reach Bramble Eyre, though I do wish we had taken the time to restock at Rippling," Zinder said, chomping on a piece of dried meat as they sat down in front of the cart. Tapper had wandered off to the right, nosing at a few rare shoots of grass. Kion finished off his own chunk of meat. He thought back to the feasts Dalia had prepared for them at Farmer Marlund's. It would be a long time before they tasted such delicious fare again.

"If the rest of the forest is this full of dark and gloom, we can't reach the end of our journey fast enough," Tiryn said. Having already finished her meal, she lay huddled between two wheels of the cart. Rimewinter lay unsheathed beside her, its soft blue light warding off the encroaching dark. Far away, a lone owl hooted into the night. Kion thought of the shadow hunters again, but if any were hiding in the woods, he had no way of knowing. An army of haukmarn could have been hiding in that darkness for all he knew, so deep it was, and so complete.

"Have you ever visited Bramble Eyre on your travels, Zinder?"

"No, though I did pass it by when I first came to Inris. It's a grand old castle; the battlements are crafted to look like giant thorns. A marvel of stonework to be sure, but I never set foot within its walls. I look to amend that this time around."

Kion sat among the roots of the fallen tree, staring up at the cross-stitched sky, ablaze with trails of sparklight. The glittering traces moved in no discernible pattern, but deep down Kion had always believed there was some purpose to their dance.

"I wonder what Lord Grundstaff will be like?" Tiryn said. "I can hardly believe Kion is about to stand before someone of such importance."

"Let's hope he's more welcoming than Forglen," Kion said.

"That remains to be seen," Zinder said. "With the blade-warden dead, the margrave and the fane frittering away in their palaces, and the daysmen of Charring and Rippling a traitor and a tyrant, the leadership of Warding has proven to be sorely lacking."

"I'm sure Lord Namril will be different," Tiryn said.

"I confess that I share Zinder's doubts," Nurien said.

"Have you seen something that we should know?" Kithian said.

"It takes no Vision to see that the war goes on unchecked in the north. The settlements of Inris are falling one by one. If there was someone noble in a seat of power, would he not have arisen by now?"

"True. Yet it may be for that reason that you and I have returned, to give the Four Wards the leaders they need."

"They resisted us before, as you well remember."

"Yet they embraced our aid in the end."

"At the barracks in Rippling they barely said five words to me," Kion said. He left his perch among the roots and unrolled his knapsack. It was high time they got some sleep. "I hardly feel like a soldier, much less a leader."

"The war has only just begun," Kithian said, his voice full of promise. *"Much will change before it is done."*

"The sword's right, lad. Your day will come, you and Tiryn both. Who knows but that the fane will be kissing your shoes before it's all said and done," Zinder said.

"When the sparks stand still," Kion muttered. "But I appreciate the thought."

Zinder finished the last of his meat and trundled off to his own bedroll. Kion slid under his blanket, his gaze returning again to the glittering sparklight. Whatever final purpose lay behind their nightly courses, the wandering sparks, like the wandering men and women who walked beneath them, had this much in common: that as long as they remained, darkness would never wholly rule the night.

The bronzewoods made the forest dark enough already; they didn't need a full day of rain to add to the gloom. But that was just what they got. And not only the first day, but the leaden clouds persisted for three days straight. The deluge came and went, pouring down buckets and barrels and then shutting off abruptly. Tapper proved unshakable against the drenching assault and never once foundered in the mud. He would no doubt keep going if the road turned into a river. And if the rain kept up like it was, he might get the opportunity.

But though Tapper's spirits never flagged, those of his masters were another matter. They were wet by the first day, soaked by the second, and bailing water out of the cart by the end of the third. In vain, they searched for shelter during the downpours, but as always, Fathomwood shut itself against them. At the end of the third day, they finally found a clearing beside the road with enough hanging boughs to protect them from the driving rain. It lay amidst a rare stand of red oaks that had taken root defiantly amidst all the bronzewoods.

To keep their spirits up, Zinder tried to hum because Tiryn wouldn't, but, except for a few smithing songs, he couldn't carry a tune if he tied it to his wrist. Instead he gave up and simply mumbled the words of songs he knew under his breath. Kion was surprised to discover that there were so many songs dedicated to hats and smithing until he realized that Zinder was simply making most of them up.

Kion kept waiting for the music to reawaken in his sister, but though grief was no longer etched as deeply in her face, no songs sprang from her lips. But busyness can be a balm for sadness and Tiryn certainly exemplified that proverb, occupying her time in learning the beast speech, trying out new words and phrases on poor old Tapper, who, as he did with the rain, bore her attempts with endless patience, though he himself proved to be a thoroughly taciturn creature and rarely said much in reply.

In the midst of the drench and the drudgery of life in a drowned cart on a muddy road in a dark forest rolling toward a doubtful end, Kion's thoughts turned to Dalia. Her plea at the docks had touched him, though it took him some time to admit that to himself. He probably would never see her again, but knowing that someone somewhere was thinking of him and worried about what he might suffer during the course of the war encouraged him that he was not fighting for himself alone, nor for some vague ideals; he was fighting for home. Not his own, but for the homes of others like Dalia and her family. Dalia may not have continued on with them, but the little home on Knuckle Street in some manner did. The haukmarn, and perhaps even some of the leaders of his own people, might resist and assail him, but a rat-catcher's daughter and her family were hoping for —and needing—him to prevail.

On the third day of rain and the fourth day of their journey through Fathomwood, they came at last to an actual camp beside the road. Though overgrown in places, it had been carved out long ago as a resting place for travelers making the long journey through the woods between Madrigal and Rippling. A single low cairn with a hollow on top had been formed of piled stones. The hollow had been sealed with mortar to form a basin for rainwater, which was, not surprisingly, full to the brim, though none of them was the least bit thirsty.

When they had wrung out their clothes as best they could and drained the cart of standing water, they arranged some fallen branches into a pile and built a roaring good fire. The wood was bloated with water and would never have taken in normal conditions, but Truesilver's fire was of another order. It burned red and raging from the very first moment. The soggy wood could not resist succumbing to its flames. The heat forced them to stay well back from the blaze, even Kion, for he set Truesilver off to the side in order to enjoy the fire's warmth along with the others.

"I think I know how Unwith's rats feel," Zinder said, tossing the last of his poor, bedraggled hats into the circle of gear they had made around the fire. Hats of every conceivable color, shape, and style lay strewn about, basking in the restorative glow of the crimson blaze. Zinder had his unshod feet propped up on a log, his toes wriggling in the open air.

"What about Mr. Unwith himself?" Kion said. "Tramping through the sewers, he has to get awfully wet."

Tiryn had barely spoken a word that wasn't to Tapper or Nurien that day, but the fire went a long way toward warming her dampened spirits.

"I imagine it helps him endure his toilings knowing that he can come home to a fire like this in the hearth. Well, not like this exactly, but you know what I mean. Knowing you'll have a fire at the end of the day makes the cold and the damp easier to endure."

"But that's the thing, isn't it?" Zinder said. "There's not always a fire to come home to. And on those days you need persistence. Sometimes life is pleasant and you hardly notice the hours passing by. That's the way it is for me at the anvil. But other days you have to scratch your way through with everything you have in you. There's not always the promise of a warm hearth awaiting you. But you press on. You don't give up. And then, wonder of wonders, you find the fire's there, just when you need it most. But if you don't persist, you'll never find it."

Kion stared off into the bottomless shadows of the woods. "Perhaps Bramble Eyre will be our fire at the end of this road."

"That remains to be seen. We won't know until we get there. It's just like in the story of Fister."

All traces of the forest's gloom vanished from Tiryn's face at the mention of a story. "The story of Fister? Oh, I've never heard that one before. Oh, do please tell it. If ever we needed to hear a story, it would be on a day like this one."

Zinder's eyebrows did a little wave. "Why of course, lass. Stories are medicine to the spirit. And I quite agree. We could use a good story right about now." And with eyes a-twinkle in the fluttering firelight, he launched into his tale.

Chapter 23

FISTER THE MAGISTER

Zinder rose and paced before the blazing fire.

"Once there was a man who was so persistent, soooooo persistent, that he spent the night in the belly of a dragon and lived to tell the tale."

"Oh, really?" Kion said.

"He must have been quite persistent," Tiryn said. "Was he a great warrior? Or clever like Curmelion?"

"Perhaps he was a rat-catcher. Mr. Unwith said it takes quite a bit of persistence to hunt them down," Kion said.

"No, he wasn't a warrior or a wise man or a rat-catcher. He was a magister."

"A magister? Is that some sort of ruler or official?" Kion had never heard the term, but it had that sort of ring to it.

"Oh, no, a magister is someone who can craft magic into things."

"So he was a wizard, then?"

"No, a magister and a wizard are not the same thing at all. Wizards do magical things, but magisters *make* magical things."

"Like some of the nynnian devices you've told us about?" Tiryn said, her cheeks by now rather rosy from the fire. "Many of them sound quite magical."

"Well, no. Nyn can't make magical things. And besides, nyn are real, but magisters are just in stories,"

"Oh, well, that's too bad," Kion said.

"All right, we're bogging him down. Let's let him get on with his story."

"Yes, and pleased to do so! So now, this magister was called Fister."

"Fister the Magister?" Kion said.

Zinder cracked a knuckle.

"Sorry."

"Yes, Fister the Magister. Now Fister was an enterprising sort. He made all kinds of magical things, mostly of the domestic variety. Brooms that would sweep up a room on their own, pendants that would keep the bugs out of your bed, and windows that let you see out but not in, that sort of thing. So overall, not the most impressive practitioner of his craft. But he was well-liked and charged honest prices and had earned a bit of a name for himself in the lands he traveled.

"But one day, after a business arrangement had gone sour and he'd been forced to take back a device that hadn't worked as planned, he was riding through the Pairless Woods."

"Don't you mean 'perilous woods'?" Kion said.

"No, these were the Pairless Woods. I don't know why it was called that. Not too many pairs there, I suppose. Everyone going about on their own. At any rate, on with the story! So, Fister was riding his trusty steed Meloncollar—"

"Sorry, don't you mean Melancholy?" Kion interrupted again.

"No, Meloncollar! His name was Meloncollar, as in collar of melons. He had a strange orange stripe around his neck, I think. Anyway, Fister was riding his *horse* through the *woods* when a great dark shadow blotted out the moon. And Fister knew that it was no cloud, for that night there had not been a single one in the sky. Rather, it was the worst thing you could ever hope to meet on a dark road at night in the middle of the woods. It was…a dragon."

Tiryn took in a sharp breath.

"The dragon swooped down loud as thunder and swift as lightning. Fister barely had time to think. But barely any time is more time than no time. And when you're about to be swallowed by a dragon, barely any time can mean an awful lot. In those precious few moments before he was about to be made a meal of in one gulp, Fister reached inside his pocket and pulled out his pocket watch—a wonderful place for a pocket watch, don't you think? Now, Fister being a magister, this was no ordinary pocket watch, but a *minute* watch."

"Wait, a minute watch, you mean? What other kind of watch is there?"

"Not a minute watch, a '*minute* watch,' my-NOOT, as in tiny, small, exceptionally the opposite of large."

"Ah, ah, a minute watch. Sorry, I must be getting a little sleepy," Kion said.

"Well, then, all the more reason to keep quiet and allow me to finish my tale."

"Yes, Kion, please let him finish," Tiryn said.

"Right. Go on."

Zinder cleared his throat with pretended affront. "Soooooo, Fister took his minute watch and wound it backwards, which is the only direction a minute watch will go when it's full-sized. For when you unwind a minute watch it makes whoever has its chain about his neck, and whatever else he's wearing or holding, the size of a pin. So, *tweep!* Fister grew ever so small and, tiny thing that he was, he slipped into one of Meloncollar's saddle-bags. How he managed that on the back of a horse at full gallop, I'm not sure, but strange things happen when you're about to be swallowed by a dragon.

"Fister had made the device for times when customers got especially angry and he found it necessary to duck away unnoticed and now—thanks to its *timely* magic—he was safe inside the saddlebag, but poor Meloncollar—along with all his baggage —was safe inside the dragon. Which is to say, not safe at all. The poor beast was instantly crushed and crunched into a dragonish snack.

"But our good man Fister remained alive—at least for the moment—for the saddlebag he'd got into was also a magical bag which was enchanted to never wear out even in the harshest winds and the bitterest rains. But though the magic in it was strong, and one of Fister's better pieces of work, it wasn't designed to withstand the acid of a dragon's stomach, not to mention the terrible heat that burned inside the awful beast. Almost at once, the bag began to seethe and sizzle and Fister knew that he had to think of some way out.

"Unfortunately, it's one thing to think in the nick of time of the first thing that pops into your head and then do it. It's quite another when you have the long, slow boil of a dragon's stomach seeping in all around you. The magic might hold a minute, it might hold an hour, but there was no way to know for sure. And then of course the bag kept sloshing about and Fister was so incredibly small you can imagine what sort of trouble he had collecting his thoughts.

"But Fister *was* a magister, after all, and sooner rather than later, that marvelous mind of his came together to form a plan. Working his way around the jostling contents of the bag— dodging huge ink bottles and sacks of coins and avoiding getting tangled up in his favorite handkerchief—at last he made it to the music box he had so recently crafted and which had been the cause of his nighttime ride to begin with. 'If only I hadn't bungled it, I wouldn't be in this mess,' Fister thought, but there was no sense wasting time on self-pity. He pushed and pried and stretched and strained in order to wind it up. It took him a good long bouncing-all-around-the-bag while to get it into position. And once he got the box wound up, it took him another good bit to turn the key which opened the box and then even more time to get enough leverage to open the lid. But right before he opened it, something happened which gave him pause.

"The jostling and moving all but stopped. It took Fister a moment to realize what had happened. 'The dragon must be asleep,' he said to himself. 'Or lying down at least. He's finished his nightly terrors and is back in his cave, I'd wager. He'll be wanting to sleep off his meal. All the better for my box!'

"Fister knew a thing or two about dragons, you see. Once they've had a meal, they can barely stay awake long enough to get back to their cave and digest it. For they do their best digesting while asleep. And they're not nearly as fierce or formidable while in that state. They're more irritable, if that were possible, but far less inclined to fight and terrorize and meddle in other people's affairs until they've gotten in a good night's sleep and gotten their meal all the way down. So, just as the dragon went still and began to rumble with the loudest, most awful and horrible dragon-sized snoring you can imagine, Fister sprang the box open. And then the terrible, shambling snores were replaced—at least inside the dragon's stomach—with an even more dissonant and jarring sound, the melody of a music box gone bad. Not just bad music, mind you, but imagine a music box that sounded as mad as a badger and as loud as a hornet's nest inside a big brass bell—a bell that you had your ear pressed right up against. If you can picture that, that would be only a little—a little, mind you—of what that music box sounded like.

"Fister had made it for a poor old merchant's wife in the village seven miles down from his. He must have been half asleep when he crafted it and he'd certainly been working far too long into the night for several days in a row so that he'd forgotten to test it. It was supposed to create music that would give a perfectly restful night's sleep—without fail—to anyone who could hear it. But instead, after trying it out for three nights in a row, the merchant sent it back saying that it had entirely the opposite effect. Instead of keeping the listener blissfully asleep it kept them painfully awake. It was impossible to sleep while it played and—even worse—once it started playing it would not stop for a full eight hours, even if you shut the lid, for the gears would go on grinding out their mechanical maleficence until the terrible tune was finished. The merchant would have bashed the thing to bits, only he wanted his money back and so he sent for Fister to come retrieve it.

"And now the music, painful as it was for Fister's little ears to endure, blared throughout the insides of the dragon like a symphony in revolt. It did not take long for things inside the dragon's stomach to shift. For though the dragon couldn't really hear the music over all its clamorous snoring, it could feel it, and that was enough for the box to do its work.

"The dragon tossed and turned, struggling to find the right position to sleep. It stretched and curled. It itched and yawned with a fiery glow. It poked and prodded, twisted and yanked, shook and shivered, but nothing would help it suppress the mind-stabbing music. And then the breathing stopped. For dragons can be whisper quiet when they want to and can hold their breath for half an hour or more. And in the silence the dragon heard the faintest echoes of the song inside it. That grating, unbearable, miserable excuse for a song! The most un-sing-songy melody you ever heard, the tasteless, tuneless crankings of a music box gone wrong, the dreaded clangings of the most *unmusical* box in all the world.

"At last the dragon took in another breath and spoke.

"'What in blazing treachery is that noise? Why, I do believe it's coming from inside of me. And it's—it's the most awful sound I've ever heard. I don't believe even a dragon could conceive of a sound more cruel and maddening. It must have been something I ate. Was it the sheep? No, it couldn't have been that. The cows? The pigs? That strange, riderless horse? The sea lion? Yes, that's about as awful a sound as a sea lion makes, but no, the sea lion was more than three days ago. I would have noticed it before now. And how could it still make any sound when it's dead? No animal can bellow and carry on like that after it dies.'

"And the dragon went on like that for some time, for dragons enjoy talking to themselves and almost never just think their thoughts when they could say them out loud. They have to keep up their conversational skills on the off-chance they might have to bandy words with some bothersome human negotiating payment for not ravaging their village or some other such inconvenience.

"But all the while the dragon was reasoning to itself, things were getting hotter and more uncomfortable for poor little Fister. The magic of the saddlebag started to unravel and little drops of acid seeped in with hisses and pops and an awful, caustic smell. If Fister didn't find a way out of the dragon soon, the awful *unmusic* box would be burnt to a crisp and his only hope of getting out would be lost. He could rewind the watch and make himself big again, but that wouldn't solve his problem. It might cause the dragon some momentary discomfort, but he would still be inside the dragon and that pungent acid would be eating at his skin and not just his magical bag.

"As the awful scent clawed its way up his nostrils and he started to choke, at last he remembered something. The conch! Yes, he'd brought that along as well, for the old merchant's wife was hard of hearing and he'd thought maybe all she needed was a Conch of Abundant Sound to properly hear the music. Unfortunately, that had only made matters worse. But what had been the merchant's wife's problem might now turn out to his advantage.

"Out came the conch and in went the magister, right into the music box and the lid closed right down on top of him. He wasn't sure how he was going to get out, but that didn't matter just now. The air was much better inside the box and here the conch could do its work—or so he hoped. Taking up the smooth ivory shell and placing it right up to his mouth, he spoke.

"'Oh, great dragon, the sound that you hear is the curse of Fister the Magister, whom you have so undeservedly swallowed during your nighttime feasting.'

"The dragon gave a start and its whole body tensed.

"'A blister inside my stomach? A cursed talking blister? But my, it's hard to hear with all that racket.'

"'A magister,' Fister tried again, shouting at the top of his voice. 'You've swallowed a magister.'

"'Oh, yes, I can hear you now. A magister you say? I've heard of things like you. You must be human. Come to think of it, I did think I saw a human on that horse but it disappeared right before I swallowed it up. And I didn't feel a human shaped thing go down my gullet. I know their shape and that was nothing like it.' The dragon's voice grew sinuous and cunning now that it was doing more than just talking to itself.

"'No matter how I got here. I've cursed you with this music to never sleep again until you let me out.' The acid smell was starting to come back. Fister thought he heard the first sizzles of it touching the outside of the metal box.

"'A curse, you say? I didn't know magisters went in for that sort of thing.'

"'Yes, well, it's my latest novelty. Created by accident, to tell the truth, but useful in times such as this.'

"Fister tried to keep the panic out of his voice. The sizzling sounds grew more and more troublesome, even over the horrid song of the grinding gears.

"'You don't say. And yet, if that's all it is, this faint little song, I'm afraid you'll have to come up with something better if you want to strike a bargain,' the dragon lied. The song was driving it mad, but it didn't want to let on and weaken its position.

"'Faint though it be, the magic of the curse lies not in the loudness of the song, but in the song itself, you see. All it takes it the barest whisper of it to drive a person, even a creature as enormously clever and accomplished as yourself, into an eternity of sleepless nights. You'll never fly again until you get your rest. And only I have the power to make the music stop.' Of course in this Fister stooped to stretching the truth, for the music would stop on its own after a few more hours even if the box wasn't eaten away by the stomach acid first. But he was in fact the only one who could stop it before then. For he had snagged the key to the box on his way in and all he had to do was jam it into the gears to bring the song to a screeching halt.

"Now dragons can be very patient in most circumstances and

so the dragon considered briefly toying with his victim a little longer. But when it comes to food and sleep, no dragon can manage to stay patient for long and the music was indeed terrifically awful.

"'Fine, fine, fine. If you stop the music, I will let you go. I'm not in the mood for human flesh just now anyway.' And here the dragon stretched the truth itself, for dragons are never entirely satisfied. If they were, they wouldn't be dragons.

"'You have to let me go first. Only then will I stop the music.' Fister knew it was best to be very specific when dealing with dragons.

"'What? What's that you say? I can't hear you over that infernal noise!' the dragon lied again.

"The stench of the acid was overpowering now. It would eat up the gears and stop the music in a matter of moments at this rate. In response, Fister wiggled his way over to the tines where the music was loudest and, stopping his own ears with his second and third favorite handkerchiefs, he turned the tiny hole of the conch toward the source of the nightmarish sounds.

"'Stop, stop, stop! You're making it louder now, not shutting it off. Very well, you pernicious prattler. I'll have this song out of my guts this instant and if you don't stop the music at once I shall make a mouthful of you all over again!'

"And with great heaves and retches and writhings and more violent movements than poor Fister had ever thought he could endure, the box—once silvery and beautiful, but now half-eaten away on three sides—shot out of the creature's mouth. Of the saddlebag and Fister's poor horse Meloncollar, no trace was to be found, but Fister clunked and clattered and shot free. He knocked his head four times, flipped over three times, and almost passed out twice, but he was free. He was free! The cave air, even laced as it was with dragon stench, was a thousand times sweeter than the inside of the creature's belly.

"Fister jammed the key into the gears, figuring he would honor his end of the bargain and then slip away unnoticed.

Dragons were said to have the keenest of senses, but he doubted even a dragon could spot something as small as him.

"The key went into the gears, just as planned, and promptly flew out through one of the burning holes in the side of the box. The *unmusic* blared on.

"'Stop it! Stop it I say! You promised!' the dragon roared, a hundred times louder on the outside than on the inside. It was almost as bad on Fister's stuffed ears as the *unmusic* of the box. The dragon flinched and flexed and leapt to its feet, driven into a mindless rage by the magical sounds now reverberating throughout its cave, louder even than the dragon's horrendous bellowing. It was going to pounce on the box and flatten it—and poor little Fister at the same time. Only the debilitating, grating din kept him from springing with the quickness and power he otherwise would have had.

"And for the second time that evening, Fister had to act upon the first thought that came into his head. The next moment his hand was on the watch and—*pooooom*—the hands of the minute watch wound back up and up came Fister. The dragon was so blind with fury, it couldn't make sense of what was happening. All it saw was the box and that box had to be destroyed.

"Fister fumbled about for the key. At his full size it would be a small thing to shove it in with enough force to break the *unmusic's* power. There! It glittered on top of some rocks halfway to the mouth of the cave. It lay just between two large cracked cow bones. But it was too far away. The dragon sprang upon the box, hurtling from its bed of sparkling gold and silver treasures, and landed with a deafening *grrruuuuummm* onto the cursed box. Fister had dashed for the key at the same time. And although he did not reach it, his desperate lunge landed him right beside the dragon's great horny snout.

"The dreaded *unmusic* went silent and for the first time in a long time, the dragon breathed a contented sigh.

"'Oh, sweet silence. I, Harglond the Devastating, have vanquished the horrible *unmusic* at last,' the dragon said, and it collapsed, far more spent and out of sorts from the twisted tunes than it had realized.

But now Fister had to think fast for the third time that night. He was face-to-face with a live dragon now. The creature's great head loomed before him no more than hand-breadth away. With the *unmusic* box destroyed, Fister had nothing left to bargain with and there was no reason the dragon should not just swallow him again out of spite or hunger or both.

"So, once again, Fister did the first thing that came to mind. He slipped his clever little minute watch off his neck and onto one of the great horns which rose from Harglond's snout like a frozen wave of ivory. It warmed Fister's fingers as they brushed against it. The dragon's great eye snapped open, as large as Fister's head.

"'So, you're here after all. And after spewing forth the contents of my stomach, I feel that I am suddenly hungry again.' The head rose, but while Harglond spoke, before the head could rise too far, Fister's industrious hands—hands that had crafted so many marvelous and delightful things—worked their final magic of the night.

"He unwound the watch.

"'I'm afraid, my dear dragon, it's time you learned some manners,' he said.

"The dragon's great eye went wide and then got smaller and smaller and with a rush of air the great beast turned into the size of a lizard no larger than a newt. A lizard that now wore a tiny chained pocket watch around one of its itsy-bitsy horns.

"'Traitorous tale-teller! This was not part of our bargain,' the tiny Harglond squeaked, its voice no more threatening than that of a terrified field mouse.

"'Neither was your eating me again once I got free,' Fister reminded his diminutive enemy.

"'Turn me back to my normal size at once or I shall roast you alive! I'll gnaw your flesh from your bones.' The once terrible lizard took to the air, flapping its way up to Fister's head, murderous intent sparking in its pathetic little eyes.

"'I'm afraid I can't help you now. My hands are far too large to unwind the watch and your claws are far too cumbersome and ill-suited for such delicate work. No, I'm afraid you're a dragon in name only now. You'll be lucky if you can terrorize the rats.'

"A jet of flame erupted from the creature's slit of a mouth, but it did no more than singe two or three hairs on Fister's eyebrows. He swatted the thing away and sent it plummeting into the pile of treasure. If it came out again, Fister never saw it. After waiting a moment to see if it would return he took a good long look at the riches.

"'No, I know the stories about what happens to those who take a dragon's treasure—even if the dragon is no longer around,' he said. 'It is all yours, my false-hearted friend. Guard it as best you can.'

"And with that he turned and walked out into the night, leaving the shattered and still smoldering music box behind him. And so by persistence and some *timely* thinking, our hero endured a night in the belly of a dragon and in the end bested it without might or blade, proving that no matter how dark things become, if you hold on for all you're worth and never let go, things will all be made right in the end. And so ends the story of Fister the Magister."

Tiryn clapped and Kion nodded in approval.

"I do have to say, right up until the end I didn't see how the poor fellow was going to make it out," Kion said.

"That story has the ring of truth to it," Kithian said.

"That's just it, isn't it?" Zinder smoothed his mustache in contented fashion. "You never know what it will take to get out of a scrape. Fister tried everything he could, but a dragon's still a dragon until you've beaten it. You can't ever give up fighting until you've undragoned it. Just like dogged old Fister the Magister."

"Well, we haven't faced any actual dragons, but I won't stop fighting Vayd and his armies until they're undragoned as well."

"You'll beat them, Kion," Tiryn said, her eyes beaming in the crimson light from the fire. "And you have something far better than a watch and a music box."

"Yes, you have your friends. It will take all of us together to defeat this foe."

"And more besides," Nurien said. *"I believe we shall discover another swordspeaker soon."*

Tiryn and Kion shared a look. Another swordspeaker. What would that mean to their little company and who would it be? So much would be decided in the days ahead. And Kion, for the first time since donning the tabard of a Warding soldier, began to hope that things might actually turn out for the better from this trip to Bramble Eyre. Zinder's story had a great deal to do with it. Odd how stories of others overcoming great challenges give us courage to overcome our own.

It would take a great deal of persistence, but he would do whatever it took to undragon Vayd Mokán.

Chapter 24

DARK WATERS

Their fifth day in Fathomwood brought more dark skies, but the rain stayed away, at least along the path. The clouds lost some of their denseness, closer now to the color of stone than of ash, more dreary than menacing. A mist clung to the forest floor long into the morning, not scattering fully until midday. Muddy patches still harried the wheels of the cart, though the road was less of a quagmire than in the days before. But just when things looked to be drying up, and their struggles against the rain at last to be behind them, a filthy runaway river gashed its way across the path. What once was a stream had burst its banks and pulled heaps of dirt and clutter down into it. Leaves, twigs, branches, and logs sped by, helpless prisoners of the roaring water. Though the channel was only about three cart lengths across, it ran too swift and deep to ford.

"Horn toads! Well, doesn't that just douse our fire," Zinder said, hopping out of the cart before it came to a full stop. His boots sank ankle deep in the mud, but he took no notice and plodded ahead for a closer look.

"Oh, my," Tiryn said, as the cart ground to a halt before the reckless waters. Tapper stopped and for the first time his foot kept still. He had enough sense to know that even the best mule in the world had no business crossing something like that.

"As fast as that's flowing," Kion said, "it will take at least two days before it recedes enough to cross."

"Even more if the rains return," Kithian said.

Kion and Tiryn joined Zinder at the river's edge. It may as

well have been a stone wall. Nothing short of wings would get them over it.

"Nurien," Tiryn said. "Couldn't we make a bridge—the same way we did in Tinesplitter Bay?"

"Forge-hammers, you've hit it, Tiryn!" Zinder said, stamping his foot and splashing mud on the others. "Oh, sorry."

"I am afraid that will not work," Nurien said. *"This water is too impure. Any ice I tried to make from it would be so brittle it would break the moment it was formed. We could use water from the water-skins, but even then the bridge would not be able to withstand such a current."*

Zinder stomped his foot in frustration, and with the same result. "Sorry," he said again.

"We will have to look for another place to cross," Kithian said.

"Fire and ice. The cart won't fit through these woods. The trunks are as tight as my fingers and the underbrush as thick as wool."

"Then we will have to leave the cart behind," Kithian said. The words fell heavily upon the company.

"But we just got the cart," Zinder said. "And it was a gift from Marlund. We can't simply toss it away because of an over-ambitious stream."

"No other path is open to us," Kithian said. *"We must seek for a safer way across or else wait until the current subsides."*

"I don't like the idea of leaving the cart behind. But we don't have time to wait for the current to die down," Kion said.

Tiryn cast a long look back at the cart. "If we have to, we can load what we need most onto Tapper, and carry the rest."

Going off the path would slow them down a great deal, but not as much as staying there for three or four days. It took some coaxing, but Zinder finally came around. Tapper was content to have the greater part of their baggage heaped on top of him and Zinder asked Kion to see if the animal minded the new load.

"I can carry this and more. My back is strong as an oak," Tapper said and his foot started going again.

They had to leave some of the food behind, cutting their supply down to only four days. Since it would only take two more to reach Bramble Eyre—provided they could find a way around the river—that seemed like it would do. The extra waterskins, the bedrolls, and all of Zinder's coin and tools came with them as well. They took several vials of oil for Truesilver, but left behind a few to save weight. Most importantly, they fastened all the glaives to the sturdy mule. Kion's armor and the claymore took some doing, but Zinder's knotting skills were second to none and eventually they got everything in place. Their clothes, some of the food, and the other waterskins they carried in their own packs and Kion tied an extra vial of oil to his belt.

With a last, forlorn glance at Farmer Marlund's cart, Zinder turned and followed his friends into the dark and somber woods. It was an ominous change, as though going from day to night and from summer to fall all at once. Walking beneath the bronzewood canopy, they could see for the first time the plum-like fruit which grew upon the limbs. It was dark and hard-looking.

"Is it any good to eat?" Tiryn said.

"Not if all the world were full of cram," Zinder said. "Bronze-wood fruit is poisonous. It'll make you sick for days if it so much as touches your tongue."

One unexpected turn of fortune awaited them in the forest, though. Within the depths of Fathomwood the thornbristles were far more scarce. And a good thing, too. For if they'd been forced to hack their way forward, they might have lost a day or more battling through the underbrush.

As it was, they trudged south along the edge of the river. The light from the glaives offered a small amount of cheer against the gloom, but even so, Fathomwood grew more eerie by the hour. Nothing stirred, not even the leaves. The rushing din of the waters was ever beside them, but beyond that, it was as if the whole forest was locked away in silence and the key nowhere to be found. The quiet pressed in on them in a way that made every word seem like an act of defiance.

As if all this were not enough, they had not been long in the woods when Nurien shared some troubling news. *"Whatever pursues us draws closer. Now that we no longer walk under the sun, perhaps they grow bolder. I sense they will reveal themselves soon."*

"Then let's leave the woods. Let's go back to the path and wait until the currents subside," Tiryn said.

"And lose more time?" Kion said. "I'd rather take my chances against these mysterious hunters than the threat of starving in this place if we don't reach Bramble Eyre in time."

"I fear you're right, lad. There's nothing for it but to continue on braving the eaves of Fathomwood," Zinder said.

Tiryn stepped on a twig and let out a screech, a lightning bolt of sound which shot like a spear through the silent wood.

"Sorry. But I can't help but think that something awful is about to happen," she said.

"We must continue on as we decided," Kithian said. *"Nothing has changed. If whatever hunts us chooses to reveal itself, we will drive them back with fire and ice."*

Tiryn chewed on one of her braids. She would not feel safe as long as they were still being hunted, but what else could they do but continue on?

Truesilver's light might draw the attention of their pursuers, but Kion was more than willing to face them. They had followed them long enough. Better to confront them and end the mystery than to take each step in shadow and fear.

The little company plowed deeper and deeper into the woods. Long and arduous hours of weaving through the thick growth followed. Doubt gnawed at Kion's mind. It might take days before they found a way around this river and they were getting farther and farther from the path. With no sun to guide them, and no animals to ask for help, they might never find their way out of this unending arboreal maze.

But he kept his doubts to himself. If he had learned anything, it was that it was never wise to question his glaive. Kithian had not failed him yet. And the few times Kion had chosen not to listen to him had only led to sorrow and regret. It wasn't Kithian's fault that the river raged on to the south. Perhaps they should have gone north instead, but they had gone too far to turn back now.

Kion's faith in Kithian was vindicated when, upon the brink of dusk, the river at last joined itself to a lake. The waters ran right up to the roots of the trees. Like the stream, the lake had also swelled beyond its natural boundaries. The river spilled into it in a small waterfall, tumbling furiously over a series of rocky steps. The rushing roar was loudest at that point, but beyond it, the waters at last grew silent. Kion's pack grew less burdensome. The black waters faded to shadow as the sun dipped below the tree line.

"Well, look what we have here," Zinder said. "This is the place to cross or I'm made of linder cheese."

"The water is not pure enough at the head of the river for an ice bridge," Nurien said.

"Farther south it looks clearer," Kithian said. *"Let us journey on a little more."*

Kion's momentary relief faded. They had not conquered the waters just yet. His pack grew heavier again, but he shouldered it without a word and together they set off along the submerged shoreline.

Once Nurien judged the waters to be clear enough, Tiryn pulled out her glaive and crept down to the edge of the dark lake. Removing the crystal pommel, she knelt and placed the dagger's hollow handle into the lake. In the fading twilight, shimmering blue ice with almost a light of its own formed around the partially submerged trunks.

"Dark as it is, you knew the waters were pure before I put you in the lake, didn't you?" Tiryn said.

"Water is my gift, as fire is for Kithian. I can sense its qualities in

the same way you can read the skies and know that a storm is coming.
So I have been made."

The trees grew far too thick for them to find a clearing where they could camp, so they slept that night with their backs against the bronzewood trunks in a triangular arrangement with Tapper in the middle. Kion had no illusion that the night would be a comfortable one. He slept with his pack on as a cushion, but that didn't save his legs from the roots. What he did not expect was to be awoken half a dozen times by Tapper. The mule had never tapped in his sleep before, but on this night he would not stop, even after Kion woke him and had a word with him. Tapper apologized, but went right back to tapping the moment he fell asleep again. Eventually Kion got up and moved a few trees away, but the wood was so quiet, it made little difference.

When the sun finally rose above the mist which covered the lake, the companions awoke to a hasty breakfast and made their way to the water's edge. Kion and Tiryn took the lead, with Zinder guiding Tapper behind.

"I am sorry I kept you awake," Tapper said through his whinnies. *"This crossing the ice has me troubled. What if I fall? I might spill all your things."*

"Well, do you think if we let you swim, you could make it across that way?"

"Of course I could swim it—easily. But not weighed down with the bundles, and who among you is strong enough to carry my load? No, I think that I will just have to try my hooves upon the ice."

But when Tapper's fears were shared with Zinder he came out strongly against the idea. "Shar's dome, the mule's right. One slip and he'd go into the drink and all our things with him. No, it won't do. I'll rig us up a sled with the rope and the bedrolls and you and I can haul the gear over the ice while Tapper swims alongside us."

Kithian and Nurien approved and so they unloaded the baggage and Zinder set about fashioning his makeshift sled. Once it was finished, he and Kion loaded it up. Meanwhile, Tiryn and Nurien brought forth the first span of ice. It ran across the water, a blue slash etched upon the face of the ebony lake. It did not travel far before disappearing into the chalky mists blanketing the surface.

Zinder had formed the sled using hooks and clever netting made from rope and a bevy of knots. Together, he and Kion eased it down onto the ice. Tiryn went out front, extending the bridge whenever they reached the end of a span. Tapper swam alongside, quietly enjoying the water and remarking how perfectly easy it was to travel without anything to weigh him down. He was a mostly sensible animal, but he did have a few vanities.

"This takes me back to Tinesplitter," Zinder said as they crept along, careful to keep their footing and stay away from the edges of the bridge. "Trik and Trak drove me half mad with their foolishness at times, but I do miss them after all."

The words had scarcely left his lips when the ice bridge gave a terrible shudder. The span in front of them shattered. Shards and water sprayed in every direction. A smoke-green shape erupted out of the lake. With a screeching roar, it shot above them, climbing into the air upon enormous wings veined in sickly green webs, like the cracked glaze of a vase. Great legs of scaled muscle hung below a thick, lizard-like body. The glistening limbs ended in gnarled claws longer than Rimewinter's blade. Unnatural eyes, dark and devoid of life, stared at everything and nothing at all.

"*A drakyn!*" Kithian's voice rang in Kion's ears.

"*How did I not see this?*" Nurien said, her voice shaken.

Kion grabbed his sword, but he never drew it from its sheath. With the swiftness of a striking snake the drakyn's tail whipped around, hitting him full in the chest with the force of a charging stallion. The blow sent Kion hurtling into the water, crashing through the surface yards away from the bridge. Truesilver flew from his hands and sank into the deep. One moment the blue sky stretched above him, the next he plunged into the enveloping black. His arms churning, he regained the surface and the world of light and sound returned.

Tiryn let out a wail of terror. Zinder's hopeless cry followed, but the drakyn's wings buffeted the two of them with a blast of air and they fell from sight, whether into the lake or onto the bridge Kion couldn't tell.

He willed his arms to swim back to the ice, but the blow from the tail had left him in a daze. The world shifted and shimmered and his strength faded. The dark waters pulled at him as though great chains had sprung up from below. A spot of gold flashed in his eyes. It was the last thing he saw before he went under. His mind flailed about for some way to stop his descent, but his limbs refused to obey. For the drakyn's tail had done more than bludgeon him. The spikes had opened a vicious tapestry of wounds upon his chest.

"I feel you fading, Kion. It is the drakyn poison," Kithian's voice cried out as a light in the darkness, a darkness swiftly smothering Kion's mind. *"Call me to yourself while I am still close!"*

But the poison ran through Kion's veins swift as kindling fire and all strength left his arms and hands. Even if he called for Truesilver, he could not hold on to it.

He plummeted through the depths, his body swallowed in a chasm of night. His mind shouted into the darkness in wordless horror. He was not ready to die. Who would stop Vayd if he did? And who would take care of Tiryn? Despair quickened the poison as it sped to his heart and the darkness deepened. The cold chill of death which he had tasted in Whitewind visited him once again, but it was stronger this time, more undeniable. Was this what his father had felt on the battlefield outside of Roving? Or his mother as the rocks of the Tinesplitter mines came crashing down upon her? To feel the specter of death loom over you and know that you are powerless against it is to know at last the terrible hardness of the world. If only he'd had more time. Just a little more time…

This would be a hard burden for Zinder and Tiryn to bear.

The pressure mounted in his ears as he sank. It gripped his head like a vice. His lungs were two dead weights pulling him under and they grew more and more unbearable by the moment. His limbs went still. He was a prisoner inside his own flesh. His body had become his tomb. He faded, adrift in a great void, alone.

"Please, I want to live," was the last thought he had. Then the world of light and air faded and Kion Bray drowned in a great sea of unknowing.

"This is a hard, a cruel path to tread," came Kithian's voice to Tiryn up from the depths, more heavy and empty than she had ever known it before. *"It shakes me to the very metal. Oh, wicked turn that brought you to so swift an end, Kion, my dear glaivebond! Too brief was our time together. And now, farewell. May we meet again when the world is reforged."*

And if swords could have shed tears, Kithian's would have joined the bitter waters of that dark lake.

Chapter 25

ADRIFT

It happened. The vision came true. Only it wasn't the young soldier from Dunach who had drowned, it was Kion. And he had not risen up out of the water on the back of a dragon, it had been the thing to send him under.

"Kion, no…" Her strained whisper vanished into the mists. He was gone. And with him, her life came tumbling down around her. No father, no mother, and no brother. She was alone now in all the world. A leaf borne away by a cruel and desolate wind.

Tiryn would have sunk into the waters with him, or at the very least into the depths of despair, had Nurien's voice not called her back to the cold harsh unforgiving present.

"The drakyn is coming around for another pass. Tiryn, we have to bring it down!" The stark words left no room for any emotion other than raw fear.

She turned to face the drakyn as it wheeled above the waters, an oil green marring of the sky. "Tell me what to do," she said, as if in the midst of a dream. Oh, if only this were just another vision and she would open her eyes at any moment and come out of it.

"Aim for the wings with my darts."

Tiryn gripped the dagger and raised it skyward. There was no time for sorrow, no time to think. She moved without purpose or feeling.

"Glaivefrost."

A hail of bright blue knives of ice shot from the crystal wings of Rimewinter's hilt. They went in pairs, each set leaving half a breath after the one before. The first two dozen missed wildly. The creature was too high and Tiryn's aim too poor.

Zinder, his face pale as ice, managed to scrounge his coalwood crossbow from the baggage and now worked to load it. He was a dead-eye shot, but a single bolt would not take down a creature of that size.

The drakyn dove, its tail winding back for another strike.

Tiryn half thought of letting the creature take her, of not fighting at all. What did she even have to live for? Yet the cool grip of her glaive cleared her mind and quickened her to the danger. The drakyn whirled, coming in for another strike. She adjusted her aim. A flurry of darts shredded its left wing. The creature spasmed and shrieked, the movements throwing off its trajectory. The tail smashed into their gear instead, sending it into the lake. Zinder got off a cracking good shot on the creature's underbelly as it barreled past, but it wasn't needed. The creature's wing was in tatters and it could no longer remain aloft. It foundered on the surface of the lake, struggling to rise and then, with a skin-tingling cry, plunged into the water.

"Tiryn, the gear!"

Her eyes flicked to the sinking bundle, still held together by Zinder's knots, but already only the barest shadow above the water. Tapper swam near it, his eyes still rolled back with the fear of the drakyn.

"I can't save the baggage," Tapper said. *"And one of the masters is lost. Oh, dear, oh, dear, I'm not a very good mule, after all, am I?"*

Tiryn had no time to wonder at how easily she comprehended his words. Nor did she have time to console him.

"Glaivefrost."

She aimed for the gear and this time larger missiles, icy balls of Tinesplitter blue, sprang from the hilt and covered the sinking baggage in an icy cocoon. Within moments, it bobbed to the surface, the claymore and double sword poking out, but all else shrouded in a cloud of ice.

"We have to save Kion," Tiryn said. How long had he been under? There still had to be time.

"He is not within my glaivesight," Nurien said. The coldness of her voice gave way to deep sorrow. Now that the drakyn was gone, she allowed the horror of the loss to sink in.

Zinder went down, pounding his fist on the ice. "Kion, Kion, Kion!" he shouted. But his voice rang out empty and stricken above the trees. "Oh, lad, why? Why? Why did you go? Why did you leave your poor old Zinder? I promised to protect you and… and I couldn't…I'm sorry, Dorn…"

The words barely reached Tiryn's ears. She kept scanning the waters. Where had he fallen in? It had been on the south side of the bridge, but where? Everything had happened too fast to remember. Why couldn't she remember? How could this be happening? Kion was a swordspeaker, the Sword of the North, a hero. Heroes were not supposed to die. Not like this.

She dove off the bridge, and swam, calling out, "Kion! Kion! Where are you?"

She knew it was hopeless. Zinder knew it too, but he dove in after her.

"No, Zinder, what are you doing? You can't swim!" Was he so overwhelmed by sorrow that he meant to throw his life away? Could she blame him if he was?

Zinder flailed, taking in great gulps of water. "I…failed him…failed to…save…"

She could not lose Zinder too. Tiryn rushed back to him, catching hold of his collar just before he went under. The gray traveling hat he'd worn—his favorite—sank beside him, but Tiryn feared losing him if she reached for it so she let it disappear beneath the water. Zinder did not even notice.

"We must return to the bridge. There is nothing more we can do. Kithian has gone to sleep. That can only mean one thing." Tiryn steeled herself against the next words, but Nurien had to say them. Like a healer snapping a bone back into place, she had to tell the sharp, hard, sudden truth. *"Kion is no more."*

The sorrow of their trek across the ice was too deep to tell. No words did Zinder or Tiryn share between them. Tapper made not one whinny or snort as he pushed the frozen bundle of gear before him through the water. Neither did Nurien speak. There is a silence in forsaken woods and a deeper silence still upon a lake in such woods, but no silence could surpass the one born from the grief that Tiryn and the others bore that day.

When they reached the shore, they pushed the frozen gear onto the mud and settled themselves among the exposed roots of the trees. Tiryn held her tears during the march across the lake, but on land they came, a torrent of sadness and disbelief, hot and wailing and without hope. Zinder's tears were quieter. He simply rocked back and forth, staring out at the ice bridge, the last place he had seen his friend alive. The mists had cleared, but Tiryn wished they hadn't. To be able to see the place where her brother died was the last thing she wanted. And yet, like Zinder, she could not pull her eyes from it.

Tapper huddled beside the frozen bundle, his head hung low. In time, he took to licking the frozen ball in an attempt to melt it sooner. It was his way of making himself useful, of showing sympathy for his masters.

Why did he have to be taken from her so suddenly and without warning? Why did he have to go to where she could not follow? Who would tease her now when she slipped on the wet grass? Who would pull her blanket over her in the middled of the night when he thought she was fast asleep? Who would give her that look of brotherly pride when she showed him one of her sketches? A thousand memories of their shared life together flashed through her mind and vanished the next moment, no more than mist upon the waters. How, how, how was she to go on without him?

The sun was well up in the sky by the time her crying ceased —how harsh the light seemed, and how cruel. Zinder, who only ever seemed to sleep about every other day, and then not for long, had passed out from the sheer weight of anguish. It was too great a burden for his nynnian heart to bear.

"The vision," Tiryn said. Her throat cracked and the words sent a stab of pain through her chest, but she, who of all was most content with silence, for once could endure the silence no longer. "It was all there in the vision. If only I could have seen things more clearly, I might have saved him." She grabbed hold of the driftwood necklace, thinking of the children of Whitewind who had lost so much, yet she found no comfort in its touch as she so often did.

"Yet, you at least had some presentiment of it. Where was my Vision? Why did I not see it? I should have seen the water drake coming. I should have warned you. Oh, Tiryn, I have failed you. Failed Kion. Failed Kithian. I thought when you rescued me from Tinesplitter that the Mastersmith had given me a second chance. Now I am not so sure. Everything is webbed in doubt and darkness. Our quest to save the Four Wards has come to an end before it ever truly began. For without Kion and Truesilver, we have no hope of defeating Malix and Vayd's armies. I could not even save one swordspeaker, much less the world entire." The light in Rimewinter's crystals and from its blade had gone dark. Apart from its marvelous craftsmanship, the blade could have been mistaken for no more than an ordinary metal dagger.

At these words something shifted within Tiryn. Some hidden reserve of strength welled up inside her, stronger than grief, more powerful than pain. For that moment she saw past her sorrow, past her failure to discern the meaning of her vision. In that moment, she saw Nurien not as a glaive nor as some great weapon passed down to her from of old, but she saw her as a friend. No, more than a friend—the bond between them had made Nurien in some ways a part of her very self. And she could not bear to see that part of her lost to sorrow. As great as the pain of Kion's loss was, the fear of losing that part of her which Nurien had claimed was just as horrifying. And so, out of love for Nurien she spoke.

"Nurien, you are not to blame for Kion's death," she said. "As much as I would like to blame myself, it is not even my fault. You told me that our gifts are given to us for a reason. If my Sight failed and your Sight failed it is not because we wanted it to happen. It is because you and I are broken vessels. We do not see as clearly as we ought. Isn't that what you told me? But as poorly as we see the future, we are not blind. I did see something. I just didn't know what it meant. And your vision saved us from the bandits on the road to Tiller. It seems to me that if the Sight is a gift we can't demand that it always be given in the exact time and way that we want. Please, don't blame yourself for Kion's death or for Kithian's loss. It was not your fault. I know that you would have done anything to save him if you could. And I would do anything to have him back now. But there is nothing we can do."

Faint motes of light reappeared in Rimewinter's crystalline pommel. *You may be only a girl, but you speak with a wisdom beyond your years. All that you say is true. This path has been laid before us and we must follow it as best we can. Still, I am sorry for your loss, and for mine.*

A fresh surge of grief swirled inside Tiryn. How strange and fickle emotions were. One moment she was consoling her friend, the next, reeling and devastated and in need of that same consolation. She would have cried again, but she had no more tears to shed.

"I don't know what I'll do without him. My worst fear has come to pass. I was so afraid of losing him in the war and I lost him before he ever fought in his first battle."

You are not alone. I will be with you always. And we have Zinder with us as well. I daresay he loved Kion like a son.

Tiryn gazed upon their dear friend. His clothes were in disarray and his eyes were still pink around the edges from his tears. No hat graced his cotton-white head. His coalwood bow lay discarded at his feet. No one had been more faithful to her brother. He was the closest thing to family either of them had left. Her own family was gone now. But Nurien was right. She was not alone. She had Nurien and Zinder and even Tapper. They could never replace her brother in her heart, but they were dear to her in other ways. She had to cling to them now like the wreckage of a ship, dragged about upon the churning, battering waves in a sea of grief. A wave might come soon and pull her under for good, but for now, she held on.

But only just.

Chapter 26

WHEN THE STRAINS RUN DRY

Zinder did not wake until mid-afternoon. But when he did, he ate two or three days' worth of dried meat. Though they still had a good amount left, the oat cakes were ruined from the fall in the lake. While he slept, Tiryn had shattered the ice around their gear and set things out to dry, but the cakes could not be saved. That meant they only had enough food for two or three days unless they rationed it out. Zinder had already eaten whatever extra would have come from Kion's share. Tiryn could hardly blame him, but they would have to be more careful with their provisions going forward.

"I'm sorry, Tiryn," Zinder said. "I forgot myself. It won't happen again."

"You have nothing to apologize for," she said. The return of Zinder's appetite was an encouraging sign. It meant that he had not lost all hope.

Wordlessly, they packed the gear back onto Tapper and departed, not sure where they meant to go, but only knowing that they had to flee the cruel cursed lake that had claimed the one they loved. They wandered on in a vaguely southern direction. Their feet barely lifted from the ground. They moved simply to be moving. When night came they ground to a halt, their feet heavy with sorrow and weary of the burden of life. Tiryn could not take another step. Neither could Zinder. Even Tapper looked spent. What strength had kept her going she could not say. In truth, she marveled that she was able to walk at all.

Away from the water, they had no difficulty finding enough dry wood for a fire, but now that Truesilver was gone, they had to make it the old-fashioned way. Zinder labored for some time until he got the flame to take, but even when it did, the warmth it brought lacked any cheer. Indeed, Tiryn barely felt the warmth at all, so cold and numb had she become.

"We have wandered long enough without purpose," Nurien said that night as Tiryn and Zinder sat staring into the fire. *"We should make for Bramble Eyre in the morning."*

"I honestly do not care where we go," Zinder said. "Kion is lost. Our quest to save the Wards died with him. But I will follow wherever you go, Tiryn. That is all I can do, but not much else, I'm afraid."

"Though you are not soldiers yourselves, you can at least bring the message Kion was tasked to give," Nurien said.

"Nurien is right," Zinder said. "We've come all this way, we might as well finish the task. And we'll be able to restock our provisions there."

Tapper's foot started tapping again. His hooves had been silent until then. Animals do not feel grief the same way that humans do, but in some way he shared in the emotions of his masters.

"I agree," Tiryn said. "But what do we do after that? Rimewinter and I are not enough to win the war."

"We must find another swordspeaker. We may find one at Bramble Eyre. If not there, then perhaps in Madrigal. Wherever there are people, the glaives might awaken. But out here in the woods, there is no one to hear their call."

"Madrigal will be safe," Zinder said. "Like Bramble Eyre, it is the only place that has never fallen to the haukmar forces. You would like it there, Tiryn. It's a fine place for someone who loves beauty and growing things."

When she was younger, Tiryn had always wanted to see the chief city of Inris, the great jewel of the north, the City of Gardens. It was said that there were more flowers in Madrigal than there were people in the whole of the North. But flowers seemed flighty things in the wake of Kion's death. Could their colors ever brighten her spirit as they once did? Could her eyes still see beauty when so dimmed by sorrow? And Madrigal was so far away. It might be that the haukmarn would conquer it before she ever beheld its marvels.

"I don't know, Zinder. My heart is turned to dust. It's a wonder I can still breathe. I miss him so much."

"Yes, lass. I miss him too. So much that I can't bear to think of it. The sorrow is too great for me to endure." Zinder sniffled and took in a rattling breath. A vague and distant grayness wandered into his eyes. "May I ask you a favor, Tiryn? You don't need to grant it. I'll understand if you say no. But it would help an old nyn's wounded heart if you could…Would you…would you sing a song to lift my spirits? Just one?"

A song. Such a small thing. That was all Zinder had asked. Back in Furrow, she must have sung to him a thousand times. Even during their search for her mother she had sung songs when the road was long and uncertain. It had helped to keep them going. And yet, the songs had been all for naught. The songs gave them strength, but to what end? So that Kion could watch Mother die? At least he had been able to see her one last time. Tiryn had not been granted even that. More than anything, that is what had killed the music in her heart, not being able to see her mother before she died. All that suffering to reach her and Tiryn had not even been able to look upon her face. The music had failed her. Her songs had been sung in hope and that hope had proved vain. And now here was Zinder asking her to revive that false hope. A hope which had betrayed her.

It ought to have been a simple thing, a way to comfort him in his grief. But he may as well have asked for her to make the sun to shine in the night. It was not something she could do, no matter how much comfort it would bring, she simply had no voice to lift in song.

"I'm sorry, Zinder. I can't sing. Not now. Not ever. The music died with my mother. And now, with Kion gone…"

"I see," Zinder said, and turned, crestfallen, to stare into the night. A horrible fear struck Tiryn's heart as she looked at his face. For it was as if Zinder had been taken away and someone else put in his place. All light and life withered from that once bright countenance. The skin turned ashen in the firelight. Was that how her own face looked? It was surely how she felt. Her mother's death had taken her music, how could her brother's bring it back? And yet Zinder had not asked her to sing for Kion or Mother, but for him. He who had given them so much had asked for something so small, and Tiryn, holding tightly to her own sorrow, had refused. But it wasn't just the refusal of the song, it was the refusal of hope. For a song is only a vessel for something larger—love or dreams or wonder or hope. And hope was something both of them desperately needed in that moment. To deny it would be as cruel as denying food or water or air. She could see the want of it in his eyes. Zinder needed hope. He needed it to go on. Without it his body might live on, but as an empty shell, devoid of life. He would dwindle and fade and the old Zinder, the friend she so dearly loved, would decay into a hollow mockery of the clever, skillful, brave person she knew. No, to refuse to sing in that moment was not simply to choose silence and grief over friendship and hope, it was to doom Zinder to a hollow, empty fate, and herself along with him.

For the second time since Kion's death, a serendipitous strength welled up inside her. It was not born of any quality within herself, but out of love for her friend. In the same way that Tiryn could not bear to watch Nurien suffer, blaming herself for failing to see the peril of the drakyn, Tiryn could not let Zinder slip into darkness and despair. She could not abandon him in that way. And so, with a voice that almost seemed to come from someone and somewhere else, she said, "Wait, Zinder. Perhaps…perhaps I will sing after all. For you. For both of us."

And from out of the depths of her own shattered hopes she
drew forth this song.

Far off the strains they sound
The soaring notes abound
And all who hear them sigh
Uplifted by the sound

Those voices raised in song
They carry us along
In currents none can see
A river steeped in song

The music carries far
Until a rising bar
Stops up the rippling stream
From traveling so far

And then the strains run dry
Though none can fathom why
The silence stings like death
And all our throats go dry

We wander parched and lost
And bitter is the cost
When we can sing no more
The melody is lost

Yet though we wander long
Lamenting all that's wrong
The rains shall come again
And music before long

Shall rise anew like spring
And through the valleys ring
Oh, wondrous blessed song
A new hope shall us bring

The strains will ne'er run dry
Our song shall fill the sky
With music born anew
The strains will ne'er run dry

As the last notes went silent and the forest settled once more into stillness, two wonderful things occurred.

Zinder's face showed the barest glimmer of a smile. But like a candle flame in the deep of night, it was all the brighter for the darkness around it.

And in that smile came the second gift. For the smile did not merely die upon his lips, but somehow, beyond all hope or expectation, that smile—feeble, faint, barely visible though it was—found its way onto Tiryn's face as well. And Tiryn looked up at a window in her mind, as if far off in the distance, and saw not one but two candles flickering there, one for each of them. And in that vision and through that song, she knew that they would pass through this grief in the end. However long it might take, it would pass.

For the music had been born anew. And with it music's handmaiden. Hope.

Chapter 27

THE NIGHT COMES ALIVE

Sleep had not taken Tiryn for long when Nurien's voice flared in her ears.

"Awake, Tiryn, and ready yourself. The shadows move against us."

Tiryn was a light sleeper, but even she surprised herself by how quickly she sprang to her feet, dagger in hand.

Zinder lay curled in a dark bundle against a tree. Tapper was already awake, his foot tapping like mad. He sensed the peril, too. A moment later came the same wild panic that had seized her on the streets of Rippling. Something moved in the shadows. And the pall of death hung close upon the air.

"Zinder, wake up," Tiryn said in a loud whisper, but not nearly loud enough. They were the last words she said before the night came alive around her.

What she had taken for shadows peeled away from the trees like shed bark, coalescing into dark-robed little men. They were stocky and broad-shouldered, and so covered in ragged cloth that only their bony hands and hooked noses were exposed to the night air. Their skin was ashen, the same color as the hauk-marn, and yet they were only a little taller than Zinder. Clutching long pointed daggers, more like spikes than actual blades, they swept in to attack with graceless, jerking movements, but wild and swift as the wind, as if moving from a fearful compulsion rather than any design of their own.

Tiryn spun about, unsure of what to do. Dozens of the dark men rushed in on every side. A numbing deadness preceded them so that she felt their presence even before they reached her.

"You must fight, Tiryn! Use the glaivefrost!"

Tiryn thrust her blade toward the figure closest to Zinder. Her arm trembled. Words caught in her throat. The dark-robed men rushed on. Nearby, Tapper shrieked and bolted into the night.

"Glaivebond, now!" Nurien's voice was hard as stone, yet even that could not wholly shake Tiryn free from her paralyzing fear.

Not until one of the shadow men raised a dagger to skewer Zinder in his sleep did Tiryn's voice come rushing back.

"Glaivefrost!"

Rimewinter flashed and two darts pierced the attacker in the side. Either the man weighed almost nothing or Nurien's darts had been infused with extra fury, for he flew away from Zinder, impaled upon a tree. His nose and hands shriveled like a burnt husk and his thick limbs and torso collapsed as though made of air. All that was left a moment later were two icy spikes pinning a set of dark tattered robes to the trunk of a bronzewood tree.

None of the other attackers so much as paused to note his death. Two more descended upon Zinder, but now he was awake and, swift as his attackers came, they could not match the elusive nyn. At once seeing the danger, he tumbled away so that their long weapons buried themselves in the roots of the tree where he'd been sleeping.

"Tiryn, behind you!" Nurien's warning came just in time.

Tiryn whirled to meet another pair of attackers who meant to run her through. She flailed with Rimewinter and somehow managed to deflect one of the attacks, but the other dagger sliced through her shirt.

She cried out in shock, but by some special mercy it tore only the fabric and failed to touch her skin. Her wonder at the narrow miss was swiftly replaced by surprise at what had happened to the dagger she'd deflected. The moment it clashed with Rimewinter, the blade was enveloped in ice. The attacker dropped the weapon to avoid having his hand overtaken as well. The sight stirred within her an unexpected courage. She may have been outmatched and overwhelmed, but she had a glaive. And she meant to use it.

"Glaivefrost!"

Fresh spikes of ice leapt toward her attackers. Four of them pierced the dark man who had stabbed her. Like the first one she hit, the man flew backwards as though struck by an invisible gust. He staggered into others coming behind him, knocking several down before he too vanished, leaving behind only his cruel dagger and dark robes. More ice darts came, some missing their mark, but the men were so thick that many of them fell, despite Tiryn's wild aim. All who were struck withered and were no more.

But still, some got through. The shadow of death grew deep around her. They rushed at her with dark knives flailing. Her life would surely have ended then and there but for Nurien.

"No, you shall not have her!" she cried.

The strangest thing happened then. A coolness shot down Tiryn's arm from her weapon, racing over her shoulder and chest and from there submerging the rest of her body in a thick blue block of ice. The protective shell turned aside all the daggers save one, but even that one was slowed and caught in the ice so that only the barest tip pierced her skin. When the blade would penetrate no further, the attacker withdrew it and began hacking through the ice, along with the rest of the dark assassins. Their efforts failed to break through, but they bowled her over and continued hacking at the ice on the ground.

Tiryn wanted to ask what Nurien had done, but, wrapped in ice, she could no longer speak. She had been trapped like this once before, but in the ice of a snowwinder, not Rimewinter's. She panicked. She could not breathe. It was only a matter of time before she suffocated. The icy shield would kill her even if the shadow men could not. But Nurien had no choice. If she had not fashioned the protective shell, Tiryn would already be dead.

The daggers chopped mercilessly into the ice, chipping away so that Tiryn felt the shuddering impact even through the thick coating. In places, it soon grew thin. The dark men swung like mad, venting their soundless wrath against the dwindling barrier.

"Hold out a little longer, Tiryn. Help is on the way." Nurien's voice had never been more kind, or felt more close. And yet was that not the same tone Mother had used when she took Tiryn from Furrow while dying on a bed of fever? There had been no assurance that Tiryn would recover from that, however much her mother might have wished to convey it, and there was no assurance now. Her deepest regret was that she could not tell Nurien how much she meant to her, and to apologize for failing her, for not being worthy of such a wondrous blade.

But through the cocoon of her protective barrier, in a strange faraway echo came Zinder's voice, shrill and furious.

"Leave that girl alone!" It came from somewhere above, but Tiryn could not see where. Yet just hearing his voice gave her a burst of hope that helped her cling to life a little longer. Her chest heaved, close to bursting, full of fire and heavy as stone. She could not bear the weight much longer.

Thumping sounds rained down around her, deep and resonant, like someone banging on a hollow log. Amidst the thumping, several of the turbulent shadows around her fell away.

"Take that, slinkers!" Zinder shouted. "That'll teach you to go after an innocent girl."

"He's beating them off of you, Tiryn," Nurien said, her voice shot through with relief. *"He's throwing the bronzewood fruit and it's hitting them with the force of stone."*

More thumps came. The frequency of dagger slashes against the ice barrier dwindled, but the dark men remaining attacked with even greater ferocity. They concentrated their blows against her neck and head. The ice flew away. At last, a small chunk dropped to the ground, freeing one of her eyes and, more importantly, the right side of her nose. She sucked in the precious treasure of air which came to her, crisp and clean and life-giving. But the blow that had saved her life was soon followed by one that would end it.

She stared into the lightless cowl, broken only by the crooked nose, her death looming within that emptiness. The cowl was a pit and the pit would swallow her. Only a well-placed shot from Zinder knocked the dagger off and the blow grazed the ice covering her head.

Yet four others rushed to strike at the opening and Zinder could not stop them all. Another dagger flashed above her for the kill.

But before the weapon could plunge into her eye, a golden beam of light pierced the shrouded head, revealing an emaciated face, the skin barely covering the skull. The eyes were dull lumps, black as coal and just as lifeless. If any emotion could be read there it was blind surrender. Not even the absence of hope dwelt within those sightless orbs. It was pure indifference, as mechanical and inanimate as the figures of Dalia's clock—no, even more, for at least those figures danced with some semblance of life. Here there was only silence and pitiless, pointless existence.

She saw all this in a burst of gold. The next moment, the wretched man was forced to use his arm to shield his face and reeled backwards as though struck. Everywhere around Tiryn the others did the same. Light swelled throughout the clearing, a miniature dawn amidst the grave-dark forest.

Zinder leapt beside Tiryn as the dark men fled, scattering as swiftly as they had come. He stood over her, his face transfixed in the light.

"What in the Four Wards..." he said.

"*It cannot be...*" Nurien said. The wonder in her voice rang strong and deep. The ice shell around Tiryn cracked and she shook herself loose, drawing a great shuddering breath as she turned to face the golden light.

She would never forget that sight as long as she lived.

Riding through the woods it came, a golden galloping beast. At first Tiryn took it for a horse, but its gait was closer to that of a deer. Only when it had drawn closer and her dazzled eyes could at last make sense of what they saw, did the creature's true form become clear. The great rack of horns, bold as lightning and shimmering like dew, gave it away. It was an elk, the most graceful and peerless animal Tiryn had ever laid eyes upon. And yet, it was not an animal at all, at least not in the usual sense of that word. For it was larger than any elk should ever have been and its skin glistened as though fashioned of hardened gold. The creature gleamed as if traveling under its own inner light, as though loping beneath some private noonday sun.

But the elk did not travel alone. The elk bore a rider.

In a moment the magnificent creature, singular and achingly beautiful as it was, faded like the setting sun beyond the hills. For upon its back rode a man, and not just any man. At first his identity remained hidden, swallowed up by the resplendent light of the golden elk. But at length the eyes, those priceless, precious eyes that Tiryn loved so well, pierced the golden beams and met her own. Tiryn stood frozen, her whole body quivering with a whirlpool of sensations: bewilderment and doubt, disbelief at the tale her eyes told her, weakness and humility at how small she was and how undeserving, fear that it might all be some dream or another false vision, but in the end and conquering all, was joy. Joy beyond the world's end. Joy beyond counting.

And at the words of Nurien all doubt and disbelief fled, as insubstantial as the swiftly vanishing shadows around her.

"Kion and Kithian have returned."

Chapter 28

CORNOC'S TALE

Kion slid down off the great flank of the golden elk. Sparks of light fluttered from the creature's fur, leaving a trail of shimmering motes behind him as he rushed into Tiryn's and Zinder's arms. Not since the death of his mother had he been so grateful to be alive. How faint and ephemeral were all his sorrows and misgivings from before. He had been renewed and restored to his sister and his friend and had once again escaped death by some special grace. To live was a dear and precious thing and none knew it more than Kion in that hour.

"But, I don't understand," Tiryn said, her face awash with tears. "You drowned. We saw you."

Zinder's face was a similar mess of drenched emotion. "This is the second time now, lad, that you've come back from the dead. If this becomes a habit, you'll send me to an early grave in your place. My heart won't take it."

Tapper ventured sheepishly into the clearing, drawn by the golden light. His long, naturally sad-looking face was transformed by the elk's radiance so that it looked in some ways, and for the first time, almost human. A knowing beyond all words shone in his eyes. Though he made not a sound, it was clear from his countenance that he felt himself as a lowly servant standing in the presence of his lord.

"Don't worry, old friend. I don't plan on almost dying ever again," Kion said, breathing deep, taking in each moment for the gift that it was, never to be repeated again. Every little gesture in

Tiryn's and Zinder's faces leapt out at him as though seeing it for the first time. The way Tiryn covered her quivering mouth, how she tilted her head to the side when she was deeply moved by something as she was now, the way Zinder obsessively smoothed his mustache and beard, and bounced on his toes, overcome with gladness, it was all so new and familiar at the same time and marvelous to see. "I'm sorry I gave you such a scare. But we have Cornoc to thank for this. I would not be here now apart from him."

He laid a hand upon the golden elk's matchless fur. The light streaming from the creature had dimmed subtly, for he no longer needed to show forth his power now that their enemies had fled.

"This golden elk is what saved you? But how?" Tiryn said, dropping her hand from her face, her lips no longer quivering, as wonder at the sight of the great beast overtook her.

"That is a tale best told by Cornoc himself," Kithian said. The elk regarded the glaive, strapped upon Kion's back, with a ponderous respect. Until that moment the beast had quietly taken in the reunion with an enigmatic smile, as though not quite sure what to make of these two-legged beings. But a profound intelligence and wisdom gleamed within his eyes and it was clear to all who looked upon him that this was no mere beast.

"Yes, Cornoc, we are grateful for your help and anxious to hear your tale," Nurien said, her voice soft and reverent, as though anything louder might banish the sacredness of the moment. But there was more to it than even that. For Nurien addressed Cornoc in a way that showed the two of them were equals in age and understanding and station. Cornoc lowered his head quietly, showing that the respect was mutual.

"With gladness shall I tell it," Cornoc said, speaking in that eternal language which needs no translation and which all understood, including Zinder and Tapper. Though it was clear that the words came from the elk, its mouth did not move. Cornoc's voice was deep as the groaning of the woods and rich

as the summer sun beating down unfettered upon the mountain heights. Peace settled upon all who heard that voice, all their cares and worries forgotten. Zinder ceased smoothing his beard. Tapper ceased tapping. And Tiryn ceased crying. To hear that voice was to hear the voice of nature itself and to become aware of one's own connection to it, so often severed by our small, hurried, and disordered thoughts and distractions.

Zinder's face glowed with its own unveiled wonder. And though he was too overawed by the voice and the beast's presence to say anything out loud, he mouthed the words, "I can hear it!" to Tiryn and Kion.

"Yes, yes you can, dear nyn," Cornoc said and his smile deepened. "For I am a solif. One of the bryt ones from beyond the frames of this world. I have come to you at Volun the Mastersmith's bidding, at the behest of the one who sustains this world and all that is in it by the unceasing work of his hammer, the hammer of his will.

"We solif have many duties in our service to Volun. Of late, I have been given the task of watching over this wanderer called in your tongue by the name of Kion Bray. I have watched him from afar for many days now, though often I have been called away upon other tasks and my vigilance has suffered. But when he is most in danger, I am drawn to him, and so it was that I came to him in the winter storm and shielded him from the cold in the northern reaches of the land and cast him into an enchanted sleep. And again, I came upon him at the lake when the grundrak attacked. And as before, I protected him even as he fell into the depths and kept the poison from reaching his heart.

"To do so, I had to cast him once again into an enchanted sleep. And so deep and profound was the sleep this time that it was indistinguishable from death, even to a glaive. Thus Kithian went silent, for a glaive's life is tied to that of its glaivebond and it cannot endure beyond his passing.

"Still, the sleep would have been in vain had not the grundrak unwittingly aided us. For the creature, taking Kion for dead, and sorely wounded itself, dragged him into its lair, a hidden cave within the depths of the lake, there to feast upon his flesh. Yet its wounds were so *grievous that it gave no thought at first to satiating its hunger and instead curled up beside its prey and drifted off into the dark abyss of dim-touched slumber. But all of this, as yet, I did not know. I knew only that Kion lay sleeping beneath the waters, the flame of his life still flickering, however dimly.*

"I could not search the lake, for solif are beings of light and our bodies cannot pass farther beneath the waters than light itself may go. And yet, Volun does not send his servants to ends without purpose. I searched the land and sought among its creatures for a way to reach him. Long it took me to find that way, but find it I did. Through a twisted tunnel with many false turns and paths I found at last a hidden way into the grundrak's cave. It was too small for the grundrak and yet it brought air and the smallest sliver of light from the world above into the creature's hidden lair.

"With stealth I entered the cave and laid upon the monster an even deeper slumber from which it might not awake for many days. Then putting forth my power in another form, I broke an opening in the rock and carried Kion away.

"After the return through the underground path, I laid him down and set to work by my arts to draw the poison from his wounds and heal his broken body. Long I labored to draw it forth, for it had penetrated deep. When at length he had been cleansed of the vile taint, I removed the enchantment from him and he opened his eyes."

Tiryn wiped away fresh tears, reminded once more how close Kion had come to death.

"We spoke briefly in the wood of my purpose in coming to him, and I shared with him some of the tale of his rescue. But Kion was anxious to recover Kithian and so, permitting him to ride upon my back, we returned to the lake with all speed. Ere we had lighted upon the shore, Kithian awoke and called out to him. And you may imagine something of the joy of that reunion as it is like unto that which you know in this hour."

Nurien's voice broke into his tale, saying, *"Indeed we do."*

"But though Kion could hear Kithian's voice and sense him, True-silver lay yet at the bottom of the lake, too deep to swim and too far for

Kion to call him to his hand. So Kion dove, striving to reach as far as he could before calling out to his glaive to fly into his hand. And though he failed twice, he persisted and on the third attempt pushed himself deep enough for the blade to reach his hand at last.

"With Truesilver recovered, Kion's thoughts turned to his companions and we soon picked up your trail. Not long had we followed it before I sensed that we were not alone in our pursuit. Before us went something dark and malevolent, a presence I had not known until that hour. They went forth as a mockery of light, arising, as I perceived, by some misuse of the Spark. These shaydvorn, as I call them, are like unto the dim-touched, though rather than twisted mockeries of animals, they are the tortured imitations of men. They have the form of men and yet they bear the marks of Shadowriven's handiwork, which mars all that is good and beautiful and which can create nothing of its own power, but only warps that which is."

They stood in silence at the end of Cornoc's tale, pondering its full meaning, for it offered as many mysteries as it answered. Even Kion and Kithian, who had heard much of it before, mused quietly upon the many things which Cornoc had revealed.

Zinder, not surprisingly, was the one to break the silence. "You are one of the golden ones, then." He bowed low and gracefully, sweeping his hat from his head. "It is an honor beyond reckoning to stand in your presence. And yet, the honor is all the more profound for you have saved Kion and brought him back to us, along with his glaive. In so doing, you have given us a gift without price."

Tiryn followed with a deep bow of her own. "Truly, we are in your debt, Cornoc. You have not only saved my brother, but in doing so, you have knit together the pieces of my shattered heart and made it whole again." Tiryn had always longed to see one of the fabled golden beasts and yet now that she had, her eyes were ever drawn to Kion and the presence of the solif was a small thing in her sight compared to the wonder at seeing her brother alive once more.

"I echo the praise of my companions for your actions, Cornoc,"

Nurien said. *"The ways of the solif and the paths they tread are usually beyond even my Sight to perceive, and known only to One, which makes your appearance here all the more surprising. It is not in my nature to welcome surprises, yet your presence among us is a most welcome thing."*

Cornoc nodded, a slow and measured gesture which, like all the solif's mannerisms, seemed to be born of long reflection.

"And yet if you know anything of our ways, the solif never alight in one place for long. For we are movement and light, and as such never tarry in one place. Indeed, now that my tale is finished, it is time that I must go."

Kion feared this might be so, for during all his time with Cornoc he had the sense almost of riding an arrow to its target. All had flown by so swiftly that he hardly remembered anything since the drakyn struck him from the bridge of ice. And now that Cornoc's purpose had ended, it was no more natural for him to stay than to catch a beam of light in a jar.

"Will I ever see you again?" Kion said.

"That is not for me to know. Only you may be assured of this, that even if you do not see me, I will always see you, no matter how far I may wander."

Cornoc's burnished skin glowed brightly and Kion perceived that this was a solif's manner of saying good-bye. Then, with one last wordless nod, the great elk dissolved into a spray of soundless light, its body dissipating into ten thousand glittering motes. The golden twinklings shot upwards through the trees and disappeared, like a swarm of fireflies scattering into the night.

"The solif are sparks, and it is in the nature of a spark to wander," Kithian said.

"You mean, as in sparklight? Like the streaks we see in the night sky? Is that what he meant about always watching over me?" Kion said, a bit at a loss. An ache welled up within him at the solif's departure.

"Yes, that is precisely what he meant. The sparks fly from the

*hammer of the Mastersmith and land where he wills, though few are
they who ever get to meet one such as you have."*

"I did not deserve such a gift, but I promise that Cornoc's
deeds will not be in vain," Kion said. "Even beyond what he did
to save me, being in the presence of a creature like that, it seems
as though all the world is brighter than it ever was before,
brighter than I imagined it could ever be."

He looked once more on the faces of Tiryn and Zinder and
saw written there the same wonder that coursed through his
entire frame. A golden glow lingered upon their faces, and Kion
felt it touching his own face as well.

For a moment, the veil had lifted and he had seen into the
realm of the unseen, into that world which is more real than the
one of flesh and bone, of struggle and futility, of loss and death.
He had seen with a vision that goes beyond the eyes, had known
with understanding that goes beyond the mind, had felt with a
feeling that goes deeper than the heart. He had glimpsed the
great eternal Beyond upon which the visible world is founded
and built and for a brief moment all that was fragmented and
fractured had been made whole.

And though the light now faded, having seen it once he
would never be the same.

Chapter 29

BRAMBLE EYRE

The eaves of Fathomwood turned kinder and less ominous as they made their way east in search of the road to Bramble Eyre. Though Cornoc's golden light had faded from the wood and from their faces, the ever present silence was less menacing than before. Kion's rescue by Cornoc and the wondrous awe of his presence yet lingered with him. The war seemed less perilous and his sorrows and burdens lighter than they had before. And the world was far wider and grander knowing that the solif had a place in it.

Most people had heard of the "golden ones," the secretive animals who wandered the hidden places of the world, but they were no more than legends. Kion had seen glimpses of them twice before, but had not known until now what he had seen. For it was one thing to catch a glimpse of something thought to be only a fable and quite another to be in the presence of an immortal creature made of liquid light. Yet, even having seen one and ridden upon its back, he still did not quite know what to make of the solif. Were they flesh and bone or spirit or something in between? Ordinary bodies are fixed, solid things, but Cornoc's seemed always to be in motion, as if it was always becoming that shape moment to moment and might become something else at any time.

"So, Cornoc appeared as a squirrel in Whitewind, but this time as an elk. Does that mean the solif can take the form of any animal they choose?" Tiryn said as they trekked along beneath Fathomwood's shadowed boughs.

"Have you ever seen light strike through a prism or the way it scatters upon the surface of the waters?" Kithian said. "It is the same with the solif. Just as the essence of a glaive is the metal it is made from, so the essence of the solif is light and that makes them the most changeable of all the Mastersmith's creations."

"I was wondering about that, too," Zinder said. "What form do you think Cornoc took to carry you out of the drakyn's cave? A bear or a large badger perhaps? He would have had a hard time dragging you through the underground whatever form he took, but I can't for the life of me settle on which one it could have been."

"I hadn't thought about that," Kion said. "I suppose you can ask him if you ever see him again."

"Ha! The chances of that are slim to skeleton. Those golden ones like to keep to themselves."

"That is true," Nurien said. "It is rare enough that they reveal themselves at all, rarer still that they would deign to speak to mortals. The fact that Cornoc consented to allow you to ride upon his back is an honor beyond reckoning."

Tapper's braying came in stark contrast to Nurien's measured tones. "I wish I could have spoken to the golden lord, but I was not worthy. My strength failed in the presence of those dark men who came from the shadows. My heart filled with fear. My legs never felt so weak. I don't deserve to even call myself a mule after the way I cowered and hid."

"I do not believe the fiercest lion would have acquitted himself any better.," Kithian said. "You are a creature of flesh and more attuned to the natural order. This is both a strength and a weakness. For when that order is corrupted, you feel it even more greatly. We are all fitted to a different purpose. And you have served your purpose well thus far, Tam-del-wir."

Tapper lowered his head in humble acknowledgment of Kithian's praise. "You're not angry with me for failing?"

"A faithful friend comes back when he fails and admits his weak-

ness. That is what you have done and in so doing proved yourself a friend twice over."

Kion patted him on the neck. "There were too many for one mule to handle. We do not fault you one bit for what you did. We're simply glad you returned."

Tapper lifted his head and gave his mane a pleasant shake. Most animals were like that, quick to forget and move on. In that respect they often proved wiser than humans.

They had by then come down into a little valley in the wood with a feeble stream. They stopped briefly so that Tapper could drink and they could refill their waterskins.

"Nurien, you said that we were being followed ever since Dunach," Kion said, dipping his skin into the cool dark water. "Was it by these shaydvorn who attacked you? Were they the ones who have hunted us all this time?"

"Yes, the shaydvorn, the 'new shadows,' as Cornoc called them, were the ones that hunted us. But I had never seen or known of them until this day."

"The haukmarn were new to us as well. Much has changed since the time of the Shattering," Kithian said.

"And you think, as Cornoc does, that they are connected in some way to Shadowriven?" Tiryn said.

"Only Malix would have the knowledge and the bent will to twist the Spark and cause such things to be," Kithian said.

"Yet there could be other corrupt glaives we do not know about, could there not? Could the shaydvorn be the work of some other glaive?" Kion said. Even Nurien had gone against the Mastersmith's will for a time.

"It is possible," Nurien said, musing over her answer for some time. *"But doubtful. Malix surpassed all others in his mastery of the Spark."*

"Do you think the shaydvorn will return?" Tiryn said. It was the very question Kion was about to ask himself.

"They fled at Cornoc's coming," Nurien said. *"My sense is that*

the only reason they risked an attack was because Tiryn was alone. They did not dare face both swordspeakers at once. Now that we are together, I doubt they will come again unless they come in far greater numbers."

"Cravens, the lot of them," Zinder said. "Won't try to take us in a fair fight. But might it not also be that Cornoc's light snuffed them out and there are no more of these vorns left to shadow us? I could not find a single track or trace of them after they fled."

"The way they came out of the shadows and the lightness of their steps makes me wonder whether they leave tracks at all," Nurien said. *"They seem to be made half from flesh, half from shadow."*

"And wholly evil," Kithian said.

Truesilver's warmth pulsed down Kion's back. They had avoided defeat by the shaydvorn. But he did not doubt that another attack would come. And when it did, both swordspeaker and glaive were eager to test themselves against this new threat and see whether or not these new enemies could endure the heat of Truesilver's fire.

The party stumbled out from under the cloak of the woods and onto the open road early on the afternoon of the first day of the month of Arcsand, the day after Cornoc had rescued them. Venturing out into the full light of day made the encounter with the shaydvorn and Cornoc seem all the more dream-like. And now, there they stood, blinking in the midday sun.

They had walked little more than an hour down the road, enjoying their return to the world of wind and light and sound, when they first laid eyes upon Bramble Eyre. The great stone refuge occupied the whole of a small island in the middle of Lake Stillmere, a tear-shaped cavity filled with steel-sheened waters possessing a fresh, sharp smell. Only a handful of fishing boats on the far side of the island broke the serene surface.

From afar, the castle looked worn, yet defiant, the kernel of a thing whose outward husk had decayed long ago. Moss worked its way across the yellowed stone in mottled patterns. Dark vines clawed their way up the walls. The blackened crenelations curved and came to a point like the horns of great beasts, embedded atop the battlements like trophies from long forgotten conquests. The silt-tinged walls rose and fell with the cliffs which traced three sides of the island.

Slender banners, milky white with a single golden diamond set in the field, swayed sleepily atop seven square towers, each of differing heights, each enmeshed in vines to a greater or lesser extent. They watched over the lake from high above, yet upon the corners of each of these towers four rounded turrets rose higher still, their conical roofs decked with dark shingles.

Slate-roofed buildings nestled up against the walls, but the main keep dominated the interior of the castle, dwarfing the keeps at Dunach and Roving. It sat atop a sweeping stone road, the culmination of all the castle's many defensive works. Three of its corner towers rose several stories above the main keep, but a fourth tower rose higher still, and thicker than all the others combined. The same horned crenelations ran along the tops of the keep, stained black like half-burnt logs pulled from the fire. Despite a few missing shingles on the towers, some crumbling stonework, and several boarded-up windows, the fortress left an impression of undaunted strength. However hard they beat against it, the twin powers of time and the elements had not been able to pull it down.

On the western shore, dark iron gates opened onto a narrow bridge of stone less ancient than the castle itself. A wide field opened up along the shore before the gatehouse. Like the bridge it protected, the gatehouse was not nearly as ancient and beaten down as the island castle itself. The gate was wrought from thick strands of metal, twisted and formed to appear as though made from thorn-covered vines. Half a dozen soldiers manned the gates. They wore straw-colored tabards over battered chain mail coats. The tabards had an empty circle traced in black with triangular spikes in each of the cardinal directions.

Kion had made sure to don his emerald tabard at the first sight of the castle. Though now that he had seen the sort of heraldry the soldiers wore, he doubted his decision. It looked as though Namril used mercenaries to man the gate. Kion had hardly been given a decent welcome among the fane's own men. It was doubtful hired swords would treat him any better.

When they came to a stop at the front gate, he saluted the soldiers and pinned back his shoulders. It was time at last to deliver his message.

"Greetings from the west," Kion said. He clutched Truesilver's hilt to steady his nerves. He had moved the sword from his back to his side. This was less ideal for travel, but it was the manner used by soldiers. "I am Glinthelm Kion Bray. I bear a message from Windle for Lord Namril Grundstaff."

The oldest of the soldiers, a man with a tangled beard and dark eyes, looked askance at his fellows, as though Kion's presence came as some surprise, though they had been watching his approach for half a mile.

"You're a messenger? Where's your horse?" the man said, resting his hands on his belt, sizing Kion up.

Zinder shifted his own belt, not liking the frostiness of the man's tone, but Kion answered as evenly as he could.

"They could not spare one in Windle. They were expecting an attack any day."

"I doubt your message is that urgent, then, if a horse couldn't be spared. I am Tormain Gilliff. You can give your message to me and I'll pass it on to Lord Namril when I see him."

"And when will that be?" Zinder stepped up, giving the soldier a stabbing glare.

Kion tried to call Zinder off with a look, but he only had eyes for Gilliff. Oh, dear. This wasn't starting off well.

"That's no business of yours, short stack," Gilliff said.

"Pardon me, did you just call me—"

Kion placed a hand on Zinder's shoulder to keep him from

shooting off like a firework. Zinder had no patience when it came to remarks about his height.

"It's fine, Zinder. I'll handle this."

Zinder scowled, but held his frustrations in check for Kion's sake.

"Perhaps if you simply ask for shelter, the soldier will grant you lodging and we can look to deliver the message later. Though this fellow may be disinclined toward you, the code among soldiers should at least afford you that," Kithian said.

Two other soldiers moved up alongside Gilliff, giving Zinder cold looks. Was it any wonder the haukmarn found the land so ripe for conquest when there was so much mistrust among those tasked with defending it?

"Forgive us, it has been a long journey and we have suffered much," Kion said. "We are weary and low on provisions. I will need to stay the night at least before journeying on. Please direct me to the barracks or other suitable quarters and I will see about my message afterward. I mean no disrespect, but I was told to deliver my message directly to Lord Namril himself."

Tormain Gilliff's expression softened at this, but it soon became apparent that the sympathy he put forth was feigned. "Of course we would be happy to offer you shelter within the fortress. Unfortunately, you are not the only one who has fallen on hard times." His eyes strayed to the large citrine in Truesilver's hilt as it flashed in the sun. "The war has brought scarcity to all of Inris. Things have been made all the more harsh by the terrible winter. Though the war has yet to come to us directly, we depend upon other towns and cities for our supplies and those shipments have all but stopped. Our stores are near to failing. As a fellow soldier, of course we can offer you what limited resources we have, however I am afraid that we cannot extend that offer to your friends."

A simmering growl rumbled in Zinder's throat. Kion did not bother to restrain him this time. It was all Kion could do to restrain himself.

"And you call yourselves soldiers?" Zinder said, his voice several notes higher than usual. "Why, you're no better than those thimbleriggers who jumped us on the road to Tiller."

Gilliff shrugged off the remark. "There's the parade field over there. You're welcome to stay and forage for thornbristle berries if your rations run out."

Tiryn cast a nervous glance at the field and her brow furrowed. Yes, they could survive in the field for a few days, but harvesting from the thornbristles would be treacherous work. Some of the thorns were the length of a dagger blade. And Kion was not about to leave his sister and friend to fend for themselves while he enjoyed the safety of the castle.

"Mind how you respond, Kion. Ill use by another does not warrant a response in kind." Kithian's words were enough to keep Kion from joining Zinder's outrage.

But Zinder happened to catch a glimpse of Tiryn's anxious face and, as if he had heard Kithian's words himself, his manner changed. After a quick breath he smiled at Gilliff.

"Ah, well, yes. I see how it is. Your stores are low. Perhaps we can help to offset your hardship. Would you be more amenable to allowing us to enter the fortress together if we offered you a gold round? It is the least we can do to assist in the war effort."

Gilliff pretended to deliberate within himself for several moments. "Hmm, well, that is most generous of you. While it will not alleviate all our present troubles, it may be of help once trade resumes."

"We all must make sacrifices for the war," Zinder said. He had bartered with folk up and down Inris for more than ten years. He could be quite shrewd when the situation called for it, though Kion was surprised at just how generous he was this time around.

"Let us hope it ends quickly," Gilliff said.

"If we all work together, I'm sure it will," Zinder said, vague enough in his jab that the soldier could not take offense, and yet the sour look on Gilliff's face told him that Zinder's slight had not been lost on him.

"Gallants." Gilliff motioned toward two of his men, addressing them by their titles as the lowest ranking members of a mercenary company. "See the messenger and his cohorts across the bridge."

From within the gatehouse a mechanism was released. Turning, grinding, clinking sounds rumbled through the iron gates as they groaned slowly outward of their own accord. From their chorus of protest it sounded as if they had not been opened for an age.

"A nynnian gate wouldn't make such a racket," Zinder said in a low voice.

"What matters is that they hold when the enemy comes," Kion said.

Zinder gave a begrudging grunt of assent.

"I'm just happy they're letting us in," Tiryn said, quietest of all. "I'm sure Lord Namril will treat you more kindly, Kion."

He did not openly contradict Tiryn's well-meaning words, but it certainly seemed that ever since he had returned to Inris he had been treated more like an enemy than a friend. They would find out soon enough whether Tiryn's hopes about Lord Namril proved true or not.

Chapter 30

A SERVANT'S EARS

Walking through the twin gates of the castle, Kion's company set foot within a worn down courtyard. Though the sky was not the least bit cloudy, the sunlight's cheer was lost upon the faded, tired looking stone. It must have been a remarkable sight in its day, but its chief quality now, like that of a ruin, was to give the suggestion of what once might have been. From the pavement to the mortar blocks, the crumbling signs of the passage of time showed that the castle had fallen far from its former glory. For decay will come, but it can only have sway where the hand of man lacks the will or the ability to oppose it. The dire winter Gilliff had spoken of may have taken the lives of the workers needed to make the repairs, or it might be that Lord Namril lacked the resources. They had heard rumor that both the fane and the margrave had suffered a strain upon their coffers and perhaps the lord of Bramble Eyre's fortunes had taken a similar turn.

The two soldiers escorting them across the bridge had little to say. Though Kion made an attempt at conversation, he was promptly informed that they were not allowed to discuss anything with outsiders.

There was the word Kion had been searching for: outsider. He may have been wearing a tabard of the Warding army, but he was still an outsider to these people. If they knew he'd once been a shepherd, he wouldn't be surprised if they turned him around and sent him right back out through the gate. No profession was lower in the eyes of most Inrisians.

"Tormain Gilliff ordered that they be taken to the guest house," one of the gallants told the men stationed at a small booth just inside the second of two wide gates at the end of the bridge. "This one has a message to deliver to Lord Namril."

A cloud of doubt passed over the faces of the soldiers stationed there, but they said nothing. The men who had escorted them across the bridge slipped away without further word. After recording the names of the travelers in a ledger, one of the new soldiers asked Kion and the others to follow him across the courtyard. From the gate, a wide path swept up and away to the north, winding its way up toward the great preponderance of stone which rested on the pinnacle of the island: the main keep of Bramble Eyre.

The keep shadowed them wherever they went, but they did not take the road which led toward it. Instead, they marched into the lower courtyard. Large buildings, some of them quite grand, presented themselves on three sides. The purpose of many was obvious, such as the stables, smithy, and tannery, but with others it was not so clear.

A large garden, budding with vegetables and spices, ran along the northern side of the courtyard. Several servants labored there under the fullness of the sun, weeding and watering an assortment of crops. One of them waved as the group passed and the soldier escorting them returned the greeting.

The soldier addressed them as he walked. "I am Gallant Rymir. And I apologize if the reception you've received up to this point has been less than welcoming. We don't get many visitors to the Eyre and things have been a bit tense of late. But the porters have the keys to most of the buildings. One of them will take you to the guesthouse and there you will find food and rest."

He led them to a two-story building which rested against the southern wall. It was smaller than most, but in better condition. The door, like those of the other buildings, sloped to a point at the top. It stood open, and its six windows as well, offsetting the heat of the day. Inside, the cool stone floor and gentle shade offered a welcome change from the sun-baked courtyard.

A young man a little older than Kion sat with his head cradled in his arms, asleep behind a small desk. A large spot of drool stained his sleeve. His oily black hair went down to his shoulders and his face bristled with unshaven whiskers. Red blotches covered the backs of his hands. The skin was raw and red and painful-looking. The strangest thing about him, though, was that he wore a dark scarf wrapped tightly around his neck. It was thin and fraying but even so it could not have been pleasant in the full throes of summer.

On the wall behind him hung empty bags and packs of various sizes. Off to the right, an open doorway looked into a room filled with empty wooden crates. The gallant escorting them rapped his knuckles loudly on the desk, startling the sleeper awake. The man's eyes darted about the room, as if expecting someone to assail him. After a brief moment, he shook off whatever fears or worries had followed him from his dreams and acknowledged the gallant with a curt nod.

"Sorry, must've dozed off for a moment," the young man said in a lethargic manner. He choked out a rumbling cough and this cleared his throat. "What do you want?"

"Hello, Grish. Are you the only porter on duty?" Rymir said.

Grish rubbed the backs of his hands.

"Yes, what of it?" He had a challenge in his stare, the kind given by people who get riled at the slightest provocation. His long sloping nose and pinpoint eyes exaggerated every minor discontentment.

"Where are the others?" Rymir's expression remained calm in the face of Grish's petulance.

"In the quarry. The foreman's moving a whole heap of stones today. What's the matter? You need a great big lot of porters for something?" Grish scratched behind his ear and rolled his neck, his slow movements reminiscent of a bear newly roused from hibernation, surly, and looking to lash out at anyone who disturbed him further.

"No. I was just wondering."

"Well what is it, then? You don't think I can handle it?" Grish's neck muscles tensed. He was now fully awake and twice as resentful as before. He scrubbed the backs of his hands with even more vigor.

Rymir chose to take his time before responding. He waited until Grish unclenched his jaw and took a few breaths. When he deemed that Grish's mood had sufficiently cooled, he said, "These folk bring a message for the marshal. They need to be taken to the guesthouse to wait there until he can see them."

Curious that he said "the marshal" and not Lord Namril. This was the first they had heard of that.

"The marshal won't be able to see them today," Grish said, his anger shifting to haughtiness. He was one of those people whose happiness rose and fell in relation to his perceived superiority to others in the room.

"How would you know that?"

Grish picked up on what he took as another slight. "I know many things that you don't, Rymir. The marshal has taken me into his confidence of late."

Rymir looked back at Kion and the others, offering an unspoken apology in his expression. In all this exchange, Grish had barely given them a passing glance. His only intention was to either provoke Rymir to anger—which did not seem likely, for the soldier was uncommonly even-mannered—or to exasperate him enough so that he left Grish to return to his nap. If either of these two was his aim, or even if it was something else, Kion could hardly understand how Grish hoped to get away with it. A simple servant could not show such disrespect toward a soldier without punishment. Perhaps because Rymir was only a gallant, Grish felt like he could treat him as an equal. Even so, it was a shock to hear him speak so freely.

"So, has the marshal left the castle, then?" Rymir said.

Rymir's question only served to stir Grish up all the more. "If you need to know, why don't you ask your tormain? It's not my business to report on Marshal Faedred's comings and goings."

"Very well. I'll take my leave, then." He turned toward Kion's party. "Grish will take care of you and see that your animal is properly stabled. I wish you well during your stay at Bramble Eyre. Good day." He saluted Kion and left.

A salute. At least Kion had finally met one soldier who showed him some deference.

Grish rolled his eyes at Rymir when he left, as if the soldier had been the insufferable one during their exchange and not the other way around. He opened one of the drawers of the desk, scratching his hands compulsively all the while, and rifled through it, making a tinkling chaos of *clinks* and *clanks* before producing a set of keys.

"Let's be off, then," he said, not bothering to close the drawer or give his charges more than a passing glance.

The guesthouse sat at the back of the courtyard, along the eastern wall. They passed by the barracks and other living quarters on the way. Grish shuffled before them, in no hurry, continuing to itch the back of his hands as he went. The house they arrived at was the smallest of all the buildings they had seen, rising only two stories high with two windows on either side of the door and five windows running along the top floor. The windows had quite a bit of relief work around them and ornamental pillars lined either corner of the building. Neighboring the guesthouse to the south was another two-story building of a simpler design, though it did have window boxes with flowers and black shutters, most of which were flung open.

Grish fiddled with the keys to the front door, only finding the correct one after the third try and much cursing, half of which was directed at Rymir and the other half at the "blasted visitors."

Zinder puffed his cheeks at the man's behavior, a dozen clever quips swirling on his lips, but he chose not to waste them upon someone so ill-tempered. They were guests in another's home and it would have been poor manners to grow upset because of the quality of the servants.

Grish did help them unload their things, and deposited them into the small entryway. He made a sour face when he saw the glaives.

"Are you some sort of peddlers? If so, these rotted things won't fetch much," he said.

"No, we're not peddlers." Kion fumbled for the right explanation and Zinder came to his rescue.

"Heirlooms. They're heirlooms. We're hoping to restore them to their proper state at some point." That was in its own way true enough.

Grish scowled at Zinder's explanation.

"There appear to be several rooms here," Kion said. "Is there one in particular we're meant to occupy?"

"Stay in whatever rooms you like. No one else is here," Grish said, rattling off the words as if each one were an inconvenience. "One of the chamber maids will bring you supper. Their house is just next door. If you need anything, you can bother them. I'll take your mule to the stables," he said, and made to go.

"Thank you," Kion said, giving way as Grish pushed past.

"Take care of him," Zinder said. "That's one fine beast."

Grish grunted and turned away, leading Tapper at an even slower pace than before.

"We shall look in on you when we can, dear friend," Kithian said.

Tapper brayed softly. *"This fellow has a strange smell about him, but I will be fine on my own. You need not worry. Mules can bear other burdens besides baggage."*

"The lord of the castle must be a lenient man if he allows one such as that among his servants," Zinder said.

"He reminds me of some of the farm boys back in Furrow," Kion said.

"He might have just been having a hard day," Tiryn said. "He was clearly exhausted."

"Staying up all night is hardly a sign of good character," Zinder said.

"Well, however gruff the welcome, I'm glad we get to stay in a place like this," Tiryn said, strolling down the hallway as though she'd just arrived at a summer fair. The hallway was half the width of their entire cottage in Furrow. A cushioned rug ran down its length. The main hallway led off to the left and right from the entryway to one of eight bedrooms on the lower floor. To the right the hallway ended in a spiral staircase. The entryway continued on a short distance before ending in two thick mahogany doors. "Why, it's practically the size of an inn. Can you believe we have it all to ourselves?"

Zinder doffed his hat and flung it expertly onto the coat rack just inside the front door. He took a long pull of cool air which had a slight zest to it. "It's nice to know that the war hasn't ruined everything," he said.

"It is a well-appointed place," Kithian said.

When Kion passed on Kithian's remark, Zinder said, "As if it mattered where that sword of yours slept. It's just as much at home sitting on a smith's shelf as on a bed of silk." Zinder opened one of the doors down the left hallway. "But for us fleshly sorts, this will do just nicely," he said with even more than his usual enthusiasm. "Oh my, it even has a wardrobe. Hand-crafted by a nyn, judging by the quality." He continued on, waxing about the comfort of the bed, "it's genuine Verisian cotton!" and praising the tile work on the floor, "it looks ancient, but still in marvelous condition—that's what quality gets you."

Kion chose the room next to his and Tiryn took the one across from him. They soon found out that all of the rooms were more or less the same, only that the bedding and wall hangings were of different designs. Kion ended up in a blue room, while Tiryn occupied one that was cherry red. Nurien remarked that they had gotten the colors backward, but only in jest. Zinder ended up in something he said was "blanched sepia" but which Kion would have simply have called "tan."

"We don't deserve to stay in such fine quarters," Tiryn said after they'd stowed their baggage and met again outside their rooms. "I keep thinking there must be some mistake."

"For what I paid that crooked gateman, these accommodations seem just about right," Zinder said, starting down the hall and disappearing around the corner.

"Zinder, where are you off to?" Kion called after him.

"Looking for the kitchen, what else?" A moment later came the pounding of two small fists against firm, resonate wood. "Shar's dome! This must be it, but it's locked!"

Kion and Tiryn turned into the entry hall to find Zinder standing with his hands on his hips, dwarfed before two great double doors. "I can see a loaf of bread through the crack just sitting on the table—and there's the smell of yurgenbrak cheese somewhere inside, too—it's practically calling out my name."

"Another one of your many admirers?" Kion said.

"I confess that I'm sorely tempted to pick the lock." Zinder pressed his eye up against the crack, his shoulders slumped in unrequited hunger.

"I don't think that would be a good idea. I'm sure it's locked for a reason."

"And Grish said a maid would be bringing supper. That's only a few hours away," Tiryn said.

"Hours? Hours? Look at these cheeks. I'm pale as the Wimwissle Swath. I've been living off jerky and stale water for days. I might not survive a few more hours." Zinder pulled the skin of his cheeks down to make it look like he was suffering from terrible deprivation.

"I'm sorry, Zinder. As your friend, I cannot stand by and let hunger drive you to crime," Kion said. A look of mischief passed between them, such as had passed a thousand times before.

"Ah, I see how it is," Zinder said, eyes alight and nose wiggling. "You'd rather watch me waste away than break a rule that may not even exist. I'm sure that we were meant to have access to the kitchen. We are guests after all. Breaking in would merely be correcting an oversight."

"An oversight? Hmm, well, I guess you're used to being overlooked, aren't you?" Kion said and then ran laughing back down the hall as Zinder chased after him.

"Come back here you big lug! Overlooked am I? All the easier for me to pounce on you from the shadows!"

Tiryn trailed after as they raced toward their bedrooms. Kion ran into his and would have slammed the door behind him but Zinder was right on his heels and the two of them crashed into the bed. Zinder was no match for Kion in a real fight, but in an innocent scrabble with close quarters wrestling like this Kion stood no chance against the agile nyn. Kion soon found himself face down on the floor with Zinder pounding on his back, yelling, "Overlooked! Overlooked! How overlooked am I now?"

Tiryn stood in the doorway wagging her head, but with a deep smile.

"You two," she said.

But Kion and Zinder paid her no mind and carried on for some time before wearing themselves ragged. Once the rough-housing and laughter had finally run its course, Zinder lay on Kion's bed with Kion sitting off in the corner and Tiryn leaning against the wall near the door.

Zinder, still huffing from the horseplay said, "Well, if I'm going to waste away, at least I will do so in comfort and finery."

Kion would have chuckled at Zinder's remark, but he was so winded all that came out was a soundless wheeze. Tiryn's face shone with a merry look. Oh, it was good to be together again, whatever happened with Lord Namril on the morrow.

A persistent shaking finally roused Kion from his early evening slumber. All of them had retired to their rooms after the mischief with Zinder and the kitchen door. Tiryn was the lightest sleeper and had been the first to stir when the front door opened.

"The maids have brought supper," she said. "They've opened the kitchen and Zinder has already gone down. He said he couldn't wait and sends his apologies."

"Pity the man who comes between a nyn and his food," Kion said, rolling back his blanket and setting his feet on the floor. "You go on ahead. I need to get my boots on."

"It's all right. I'll wait." Tiryn teased the end of one of her braids out of nervous habit.

Kion readied himself and accompanied Tiryn down the hall.

"Enjoy your meal," Kithian said, his voice coming to Kion's ears, though the sword remained in his room.

"And see what the maids can tell you of Namril and the state of Bramble Eyre's defenses," Nurien said from Tiryn's room. *"A servant's ears hear more than just their master's orders."*

Kion found the double doors wide open this time and a swirl of savory and salty scents greeted him from within. A long table had been set with many candles and three plates, each served with a modest, yet steamy and well-prepared quantity of food: a stout potato, a thick slice of dark bread, a smattering of tender mushrooms, a single boiled carrot, and a small hunk of yurgen-brak cheese, which, while an unappetizing pond-scum green, nevertheless radiated a husky and oddly enticing smell. The pleasant warmth of the room wrapped itself around them as Kion and Tiryn took their places at the end of the table next to Zinder.

Two chambermaids attended them, one plump and with her gray hair in a bun, the other young and quite slender, her hair tucked inside an off-white bonnet.

"Ah, there they are," the older maid said. "We're sorry about the kitchen being locked. Master Zinder was just telling us. Master Kion, Mistress Tiryn, I am Mariday and this is Livia, at your service." The two maids gave little curtsies. Tiryn's face tensed. She didn't like the thought of someone waiting on her. It made her too much the center of attention. But it looked like she would have to get used to it.

"Pleased to meet you. And it was no trouble being locked out," Kion said.

Hungry as he was, he did not wish to eat until the maids departed. Zinder was under no such compunction. He'd already finished his carrot, the mushrooms, and half of his potato.

He did at least have enough manners to swallow his latest bite before saying, "Speak for yourself, lad."

"But Grish knows that he's supposed to open the kitchen for anyone who stays here. Lands of mercy, how that boy fell so far from his father's tree is a wonder and a misery." The maid's voice was throaty and yet had a sing-song quality to it.

Remembering Nurien's advice, Kion said, "I'm sure he was simply distracted from too much work. There must be a lot to do with everyone preparing for the war."

"Too much work?" Mariday said, raising a matronly brow. "Perhaps that's the case for most of us, but not that slackhand. He's always looking for the easy way out in whatever he does. If Lord Namril weren't such a pudding-hearted fellow, he'd have cast him out long ago."

"I hope to meet your lord sometime tomorrow," Kion said. "Though all I've been promised is a visit with the marshal. Faedred, I believe, is his name."

Both of the maids' faces darkened at this.

"Ah, well, I'm afraid you won't be meeting Lord Namril on the morrow, or any time soon for that matter," Mariday said. "He left many days ago to seek the fane's aid. It takes some forty days to reach Gilding and back, and that's with no mishaps along the way. It may be some time before he returns."

Silence fell upon the room. Zinder even stopped chewing. The news stifled all the winsome effects of the savory scents upon their mood. If Namril was gone, what did that mean for Kion's future? He was to deliver the message and then put himself under the lord of Bramble Eyre's authority. More than his own future, what did the lord's absence mean for the war? Could Bramble Eyre defend itself without his leadership? These questions and a dozen more thundered through his mind.

"In the middle of a war? Could he not have sent one of his own house or a messenger instead?"

"Oh, he's been sending his men to the fane asking for aid since before the war began. Many of his soldiers died over the winter. But a fat lot of good his begging has done, you see. He's not gotten a loaf of bread for his troubles. In the end, he thought the only way that had any chance was if he went and asked personally. It's a shame seeing him driven to such ends. Forced to grovel on his hands and knees before that no-good fane we've got in Gilding. And the lord not in good health either." Her head dropped in a way that showed she had not earned her gray hairs for nothing. Yet the care in her eyes when she spoke of Namril told Kion all he needed to know about the quality of the lord's character.

"I hope he can make the journey safely, but from what you say, it appears my message for Lord Namril was in vain. For there was rumor that some of the fane's men might be coming to the castle. I see now that it was no more than that, a rumor. Nevertheless, I will deliver my message to the marshal tomorrow and see what comes of it. Is the marshal well thought of among the residents of the castle? For I have been ordered to pledge myself to the Lord of Bramble Eyre and since Namril is gone, I suppose I will be under Faedred's leadership instead."

Though Livia's expression had remained calm and attentive throughout the conversation, at the mention of the marshal's name, a faint knot formed on her brow. If she had not been so quiet and still, Kion would have missed it.

But Mariday's response made him wonder if Livia's mind had not wandered to something else and her expression was simply a coincidence.

"Oh, the marshal is fine enough as far as men of his sort go. He's a handsome shiner, I can tell you that much. And his men certainly seem devoted to him. But since his authority does not extend to the servants, I can't say if you'll find his leadership to your liking. There's one blum thing about him, though."

"And what's that?"

"He's nigh on thirty years old and has yet to take a wife. He's had more than his fair share of chances, yet there he is, alone and unmarried." From the way Mariday's head shook, one might have thought Faedred was suffering from some terrible sickness.

"Thirty and still unmarried. Well, I'm sure he has his reasons," Kion said, shooting a sideways glance at Zinder.

Zinder's fortunes in love, or lack thereof, were one of his least favorite subjects. He grumbled and waved his fork threateningly, but said nothing. He had resumed eating and was too committed to finishing off his potato to offer a retort.

"All I know is that if he knew what was good for him he'd find a nice wife and settle down."

"I suppose I'll find out for myself what Marshal Faedred is like tomorrow," Kion said.

"I hope he'll have time to see you. He's been out of the castle all day looking for a cure for our dear Grundy."

"Grundy? Is that one of his men?" It would certainly speak well of Faedred if it was.

"Oh no, why dear Grundy is our Lord Namril's son. He took ill two days ago and Lady Valissia—that's Namril's wife and Grundy's mother of course—well, she and the rest of the servants positively adore Master Joromar, or Grundy, as we call him. He's about your age, Master Kion, and as strong as an ox, or was until he took ill."

Tiryn perked up at this, finally working up the courage to join the conversation.

"Do they know what's wrong with Master Joromar?" she said.

"Spademaster Tellman is our chief healer here at the Eyre and he thinks it's the sprull. It does come often to the castle. It took

Grish's father, and Faedred's too, but it doesn't usually come in the summer or affect those as young as Grundy."

"Perhaps I could see him. I would be more than willing to help if I could."

"Tiryn's quite the healer," Zinder said. "She fixed my mangled leg up in half the time it should have taken."

Mariday's face lit up and her eyes grew moist. "Oh, that would be so kind of you. I'll have to get Lady Valissia's permission, of course, but I'm sure that if there's any chance of saving her dear son she'll agree to it."

"Yes, I'm sure she'll welcome the help." Livia nodded in quiet thanks. "We should leave them to their food, Mariday. We don't want it getting cold."

"Oh, lands of mercy, you're right. Foolish me, prattling on like this. I'm ever so sorry. It's been a pleasure to meet all of you, I'm sure. We'll bring you your breakfast first thing in the morning and promise not to keep you so long next time with my chatter."

"We very much look forward to seeing you again, ladies." Zinder hopped up and saw them to the door, returning before Kion had taken his third bite or Tiryn her second.

"Well, it certainly seems like Nurien was right," Tiryn said.

"Oh, what did she say this time?" Zinder said, spreading the soft yurgenbrak over the warm slice of bread with his knife.

"She said to be sure to find out what the chambermaids knew. 'A servant's ears hear more than just their master's orders,' was how she put it," Tiryn said.

"That's true as forgelight, that is," Zinder said. "A servant's ears indeed."

Chapter 31

THE MARSHAL'S PLANS

Once again it was Tiryn who woke Kion from sleep. After all that had happened since Windle, he had finally reached his destination and for the first time awoke refreshed and well rested. Tiryn was already dressed and Zinder could be heard humming and fidgeting about in the room next door, fussing over which hat to wear.

Kion quickly dressed, slipping on his tabard in preparation for his meeting with the marshal. It still did not feel quite right on his shoulders, and he could not imagine how any soldier could fight in it the way it rubbed against the legs. But there was nothing to be done but to put it out of his mind as best he could. He doubted Faedred would judge him by how well he wore his uniform. Then again, after his encounter with Forglen, he wasn't sure what to expect.

"Do not trouble yourself over what happens with the marshal," Kithian said, sensing Kion's unspoken doubts. The bond between them grew stronger each day so that such things no longer came as a surprise. Kithian could sense the smallest changes in his mood, even when Kion was silent. *"However great or low a man may be, his worth comes not from his title, but from the quality of his character. True nobility is tested in the heart."*

Words Kion had read in Strom's journal came to mind, how he often felt unworthy to bear the mantle of the bladewarden and longed simply to be just another soldier fighting for the fane. Being a swordspeaker did not bring the same burdens as a bladewarden, but the struggle to accept both callings was the same.

"Thank you, Kithian. I will try to remember that."

This time, Kion and Tiryn brought their glaives with them to the kitchen. Tiryn kept Rimewinter inside her vest while Kion leaned Truesilver against the wall. They found breakfast already set upon the table. The boiled eggs were barely warm, but the bread and cheese tasted just as delicious as the night before. Zinder, who had chosen a round, frog-green hat with a mustard feather for the occasion, had already finished his meal by the time they arrived, but stayed to discuss their morning plans and also to lament the state of the castle's defenses.

"The walls have as many holes as linder cheese," Zinder said. "It's doubtful the war will come here anytime soon, but the Eyre is in no shape to fend off any serious attack. And the armor the soldiers are wearing—did you see it? They may as well knit themselves sweaters for all the protection it provides. Two good swings from a sword and it would shatter like dry noodles."

"Perhaps the marshal has plans to improve the castle's defenses," Kion said. But Zinder remained doubtful, going on for some time about what was needed to get the Eyre ready for battle.

They had not quite finished breakfast when a loud knock sounded upon the front door. Before they could answer, Gallant Rymir and another soldier passed inside and proceeded down the entryway, their chain mail clinking underneath their yellow tabards, their boots pounding a steady rhythm throughout the house.

Kion and the others rose to greet them.

"Good morning," Rymir said. "I trust you found your accommodations suitable."

"More than suitable—once we got into the kitchen," Zinder said.

"Yes, I heard about Grish's failure to unlock it. For that I apologize. If I could have sent you with another porter I certainly would have." Rymir swept his arm toward the front door. "The marshal will see you now. We have come to escort you. He awaits you in the great hall."

They left their breakfast unfinished, which was all the better, for after the soldiers' arrival Kion's stomach had turned in so many knots he couldn't have eaten another bite.

Out in the courtyard, the morning sun struggled to crest the horned crenelations. Scattered clouds draped rain across the castle grounds. Zinder's bright hat held its vibrancy amidst the grayness, like some subterranean fungus growing in a cave. He turned quite a few heads as they went, which pleased him more than a little.

The march from the back of the courtyard to the curved road leading up to the keep was long and steep. The morning rain made the pavement treacherous and their going even slower than it otherwise would have been. It did not help that Kion's scabbard slapped against his leg if he didn't tilt it purposely away from his body. He tried to mimic the way Rymir and the other soldier carried themselves, but it still felt awkward and unnatural, like trying to skip while carrying a bowl of soup. As much as he had practiced wielding a sword, he had never had to wear one at his side. But it was a small thing in the grand unfolding of the war and he would grow accustomed to it in time.

As they reached the summit, a cloaked figure exited through the high-pointed arch of the keep's wrought iron gate, fashioned to look as though it were made of thorny vines, just like the main gate of the castle. The figure moved swiftly and kept his eyes down. Kion looked after him as he passed, trying to tease out what struck him as so odd about the man. A bit overdressed, that's all. Such a thick coat was unnecessary for such light rain.

"That was Grish," Kithian told him, again with his uncanny ability to guess what Kion was thinking.

"How can you be sure?" Kion whispered.

"He wore a scarf beneath his cloak."

Ah yes, the glaivesight. Kithian could see right through the cloak, thick as it was.

"He moved far more quickly than he did the last time we met," Nurien said.

Grish was a porter; he must have had something urgent to deliver or retrieve, something more important than accompanying a group of visitors to the guesthouse. Kion and Tiryn shared a questioning glance, but Rymir led them on and the incident was swept from their minds.

The soaring fortress now drew them in. They passed through its daunting gate, enveloped briefly by the fluted stonework before passing into a small bailey. The stone around the gate and on the front of the keep was riddled with mortar-filled cracks and traced with creeping vines. Tarnished bronze doors, thick and stout, stood open on either side of the main entrance.

This was the third great fortress Kion had seen and these massive bulwarks of hewn stone never ceased to inspire awe and wonder. This keep was certainly the oldest and largest of the three, and gave the impression that it had stood since the dawn of time, that perhaps all other keeps had been framed and patterned after this one. The very air had an ancient, enchanted quality, which called to him and made him long to know its history. Who had designed and built it? How long had it taken? And what great men had walked these halls and strengthened its defenses through their counsel and deeds?

Coming out of the spitting rain, a hush settled around them, though pattering echoes still rippled off the flagstones behind them. Two squat towers framed the opening. Large and ponderous brass bells could be seen through the arrow slits in each, hanging solemnly within. At the end of a short entrance hall, a gate of wrought iron bars, of the same thorny design as the others, also stood open. Four soldiers kept vigil at this second gate inside sequestered booths which housed the massive winches, gears, and chains needed to open and close both the bronze doors and the inner gate. One of the guards returned

Rymir's salute and nodded toward a much larger hall lit with flickering candle rings suspended from long iron chains. The cavernous hall was rimmed by a crenelated gallery halfway up. A slender set of stairs granted access to this defensive walkway both on the left and the right.

Old gray stones, worn smooth from the passage of many years and many feet, led to a dais at the far end. Three wide steps afforded access to a long rosewood table set with a dozen chairs, sitting along one side and facing the newcomers. Only two of the high-backed chairs were occupied. The two men there were so deep in conference that they failed to look up at the echoing tread of the latest arrivals. They spoke in hushed voices, their faces grave. One of them had a grizzled beard and hair streaked with gray which ended at his shoulders. The other had hair of similar length, but it was raven black and glistened as though he had just come out of the rain. Both wore the straw-yellow tabards of Bramble Eyre, though the younger of the two had white bars on both shoulders while the older man wore a white bar on one shoulder only. Two gallants attended them, standing at attention on either end of the table.

When Kion's party reached the foot of the dais, the men at the table looked up and Rymir gave them a cross-armed salute.

"The messenger and his party have arrived," Rymir said.

The raven-haired man's expression changed at once. His eyes flashed with interest as he looked over each of them in turn. His comely face and well-set frame marked him as Faedred, marshal of Bramble Eyre. He was every bit as striking as Mariday had said, though he had a haggard look about him, as one much worn through trouble and care.

"Ah, the mysterious messenger from Windle. Welcome to Bramble Eyre. I am Marshal Faedred Alagris and this is Flag-master Logren Brestock, my second. I apologize that I was unable to receive you yesterday, but I have had many unexpected duties of late."

Kion saluted and stepped up beside Rymir. "It is an honor to meet you. I am Glinthelm Kion Bray, recently come into the service of Swordswain Forglen of Windle, though I have orders to place myself under the command of the Lord of Bramble Eyre once my message has been delivered. Beyond the service of my blade, I fear that you will not find my arrival all that helpful as the swordswain sent me to request that any troops of the fane that could be spared be sent to aid in Windle's defense. From what I have been told, no such soldiers are here, nor are any expected. In any case, here is the letter he sent."

Kion produced Forglen's written message and laid it upon the table. After a quick reading—for it was no more than three lines long—Faedred nodded and set it aside. Kion looked for signs of disappointment in the marshal's face, but the intensity of his gaze did not waver.

"You have been informed correctly," Faedred said. "Lord Namril has been sending for men ever since an outbreak of the sprull took so many this past winter. In the end, he decided to go in person to petition the fane. I tried to dissuade him on account of his health, but he has a will of adamant at times. In any case, I greet you in his stead. Though your message may have proven fruitless, your coming could not have been more timely. For not only do I welcome the service of another blade into our ranks— and indeed the sword you carry marks you as something more than a mere glinthelm—I also see that you come with a nyn among your company and I am told that your sister has talent in the healing arts. I have need of all three of you, but at this moment your sister most of all."

Kion looked back and saw that Tiryn was as surprised as he was by Faedred's words.

"Is this regarding Namril's son?"

Faedred's countenance returned to the grave aspect it held when they first entered.

"Yes. One of the maids told us that a healer traveled among you. I only learned of it this morning or I would have sent for you sooner." He rose, a little less in stature than Kion, but far more well built. The flagmaster rose along with him.

"Tiryn, they tell me you are called. Would you be willing to see Lord Joromar now?"

Tiryn was even more daunted than usual, by the manner in which Faedred carried himself, by the magnificence of the great hall, and by the weight of the marshal's question. A stranger's life had been suddenly thrust into her hands.

"I...of course. I will do everything I can to help," Tiryn said.

"That is all that we can ask. Please go with Rymir. He shall take you to Lord Joromar's chambers. I do not wish to burden you too heavily, but we have tried everything. You may be his last chance. If he died while Lord Namril was away I could never forgive myself." Warring emotions vied for dominance upon Faedred's face, anger and desperation and something else which escaped Kion. Whatever it was, it was clear that Faedred felt helpless in the face of the young lord's illness.

Tiryn hesitated, her eyes seeking Kion's for assurance.

"I have faith in you," Kion said. "Mother taught you well. We'll join you as soon as you can."

"I could go with her," Zinder said, gazing up at the marshal, who, between the stairs and his own height stood as tall as a haukmar. "If that's all right with you, Marshal."

Faedred's distress gave way to a businesslike manner. "I would not want you to catch the sprull. It is especially dangerous for those advanced in age. Tellman our healer is the only one we've let in who was over fifty."

Zinder licked his lips and was about to explain that he was only thirty-five and that all nyn had white hair like he did, but Kion stepped in first.

"He's just worried that my sister will feel unsure in such a large and unfamiliar place," he said.

Flagmaster Logren, who had remained tight-lipped and grave throughout, finally ventured to speak. "Perhaps he has a point, my lord. The young lady might feel more comfortable if escorted by her companion."

"Very well," Faedred said. "So long as you remain outside Lord Joromar's chambers when she enters in, that should be suitable."

"Of course. With a good will, Marshal," Zinder said, tipping his stridently colored hat with a dash of elegance.

Faedred acknowledged the gesture with a polite nod. "Some of my men will speak to you later of a problem we have in repairing the castle defenses, but that can wait. Nothing is more important than the health of Lord Joromar." He nodded to Rymir. "You have your orders. Report to me if there is any change in Lord Joromar's health."

Rymir saluted and escorted Tiryn and Zinder toward one of the side doors. Zinder called back. "Don't you worry, lad. I'll keep her safe."

"I know you will. Thank you, Zinder."

Once they had gone, Faedred measured Kion afresh with a long, thoughtful look.

"Kion Bray," he said. "So tell me, how is it that a messenger from Windle comes by a sword of such magnificence?"

Kion gripped Truesilver's handle, seeking the comforting warmth which flowed into his hand. There was much he could have said at that moment. But would the marshal believe even half of it?

Chapter 32

BERANSKYRE

Kion began with the finding of Truesilver at Roving after the death of Strom and of his journey to Charring. Faedred said not a word during the whole of the account. He sat beside Flagmaster Logren and listened intently, his keen eyes studying Kion's every movement. Kion could not tell whether the marshal believed all that he was hearing or not. And the longer Kion went on, the more worried he became. But when he finished describing his fight with Vayd, Faedred broke his silence.

"You are the one who defeated Vayd at Charring? Then that makes you the Sword of the North," he said. "But that happened two months ago."

"No one has heard anything of the Sword since," Flagmaster Logren said, adding, with and eye toward Faedred, "Some say that he must have been killed in one of the battles at Fennigar or Grettling or Quelling."

"I did not fight in those battles, and as you can see I am very much alive."

A long silence followed in which Faedred and Logren exchanged glances and the three gallants stared openly.

"Can you believe this, men? The Sword of the North has come to Bramble Eyre," Faedred said. Though his expression, along with Logren's, remained cautious, the look on the soldiers' faces showed that they at least did not doubt Kion's tale.

"Might we see the sword?" Logren said.

Kion unsheathed Truesilver, the blade resting with perfect

balance in his hand, the flawless metal radiating a soft sunset glow amidst all the candled shadows of the great empty hall. The citrines in the hilt glittered with slow ponderous motes.

"The craftsmanship is without equal," Faedred said. "It truly is a masterful blade. And you can set it on fire like the tales say?"

Kion stepped away from the table. "Glaivefire."

The deep crimson flames licking the blade erased whatever doubts Faedred and Logren might have had. No one could see that fire and think that it came by natural explanation or some trick. The deep, opaque redness of the flames and the way it flickered like paper showed that this was something beyond what could be produced by the craft of men. Indeed, to those who saw it, all other fires they had seen burned pale and cold.

"By the margrave's banner, I can feel the heat even from this distance," Faedred said.

"You see, my lord," Logren said. "I told you the Sword yet lived."

"I should have learned by now never to doubt you, old friend," Faedred said. "Very well, Kion, please tell us the rest of your tale."

"Stillfire." The word quietly erased the crimson flames. He sheathed Truesilver and resumed his account, passing quickly over his search for his mother and of her death.

"I am deeply sorry," Faedred said.

Kion was grateful for the sincerity of the marshal's words, but the ache remained and he hurried on lest he falter. He told them of the return to Whitewind and Dunach, and of his time in Windle and Rippling and of his journey through Fathomwood. The only things he chose not to speak of were his rescue by Cornoc and the fact that Truesilver could speak. Perhaps he would tell them in time, but he did not want to risk his new commander thinking his tale was mere invention. Though he could demonstrate Truesilver's fire easily enough, it was much harder to convince someone that he could hear a voice coming from an object made of metal. And his encounter with Cornoc and the battle with the shaydvorn felt too mysterious and fantastical to be believed. He wasn't sure he fully understood what it all meant himself.

Faedred rose and came to stand before him. "That is quite the tale. I am not sure that it is my place to command a warrior such as you, but if you choose to honor your duty to the swordswain, I will accept you into the service of Lord Namril until such time as he returns and deems otherwise."

No doubts arose to trouble Kion's mind this time. Though he had only just met Faedred, his heart sounded no warning bells within him as it had with Forglen. The marshal at least carried himself outwardly as a man worthy of his rank. And Kion was ready to fight, ready to see his sword tested on the battlefield and on the training grounds.

He knelt upon the steps before the marshal. "I pledge to serve you with all that is in me."

"So be it." Faedred motioned for Kion to rise. "Come with me now. For I do not deem it fitting that you should serve as a mere gallant. And yet, from what you've told me, you have no formal training in the art of war. We are a separate force from the main Warding army. We answer to Lord Namril only, though he, in turn, is beholden to the margrave and the fane. In my position as marshal I stand just beneath Namril in authority, and below me we have our flagmaster and then quartermaster. Beneath them are the eight tormains charged with defending various parts of the castle. And of course the bulk of our forces are made up of the gallants, our common soldiers. But I do not believe you are suited for any of these positions."

Kion braced himself. So he was to remain a messenger, then, or perhaps be given some other non-combat role like chronicler or castle guard.

Faedred studied him for a long dreadful moment. "But there is an old title I could bestow upon you, one that has not been used in many years. It is that of beranskyre, the lord's champion.

If you can earn it, you will not lead any of our companies, but serve directly under me."

"Earn it, Marshal?" Kion said.

Faedred led him to a door opposite the one Tiryn and Zinder had left by. Logren and the gallants followed close behind. He had never heard of the title Faedred spoke of and wondered how long he would have to serve before he earned it.

"Yes. Besides fighting in the Eyre's battles, the lord's champion is tasked with fighting any duels issued against the lord himself. And for that, he of course has to be a greater warrior than his lord. While I do not think you would have much difficulty besting Lord Namril if he were here, as he is getting quite on in years, since I am currently the acting lord of Bramble Eyre you will instead have to best me."

Kion broke his stride at the unexpected news. A duel with the marshal of Bramble Eyre had been the farthest thing from his mind when he awoke that morning.

"You do have a set of armor, don't you?" Faedred said, clapping him on the back. The blow was meant to be friendly, but Kion felt it through his whole chest.

Kion forced his grimace into a smile. He took a quick survey of Faedred before he passed through the door. He carried his frame more lightly than might be expected for a man of his build. Though Kion had bested Vayd and many others since, this time he would not have the advantage of Truesilver's fire. It would be a straight fight, based on skill alone. Was he up to the challenge? And what would happen if he failed?

The training yard lay open to the sky in the center of the barracks. The rest of the building bounded it on every side with a balcony running around its length, just as in the great hall, though this one was far narrower and smaller.

Kion had been escorted back to the guesthouse to don his

armor before the fight. A gallant assisted him, but he didn't get the fitting as properly as Zinder would have. Kion adjusted it as best he could and followed the soldier back to the barracks where Faedred awaited. The marshal was not alone. Close to fifty soldiers crowded the balcony, called out from their normal duties across the keep to watch their leader fight the Sword of the North.

Only Faedred, Logren, Kion, and the gallant accompanying him occupied the courtyard itself. Straw-padded sparring poles and weapon racks of all shapes and sizes lined the walls. The sun hung just above the eastern side, warming the dark shingles of the roof and casting spindly shadows upon the chipped and faded flagstones.

Faedred wore lamellar armor of blackened steel with silvery vambraces and leg plates. The armor rested comfortably on his frame, well-oiled and supple. Though Kion had fought in armor several times, he did not wear his nearly as well. Looking into Faedred's eyes as he took his place in the center of the courtyard, it was clear that he expected to win. Was this some sort of trick, then, to humiliate him? Was he only different from Forglen in his polished mannerisms and air of cool command? The soldiers along the balcony were of the same mind, looking down on this young warrior not as some fabled hero, but as a lanky upstart who did not belong among their ranks, much less deserve to bear the mantle of the lord's champion. Kion had known hostile crowds before, in his duels at the Seven Fires festival. Though this crowd was not as openly hostile as those had been, Kion wished he had Zinder there so that he could have had at least one person in his corner.

"*Oh-rah*, men!" Faedred shouted to the soldiers above, which Kion took for some sort of battle cry.

"*Oh-rah! Oh-rah!*" The men shouted back in unison, their voices booming like a great drum.

"I have summoned you this morning to bear witness to a duel between myself and Kion Bray, also known as the Sword of the North. Should he win, he will be granted the title of beran-skyre, the lord's champion, and serve alongside us as our brother in battle. But like all soldiers, he must earn his rank. If he fails, we will send him south to Gilding with his sword between his legs!" He said this with a rakish grin and winked at Kion, but his men took up the jest in boisterous fashion.

"Oh-rah!" they shouted again, though less in unison and the cry came amidst harsh laughter and mocking exclamations. Between their unexpected derision and the realization that he might once more be sent on some vain errand and forgotten, Kion's hopes wavered. It was beginning to look as if the marshal did not want his service any more than the swordswain. And could Kion fight alongside soldiers after a welcome like this?

"Pay no heed to the crowd." Kithian's quiet voice overcame the raucous courtyard. *"Battles are fought with actions, not words."*

"Do you think I can win?" Kion said in a low voice that was lost amongst the din.

"Yes. With a glaive in your hand, you can win any battle. But that does not mean that you will. Be cautious. Feel him out and wait for an opening."

Faedred motioned for silence.

"Enough jesting. Save your cheers for after the fight. Flag-master, explain the rules to our challenger."

Logren's voice, weathered and thin as it was, redounded in the enclosed space. "The rules are simple. The first to score three hits wins. Hits are valid anywhere but the hands and the feet. Understood? Very well, don your helmets, touch swords, and begin." He withdrew to the far side of the courtyard.

Kion pulled on his father's helm and lowered the visor. Faedred did the same. His eyes glinted within the narrow slit. His longsword was equal in length to Truesilver. The crossbar of the hilt ended in sharp prongs and the pommel had the shape of a diamond with a hollow center. The two warriors drew together and touched swords.

The gallery above went still as stone.

Kion braced for a sudden attack, but Faedred drew back and set his guard, holding his blade in an almost casual two-handed plow stance. Kion held Truesilver in a similar position, though with his blade more extended, ready to thrust or parry. He kept his ground, following Kithian's counsel and waiting to see if Faedred would take an aggressive approach or try to parry and counter.

Faedred took his time, sizing up Kion in his own fashion. Then he shuffled forward. His footwork was flat, but quick. It was as if he never took his feet off the ground. He moved forward only by quarter steps, each time pausing to gauge Kion's defenses. Kion gave a little ground, but not so much that their swords did not touch once again. He read in the touch and in Faedred's movements that he would not press the attack. He would wait and seek to counter.

Very well. It fell to Kion to make the first move. He raised his blade and burst forward with a lightning-quick lunge. Faedred countered and Kion twisted his grip, his blade sliding off Faedred's for a hit on his chest, but at the same time Faedred reversed and landed a blow on Kion's side. The impact reverberated like a brass bell straight through his bones.

Logren raised two fists. "Draw. No point scored." So that was how it was to be. A hit had to be clean.

A few scattered shouts rang out from the balcony amidst a general murmur. The two combatants pulled back and set their guards once more. No points had been scored, but Faedred's blow left Kion smarting. Though smaller in stature, Faedred was as strong as Dougan Shaw, Kion's old tormentor back in Furrow, perhaps stronger. Kion would need to look out for the counter next time.

"He is well seasoned and patient," Kithian said. *"But you are ready to meet this challenge."*

Kion gave Faedred a moment to see if he would change tactics, but the marshal stayed in the same stance as before, inching forward, but otherwise not making any attacks. Kion gave a little ground before touching swords and extending forward. This time his blade swept in low for the legs. Faedred made an attempt at the parry, but Truesilver was too quick and landed a hit on his shin. Kion again missed the counter, despite watching for it, and Faedred landed a glancing blow on his forearm.

"Draw."

At least Kion wasn't left with a stinger like the last time. He shifted his chest piece. The pain from the first blow had dulled but not gone away.

Kion wasted no time in going on the offensive. Until Faedred showed him otherwise, he would take the role of the aggressor. And so the battle went on. Kion lunged, Faedred parried and countered and they drew again. They withdrew, came back together, and the same sequence played out again. It happened five, six, seven times, all with similar results. Neither of them would land a blow or Kion would but Faedred would counter. Neither fighter could score a clean hit.

"He's trying to wear you down," Kithian said, his voice cutting through the cries from the gallery for Faedred to press the attack. *"He's letting you strike first, knowing he can counter, which is his strength. He knows you are the younger fighter and have the greater speed and quickness, but you cannot keep up the attack forever. Eventually you will tire. You must change tactics before that happens."*

Change tactics. Kithian was right. Already Kion's chest heaved and his hair was soaked through and the last blow Faedred had given him came down like a hammer on his shoulder. Despite the pain, he still had plenty of strength left in his arms, for Truesilver weighed a fraction of what a sword that size should have, but his legs were starting to feel the weight of the poorly fitted armor. But what could he do? He could not force Faedred to go on the offensive. Or could he? If Faedred was waiting for Kion to grow weary before he struck, what if Kion could make him believe that he was already worn down and bait him into an attack?

Faedred initiated another cautious advance, pressing Kion to respond, but this time he did not stand his ground. He shifted backward, letting Faedred come on. He kept giving way until he drew near to the weapon racks along the wall. The din of the gallery rose, the soldiers clamoring for Faedred to strike. The marshal, goaded by his men and beguiled by Kion's feigned weariness, charged in. But rather than a straightforward thrust as Kion expected, he let fly a frenzied tapestry of slashes. It was all Kion could do to fend off the strikes and keep his footing. The weapons on the racks behind him shook. Before he could be forced into them, Kion leapt to the side with a quickness that surprised even himself. It certainly caught Faedred off guard. One moment Kion was in front of him, desperately parrying his strikes, the next he was darting away to land a telling blow on Faedred's side. This time Faedred had no counter.

Logren lifted his left fist. "Point for the challenger."

The spectators went silent save for a few low groans of disbelief.

"You're heartier than you look," Faedred said, rubbing his side. Now it was time for his ribs to sting. "And quicker too. Well played."

Kion acknowledged Faedred's compliment with a nod. He had to give the marshal marks for character. Not many commanders would take being outshone in front of their men in this fashion.

"But you haven't won yet," Faedred said. "I still know a few tricks. Let's see how you handle them."

They touched swords and the fight began anew.

Faedred proved that his words had not been idle boasting. He came at Kion with feints and half-lunges now, disguising his attacks with careful movements and calculated thrusts. It was as if Kion were facing an entirely different fighter. He no longer looked to press Kion into the attack and wear him down since that tactic had failed. Instead, he sought to confuse Kion by mixing in aggressive moves with more defensive ones, keeping him off balance, unsure of what would come next. Kion found himself giving ground now not intentionally but out of necessity. It felt more like he was being schooled in battle than actually fighting. Yet still, just as with the leap, he surprised himself by parrying Faedred's unexpected attacks when they came. Each time he saw them only at the last moment, but each time he reacted just in time to deflect the strike. Even so, he was so busy trying to grasp Faedred's tactics and counter them that he could find no way to strike back on his own. The rumbling from the balconies rose higher. The marshal had not yet landed a hit, but he had regained the upper hand.

"He is attempting to use his superior experience in battle to overawe you," Kithian said, his voice once again countering the daunting effect of the crowd. *"Do not be drawn in by his displays of skill. Countering is not your strength, but you found a way to do it before and you must find a way to do it now. Be patient. Wait for your moment."*

Kithian's words steadied Kion's nerves. He settled in and waited. He studied Faedred's attacks now. If Faedred meant to school him, he would learn what the marshal had to teach. His legs ached and true weariness set in, but Faedred's strokes were also dipping in speed and strength. As long as Kion could hang on, he would have a chance to strike back. Then it happened, just as Kithian had said it would. Faedred repeated a sequence he had used earlier. He may have already repeated it several times, but whether from his ebbing endurance or Kion's patient study of his technique, Kion recognized it this time. It came in a series of feints and flourishes, but at its heart it was simply a reverse sweep. And Kion knew the counter. He ignored the flourishes this time and the initial thrust, driving his sword high so that it glanced off Faedred's neck guard and then he twisted away from the marshal's reverse to avoid the equalizer.

"Point for the challenger. Two-nil," Logren said, giving Kion a nod of quiet respect. A resounding silence fell upon the gallery.

"Not only quick, but you've got a mind to match the sharpness of your sword," Faedred said. "I admit that things are not looking well for me, but until the battle's over, there is always hope."

Again, Kion had to respect the marshal's character. It was not a battle for life and death, but Faedred's reputation as a warrior was in play, and in the full view of his men. Kion doubted that he would have taken things in such stride if their roles had been reversed.

"Yes, there is always a chance," Kion said.

"Shall we?" Faedred said. His shoulders rose and fell in weariness, but his eyes gleamed with a silent confidence. He had not given up.

For the third time they touched swords, but by now, Kion's youth and the superiority of his weapon came fully to bear upon the fight. Faedred attempted a few risky thrusts, but they only resulted in draws or misses as Kion's quickness allowed him to respond more easily than before. It was not that Kion was not exhausted as well, only that his tiredness had less of an impact on the quality of his swordplay. Faedred had the greater strength and experience, but he also had the heavier sword and the slower reflexes. The men in the gallery had little to cheer about in this third round of battle. Though Faedred did his best to make a game of it, he had already spent himself in the previous exchanges.

Faedred went for a desperate lunge, overextended himself, and slipped. Kion almost felt bad for how easily his final touch upon the marshal's shoulder came. As the last blow landed, this time there was no quieting of the gallery. Instead there came a wave of sighs followed by a slow, solitary clapping. It was soon joined by another pair of hands and then several more. Though grudgingly given, and with no great enthusiasm, the soldiers acknowledged Kion's victory with a soft rain of applause. Subdued as it was, to Kion's ears it may as well have been a thunderstorm. At last he had gotten the chance to prove his worth as a soldier. On this day, he was more than a mere whispered legend from the battle of Charring. He had not needed Truesilver's fire to win this battle, but had bested Faedred through his skill and Kithian's counsel and encouragement. He likely would not have won with any other sword, but it had still been his arm that landed the blows.

"Third point—and the match—to the challenger, Kion Bray," Logren said, coming toward the two fighters. He clapped along with the men in the balcony.

"Well fought, glaivebond. Well fought," Kithian said.

Faedred pulled off his helmet and raised Kion's arm to the sky.

"Behold your champion," he said, lifting his voice to the men gathered above. "The beranskyre of Bramble Eyre!"

And now the applause came in earnest. There were even a few whistles and whoops and grins of surprise, though several shook their heads. None of them had wanted the outcome that occurred, but they were men enough to admit defeat. Just like their leader.

Kion could see in that moment why Faedred's men were drawn to him. He was a skilled warrior, but not arrogant about that skill, and not above admitting when he had been bested. His willingness to even offer the challenge to Kion and grant him the possibility to earn this title showed that he valued men not for their position and background, but for their individual skill and quality. And he not only gave Kion the chance to prove himself, he allowed him to bask in his victory. Kion took off his helmet and looked into the face of the man he'd just defeated. A great weight lifted from him. He had found a leader he could serve under at last. And now he could truly call himself a soldier.

Chapter 33

BED OF SORROW

Winding through the inner workings of the keep at Bramble Eyre was like passing through the heart of a mountain. Tiryn had never seen so much stone in one building. It was a wonder this tiny island could hold it.

She and Zinder, led by Rymir, passed through hall after hall in silent awe at the fitted stonework, the faded but finely woven tapestries upon the walls, and the myriad lanterns and sconces which gave shadowy light to the dark, tomb-like passages. They went through enough doors to outfit half the houses of Furrow. And when a passage did not end in a door, it ended in an iron gate, guarded by one or two gallants, who nodded to Rymir and let them through, though not a few gave Zinder some curious looks. Then at last, the long-absent daylight streamed in through arched windows as they ascended what seemed to be an uncountable number of spiraling stairs to a door near the top of the great tower in the southeast corner of the keep.

As they ascended the last few steps, a piercing song wove its way through the tower.

How dear the memory
You sitting on my knee
That bucking, bouncing horse
Oh, fond, sweet company

Of laughter was no lack
You rode upon my back
Such romping raucous trips
Oh, bring the laughter back

You used to run and play
In your wild carefree way
And I would hold your hand
Together all the day

And now that you are grown
And to the four winds flown
Your memory's all I have
For I am all alone

It was the same song played by the Unwiths' clock, the same one Mother had so often sung to Kion and Tiryn, but Valissia had changed the words. She had turned the song into a desperate plea for the return of her son. And her voice, lilting and subtle, yet keen with sorrow, called out to Tiryn and her heart grew heavy within her at the thought of the suffering behind the melody. All the majesty of the great castle peeled away under the weight of what now lay before her.

Two soldiers stood stiffly at attention outside the door where Rymir halted.

"This is the healer Lady Valissia sent for," Rymir said.

One of them opened the door and went inside, returning after a muffled conversation.

"You may see Lord Joromar now," he said.

"Well," Zinder said, "I'll wait here for you. I only wish I'd thought to bring a book to pass the time."

"We have a library on the main floor," Rymir said.

"Now why didn't you tell me that before?" Zinder clucked his teeth disapprovingly.

"I'd be happy to take you there afterward."

"I wish you didn't have to wait, Zinder, but thank you for coming with me," Tiryn said. "I'll be back as soon as I can."

A bitter tang washed over her as she entered the room. A single lantern bathed the room in a weak glow that seemed half shadow, half light. The quarters were large and full of cabinets, chairs, a desk, and other furniture, all expertly crafted. Four figures clustered around a large bed with a pleated canopy, three women and a young man. Tiryn at once recognized Mariday and Livia, whose faces glimmered with quiet hope in the subdued light. Mariday's manner was so still and withdrawn, it was as though she were a different person.

The other woman wore a long sweeping dress of sable fabric which had the appearance of a funeral garment. Within the hood which draped her head her sapphire eyes radiated the wisdom and care of someone who had lived through much, though her face had lost none of its beauty. It was she who came forward to meet Tiryn.

"Thank you for coming," she said. Her voice was gentle and sonorous but tinged with fear. Echoes of the melody from the stairs ran through it. She spoke with hushed tones, as though anything louder might upset some fragile and invisible balance within the room. She latched on to Tiryn's hand. "I am Valissia, Joromar's mother. If there is anything you can do, please help my son."

"I will try, my lady," Tiryn said, even more softly than Valissia. The urgency in the lady's expression only made Tiryn's burden all the heavier. Looking into her eyes, Tiryn knew that of all the wealth she possessed, her son was far and away her greatest treasure.

Valissia walked Tiryn to the bedside, the maids withdrawing to a respectful distance. The fourth person in the room was a young man who had Grish's angular chin and sloping nose, but was otherwise a much rounder person with maple-brown hair. His cheeks were pink as a piglet, his eyes red from tears, and his clothes were ruffled and spattered with dirt. He looked quite out of sorts, and rather out of place amidst the elegant surroundings, but managed a snaggle-toothed grin and a bow as genuine as it was clumsy.

"This is Havrick, one of our gardeners and Joromar's dear friend," Valissia said.

"Pleased to make your, er, well, um...yes." A great lump in his throat stopped up his words.

"It's nice to meet you as well," Tiryn said.

Havrick shuffled away to give Tiryn room beside the bed. But he stood watching her with grief-swollen eyes, mercilessly wringing all the shape and form out of an old straw hat. He swallowed the knot in his throat with a great *galumph*. "We've tried everything—everything," he said.

With each moment spent in this room and with each desperate word and each tortured look, Tiryn's task became all the harder to bear. She had some skill in healing, yes, but nothing to warrant the hope glimmering in their eyes. They needed someone like Mistress Shona, the healer of Furrow, or Mother. They would know what to do. And yet she was here and they were not. She must face this task alone.

But when she looked upon the sleeping form of the young lord, the weight of her doubts and misgivings lifted. For she saw before her not a life hanging on the edge of doom, which might slip through her unworthy fingers at any moment, but simply a young man, and a very large young man, whose face, though pale and somewhat wasted from whatever disease now wracked his body, glowed with a kind, endearing light. He had an honest, plain look about him, an unadorned innocence which drew her to him and made her long to heal his sickness not because of the distress of the people around her, but simply for his own sake. He was someone in need and a warmth surged through her as though her own brother lay suffering there.

Apart from the general goodness in his face, Joromar's defining trait was his shockingly red hair. Though wet from fever and darkened under the dim light of the lantern, its burnished coppery sheen bordered on orange at the tips and no darker than rust at the roots. Valissia's hair was mostly hidden within the shadows of her hood, but her features were so soft and fine and her frame so small and slight that it was hard to believe this great heap of a young man was truly her son.

Tiryn reached out to touch him when her vision of the drowning soldier came back to her, unbidden. Since Kion had not died, the vision might have been about someone else. The soldier in that vision had been in a bed just like Joromar was now. And under that bed—and this is what captured her thoughts—had been a mortar and pestle, the tools of the healer. Did this mean that she had been brought to save this young man? And yet the soldier had died. Did that mean Lord Joromar would die as well? More likely that the vision had nothing to do with him. But even if it did, she told herself the same thing she had told Kion once, "we can change our dreams."

She touched his forehead and found it wet and almost scalding. The heavy tang in the air told her that some oriloam balm had been applied to his skin. This was the usual treatment for the sprull, a wasting disease that took the lives of mainly the old, and usually during the winter. And there was the faint greenish glimmer to his lips, a tell-tale sign of that disease.

Tiryn turned to Havrick. "Mariday said that one of the other gardeners, a man called Tellman, has tried to help him. Why is he not here?"

Havrick wrung his poor straw hat near to ribbons. "That's what makes it all the worse. Tellman came down with something just last night. We think he may have caught the sprull from spending so much time at Grundy's side."

"How terrible." So it was the sprull. Tiryn was glad Zinder had stayed outside. "And the oriloam has had no effect?"

"Not a bit," Havrick said.

"Have you tried rissel sprig?" This was a common remedy for other sicknesses. Even if it did not cure them, it eased the discomfort brought about by fever and other aches.

"Yes, we rubbed whole heaps of it onto him."

"What about asper nettles?"

"That too." Havrick gnashed his snaggly teeth.

Tiryn asked about a few other remedies, none of which she expected to discover had done anything, but found that they had tried every one of them and nothing had worked. Havrick grew more distraught as the litany of failed medicines was recited, and that spilled over to Valissia and her maids, raising Tiryn's anxieties as well. It was not long before she had exhausted every healing herb she knew.

"Ask them if they have tried cherrum vinegar." Nurien's voice came so forcefully in contrast to the hushed tones that it gave Tiryn a start.

"Is something wrong, Miss Tiryn?" Havrick said.

"No, no. I was just wondering if you've tried cherrum vinegar?"

Havrick's face formed a plump puzzle. "Cherrum vinegar? Why, no. That's only for rashes, isn't it?"

Tiryn had never heard of cherrum before so she wasn't sure what to say. "Do you have any?"

"Not that I'm aware of, though there may be some in the storeroom. Tellman keeps an awful lot of strange things in there."

"Cherrum vinegar is good for rashes, but also for other things," Nurien said. *"Since the remedy for the sprull did not work, we must consider that he could be afflicted with some other condition."*

Tiryn tried to appear deep in thought as she listened to Nurien's voice. She doubted she would ever get over the awkwardness of hearing a voice in the midst of a room of people who had no idea what it said.

"Perhaps if we could find some, we could see if it helped," Tiryn said. What disease did Nurien suspect Joromar might have?

"Cherrum. I see," Havrick said, but still looked confused.

"Havrick will take you to look for it as soon as you leave," Valissia said. "Are there any other remedies you know of?"

"It's hard to say. How long has he been like this?"

"We found him passed out the day before last. Mariday went to wake him when he did not appear for breakfast," Valissia said.

"Ask what he was doing the day before he took ill," Nurien said.

Tiryn passed along the question, substituting Nurien's stark tones with softer ones.

"Working in the quarry, like he does on most days. I've told him he doesn't have to go down there, but he insists on helping, to get as much of the repairs for the castle finished before his father returns."

"Where is the quarry located?"

"Beneath the castle," Valissia said as Tiryn passed the question on.

"That is helpful to know."

"He works along with the other commoners?" Tiryn said, unsure of what to say when Nurien posed no further questions.

"Yes, he's always been like that. He takes after his father in that way. The two of them treat their servants as if they were family."

"'Tis true," Mariday put in.

Hearing this made Tiryn's heart go out to Joromar all the more. She had never heard of a noble who treated his servants that way.

"And he has not woken since?" Tiryn said.

Valissia shook her head.

The sprull often came on unexpectedly like that. Someone in poor health would not last three days in the worst cases, but Joromar was young and strong. He would last a few days more at least. But what if it wasn't the sprull? He could have far less time.

Tiryn waited, hoping Nurien might say something more, but the dagger remained silent from its place inside her vest.

"There is still time. If I can find a remedy, I will," Tiryn said. If it depended solely on her, Joromar had little hope. But she had a hidden ally in this fight: Nurien. She was far older and wiser than all of the people in the room put together. If Joromar was going to be saved, it would be through her and not Tiryn. And it looked like a journey to the storeroom was the place to start.

"Please, Tiryn, you must save my son," Valissia gripped both of Tiryn's hands. Desperation throbbed in her fingers. "He is a strong young man. He has beaten death before. I am trusting that by your hand he will beat it once again."

"I promise you that I will do all I can," Tiryn said, trying not to let the burden pull her under, but as she passed through the door it seemed as though the whole of the castle now pressed down upon her.

Chapter 34

HUNTING FOR A CURE

Tiryn pinched her nose shut.

"Phew! Smells like wet rags," Zinder said as Havrick heaved open the massive oaken door to the storeroom. "Wet rags left to rot for months in a vat of pickled beet-juice." Though he fully understood the reason for their visit, he was a little disappointed that they had been forced to skip the library for now.

The storeroom lay far down within the depths of the fortress. It was used not only by Tellman and the other gardeners to store foodstuffs for the kitchen, but at the far end, two black metal slabs formed the doors to what Havrick told them was an underground dock. From there shipments were brought in from faraway places and so crates and barrels of oil, cloth, coal, spices, salt blocks, and metal ingots sat alongside stacks of wood both cut and uncut, scattered about the dank, maze-like room. A straight path ran through the middle of this arrangement, with goods stacked in rows on either side.

"This is quite the storehouse," Zinder remarked, his voice muffled by his hand over his mouth.

"Yes, well, many of the crates are empty just now, but it holds quite a lot when the stocks are full. Sorry about the smell," Havrick said, though it did not seem to bother him. His mangled straw hat now sat atop his head, looking as if it might fall apart at any moment. He grabbed the lantern beside the door as they delved into the shadowy room.

Rymir, who brought up the rear, did not seem to mind the

stench either. Tiryn gradually unstopped her nose and found that it was not as bad as she'd first thought. Zinder was certainly exaggerating. It was only like wet rags left to rot for a few days, not months.

Havrick took the first row on the right.

"There are twenty or so boxes here where Tellman keeps his experiments, as he calls them. He's more or less self-taught when it comes to the healing arts. Quite the smart fellow. Almost as smart as my da. Here. Let's take these four on the top first and divide them up, one for each." He handed Tiryn the lantern. Havrick and Rymir pulled one box for each person down off the stacks and they sorted through them, emptying them to ensure that nothing was missed. Some of the things inside were so covered in dust it took time to tell what they were.

They found a large number of tin containers with various powders, bundles of dried plants, and several vials filled with strange liquids, but no cherrum. So they packed everything back up and put it away before bringing down the next set of boxes. It took them a good quarter of an hour to go through the first batch and about the same for the second. The second batch yielded the same curious, but fruitless results, as did the third. But on the fourth round, about halfway through their rummaging, their persistence paid off.

"Sparks! That's cherrum vinegar or I'm the fane's footman," Zinder exclaimed, holding up a flask of purple leaves to the lantern light.

"Hoo-diddly! Well done, Master Zinder," Havrick said.

"Yes, well done," Rymir said. "Lady Valissia will be glad to hear of this."

"I can't promise that this will cure him," Nurien said. "But there is a fainting sickness that comes in summer called lumdrost. It usually comes from working too hard in places with little air and dangerous fumes, such as might be found in the quarry beneath the castle."

Tiryn vaguely remembered reading about such a sickness, but had never known anyone who had it.

"Havrick, if this doesn't work, is Tellman well enough to speak with? If so, he may have other things we could try," Tiryn said.

"No, but he may have taken a turn for the better. It wouldn't hurt to check."

"Very well. You have a mortar and pestle nearby, I believe you said."

"Yes, just across the hall in the Mixing Room."

They hurriedly packed all the items they'd removed and left.

"Curse me for not being a better herbsman myself," Havrick said, opening the door to a small room with two tables and two mortars and pestles. "I ought to have been, you know. My da was the Spademaster before Tellman. One day when I'm older, I hope to follow in his footsteps. Tellman's been teaching me, but I'm slow and still have a great deal to learn and even he didn't know everything that my dear old da did." Havrick's sincerity was as plain as his face.

"I'm sure you'll make a wonderful spademaster someday," Tiryn said.

She placed several pinches of purple leaves from the flask into the mortar and crushed them. It let off a sharp, sweet, pleasant smell, much like cherries.

"That's much better than the storeroom," Zinder said. "Perhaps my poor nose will make a full recovery."

Havrick took off his hat and wrung it mightily as he watched Tiryn work. It must be hard having both his friends suffer from the same sickness that took the life of his father. Hopefully, Nurien was right and it wasn't the sprull. But if Joromar did not have it, then how had Tellman taken ill?

The leaves expelled a good deal of liquid, turning the herbs into sour-smelling syrup with an unexpected sweetness around the edges.

"We should try the vinegar on Spademaster Tellman as well," Tiryn said.

"Yes, I couldn't bear it if I lost both of them," Havrick said. "But Grundy has had it longer, so we'll go to him first."

"All right, then, let's get this vinegar up there as quick as we can," Zinder said, but the next moment he paused and let out a cavernous groan.

"What is it, Zinder?" Tiryn said.

"It's all those stairs. They weren't made for nynnian legs, I can tell you that." He wheezed and puffed, as if he grew tired just thinking about it. "But onward, onward, and up we go. The young lord's awaiting."

Zinder's eyes sparkled with anticipation. "Well? Did it have any effect?" he said.

"We'll have to wait," Tiryn said. "But we should know within two or three hours."

"That will give us ample time to visit Spademaster Tellman," Rymir said.

"And that means more stairs and no library," Zinder said. "Why can't the whole world just be healthy? Nyn never get sick, you know."

"We can't all be as hearty and hale as you," Tiryn said.

Spademaster Tellman lived in a building about the size of the guesthouse, except that it was three stories high instead of two. The porters and other male servants lived there as well.

Tellman's room was near the entrance. An older woman attended him, though she was not quite as old as Tellman or even Mariday. Havrick introduced her as Ruwena, the assistant spademaster. Her hair had faded from black to a bluish gray, but her face and hands still had a certain liveliness to them.

Tellman, like Joromar, had fallen into a feverish sleep. His hair was white and wispy, so that it almost seemed invisible when the light hit it a certain way. The same greenish tinge marked his lips, the telltale sign of one suffering from the sprull

—though it was an even darker shade than Joromar's, almost blue in places. The poor man labored for each breath and his leathery face was stretched into a permanent grimace. Havrick even remarked that he appeared to be "fading fast," no doubt due to his advanced age.

"He won't last long," Ruwena said, her voice low and rough. She gave Havrick a furtive look, and Tiryn sensed that she wished to say more, but perhaps because of the presence of strangers she held her tongue.

"Poor Tellman," Havrick said, punishing his hat again with complete disregard. How it still held together was a wonder. "It wouldn't be far off to say he's been like a second father to me since my own da passed. He's taken me under his watch and taught me everything I know about gardening and many other things besides."

Looking at Tellman's face, it was not hard to imagine gentle, quiet words coming from the now unmoving mouth. He had the worn softness about him of a life well-lived. But he was a mere shadow of a man now. Tiryn could almost see his skeleton beneath the blanket. Would this disease spread to more people soon? Would she come down with it herself? Still, the cherrum might work. They had to give it time.

After applying the vinegar to Tellman, they returned to the castle and, to Zinder's great delight—and Tiryn's as well—went and visited the library.

"It will take our minds off all this grim business," he said. And he was right.

Such a trove of literature Tiryn had never seen before in all her life. The shelves went so high one had to use a ladder to reach the top. The ladders had wheels at the bottom, one ladder for each wall. A dozen tables filled the room, along with three book stands, each with great tomes set upon them. These were great bound volumes with covers as thick as her fingers and metal clasps and framings. Everything about them said "ancient" and "profound", as though those books were great mountains which rose above the others spread out upon the plains. But even the plains were rolling and green and ripe with bounties just waiting to be harvested. Everywhere she looked were delights and wonders unending, a tapestry of well-worn spines in muted shades of brown and green and red and blue. And the smell—oh, the smell! The smell of the library was like the smell of autumn, when the dry wind sent crackling leaves blowing across the way, bringing the scent of nutmeg and cinnamon cider and other mulled spices. Oh, to step into that library was no small thing. For a time Tiryn lost herself in its depths, forgetting about Lord Joromar and Spademaster Tellman, the war, and even her mother. Here she found refuge and solace amidst the storms of uncertainty brought on by all the troubles swirling about her and she and Zinder whiled away the morning in sweet comfort, poring over books, each one as grand and wondrous as a plate full of the choicest foods.

Sadly, it did not last. The world came crashing back with the return of Havrick and Rymir just before noon. To Tiryn's hungry mind their timing could not have been worse, but to Zinder's grumbling stomach it could not have been better.

"The mind can only contemplate what the stomach can ruminate," Zinder said, closing the weighty volume he'd been lost in for the last half-hour. "But, oh, these will be fond times in my memory. Did you know they have a copy of *The Hunts of Daydrin* here? I finished the entire account of his last battle with the dragon Ashlock. And though it didn't of course tell what happened to Daydrin—no one seems to know—it did shed light on several new details I had never heard before."

Tiryn followed Havrick and Rymir from the library, but the stories she'd read still swirled inside her as they arrived back at the guesthouse to take their lunch. Mariday and Livia had brought them another modest, but filling meal. They ate with some haste in order to return and check upon Lord Joromar and Spademaster Tellman as soon as possible. Tiryn's stomach was too twisted and turbulent to eat much. She ate mostly out of necessity. Zinder, who did not suffer from the same weakness, did his part by finishing what Tiryn could not.

Tiryn's worries proved well-founded, for they found Joromar even worse than the last time. He breathed heavily now, just like Tellman, and his face was strained from his silent battle for life. The cherrum had not worked. Leaving him and the crestfallen Valissia, they returned to Tellman. He, too, had grown worse, descending into restless groanings, and his skin could have lit a candlewick. The poor old man did not have much time left and yet she still had no idea how to cure him.

They returned to the storeroom with heavy steps, their hopes wavering on the edge of a great cliff. This time, Nurien suggested belvor powder, another remedy Tiryn had never heard of. But they found none of it in Tellman's stocks. Absent the powder, Nurien suggested gremgorn extract and, after another round of scrounging through the crates, they discovered a small vial of the greenish liquid. It smelled sour and bitter, overwhelmingly so. Tiryn covered her mouth and nose with one hand while applying it to Joromar's skin. Mariday and Havrick coughed and gagged until she was done. Livia had taken Lady Valissia to rest in her chambers. She had not wanted to go, but Faedred had come and insisted upon it and so she had yielded to the marshal's request.

"Gremgorn is a potent herb," Nurien said. *"If it is snickwing fever that he suffers from, he will show signs of recovery within the hour. Though there were no reports of snickwing sightings within the quarry, it is the only other sickness I can think of which would account for his suddenly falling ill like this."*

Snickwing fever had not been heard of in Inris for many years as far as Tiryn knew, but there was always a chance it had returned. It was associated in some way with the haukmarn, though Tiryn couldn't say why. But war often brought pestilence with it, and if this was a new outbreak of that fever it could prove dire for the rest of the land. Still, it was not known to cause green lips. Only the sprull was known for that.

"Please inform me if there are any changes. If the gremgorn works, you should see it within the hour," Tiryn said.

As she headed toward the exit, Havrick made no move to follow.

"I think I'll stay behind to keep Mariday company this time, and to keep watch over dear old Grundy. I asked Grish to take over for me in the garden this afternoon so that I could stay," he said.

"Grish is your brother?" Tiryn said. She had meant to ask him about their resemblance before, but it had slipped her mind.

"Sure is. He doesn't care much for gardening these days, not since Da passed on, but it's just weed work today, nothing hard."

"That's very nice of Grish to help," she said. Two more opposite brothers, Tiryn could not recall. One fair-minded and kind, the other standoffish and surly. Even their appearance was wildly different. Havrick's frame resembled that of a giant squirrel, while Grish reminded Tiryn of the stick figures she and her friends used to make because they didn't have any dolls. But she had only met Grish once. Perhaps the comparison was unfair. Grish might have a side he had not shown.

"I'm curious, though. Does Grish always wear that scarf of his?" Tiryn said.

"Yes, always," Havrick said. "Leastways when he's out and about. It's to cover the awful scars he has on his neck. When I was little, we lived in Noath. I don't remember much about it, but when I was a few hairs shy of my first year, a lightning storm set our house on fire and killed my mother and nearly killed Grish. It left him with horrible burns. We lost most all we had and the chieftain did nothing to help and so we fled to Inris."

"How awful. So you're Noathryn, then? You don't look it," Tiryn said, recalling the tall, fair-haired men she had seen during her journey through the lands of Inris's western foe.

"Oh, my mother was Inrisian, dark-haired like Grish, and everyone says she was a true beauty. She'd been captured by the Noathryn in a raid, but my father worked for her freedom and married her. After the fire, we fled to her family, but they were too poor to offer us much help. Da wandered about for a time after that until we finally ended up at Bramble Eyre."

"Those burns must have been terrible," Tiryn said.

"Grish has suffered a lot," Havrick said, giving a few lumbering nods. "If more people knew, they might understand why he is the way he is."

"Thank you for helping our dear Grundy, Miss Tiryn," Mariday said, giving her a matronly pat on the arm. "You're a sweet ray of sunshine in all this gloom, you are."

The gesture lifted a little corner of the dread which hung over the room "Thank you, Mariday. You're too kind. Let's hope the medicine works this time."

Tiryn took her leave and met Zinder and Rymir in the hall.

"Any effect at all?" Zinder said as Tiryn struggled to gather the tendrils of her thoughts outside the doorway, which at the moment was like trying to capture smoke in a sack. Something was not right about all of this. One of the remedies should have worked. And these people were too kind and gracious to have to endure such a horrible tragedy. Joromar was far too young to be taken like this.

"Nurien says we won't know if it takes effect for at least another hour," Tiryn said.

"Who is Nurien?" Rymir said.

Oh, dear, had she let that slip? She must have been more exhausted than she realized. She darted a nervous glance at Zinder. Her tongue went dry as a rope. She looked foolishly back at the door, unable to meet Rymir's gaze, willing her mind to think of something to say.

"Someone who knows a great deal about the healing arts," Zinder said, his mind and tongue much quicker than hers.

"Ah, I see," Rymir said. It was clear that he still had questions, but he could tell from Zinder's tone that there was no more to be said on the subject. Rymir had remarkable dignity in the way he carried himself. He made all the soldiers they had met, save Aonar and Roardin, seem rough, low, and hard-hearted. Nurien had mentioned that she thought they might find a swordspeaker soon and to Tiryn's way of thinking, there could be no better choice than Rymir. Though she had only met him yesterday, he had been with her almost the whole of the day and had treated her and Zinder more like visiting officials of the margrave's court than commoners from a remote little village.

How her life had changed in just a few short days. From Kion's near loss at the lake, to the attack by the shaydvorn, to the wonder of seeing a solif, and now the fate of the heir of the Grundstaff family placed in her hands. Honestly, she didn't have time to riddle it out. The one thing she did know was that Joromar and Tellman were dying and that she would do anything she could do to save them. She had always had a love for those in need, but her mother's loss had honed it to a point as sharp as a needle. Seeing the look on Valissia's face, and on those of the servants, who talked of Joromar more as a friend than a lord, cut her to the very marrow. She knew what it was to lose someone so dear. Though she had never met Joromar, through his mother and his friends, she felt as if she knew him somehow. She could not let them suffer the same loss she had, especially not Valissia.

Yet time was running out. And with each passing hour, the mantle of death drew closer and thicker over Bramble Eyre.

Chapter 35

THE WORLD OF SUN AND MOON

Tiryn and Zinder returned that night to the guesthouse in defeat. The empty halls and rooms echoed with a dreadful silence. As wonderful as it was to have such a fine place to sleep, the well-crafted furnishings and ornate bedding could not ease the hollowness of Tiryn's failure to find a cure. The gremgorn remedy had failed. When they left Joromar's room, he was shaking visibly beneath the sheets, in the last throes of his battle with his ravenous illness. Even with Nurien's great knowledge and insight, Zinder's unflappable support, and Rymir and Havrick doing all they could, they had been unable to save the young lord.

They returned too late for dinner. Even Zinder did not have the heart to complain about missing a meal, though he did have a few pieces of jerky from their provisions to lessen the blow.

Kion wasn't there, which made the house all the more vacant and lifeless. Rymir had told them earlier of Kion's duel with Faedred and of his ascension to the rank of beranskyre. As happy as this news was, it also meant that Kion would be staying at the barracks from now on.

"Hammer and tong! They've finally given him the place he deserves," Zinder said. "This marshal looked a bit high and mighty when I first saw him, but he's got a noble spirit after all."

"Oh, you can trust Marshal Faedred," Rymir said. "He treats all with respect, from the lowliest gallant to Lord Namril himself."

"Well, if he meets your standards, that says a great deal. One thing I wonder about, though. He said that he had need of my help repairing the castle defenses. I hope he knows that I'm no stonecutter. While I can discover how to craft most things given enough time, I'm a blacksmith by trade."

"Marshal Faedred is well aware of your skill. He wishes to meet with you tomorrow at noon in order to discuss some issues they are having with a tool in the quarry."

"Well, that sounds intriguing. I only hope Joromar will be on the path to recovery by then."

Sitting down alone at the empty table, just the two of them, Joromar's and Tellman's fate consumed their thoughts. Weary as Tiryn and Zinder were, even sleep was a distant concern for they lived in fear that a knock would come at any moment, heralding the terrible news that either Joromar or Tellman had died.

"What are we going to do, Zinder? We've tried everything," Tiryn said.

Zinder fiddled with a dribble of wax that had dropped down onto the base of the lone candle in the room and failed to answer.

"You know, today when I reread the story of Daydrin and Ashlock, I had hoped to find out the answer to Daydrin's fate. Ashlock was the last creature he ever went to hunt. If the bard who accompanied him had not recorded what happened, we wouldn't know any of the tale. But he never discovered Daydrin's or the dragon's fate. And yet, whether against Ashlock or by some other hand, Daydrin did meet his end. Every hero, no matter how great, will fight a final battle. We did all that we could. It may be that Joromar will pull through. This may not be the young lord's final battle. But a dragon waits for us all sooner or later—or a sickness, or some other sudden end. All that can be asked of anyone is that he fight his final battle with all that is in him when the time comes."

Unlike most of Zinder's stories, this was not one she was glad to hear. But the story of Daydrin was not a made up one. Perhaps that was why the ending was so unsatisfying. In the made up stories like Fister the Magister the heroes always beat the dragons. Wasn't that the point of the story? That you could defeat the dragons? That you could eventually overcome any foe if you held on long enough? But when it came to the world of sun and moon, river and rock, wind and sea—the world Tiryn lived in, and Daydrin—were the dragons always destined to win?

Zinder had been trying to prepare her for the news neither of them wanted to hear, but she refused to give up. Joromar and Tellman were not dead yet. And until they breathed their last, she refused to lose hope. She refused to believe that this was their dragon.

"They never found Daydrin," she said. "Maybe he survived. Maybe he beat the dragon after all."

Zinder remained quiet. He smoothed the end of his beard and watched the candle slowly shrink, drip by drip.

"Remember that your brother has twice come to the very brink of death and was pulled back both times," Nurien said in her steady way. *"While I admit that the chances are few that they will survive, you are right to hold on to hope. We do not know the future. Not unless it is revealed to us. For now, their fate remains shrouded."*

For the first time, Tiryn found herself wishing that a vision would come, that she could know, one way or the other, whether or not Joromar and Tellman would live.

How long she and Zinder sat together in silence was hard to say. But when an angry peal of thunder rattled the windows and shook them from their tortured brooding, the candle was a stub of what it had been when they sat down. Sheets of rain made a riot upon the roof. It must have been going on for some time, but only now did Tiryn notice it.

Then came a sound more frightening than a blast of thunder. The long dreaded knock on the door.

Both Tiryn and Zinder rushed to the entryway. Was it good news or bad? With every step she swung back and forth between those two eternally distant poles. One moment she imagined herself running to the bedside of Joromar and seeing his eyes open for the first time, the terrible burden on her heart lifted at last. The next moment she plummeted to the depths, her whole body lifeless as stone, unfeeling, numb, lost in the dark as she watched Valissia kiss her son's forehead for the last time and pull the sheet over his unmoving face. But when Zinder opened the door, the swinging stopped. Her heart stopped too.

Havrick stepped out of the stormy courtyard and into the light. The anguish in his eyes plunged Tiryn's mind back into the darkness. Her worst fears were written on that forthright face.

"Spademaster Tellman is dead," Havrick said. His face scrunched up and his mouth wiggled in unusual ways as he did his best not to cry.

"Oh, dear," Tiryn said, drawing Havrick in and wrapping her arms around him. Though sadness drained her strength, sympathy for Havrick helped steady her emotions. It was awful that Tellman had died, but the young gardener of course felt it more keenly than she ever could.

"Such hard tidings," Nurien said from the dining hall where Tiryn had left the dagger. *"Life is so fragile and fleeting."*

"Well, stone kickers. That's a hard blow." Zinder placed a hand on the broad round back of the grieving boy and together they walked him into the dining room. Havrick sank into one of the high-backed chairs and they drew two more on either side. He was desperate to talk, telling them how Tellman had died quietly and how a peace settled upon his face, deeper than any that had ever graced it before.

"Just like the look on my old da's face when he passed. Like he'd worked as hard as he could and now was finally getting the rest he needed. What's the word? Satisfied, yes, satisfied, that's how he looked. He led a good long life, Tellman did. And though I only knew him the last few years of it, he often told me that these were his 'basket days.' That's what he called them. 'Life's like a basket,' he'd say, 'and every good day you fill it up and every bad day you take from it. The purpose is to fill it up, and I can say that these have been good days, Havrick, good days. Indeed, my basket's as full as it has ever been.' His wife had died, you see, and he left Dunskein with a heavy heart. But that tragedy brought him here, to serve under Lord Namril. Our dear lord will be sorry when he hears he's lost his chief gardener —if Lord Namril ever returns.

"But if he does, what will he do if his son dies as well? Oh, dear old Grundy can't be far behind Spademaster Tellman. Lord Namril's heart would give out on the spot if he came back to that. Sure as the sun rises in the morning. And then what? Why, Bramble Eyre would be no more. The Grundstaff line will have failed. I suppose Grish would stay if that happened, but not me. I couldn't bear it. I'd have to move on, like Spademaster Tellman did after his wife's passing. Too many hard memories for me here. In truth I almost left when Hostram died two years ago. I'd already lost Da and when Hostram went—he's my youngest brother, you see—when Hostram drowned I about couldn't take it.

"Dear old Grundy was with him that day. They were the best of friends back then, and I, to my shame, always frowned upon their adventures and even chided Hostram for not pulling his weight in the garden like the rest of us. After Da died, I was a good deal more serious than I am now. Thought I should step up as the man of the family because Da wasn't there and Grish was, well, Grish, and Hostram cared more about punting about on the lake or trekking in the woods than growing up and becoming a man. But all that changed when Hos died. I realized that Grundy was a capital sort and that life was more than just work.

"I daresay Grundy never forgave himself for what happened, though it wasn't his fault and he nearly drowned himself trying to save him. But he always said that he let Hos down that day. 'Didn't live up to my end of the bargain,' that's the way Grundy put it. You see, Hostram had saved Grundy's life the year before when the two of them were out in the western woods hunting briar boar. A lot of folk say there aren't any boar left in the woods, but Grundy and Hos loved to hunt for them anyway. Grundy got into a batch of wraithleaf that day and fell terribly ill. Hostram carried him all the way back to the castle—don't ask me how for even at fifteen, Grundy was a beast and Hostram was two years younger. Tellman gave him the antidote, though, and Grundy recovered. Grundy always felt that he owed Hostram his life and that he failed to repay him when the time came."

Havrick went on talking long into the night, as if words were breath and he would suffocate if he stopped speaking. If Tiryn had been in his place she would not have wanted to say a thing, but that was not Havrick's way. He unloaded his sorrows in words, and even though what he said was sad enough that Tiryn struggled to hold back her tears, his grief lifted with each new remembrance.

But beyond Tiryn's sorrow for Havrick and the double sorrow at the loss of Tellman, her mind was troubled by the story of Hostram's death on the lake. For it once more recalled to her the vision of the young man drowning. She could not help but feel that these things were in some way connected. But grief over Tellman's death and Havrick's need for companionship drove away such thoughts for now. There would be time enough to consider them later. Now was the hour of mourning. And as her thoughts drifted toward the great tower where a young lord held on to life by the barest of threads, she could not help but agree with Nurien that life was indeed so very fragile and fleeting.

Chapter 36

MORTAR AND PESTLE

Tiryn awoke with Rimewinter in hand. She usually slept beside it, but must have grasped it sometime during the night.

"The mortar and pestle."

"*Yes, from your vision,*" Nurien said, unsleeping and vigilant as always. "*What of it?*"

"I had thought it meant that perhaps I was supposed to try to save Joromar. But what if that wasn't it? What if it meant something else?"

"*That is possible. What are you thinking?*"

A cloud of conflicting thoughts whipped through Tiryn's mind. They were the fruit of midnight wrestlings with the death of Tellman and the mystery of this strange illness. Added to it, Havrick's story about the lake had implanted itself deep within her. All of this her mind had worked through even as she slept so that it came to her now in one great deluge of revelation.

"Remember that the mortar and pestle were black, made from onyx? What if they were meant to tell me the reason the young man died? What if he didn't die from drowning? What if he was killed by something created in that mortar and pestle? What if his death was *intended?*" That last word rippled across her skin and brought a chill even beneath her blanket.

"*I had not thought of that.*" Nurien's voice quickened as she caught up Tiryn's train of thought. "*That would explain why the remedies for the sprull did not work, nor the others we tried. If it wasn't a natural sickness, none of those cures would have worked. But we have no way of knowing this for certain."*

"What about the lips? Only the sprull causes the lips to turn green, but might there be something else that would cause that? Perhaps it was only made to look like the sprull."

"Yes, you are right. The lips might hold the key. If we can find some other sickness that causes that, we might find a remedy that would prove effective."

"You don't know what might cause it, then?" Tiryn said, realizing that she had placed a great many hopes on that being the case.

"No, but I know how we might discover the answers we seek."

"How is that?"

"We will search for them in the library."

Yes, of course. The library.

Tiryn launched herself out of bed and threw on her clothes with not a thought as to what they were or whether they matched or the state of her hair or any other of the usual concerns. She was off to snag Zinder and then march straight to the library. The answers they sought were closer than ever.

The library's enchantments were lost upon Tiryn during that second visit. Though marvelous treasures of paper and ink called to her from every side, she had to shut them out. Her ears could listen to one call only now. The one that would save Joromar's life.

Tiryn and Zinder leafed through tome after musty and forgotten tome in search of any sickness that would cause green lips the same way the sprull did.

They had sent for Rymir to escort them and he proved willing and helpful as always. While he did not assist in the reading, he searched and brought them book after promising book. Though they failed again and again to find what they needed, each false path led them closer and closer to their destination. For even in a library the size of the Eyre's, there were only so many books on herbs and medicines. They would find the right one eventually.

In the end, Tiryn found the book they were looking for at the bottom of a large stack in the corner. Her heart drummed like a troop setting off for battle the moment she saw the entry she'd been looking for. *A Perilous Harvest*, the book was called, and its thick binding was covered in frayed lilac cloth. The golden lettering for the title had mostly flaked off, but the imprint remained.

It was a treatise on the most harmful plants known to grow in the Four Wards. Tiryn had never known there were so many plants in the woods and fields and mountains that could kill someone or make them seriously ill. Flipping through the pages was the work of long, anxious searching, for the herbs were listed alphabetically and it was not until she came to the letter "W" that she found what she sought.

Wraithleaf — A plant with serrated leaves of deepest green. The leaves are small and easily missed as they grow along vines generally among other bushes or undergrowth. Warning: poisonous (this was written in striking green ink that had not faded as much as the rest of the text). *Highly dangerous when exposed to the skin, but especially when ingested. May induce false sleep from which a person will not awake unless the remedy (see below) is applied shortly after the poisoning sets in. Effects include fever, aches, and a color similar to that of the leaf itself manifesting in the lips, especially prominent among those of a weak constitution, with the color growing more pronounced as the poison sets in.*

Below that was a list of herbs used to counter wraithleaf poison, most of them common save something called marrowcap which Tiryn had never heard of. Tiryn let out a great exclamation as she read it, not caring that she was in a library. Neither did Zinder or Rymir, who perceived at once what the cry meant.

"So it was poison all along," Zinder said, scanning the entry.

"But who would want to poison Lord Joromar?" Rymir said. "Everyone in Bramble Eyre loves him."

"And Tellman as well," Tiryn said. "Who would poison him?"

"The same person who poisoned Joromar, or I'm taller than a haukmar," Zinder said.

Could it be possible? Tiryn, who had always assumed the best of everyone, found it hard to fathom. What could possibly drive a person to do something so heinous? To murder not one, but two people? But that would come out later—if it came out at all. First they had to make this remedy and see if it worked. There was still a chance that it wasn't wraithleaf poisoning. But the greater fear was that they were too late. For the entry had said the remedy needed to be applied "shortly after" contact with the wraithleaf and Joromar had taken ill three days ago.

"Nothing matters now except getting this to Lord Joromar," Tiryn said. "I'm only worried about this marrowcap. I've never heard of it, have you, Zinder?"

"Can't say that I have."

"Neither have I, but Havrick might know," Rymir said.

"*It is not known to me either,*" Nurien said.

"Right, let's go find him and see what he says," Tiryn said. She hastily scribbled down the list of ingredients in the little notebook she carried in her satchel and they raced out of the library.

At the gate of the castle, Rymir said, "After we retrieve Havrick, I'll accompany you to the storeroom. Then I'll have to send for Mariday to escort you up the tower. Faedred is expecting me to bring Zinder to meet him in the quarry."

"Oh, bother," Zinder said, tugging on the brim of his hat, a white, four-cornered affair with dueling ink-blue feathers on either side. "I forgot about that. I'd prefer to see the young lord recover, but I suppose I need to see about this quarry business. I still haven't gotten to see him, you know, and I'm rather anxious to find out what all the fuss is about. But no matter. I know my place. And besides, Tiryn, you and Nurien have done all the work here."

"Not quite. Your encouragement and high spirits have meant more than you know. But there will be plenty of time to meet Lord Joromar once he's recovered."

"Pardon me, but this is the second time you've mentioned Nurien," Rymir said. "Do either of you care to explain to me who this person is?"

Tiryn's and Zinder's eyes met. They had agreed to keep the true nature of the glaives a secret, but Rymir was as trustworthy as they came and they'd spent enough time around him the last two days that it might be easier just to let him know and not have to be so careful.

"Well, it's an unusual story," Tiryn said at last. "I'll tell you along the way."

Rymir took the news about the glaives as well as could be expected. He admitted that he did not fully understand, but he did not openly question it. In truth, there was no time for questions. By the time Tiryn finished, they'd huffed their way down to the lower courtyard and collected Havrick.

Havrick was both thrilled and disturbed by the news that they had a cure, and that Joromar may have been poisoned.

"Wraithleaf! Of course! It's just like before. How could I have missed it? His lips look exactly the same. I just never thought..." His eyes darkened and he mumbled to himself, "Oh no, how could you?" The color drained from his face and he stood in the midst of the rows of cabbage looking this way and that, as though he no longer knew where he was.

"What's wrong?" Rymir said. "Are you all right?"

The words snapped Havrick out of whatever fit had come over him. He passed his hand over his face and took in a long breath before letting it back out in a blustery sigh.

"It's nothing. I'm sure we can find marrowcap among Tellman's stores. Let's go see about making that cure for Grundy," he said.

"Fair enough," Zinder said and they took off back toward the keep, but as they pounded their way across the courtyard, he added, "Care to tell us what's troubling you?"

Havrick winced, his generous cheeks piling up into two great mounds. "I—I'll tell you after we've given the cure to Grundy."

Tiryn's excitement about finding the cure went up in smoke at Havrick's startling reaction. It was not like him to hold something back. But she laid aside her concerns for now. Joromar's life still hung by a thread. They had to get to the storehouse as soon as possible.

They reached the keep, half-running and out of breath. Rymir took them down to the storage rooms and went to fetch Mariday. Zinder left with him, both sharing their confidence that this time the cure would finally take.

Havrick had recovered his senses by the time they reached the storeroom and they had little difficulty in finding the ingredients for the remedy, even the marrowcap, which was a long, tall, dingy-white mushroom that Tellman kept in a clay pot. They raced at once over to the Mixing Room to concoct the antidote. Though Tiryn had used the mortar and pestle there to prepare the other remedies, the implements now took on an ominous aspect. Had the poisoner used these same tools to prepare the wraithleaf for Joromar and Tellman?

Mariday came rushing up, heaving and winded from having hastily hauled her aged frame down into the lower reaches of the keep. "Is it true?…Have you truly…have you found…the cure?"

"We hope so," Tiryn said, holding up a jar with the malodorous concoction the book had called for. It stank of rotten melons festering in the sun. But all that mattered was that it worked.

"Come now, then." Mariday pushed them out into the hall and hurried toward the stairs despite still being out of breath. "So, what do you think…the poor boy is…suffering from?" Mariday was taking the stairs two at a time, along with Tiryn and Havrick. How she managed to get any words out was a wonder, for Tiryn was breathless herself, and she had not been running as much as the elderly maid.

Havrick, who was more used to stairs, answered. "Tiryn thinks Grundy may have been poisoned." His voice was flat, completely devoid of emotion. Nothing at all like his usual sincere manner.

"I would like to know why he is taking this news so strangely. There is more to it than his love for Joromar," Nurien said.

Mariday tottered and nearly fell. "Poisoned, you say?" She clenched her mouth shut and righted herself, adding in a whisper, "But who…who could have…done such a thing?"

Havrick was behind Tiryn on the stairs, so she could not see his expression, but she could hear the deep anguish in his voice. "I…I…I think it might have been…" But he could not bring himself to say whatever he was thinking.

Mariday stopped dead in her tracks at the top of the third flight of stairs. After taking several moments to catch her breath, she said, "It was Grish, wasn't it? He's the only one in the castle who never took to our dear Grundy."

Havrick took off his hat and wrung it for all it was worth—which was not much at this point. "Oh, Mariday, I didn't want to tell anyone, but after Tellman died, Ruwena told me she overheard Grish and the Spademaster arguing in the shed the night before Grundy took ill. He came seeking some recipe, a remedy, she thought, though she never heard which one. But Tellman had quarreled one too many times with Grish and was in no mood to reconcile. He sent him away empty-handed. Grish cursed him something awful and stormed out, yelling at Tellman that he would regret his decision. She thought it was just another one of his idle threats, but after Tellman died, she said the words kept coming back to her so that she had to tell me. Like her, I thought it was probably just Grish's anger talking. He never cared for Grundy, it's true, but he had no cause to kill him."

At last, Havrick's odd behavior made sense. The news that Joromar might have been poisoned cast undeniable doubt on Grish's actions. His heart was torn between the love of his brother and the love of his friend.

"Oh, Havrick, I'm so sorry about all of this." Tiryn laid a soothing hand on his shoulder. "You're right in the middle of all this with your master, your brother, and your friend. But we don't know for sure that Grish did this. Did you talk to him about what Ruwena said?"

"No. I went to find him first thing this morning, but he wasn't in his room. The guard for the servant's quarters said he never came back last night. I fear he may have run away after Tellman died, knowing that he would be suspected. But either way, I can't bring myself to think he'd ever do something so vile. Grish had his rough edges, but he was my brother, after all."

"Oh, my dearest Hav," Mariday said, hugging him with all the strength her stubby arms could muster.

"It's all right, Mariday," Havrick said. "What matters most is that we save Grundy. The rest will sort itself out, I hope."

"Grish may have done this terrible deed, but the reasons remain hidden. Perhaps we can have Kion and Kithian question him," Nurien said.

Gathering up their strength—Havrick most of all—they mounted the stairs once more and labored up the remaining flights. Tiryn's legs wobbled with fatigue by the time they reached the top, but there was no time to recover. She leaned on Havrick as they entered the room. There they found Valissia, dressed in another dark but elegant dress. Livia attended her, standing in her lady's shadow. Beside Valissia, dark and close as a second shadow, stood someone Tiryn did not expect to see:

Faedred, marshal of Bramble Eyre. He wore the coal-black attire of mourning, just as Lady Valissia. In the cold, thin light of the chamber Tiryn suddenly had the terrible fear that they had come too late, that Lord Joromar was already dead.

"Greetings, Tiryn," Lady Valissia said. The defeat Tiryn had anticipated was absent from her voice. There was still time. "Faedred tells me you may have found the cure."

The perplexed look on Tiryn's face drew forth an explanation from Faedred. "Rymir told me. He said that you believe it is wraithleaf that has stricken Lord Joromar. I left Logren and Kion to meet your nynnian friend and came at once. I wanted to be here in case he awoke."

"If you can save him I will give you whatever you ask," Valissia said.

"I just want him to live. That is all the payment I need," Tiryn said. She withdrew from Valissia and Faedred and went to Joromar's bed. The young lord lay unmoving there, his once robust red hair lusterless and brittle-looking, his face shrunken and corpse-like. She placed her hand near his mouth and nose and could not even feel him breathing. Touching his wrist, she felt the barest traces of life flowing within his veins. She had to hurry.

She took the rotten-smelling, ash-green paste, and rubbed it into his neck. Joromar's skin was coarse as sand, but the remedy brought moisture and suppleness back wherever it touched. When Tiryn had used every last bit of it, she rose from the bed. Between her spent legs and the heaviness of so many eyes upon her, it was a wonder she had the strength to stand. Valissia and Faedred drew alongside her. Havrick and the maids remained at a short distance, but strained to see any signs of change in the poor, beleaguered young lord.

"The book where I found the cure said that we would know within a few minutes whether or not it worked or...or whether he is too far gone," Tiryn said. The whole room stood as if on the head of a pin. They scarcely dared to breathe. Never had hope and fear waged such a battle in Tiryn's heart. Back and forth the two enemies fought for long voiceless ages with no clear sign of which would emerge victorious. But as time wore on, the silence became a roar, and that roar was the sound of the triumph of her fears. No change came, though the six people in the room waited for nearly an hour.

The bright hope Tiryn had carried with her when she entered dwindled and died. The faces of those around her grew more and more grave. Only in Valissia's eyes did the light of hope still shine, but even there it flickered. Somehow, Faedred took the failure of the cure the hardest. He stared off toward the curtained window like a man condemned, as though it were not Joromar who was dying, but he himself. Joromar was his lord's son, so surely Faedred cared for him for that reason, but Tiryn wondered why he of all those gathered should appear the most stricken by this latest failure to save the young lord's life. Even Havrick, who had double cause for distress over all that had happened, endured the withering moments with more fortitude.

Tiryn latched on to the driftwood dagger that hung from her necklace, searching for some last shred of hope. She found only one, and it wasn't much hope at all. That she must have been wrong about the poison. Or at least that it had not been wraith-leaf. But the green lips and the other symptoms made it seem all but certain.

Either way, she still had no answers for the devastated faces around her. And her ignorance was leading to the death of Joromar Grundstaff.

Chapter 37

THE BROKEN WELNOD

Two mismatched figures descended the rough stone ramp into the quarry. The taller one held aloft a swaying lantern, which bathed the nearby rock in a shifting bloom of coppery light. The particulars of the figures remained lost in the glare, but Kion could tell by the lightness in his step that the shorter one was Zinder. There was also the fact that Kion and Logren had been waiting for him down here in the heart of the cavern for some time.

The cavern was roughly as wide as the keep under which it sat, though not as long and only two stories deep. Every side of the rectangular chamber was fronted in chiseled rock, scored and scarred by centuries of labor. Workers wove their way amongst a dozen or so rough hewn pillars, round as millstones. Their endeavors were aided by the light of the lanterns which hung from massive chains and crisscrossed the quarry like fireflies caught in a spider's web. Most of the men hauled rock into one of several carts. A few worked away with pounding hammers and humming saws to fashion some of the free-standing stones into more manageable sizes. A thin, slightly bent man with dust-filled hair directed their efforts. Logren had pointed him out to Kion as the quarrymaster, Ravius Trimble, though Kion had yet to formally meet him.

"A castle is a living thing," Logren had said when they descended the ramp earlier. "It is not built once and then left to stand through the centuries against wind and rain, frost and sun, moss and vines, birds and insects. Its very existence is an affront to nature. Even when not under assault from enemies, it is under assault every day from the weathering effects of time and all its allies, who strive to pull down the great works which man has built. Nature is time's battering ram, a far greater foe than any that will ever come against our walls. And so a castle is constantly in the process of being repaired and rebuilt. But for the efforts of the quarrymen and the Grundstaff family down through the years, Bramble Eyre would have fallen into a crumbling ruin long ago."

Logren had the air of an instructor about him, at least when Faedred was not present, for then he deferred to the marshal. In the short time Kion had known the two men, he had learned that they complemented each other remarkably well. Faedred was decisive, confident, and devoted above all else to the protection of Bramble Eyre. He worked with an intensity and a discipline in all that he did. And he demanded that same intensity and discipline from his men. But they seemed to love him all the more because of this and not in spite of it. If he asked something of them, they invariably went beyond it and did even more. But Logren's words of caution and counsel helped temper the marshal's unrelenting nature, for even the best of men could not do all, nor was he always right. And Faedred, to his credit, was willing to listen to and, more often than not, heed the older man's advice. Faedred always acted in such a way that two things were clear: that he thought of his men not so much as soldiers under his command, but as brothers it was his duty to protect. And because of that duty, authority came naturally to him. He did not so much command his men as ask them to fulfill the duties to which they had already pledged themselves. And he never asked from them anything in such a way but that it was meant for their benefit or the benefit of the Eyre.

The lack of soldiers from the fane or the margrave had caused Faedred to push for improvements in the defenses of the undermanned castle. Lord Namril had long put off the much needed repairs after a series of lean harvests and the closing of the mill at Glenwither, upon which much of the Grundstaff fortune rested. With war looming and Lord Namril no longer present, Faedred had pleaded with Valissia to grant him the funds to make repairs to the most vulnerable parts of the castle, but that request had only recently been granted and so the work had only just begun.

"Welcome, Master Hamryn," Logren said as they met Rymir and Zinder at the base of the ramp. Dust and fine gravel coated the surface, as it did everything else in the quarry.

"At your service." Zinder doffed his white cap. Kion had never seen that particular one before, but that was only mildly surprising as Zinder seemed to produce them almost out of thin air.

"It's good to see you again, my friend. It feels like I've been gone a month," Kion said.

"Oh, really? I barely noticed." That tell-tale mischief glinted in Zinder's eyes.

"And I thought nyn were supposed to have such keen senses."

"One thing I can see is that your fashion prospects have improved since I last saw you. Is that genuine bear fur on your tabard?"

"Indeed it is. It looks like I'll be serving in the forces of Bramble Eyre for a time," Kion said. The yellow tabard he wore not only had a rim of fur around the collar, but a large design in the shape of a bear claw stitched upon the chest inside a circular field of forest green. He hadn't gotten used to this new tabard either. It felt more like something that should be worn for ceremonies than battles. "But tell me, how is Tiryn and, more importantly, how fares Lord Joromar?"

"Tiryn's doing well, under the circumstances. She has someone to look after and she's been more than up for the challenge. She thinks she may have finally found the cure."

"Let us hope so," Logren said, dropping his usual somber air. "I fear for Lady Valissia should he not recover. Lord Joromar is far too young to die." After a moment's pause, he stiffened and the soldier in him returned. "Now, to our concerns within the quarry. As you can see, the men are busy cutting and loading the stone that we have already extracted, but we need to cut several large blocks for a section of the western wall in need of repair. However, we are not able to cut stone from the quarry fast enough. At our present rate, we will run out of stone within an eight-mark and it will take us months to finish the repairs."

"I see. Rymir mentioned something about some of your tools being in need of repair?"

"Yes. It's our welnod. It has ceased to function and we do not have the skill to repair it."

"Ah! A delving fork, you say? Well now, you're in a fine fettle, then, aren't you? Hard to do any serious quarrying without that. Where is the little clinker? I'll have a look."

"The quarrymaster has it," Logren said. He led them through the dust clouds into the heart of the racket at the center of the quarry. Summoning Ravius over with a gesture, Logren introduced them and asked to see the welnod. Ravius lumbered off behind a pile of stone, soon returning with a thin box of blackened metal.

"It lasted longer than most. This one's more than ten years old," Ravius said.

"It must be of exceptional quality," Zinder said, taking the box. Opening it revealed a two-pronged fork with rounded tines as long as the handle. The whole thing was about the length of Kion's forearm. Its silvery metal glistened with oil even in the spotty cavern light. Zinder let out a low whistle. "She's a beauty all right. I've never seen one finer."

"You think you can fix her?" Ravius said, staring hard at Zinder.

"I'll do my best. I've never built one myself, truth be told, but I can repair anything given enough time and I've always wanted to try my hand at making one of these. Give me two or three days and I should have her working again."

"We'd be more than grateful."

"Indeed," Logren said. "You will be well compensated."

Zinder, who was a natural born businessman, nodded with satisfaction. Their funds were not exactly running low, but one never knew what needs might come up and there was always the expense of new hats to consider.

Logren left them after they departed the quarry, and Rymir and Kion headed back to the barracks for they had missed the midday meal. Zinder was of course more than willing to accept their invitation to join them.

"It is near the smithy, after all," Zinder said, making a pretext. He no doubt could have taken his meal alone at the guesthouse (and knowing him, he might just eat there as well once he'd finished at the barracks), but Kion was glad of his company. The soldiers of Bramble Eyre had welcomed him for the most part after he'd proven himself against Faedred, but nothing could replace time with his old friend.

"I will take you to the smithy once we're finished," Rymir said. "I believe Marshal Faedred wanted to meet with you, Beranskyre, after his return."

"Oh, yes, it's Beranskyre, now, isn't it?" Zinder said. "Yes, well, I forgot to congratulate you. First Sword of the North, now Beranskyre. I wonder how many titles you'll have by the time this war is over?"

"I'm not sure if I deserve the ones I have."

"I heard your duel with the marshal was quite impressive. He gave you all that he had and yet you bested him three-nil. No one's ever done that," Rymir said.

"Well, Kion has the superior sparring partner," Zinder said. He was only a passable swordsman, but he was the only sparring partner Kion had ever known.

"That and I had the superior blade," Kion said.

"I say you would have beaten him in any case. You have more skill than you know," Kithian said. Though Kion appreciated his glaive's praise, he did not fully agree. A glaive brought out the best in its wielder and Kion had never fought so well with an ordinary sword.

"All the titles and honors in the world are nothing if we don't win this war. We're almost to the second month of summer and still the fane has sent no relief," Kion said.

They made their way out of the castle and down the steep road to the lower courtyard where the barracks and lunch awaited.

During the meal, Zinder ate not only two helpings of potatoes, peas, bread, and soup, he devoured Rymir's descriptions of the castle defenses and its history. Kion listened with the same eagerness, even to things Rymir had told him before, for it was all still so very new to him. Kion had been shown all over the walls, towers, and keep during his first day under the marshal's command. From the ancient armories, to the tower-mounted bolt throwers and barrels of arrows on the outer walls, to the murder holes and trapdoors to attack invaders once they penetrated inside, to the dwindling storehouses of food and the hidden underground spring which would supply them during a siege, Kion had seen all that comprised Bramble Eyre's defenses and made it one of the most renowned of all the strongholds of Inris. It had stood for nearly five centuries and had never known defeat. The bridge to the shore even had hidden mechanisms which could be triggered from the gatehouses to cause it to collapse, cutting off access from the mainland.

To a plain shepherd boy it had been like walking into another world. A world of craft and skill and endless amounts of labor and riches all expended for a singular purpose: to keep the people within its walls safe, and the lands of Inris at peace. So many had labored here through the years with that dream in mind. It made Kion all the more committed to defending it, not only for the people who now dwelt within, but for all those who had come before and kept it standing.

The three of them could have sat all afternoon at the table discussing tactics and the art of castle warfare. For though war is an ugly thing, the craft of war and the ingenuity it demands is not.

"Though the beranskyre has learned much in his short time with us, he has taught us many new and surprising things as well," Rymir said. "I'm told you met with the marshal, the flag-master, and the tormains to discuss your encounters with Vayd both in Charring and on Tinesplitter Isle. You also told them of your encounter with the shaydvorn in the woods. That troubles me even more than the haukmar threat. For if it had not been for your enchanted weapons, he said that you would not have survived. What will we do if such creatures attack our scouts who daily roam these woods?"

"Ah, so you told the leaders here about the glaives, did you?" Zinder said. "Well, Tiryn and I had a talk with Rymir about them as well. He knows what it means to be a swordspeaker."

Though the news surprised Kion, he was glad to hear it. Like Zinder and Tiryn, Kion had come to trust Rymir as much as anyone during their time in the castle. He held only Faedred in higher esteem. The quality of Rymir's character was shown in a quieter way, but Kion was grateful to have found two such warriors amongst those defending Inris. Though no one could rise to the view he had of Strom Glyre, he saw a little of the bladewarden in both of them.

"I didn't tell Faedred and the others about their voices yet," Kion said. "I didn't think they would understand. But I plan on showing him the other glaives and I was thinking of telling him about the full truth then. Kithian and I discussed it and we decided it would be best if he knew."

"Kithian is the name of your sword, then?" Rymir said.

"Yes. Perhaps I can show you the other glaives as well sometime."

"I should like that very much," Rymir said, his eyes sparking keenly.

Toward the end of the meal their talk turned, albeit unwillingly, to a different subject. For one of the cooks who brought Zinder his second helping informed them that Faedred had returned from his visit to Lord Joromar's chambers and that word had quickly spread through the barracks that the latest cure had failed. It was widely expected that the young lord would not last through the night.

Zinder and Rymir then spoke of Tiryn's various attempts to cure the stricken lord. They told of Tellman's death and their visit to the library that morning. In hushed tones they also mentioned Tiryn's suspicion that the poor boy may have been poisoned, though they had no idea who might have done such a thing or why.

"I hope we get answers soon," Kion said.

"And that Joromar recovers," Rymir said.

"I've got my hopes pinned on Tiryn and Nurien. If anyone can save him, it's those two," Zinder said.

They finished their meal in a much more somber mood than how it began and rose to wish each other well. Zinder went off with Rymir to the smithy and Kion went up the third floor of the barracks where Faedred had his chambers.

He spoke with the marshal for a time of Joromar's health. Kion almost did not recognize the marshal as he spoke. His countenance could not have been more grave had Bramble Eyre itself been overrun. Seeing how troubled the subject made him, Kion soon shifted to talk of the glaives and their true nature, and of the ways of the swordspeaker. He told him the names of the two weapons, and also the names and what he knew of the unawakened glaives they had brought with them from Tinesplitter Isle. Faedred's aspect changed as Kion unfolded the legend of the glaives and the marshal listened without comment for several long minutes until the very weapons Kion spoke of were brought in and laid out upon a large table.

"Would you permit me to touch them?" Faedred said. As light from the courtyard poured into Faedred's chambers from the three large windows on the western wall, the marshal removed his black leather gloves with great caution, but then hesitated, as if Kion were the leader and he the soldier under his command.

"Of course," Kion said.

"He believes that touching one of them might awaken it and impart to him the gift of swordspeaking, but that is not the way. The call must first be given before one can respond to it," Kithian said. The remark took Kion by surprise, for Kithian had informed him that the marshal was usually hard to read. Kion would have conveyed these things to the marshal, but Faedred spoke first.

"This one is Gorven, I believe you said? By the Warding Wall it's so heavy I don't see how anyone but a haukmar could use it in battle." The marshal hefted the hammer. Rotted and pitted as it was, it had lost whatever detail or signs of craftsmanship it once had. Yet, Faedred cradled it as though it were an object from the fane's own treasury.

"The weapons lose their weight in the hands of a sword-speaker," Kion said. "To wield one is to feel as if you were born to it, as if the shackles of this world had been lifted and you held in your hands something from beyond the Boundless Depths." Looking at the way the marshal held the weapon, he thought the same thing he did when looking at Rymir. Faedred would make a worthy swordspeaker indeed.

Faedred set the warhammer down with great care.

"And do you know what powers it possesses?"

"Well, Gorven's other name is Mountainfall. And from that name you might guess that the gift of this weapon is—"

But Kion's explanation was cut short by an urgent rapping on the thick door to Faedred's chambers.

A hurried, and yet hopeful voice sounded from the hall. "Marshal, permission to enter. It's the healer, my lord. She has a message for you. She says it is quite urgent."

From the concern on Faedred's face, it was clear he meant to order Tiryn in, but he was not given the chance. Tiryn burst in as soon as the soldier finished. She came to an abrupt halt, flushed and scarcely able to draw breath, her auburn braids well on their way to unraveling.

"I know...I know the way to...to save Joromar," she said. "This time...I won't fail..."

Chapter 38

THORNS AND THISTLES

Tiryn rushed to the table and locked her eyes onto the battered morningstar. "There it is…Kion, take Grimbriar…We must hurry."

Kion picked up the unwieldy weapon with both hands. The oversized head felt like it was made of lead. "Why? What does this have to do with Joromar?"

"I can't…I'm too…out of…breath…just…come." Tiryn barely managed to huff out the words while pulling Kion toward the door.

"Tiryn, are you certain you have not come down with something yourself?" Faedred said.

Tiryn was clearly not acting herself. So much so that even the marshal grew alarmed.

"It is all right, Tiryn. I will explain it to Kion since you are still winded from your flight," Nurien said. *"Remember how Tiryn placed Truesilver in your hand when you had nearly frozen to death? We believe that may be our last chance to save Joromar."*

Kion glanced at Faedred, whose concern only deepened at the unnatural silence as Kion listened to Nurien's words.

"Forgive me, Marshal, Tiryn's dagger has shared what they are planning. For some reason they think Lord Joromar may be a swordspeaker, and that if he can touch this glaive it may save his life."

"We are not certain. But Tiryn had a vision and based upon that, we believe Barazain might be the weapon he has been called to. But

have the others sent as well. We will try all of them if we have to. This is Joromar's last chance."

"I can see it in your eyes. You were speaking with one of the glaives just now, though I cannot tell whether it was your sword or Tiryn's dagger," Faedred said.

"Yes, they want us to bring not just the morningstar, but all of the glaives."

"Very well, we will go together." Though the marshal grasped the nature of Tiryn's request even less than Kion, he fell naturally into his air of command. "Gallant, have a cart readied in the stable and find men to carry the rest of these weapons down. Have them brought to Lord Joromar's room. And make haste."

"Zinder is already preparing a cart. We met him in the guesthouse. We went there first to seek the glaives, not knowing you had taken them here," Nurien said. *"It took us some time before we found out where they had gone."*

Kion told Faedred about the cart as they bounded with Tiryn into the hallway, down the stairway, through the main hall, and out into the courtyard. The stables were right next to the barracks, and Zinder and some gallants already had the horses harnessed and waiting.

"Good, she found you!" Zinder said, waving them into the cart and handing the reins to Faedred. "It's a mad idea, isn't it?" His chest was heaving and he was nearly as spent as Tiryn, but his eyes burned with hope. "So mad it just might work!"

As soon as the other soldiers brought the rest of the glaives they jumped into the cart and off they went.

Kion rode beside Faedred, and Tiryn and Zinder rode with the gallants in the back. Not since his wild trip with Zinder on the road to Charring had Kion gone through such a whirlwind of reckless peril. But this ride surpassed even that one in its thunderous roar and breakneck pace. At times, it felt as though the horses had taken flight and at times the cart actually did, bouncing over the pavement like a stone skipping across a lake. Kion clutched his seat, fearing he might be thrown onto the road at any moment. They charged up the hill to the keep as though it were flat. Faedred showed no fear, even when they barreled around the bend with no more than two wheels touching the ground.

Yet for all the danger and thrill, the ride ended almost as soon as it began. They gathered the weapons and launched themselves at full tilt into the keep.

"What about Tiryn's vision made you believe that Joromar might be a swordspeaker?" Kithian said as tapestries, windows, and doors flew by. Everywhere they went they caused a stir among the servants and guards, who had no idea what the marshal and those following him were about.

"She saw a young man dying. He had lips the same color as Joromar, though he looked like one of the stable boys we found in Dunach. Beneath his bed was a black mortar and pestle with uncrushed thorns inside. At first we thought only that it meant that Joromar had been poisoned. But in visions one thing may have many meanings. After the cure for the poison failed to revive him we nearly lost all hope. But the remedy may have staved off his death for a little longer and that is when Tiryn recalled the thorns in the mortar."

"They were thornbristles?" Kithian said, a knowing tone in his voice.

"Yes, I failed to ask Tiryn about them before, but when the cure failed, we thought we might have missed something and so I asked her to describe the thorns more closely. When she did, I knew it must mean that Grimbriar had something to do with all of this, for thornbristles are his reagent."

They arrived spent and gasping at the base of the main tower. They were forced to take a short rest before mounting the steps. Kion had difficulty keeping pace with Faedred, and Tiryn and Zinder, who were exhausted after so many trips up and down the stairs, faded behind the both of them.

"Go on without us," Nurien said from half a flight below. *"The*

important thing is to reach Joromar in time. His life wavers in its last feeble throes. Every moment is dear."

Kion pushed through the white heat blazing in his chest and staggered into the room at the top of the stairs just behind Faedred and the other gallants. A woman in the dark dress of mourning with a hooded cowl, her beauty unsullied by the many tears upon her cheeks, sat beside an ornate bed. Several servants huddled beside her, but Kion paid them no heed. He forced his legs to carry him to the bedside where a tall, broad figure lay lifeless beneath a finely woven blanket.

"It's too late." The words came involuntarily from his lips. He knew what death looked like. Joromar's lips were the dark green of bronzewood leaves. His skin was the corpse shade between gray and white.

The woman, who was surely Lady Valissia, said nothing, only bowed her head to hide another wave of tears. The servants did not have the heart to look up.

"No, you still have to try," Faedred said, forceful and defiant, like a soldier surrounded who meant to die fighting.

"Do not esteem lightly the power of the glaivebonding. By all appearances, you yourself were dead in Whitewind," Kithian said.

They were right, of course. It would do no harm to place the weapon in Joromar's hands, beyond perhaps the raising and dashing of false hopes.

"Forgive me, my lady." Kion brushed past her and pulled back the blanket. There was no point in waiting any longer or offering any further greeting. He could deal with the formalities once it was all over.

Kion turned over Joromar's shovel-sized palm. Joromar's arm, pale and wasted as it was, far surpassed the thickness of his own. The poor young man would have made a fine warrior. Kion was sad that he would not live to fight for the Four Wards and that Kion would never get to meet the person behind the kind, generous face. With a defeated sigh, he placed the gutted handle of the great morningstar known as Grimbriar in Joromar's hand.

The handle sat there for the space of one breath…two…three —if anyone had actually dared to breathe. But in the end they were forced to. For nothing happened. The morningstar remained in its decayed state, and Joromar's body would soon do the same.

At that moment, Tiryn and Zinder at last stumbled into the room. Zinder clutched at his side, but Tiryn was worse off still. She had no strength left and fell into one of the gallants' arms.

"Did it…?" she said. "Oh, no…we didn't…come…in—"

She did not finish. At that moment, the window to the room burst open, the thick curtains shaking in an invisible wind. A great golden light lanced through the opening, bending to strike Joromar full in the chest. The beam scattered into a thousand needles of light. They swirled over his motionless frame before sweeping over the astonished figures gathered around him in rivers of shimmering motes. Joromar's skin turned brass wherever the pinpricks of light touched it and the metallic sheen spread in a burning consummation. In a flash he went from a weak, lifeless form into a shining statue first of bronze, then gold, then platinum, then a blazing white too intense to see.

A harrowing energy pulsed through Kion. It set his whole being thrumming with a feeling of freedom, like what the first flowers must feel upon the awakening of spring. It was something akin to the inner blaze of riding Cornoc, only deeper and more enduring, as though whatever wild promise now whirled about the room was no mere passing thing but was meant to stay. And Kion knew at once that Joromar not only had come back to life, but that his life would be forever changed. He may have been the lord of an ancient and storied castle before this day, but as the light faded and the curtains fluttered back into place upon the windows, Joromar Grundstaff had become something greater still. He had become a swordspeaker.

Chapter 39

GRIMBRIAR

The brilliant light withdrew from Joromar's room as swiftly as it came. Only the faint and inexplicable smell of upturned soil gave any indication that something unusual had happened. The rancid stench of pungent herbs and feverish bedclothes which had permeated the air moments before—and which gave the strong sense that death lay very close—had vanished completely.

But two other changes in the room were far greater than the strange lingering scent. One of them was the sight of Joromar, sitting up on his bed, his fiery hair glistening, his skin flushed and ruddy, and his eyes two flashes of wonder and disbelief. His arms were wrapped around his mother, her hood cast back and her jet-black hair flowing over her shoulders like a dark river singing in welcome of the dawn.

"What happened to me?" Joromar said. His voice had a rattle to it from having not spoken in so long. He cleared his throat with a great blast of air, as though expelling the last traces of sickness and sleep which remained. "How long have I been here?"

"Three days. Three terrible and interminable days. Oh, Joromar, I thought I had lost you." Valissia renewed her embrace with even greater intensity.

"We thought your boat was sunk for sure," Havrick said, for once giving his poor hat a rest from his wrenchings. The whole room erupted with effusions of relief and everyone spoke at once. So great was their excitement that they failed at first to mark the second great change in the room and that was the appearance of the weapon that had been placed in Joromar's hand.

But another voice spoke amidst this chorus of joy, a voice which eclipsed all others in Kion's and Tiryn's ears and caused them to take notice of the marvelous transformation in the once battered and rusted morningstar.

"You have wandered upon the shores of death, glaivebond. So long did you resist my call that I began to lose patience. For I am not the patient sort like my friends Kithian and Nurien, who I am pleased to see are here as well. All the same, it is good to finally hear your voice, and to have found my own again. From those around you I learn that your name is Joromar and that you are well-loved by those who know you. I fear you will find that the same cannot be said of me. For I am too forthright to garner such esteem. But what I lack in fair words I make up for in steadfastness. You shall find none more loyal among the Mastersmith's servants than myself, for I am Barazain of the Thorns, though in the wider world I am also known as Grimbriar."

The voice was indeed grim like its namesake, yet also thick and resonant. It was not unkind for all its gruffness, only lacking the polish and care to make its kindness more apparent.

"Well met, old friend," Kithian said, his voice full of familial affection.

"Indeed. You have awakened just in time. We have much to speak of," Nurien said. She, too, spoke with gladness in her voice, but tempered by the old sorrow which never left her for long. *"But that can wait until your new glaivebond has come to reckon with what has happened."*

"Yes, it can wait, though I already have some notion of how things must be if you and I have returned," Barazain said. The same sorrow in Nurien belonged to Barazain as well, for he had agreed to follow her to Tinesplitter Isle where both their glaive-bonds had perished.

Joromar had laid Grimbriar aside when his mother came, but upon hearing the glaive's words he took hold of it once more. It was clear from the way he regarded it that he could tell the voice came from the weapon, but it was equally clear that his mind struggled to find some other possible explanation. As those around him noted his foggy expression and the way he stared at Grimbriar, the fervent talk around him died away and all eyes were drawn to the transformed weapon.

The spiked ball which crowned the leather-bound handle glistened as though it lay beneath some secret light. The metal spikes and head possessed a subtle, almost wooden hue. If not for their gleam and supreme smoothness, they might have appeared to have been made from oak, but as it was, they were more of a sepia-tinted brass. A finely cut emerald rested on the handle beneath the head. Like everything else about the weapon it was immense and would have bought half the land in Furrow had it been sold. It caught the light and pooled it into iridescent points the way the sun's rays ignite the folded edges of briny waves. The setting for the gem was an intricately fashioned circlet of thorns. The leather of the handle also evoked the suggestion of wood, only this time of a yellowy shade, like sandalwood or freshly cut pine. Another emerald, even larger than the first, topped the end of the handle, giving off subtle scintillations of its own.

Joromar turned the morningstar around in his hands. His own hazel-green eyes turned an even deeper shade of green as he marveled at the weapon he now held.

"Mother, did you hear those voices?" he said.

Valissia's eyes drew into sharp focus, waking from her blissful dream. "What voices, my son?"

"Grimbriar, one of them said his name was. And there were two others that answered him. Did you hear them? I see three people who are strangers to me, but the voices did not come from any of them."

Valissia's brow creased and she gazed about the room. "Grimbriar? There is no one here by that name. It could be the lingering effects of your fever. You were burning up."

Kion bowed his head by way of deference to the lady and her son. "If I may have permission to speak, my lady?" he said.

"You may speak freely. You are among friends." Valissia moved to the side, allowing Kion to address her son more easily, though the concern on her face failed to lessen.

"Greetings, Joromar. My name is Kion Bray. My sister, along with others, has been laboring to cure you. It warms my heart to see you awake and well again. I know you must have many questions, and I may not be able to answer them all, but I can tell you why you're hearing those voices, for I hear them as well."

Joromar gave him a reflexive smile, as broad and generous as his large face would allow. A vivid curiosity dominated his expression.

"Yes, well, speak on. I'd love to know what in the fathoms is going on, and why I'm holding a blasted morningstar in my hands while lying in bed surrounded by half the castle," Joromar said with a hearty laugh.

"Blasted morningstar? Is that all you think I am? Well you are young and so perhaps may be forgiven, but you have much to learn," Barazain said.

"Easy, friend. He's been near death for three days and the knowledge of the glaives has been lost for an age. Let us allow Kion to set things straight before pressing ahead," Kithian said.

"Very well, I defer to your authority," Barazain said, though his tone lost none of its sharpness.

All this only caused Joromar's unease to grow. "And did you hear that, too? Green goodness, what is going on?"

"I believe it would be best to explain it to you in private. It will be hard enough for Lord Joromar to understand on his own," Kion said. "Lady Valissia, may we have a brief moment with him alone? Afterward he can explain it to you himself."

Valissia folded her hands in her lap. "I'm not sure that I understand," she said. "He only just awoke. Are you certain this should be done now?"

"It's all right, Mother. I'm sure it won't take long." Joromar covered his mother's hands with one of his own. He showed surprising tenderness for one with such massive, maul-like hands. "Something tells me that what this Kion fellow has to say is going to be important."

Valissia searched out Tiryn with her eyes. "Are you certain he's all right? This voice isn't some result of the sickness?"

"No, my lady." Tiryn said. Of all the joyous glows on the faces, only Valissia's and Havrick's exceeded hers. "It's actually something very good. Only Kion's right. It would be best to tell Lord Joromar on his own first."

"I understand what this Grimbriar refers to," Faedred said. "And you have no need to fear, Lady Valissia. I will explain to you what I know in the hall while they talk. That will help prepare you for when Lord Joromar tells you afterward."

"This is all so very strange," Valissia said.

Havrick muttered under his breath, "You ain't joking." Both Mariday and Livia shared their mistress's disoriented look.

Valissia looked to Faedred, taking assurance from his clear, undaunted eyes.

"Do not trouble yourself, my lady. Tiryn did save your son, after all. She and her brother know what they are doing. Come, let us wait together outside." Faedred drew her up and Valissia allowed herself to be escorted from the room.

Kion, Zinder, and Tiryn, were left alone with Joromar and the three glaives.

"Well now, before you tell me who this mysterious Grimbriar is, do you care to tell me who you are? From what Faedred and your brother said, I'm guessing that your name is Tiryn and that I owe you a great deal of thanks for saving me from whatever it was that put me in this bed."

"Along with Nurien and Havrick and many others," Tiryn said in her shy, awkward way.

"So you two are brother and sister, but what about yourself, Master Nyn? How do you find yourself wrapped up in all of this? Nyn are not known for their skill in healing as far as I've heard," Joromar said. He had an easy, familiar way of talking that, despite his befuddlement, made it clear that he was more than eager to hear what they had to say.

"Well, Lord Joromar—" Zinder began, sweeping his cap from his head in flowery fashion.

"Please, call me Grundy," Joromar said. "Everyone else does, except for my mother and father and Faedred."

"Fair enough, Grundy. I serve as the guide and steward and general instigator for these two waifs. And once upon a time I was a smith of some renown. Zinder Hamryn, you may call me, or Hammer of the North, whichever you prefer."

Grundy scratched his ample chin, giving Zinder an approving eye. "A blacksmith. I see. We could certainly use some decent ones here at the Eyre. And now you, Kion Bray. From your tabard I take it you're now the beranskyre of Bramble Eyre? Goodness, how long have I been asleep?"

"Too long," Kion said, "and there is much to say about your sickness and the war and why we are here at all, but first I must tell you of Grimbriar." Kion drew close to the bed with Tiryn and Zinder flanking him. "Grimbriar is one of the names of the weapon you hold in your hand. But this is more than a mere morningstar. It is a glaive, a living weapon, forged by the Mastersmith of old to aid the cause of men. Glaives have wills of their own, but only a select few can hear their voices, those known as swordspeakers. I and my sister have this gift. And now you have been called by Barazain to embrace the same call, to take up your weapon and stand alongside us as we fight this war, a war to decide whether the Four Wards shall endure, or whether a scourge and a darkness will destroy us all."

Grundy's gaze went once again to the glistening morningstar in his hands. Its two great emeralds cast a verdant luster across his frame. The light glimmered with the echoes of spring and of all things green and growing. In that light, his face not only no longer appeared sick and wasted, it was as if it had never known sickness, nor ever could. Indeed, he appeared to be the healthiest, most vigorous man they had ever seen.

Yet, the mask of confusion he wore remained. "…But how can such a thing be?" he said.

"How can anything be?" Barazain said. *"Only by the Mastersmith's will. You may as well ask why the moon traces its courses or the birds sing to the dawn."* Once again, his manner of speaking was frank, yet not rude. He simply stated his thoughts without subtlety or guile.

"But the moon and the birds and how they behave are part of the natural order of things. Only men can speak, not weapons," Grundy said.

"Ah, I know what you mean, Lord Grundy," Zinder said, chuckling. "I felt the same way when Kion first started babbling on about his sword, Truesilver. I feared he'd fallen into a hole in his mind and would never come out. But I've come to believe what he and Tiryn say about these weapons, though I've never heard a word from them myself. You can trust whatever it is that morningstar is telling you, nyn's honor."

"There is much about this world unknown even to the glaives," Barazain said. *"That it should turn out not to be the way you imagined should not surprise you. The world is a perpetual surprise to those who have the honesty to see it as it is."*

Grundy shook his head and turned the weapon in his hand round and round, as if expecting to find this was all some clever trick. Though Barazain was right in saying that the world often turns out to be much different than we imagine, few find it easy to take such changes in stride. Most prefer the familiar, the well-known, the dependable and predictable things. The unexpected can frighten, upend our understanding, make us feel unsafe, exposed. Kion, too, had wondered whether or not he had gone mad when he first began hearing Kithian's voice.

"So you're saying that you and Tiryn hear all of this talk as well?" Grundy said.

"We do," Kion said, sharing a glance with Tiryn.

"My weapon is a dagger called Rimewinter," Tiryn said. "I don't quite understand what all this means either, if that's any comfort. But I know that the glaives were sent to us for a reason. And that it's no accident that they have come to us now, just as the haukmarn have come. Truesilver and Rimewinter have already saved us many times over. And Grimbriar is the reason you are alive right now. It wasn't my skill as a healer that saved you, it was the life-giving power of the bond between you and your glaive that brought you back from the brink of death."

"Join us, Joromar," Kion said, forgetting the young lord's station and grabbing him by the shoulder as though they were brothers. "The haukmar armies march across our land, conquering at will. As swordspeakers, we may not be able to win this war on our own, but we can fight alongside the Warding army until we find a way to hunt down the haukmar leader, Vayd Mokán. We stop him and we stop this war. Are you with us, Lord Grundstaff?"

Joromar's mountainous shoulders rose and fell with a mighty sigh. Doubt riddled his face and Kion wondered whether, given all that he had gone through, they were asking too much of him too quickly. But doubts or no, Joromar now understood the call he had been given. Now it was up to him whether or not he chose to answer.

Chapter 40

SECRET IN THE WATER

Grundy cast his blanket aside and set his bare feet down on the cool stone floor. Ah, it felt good to be up and take in a great lungful of fresh air. His legs and back were awfully stiff and he had a powerful ache in his stomach, but then he'd been asleep for three days from the sound of things so that was to be expected. Other than that, he felt howling good.

He had fallen asleep to a very different world, one where he went and did as he pleased, a proud son and the heir to the Grundstaff line, one where the only people he had to answer to were his mother and father. Despite this, he had never lorded his title over the others who dwelt in the castle. In fact he went out of his way to treat them as friends, so much so that he'd won the favor of most everyone in the Eyre. He rather enjoyed that life and had always supposed that it would go on and on just as it always had. But here he was, fresh from lying on his deathbed, speaking to three complete strangers who told him even stranger things.

And yet, he could not deny the truth of what they said, any more than he could deny hearing the voices of the glaives. They were not voices in his head, but ones he could hear in the same way he heard Kion's, Tiryn's, and Zinder's. And this morningstar…that had captured his thoughts most of all. It was a work of supreme craftsmanship, of that, there was no denying. But there was more. The feeling when he held it in his hands was mysterious and marvelous all at once. It was like touching the lifeblood of the world itself, like touching Spring. The same invisible, renewing power which brought nature back from death year after year ran in some way through its haft. Touching it, he knew the world in a way he had never known it before. It was more vibrant, more real, more infinitely wondrous than ever, and at the same time more simple, as true things always are.

Grundy didn't know half of what all this meant, but he knew enough to know that they were telling him the truth. And deep down, he had always known as well that Bramble Eyre would play some part in this war. He just always thought that part would be determined by his father and not him. But his father had been gone for far too long and now this unlooked-for band of companions had come to the castle at their hour of greatest need.

"I suppose I'm with you, then," he said, yet even as he said the words he wondered if he had any idea just what he was committing to. "On one condition."

"Yes?" Kion's eyes darkened.

"What is it?" Tiryn said.

"There's to be no more of this Lord Joromar nonsense. It's Grundy, you hear? Let's get that straight from the beginning."

Kion and Tiryn shared a satisfied smile and Zinder let out a whistle.

"Of course…Grundy," Kion said, his smile widening.

"Well, how about that?" Zinder said, stroking his beard.

Grimbriar let off a burst of yellowish-green light. *"Very well. Then let us get down to the root of things. You spoke of a war, Kion. Who are we fighting and when is the next battle?"*

"Now, now, Barazain, slow down," Kithian said. *"There is much to be said and done before we are ready to fight again. We are not under immediate threat in any case."*

"Yes, well we seem to be in some sort of castle. But unless the enemy is at the gates, surely you don't mean to stay here?"

"We will discuss such matters in due time," Nurien said. *"We*

have kept Joromar's mother and friends waiting in the hall far too long. They are no doubt anxious to speak with him and ensure that he has made a full recovery. Now is not the time for talk of war and battle."

"Yes, I agree with…Rimewinter, is it?" Joromar said.

"You may call me Nurien."

"Nurien, yes, I agree with Nurien. I need to speak with my mother."

"And I am Kithian. Well met, swordspeaker. Please, call in your family and friends and we will speak with you in greater depth some other time. Barazain, go easy on your new glaivebond. It is hard enough when someone has just been called, much less when they are called back from within a hair's breadth of dying."

The voices of Kithian and Nurien were so very unlike Barazain's. While they spoke with gentle wisdom, Barazain spoke with unabashed directness. Grundy was no stranger to action and plain speaking. His best friend in all the world, Hostram, had been that way—and gotten the two of them into heaps of trouble because of it. Some of that had rubbed off on Joromar. Since Hostram's death, whenever he felt like doing something a little unruly he always told himself that he was simply "honoring Hos's memory." But he was in no mood for anything rash at the moment. There were too many questions that needed answering first.

"Yes, well, pleased to meet you, and thank you for all the answers, such as they are. I can't promise that you won't regret asking me to join you once you get to know me," Grundy said. "But I'll do whatever I can to help. Just now, though, I think I will talk to all these worried folks out in the hall and get a little food in my belly. I've got a terrible hunger."

Zinder let out a crackle of a laugh. "Ha! Now that's my kind of fellow. I like him already."

Grundy let Havrick row for once. Mother had insisted upon it as a condition for letting him out on the lake. She had tried her best to dissuade him from going at all, refusing to believe the evidence of her own eyes, that he had made a complete and full recovery. In fact, he could not remember ever feeling better.

But he needed to clear his head, to make sense of all this madness that had fallen upon him like a heap of rocks from the quarry. The lake had always been his place for that. Yes, there were usually a few scattered fishing boats out along its crystal expanse, but the serenity of the open water, together with the aquatic scents, pristine air, and shimmering sunlight gave expanse to a man's thoughts in a way that could not be found within the confines of an ancient castle.

Grimbriar lay at Grundy's feet in the bottom of the hull. Though it was awkward speaking in front of others to what appeared outwardly to be a lifeless weapon, he sensed that he would be missing something if he left it behind. Barazain may have had a few rough edges, but Grundy didn't mind. He was one of those rare few who had the knack of getting along with people of every mood and stripe.

Barazain was an odd sort. He reminded Grundy of some of the fighting instructors he'd had. None of them stayed for long because Grundy, affable as he was, was not much for the discipline and long hours of practice they demanded of him. Not that he minded a bit of sweat and hard work, but it wasn't the kind of work where you got to have a laugh and banter about with your friends. No, fighting was serious work, and difficult to master. In his mind, it never won out over days out on the lake or romps through the forest with Hos or Hav or anyone else he could drag along. Even helping out in the quarry or the garden or the kitchen were preferable. At least there he could talk and joke. And so, in frustration, his instructors had always given up on him, no matter how much his father pleaded with them to stay.

Like those old instructors, Barazain intended to get him into "fighting shape" as soon as possible. Unlike them, though, he was unimpressed with Grundy's size and natural strength. In Barazain's view, wit and reflexes meant more in combat than raw physical power. Grundy needed to be "honed and ready" for when battle came. And that involved sparring as often and with as many people as he could. Grundy was glad for his mother's protective instincts in this instance, for she flat out refused to let him go with Faedred to the training hall for at least two days. So he had a brief time of peace and quiet before him. Hopefully, by then he'd have come up with an even better—and longer— excuse for why he couldn't train.

"You do not fear the water, though your friend died upon it. That is a good sign. It shows you have courage," Barazain said, in the first compliment he had given. Grundy cherished it, unsure of when he would get another.

"For a month after Hostram drowned I didn't go, but then my sorrow turned to anger. Anger that the waters which had given us so many memories should have taken my friend. And so I went out on the lake in defiance of what they had done, to show them that I would not let them cow me into submission."

Havrick scrunched his nose. "Talking to that weapon again, are you?"

"Sorry, it's hard to get used to, isn't it?" Grundy said.

"Oh, I don't mind. It's actually sort of funny. What's that thing's voice sound like?"

"Honestly, I don't see how this simpleton is the boon companion you say he is. Listen to the way he talks. Does he not know that I am called Grimbriar? I have heard you tell him so several times. But he insists on referring to me as a weapon or a thing, as though I were some common object with no life of its own. You ought to be talking with Kion and Tiryn and planning for the war, not out with this bumpkin paddling about when there are important things to be done," Barazain said with his usual spice.

"His voice sounds a bit like thunder—especially when you refer to him as a thing. Be sure to call him Grimbriar from now on. Otherwise I'll get an earful," Grundy said, though in truth he did not care all that much if Barazain got a trifle hot from time to time. It was actually rather amusing.

Havrick, who often took things far more seriously than he should, gave the weapon a tremulous look, as though it might rise up and strike him of its own accord. "Right. Wouldn't want to anger the—" He stopped himself before he committed another verbal offense. "Wouldn't want to make Grimbriar mad, I mean."

"Yes, I hope we can all be friends," Grundy said, letting out a low, tumbling laugh. Friends with a morningstar. How did that make any sense? He still felt sometimes that he must be dreaming. "So, Havrick. I didn't just invite you out here for another one of our excursions. I wanted some fresh air, to be sure, but I also noticed that when you and Mother and Faedred were talking about my illness you were reluctant to give many details. So now that we're out here alone, I want the straight truth. How did I get sick? I went to bed three nights ago feeling a little queasy in my stomach and that's the last thing I remember. Was it something I ate?"

Havrick took off his crumpled straw hat even though the sun pounded down as hard as ever. A tug-of-war played out on his face, mirroring the one in his mind. Havrick was an honest person. And he preferred to choose the right thing when he could. But he struggled with how to choose when the right thing wasn't clear.

"Well, you see, Grundy, the thing is..." Havrick said. He started and stopped several times while his moral sense and love of his friend wrestled against each other. "I'm not supposed to tell you anything—at least not for now. That's what Lady Valissia and Marshal Faedred made me promise. They were worried it might be too much of a shock to you and cause you to worry. They even asked the newcomers, the ones who saved you, to wait until we could be more certain about what happened..." Havrick squirmed in his seat and kept glancing out at the water, as if he would rather have thrown himself in the lake than be sitting in the position he now found himself in.

"Now, Havrick, I don't see what good there would be in that. You said even my mother doesn't want me to know?" Grundy said. He knew that Havrick was loyal to him even above his father and mother. Friendship brooks no outside ruler or master. It is a kingdom unto itself, its authority beginning and ending with those who make up its sacred circle. Grundy had no doubt that Havrick would tell him everything if pressed, which cast the dilemma back into his lap. Did he go against the wishes of his mother? There he wasn't sure. It was not something he was eager to do. Yes, she could be far too protective and he had been a little loose now and then when it came to applying her rules, but usually only for harmless fun or an adventure. This felt more serious.

"Well, I don't think it was her idea at first, if I'm to be honest," Havrick said, searching for a way to help out his friend. "It was more Marshal Faedred's. You know how he is about making sure everything runs smooth in the Eyre."

Ah, well, Faedred was a different story. Loyal as he was to Bramble Eyre, he was even more of a stickler than Mother. More importantly, he was not one of Grundy's parents, and so Grundy felt less honor-bound to abide by the marshal's rules and less guilty about skirting around them.

"Now listen here, Hav. Do I look like I might suffer shock from some news? If anything, I might lapse back into illness from worry about these secrets of yours, now that I know they exist." Grundy unleashed a brash and cautionless grin. "Besides, remember that part from Luididis where it says that 'Friendship makes its own rules'? Have we not always gone by that law? We made a pact never to keep secrets between us and I'd say that trumps the promise you made with my mother on Faedred's account. I came within a sliver of death from what I've been told. I think you owe it to me to tell the truth." He leaned back against the prow of the boat, knowing how his words would land on his friend.

Havrick put his hat back on, feeling a great burden lifted off them by his friend's timely recitation of the cherished passage from Luididis. It was from one of the few classic works Grundy had studied and, like most things he learned that were worth bothering about, he'd shared it with his friend. Grundy was, in a way, Havrick's tutor as well as his friend since most common folk had neither the time nor the coin to pay for any sort of education on their own. Through Grundy, Havrick had strolled not only through Luididis's works, but Hemrith's *Compendium of the Natural life of Warding*, Bandalar's *Histories of the Two Wards*, and of course the many volumes of *Wanderings* by the great sage himself, Nimrain. Those had been his favorites. Grundy was no scholar and there had been much in his studies he'd found interminably dry and pointless. But Luididis had always been a bright island amidst a sea of dark waters. Many a fine and memorable adventure had resulted from the recollection of Luididis's teachings on friendship as well as other things.

It was not that friendship had to be inherently rebellious, only that to flourish a group of friends had to abide by their own set of rules, thick or thin, rain or sunshine, no matter what the rest of the world said. Of course, that could be good or bad, depending on the circle of friends. But in the case of Havrick and Grundy, it had generally been for good as they meant no harm in their mischief and explorations around Lake Stillmere.

Even if they had not been bosom friends, was not Grundy nearly an adult? Could he not make decisions for himself? He loved his mother dearly, but at times she still treated him like a child.

"Now that you put it that way. I do have to confess that it's been eating me up not to be able to tell you what I know. For more reasons than one—as I'm sure you'll see."

"Say on," Grundy said. He knew he could count on Hav.

With the boat drifting across the gentle lapping waters

Havrick unloosed all that he had been holding in. He spoke of how they had mistaken his illness for the sprull, and of Tiryn's arrival and of the failed attempts to find a cure. Grundy was shocked to hear of Tellman's death, for he was a good old soul and in fine health the last time he saw him. It took Grundy a long while before he could live that news down. At first he felt guilty that he might have passed on whatever disease he had to Tellman, but when he voiced this, Havrick was quick to counter.

"No, no, no, Grundy. It wasn't your fault. Not one solitary bit."

"Then you're saying Tellman's death was just happenstance? How can that be?"

Havrick set the oar on his lap. "Not that either. We think he was, well, which is to say, that Tiryn, well, she came upon the idea that…Well, I can't put it any plainer than to say that she thought it might be poison."

"Poison?" Grundy snapped out of his casual stretch, his whole body tight as a wire.

"Wraithleaf poison to be exact. I can't see how I missed it, having watched you nearly die from it before. But you hadn't been out in the woods so it never occurred to me that it might have been that."

Grundy tried to piece together the fractured puzzle Havrick had laid before him. Tellman's death made it hard to think. A veil of sadness draped his thoughts. He struggled through it until he dug up what he saw must be the obvious truth.

"Oh, no. Was Tellman poisoned as well?"

"Seems likely." Havrick looked even more upset by this than Grundy.

"That means someone did this to us on purpose," Grundy said.

"Sounds like you have a snake in your nest," Barazain said. *"Best stamp it out before it strikes again."*

"It gets worse," Havrick said, his face as dire as Barazain's warning. He told Grundy of the argument between Spademaster

Tellman and Grish. Havrick rushed through it, getting the bitter taste out of his mouth as quickly as he could.

"Grish?" Grundy said the word so loud a flock of birds took flight from the shore. "We've had our differences, but what in the fathoms would he do something like that for? No, Hav, he may be a sour sod, but he's still your brother and I won't believe he's gone that far off unless I hear it from his own mouth. Besides, Ruwena said he was only looking for a remedy, didn't she?"

"Yes, that does give me some hope. But that threat he gave Tellman sounds awful bad when the poor old fellow ends up dead a day later."

Grundy's stomach made an uncouth rumble. Thinking always made him hungry. At first he was certain it could not have been Grish, for what did he have to gain by poisoning him? But then again, what reason did anyone in the Eyre have for something like that? The more he thought about it, Grish was asking for a remedy for poison, not the poison itself, which also made no sense. But then a terrible memory struck him.

"I clean forgot," he said, smacking the side of the boat hard enough to bobble it. "You know I'd been staying late at the barracks the last few nights before I got sick. Faedred thought it might help morale. But he wouldn't let me eat the same fare as the men. He had porters bring in my meals from the keep—you know how strict he is about rank and station and all that nonsense. Well, that last night it was Grish who brought me my food! I thought it was a bit unusual, but the cooks are short-handed so I figured he'd been roped in to help."

"From everything you've said, I don't see that there can be much doubt as to this man's guilt. But if you need further assurance, you should seek out Kithian. He can get the truth out of anyone. It is one of his gifts," Barazain said.

Grundy was intrigued by the suggestion, but not enough to go on talking to Barazain while his friend sat there, wrestling with a whole troop of doubts and fears.

"Cragsnappers, Hav. It could have been him. But no. I still

can't believe it—I won't. There has to be some other reason. Did you talk to him? Surely you talked to him about this?"

Havrick groaned, pulling off his hat again and wringing it something awful. Though the boat drifted softly across the pearly smooth waters, Havrick might as well have been spinning in a whirlpool as green as he looked. "No, that's the worst part of it. I can't find him—no one can. I've talked to two dozen people who ought to know where he is, everyone from his foreman to the guards at the gate. He's nowhere to be found."

That settled it. Grundy would get to the bottom of this come wind or high water. "Take us back to the docks. If the gate guards haven't seen him, he must still be in the castle some-where. We'll find him. You can bet your turnips on it."

Havrick set to rowing once more. At first he put his back into it, rowing with zeal, but not long into the return journey, he slowed. "I just realized something. I didn't check with the dock-master. What if Grish took one of the boats?"

"Then there'd be one missing. Either way, getting back to the docks is our first order of business."

Havrick nodded and leaned into his strokes again. They were not far out so it wouldn't take long to return to the underground docks which lay tucked beneath the keep. Half a dozen boats issued from there every day. With the trade roads down to a trickle, fish was an even more important source of food in the castle than usual. Even so, they didn't have enough boats to keep up. Several were always kept inside in various states of repair and the two barges for hauling large loads were unsuitable for the task. Then there was the Grundstaff punt, *The Dew Skimmer,* used for family outings and parties on the water. It was twice the size as the others and in fine condition, though it had not been used for some time.

"Joromar, what does this man Grish look like?" Barazain said. His voice had a revelatory tenor to it, as if he had just landed upon the answer to an important question.

Grundy slipped out of his wonderings. "Grish? Why, he's

about Havrick's height, though far thinner. He has hair as black as night that comes down to about his shoulders. His nose is crooked and his teeth are yellow as butter. Why do you want to know? Do you think you can help us find him?"

Barazain returned the question with one of his own. *"Does he wear a scarf around his neck?"*

A scarf? Why in the fathoms would Barazain ask that? He had no way of knowing…All the blood drained to his toes as he said the word, "Yes…"

"The body of a man with a scarf is resting at the bottom of this lake. Your friend's brother is dead."

Chapter 41

FALSE HEART

Grundy's hair was still wet from his plunge into the lake. He'd had a change of clothes, though, so the rest of him was dry. Havrick sat to his right at the guest-house table, his eyes storm-tossed and vacant. At first, he had rambled on about how dear Grish was to him and how cruel a thing it was for him to have died so young. But by the time they reached the guesthouse, his words were spent and he stared ahead in silence, his only hope to wait out the terrible storm that had unleashed upon him.

Sitting next to them, Kion, Tiryn, and Zinder had all recently arrived.

Tiryn wore a dress woven with a myriad of teal threads. It was in the old style, something some former lady of Bramble Eyre had worn. Though its beauty was understated and not showy, it was far more elegant than anything a commoner would ever wear. Grundy's mother insisted that Tiryn take it as payment and Tiryn had reluctantly agreed. Kion, who had arrived from a sparring session in the barracks, was far less presentable; he looked like he might have just come from the lake as well with his tunic drenched and his dark locks running in damp strands ringing his face. Zinder was immaculately clean, though he had just come from the smithy. He was arrayed in an ebony vest with rose accents and a coal-black hat furled to one side with a white feather so long that it drooped. Havrick and Grundy looked like hayseeds by comparison.

"You both look pale as ghosts. Something important has happened," Tiryn said.

"Sure as the sun it has," Grundy said. "I wanted to tell all of you together. Because apart from my mother and Faedred—who are on their way—you might be the only people I can trust in this entire castle."

"So Havrick told you about the poison." Zinder stated the obvious.

"He did."

"Well, I for one am glad. I never liked the idea of keeping it from you, even for a day while they hunted for Grish."

"No need to keep hunting. We found him," Grundy said flatly. Havrick closed his eyes, reliving the horrid memory all over again. This whole thing was a nasty business and Grundy hated it for Havrick most of all. But there was no way around it.

"Where?" Kion said, eyes keen, as if he meant to set out after Grish the moment Grundy told him.

"At the bottom of Lake Stillmere," Grundy said, swallowing down a heavy lump in his throat. He would never forget those lidless, unliving eyes staring up at him after they got Grish's body into the boat. Grish could be hard-nosed and difficult, but that didn't mean he deserved death.

"He's dead?" Kion said. All three of them sat up in their chairs.

"Grimbriar found him as we headed toward the docks. It's only about four fathoms deep there. I didn't know glaives could see through things that way."

"Oh, Havrick, how terrible." Tiryn was swift to rise and comfort him. Kion and Zinder did the same.

"So sorry for you, lad," Zinder said.

"I'm sure it wasn't easy coming here to tell us," Kion said.

Havrick bit into his lower lip and mumbled, "It had to be done. There'll be time enough for tears when I'm alone."

Grundy had told him not to come, but Havrick insisted. He was made of sterner stuff than he looked.

"We left him covered in the boat. I ordered the dockmaster not to let anyone near it," Grundy said, hurrying to finish.

"So he drowned?" Tiryn said.

"No. He was stabbed in the stomach."

Zinder stroked both ends of his mustache. "Only one wound?"

"Yes, but it gutted him bad."

"And no other signs of a fight?"

"Not a mark on him."

"So the person who killed him knew his way with a knife. And Grish must have known him. It's hard to get in a blow to the belly without getting in close. For that it would have to be someone he trusted."

Zinder paced to the end of the table, his nynnian mind whirring. Kion and Tiryn stared at the wall, too stunned to speak. Their eyes knew the bitterness of death all too well. Grundy himself knew it from losing Hostram, his dearest friend, not two years past. But this was different. Though Grundy had not been as close to Grish, his death had been intentional. All deaths seem like an injustice, an affront to the natural order of things, yet none more so than murder. And Grish's killer roamed free, most likely still in the castle.

"It stands to reason that whoever killed Grish had a hand in poisoning me and Tellman. Maybe he was the one who did the poisoning and Grish found out," Grundy said. "Grimbriar said that Kithian had a way of finding out the truth in such matters."

"*Yes. I can tell the truth of whatever is spoken in my presence, though with those who intend to deceive it requires Kion's touch,*" Kithian said. His voice had a clear, unshakable calm to it, as though he could see through all this death and confusion to something better on the other side.

"But who to question? I don't have the slightest inkling of who would want to kill me, much less Tellman."

"Could it be someone loyal to the haukmarn?" Kion said, recovering at last from the shock. "Someone who turned to their side and now seeks to weaken Bramble Eyre from within? I only say that because it happened in Charring."

"I suppose anything is possible," Grundy said. "Though somehow I doubt it. It might be someone who wanted to weaken Bramble Eyre for other reasons though." Even now, the castle seemed shaken. Its great walls, its peerless towers, its enduring strength down through the years, tested many times and never broken, quivered in its foundations. Whether that quivering would bring it all crashing down on top of them, Grundy could not say.

"Who stands to gain if you die?" Zinder said, his bright eyes narrowing to tiny pinpricks of light. He was a curious sight with his ice-white beard and dandy hat, but aside from the glaives, he was the oldest and sharpest mind among them.

"No one, unless my parents were to die as well. If that happened the Grundstaff line would have died out and control of our lands would pass to the Alagris family."

"Faedred?" Kion said, trouble darkening his brow.

"Yes, but that's out of the question. He's always been loyal to my family. And besides, my father and mother are still alive so he would gain nothing from killing me."

"I don't like to say it, but we were told that your father was in poor health. A journey through the Savron Toths is no light matter," Zinder said.

"My father will return. Of that I have no doubt," Grundy said. Nor would he allow himself to think otherwise.

"I'm sure he will," Kion said. "In any case, we can rule Faedred out. He's too honorable to stoop to such deeds."

"Tiryn, I think you should tell them of your conversation with Livia this afternoon," Nurien said. Tiryn's cheeks blossomed a reluctant rose. She fought within herself, looking as though she wished to dart from the room to avoid the tapestry of sharp stares weaving its threads about her. But she steadied herself and cleared her throat with a mousy rattle.

"There may be another side to Faedred," she said. Coming

after her long silence, her words had the same effect as a boulder dropping into the room.

"What do you mean?" Grundy said. Faedred had been like a second son to his father and an older brother to him. There were rumors that he had been a bit restless in his youth, but after his father died and he took his place as marshal of Bramble Eyre, he had shown nothing but honor and respect to the Grundstaff family. Beyond that, he inspired unquestioned loyalty in his men.

"I'm only repeating what I've heard," Tiryn said. "Normally I wouldn't, since I don't like to do that sort of thing. I really didn't think it had anything to do with the poisoning when I heard it. But hearing you talk brought to mind something Livia told me this afternoon when she walked me back to the guesthouse. She said that she's noticed the way Faedred looks at Valissia sometimes. How did she put it? 'It's more than just the devotion that comes from duty,' I believe was what she said."

The words came to Grundy like some distant rumbling in the quarry. Such sounds usually turned out to be nothing, but that did not make them any less ominous to hear.

"Livia said that?" Grundy said.

"I don't think she meant any harm by it. She said she's only noticed it a few times when she came to attend Valissia and Faedred was not yet aware that she had come."

"Livia is awfully quiet. She's surprised me more than once for certain," Grundy said. "But no, Faedred is the marshal of Bramble Eyre. A noble man. His family has served mine for generations. I can't imagine he would ever have designs on my mother. Livia must have been mistaken. I don't doubt that she saw something. She's an honest girl. But I won't accuse the marshal of betrayal on the basis of a few stray looks."

"Is Faedred married?" Barazain said.

"No. My father always said that he was married to the Eyre. He could have had any number of noble maidens who've visited the castle down through the years, but he never had time for such things. He would rather be at the wall with his men than in a ball or a festival upon the arm of some glittering lady."

"The human heart is a fickle thing. Sometimes it sows seeds it cannot harvest. And it waters them to its own destruction," Barazain said. He sounded as glum as some of Grundy's old professors, with an emphasis on the old. Then again, the glaive was far older than any of them had been. It was more than eight hundred years since Barazain had fallen asleep, and who knew how old he was before that?

Coming as they did from his glaive, the weight of those words landed heavy upon him. Grish was dead, Faedred's honor was being questioned, someone had poisoned the Spademaster and himself, and Grundy was supposed to somehow discover the answers for all of it. On the best of days, he was hardly what might be called a diligent thinker. He read books, but only those he enjoyed, and he preferred messing about on the lake or riding through the woods on the back of a swift stallion to whiling away the hours lost in thought. Perhaps the glaives could unravel the truth. They possessed a wisdom far beyond that of mortal men. Even Zinder or the Brays would have a better chance, but it was all too much for poor Grundy, half a day removed from nearly slipping beyond the fetters of this world into the one beyond.

As if to save him from the mounting burden of his many questions, the front door banged open and Livia led Mother into the entryway, followed closely by Faedred. Mother had changed into a silk dress of leafy green—her favorite color. Her cheeks were drawn back in the protective smile that she always displayed when Grundy strayed beyond one of her many boundaries. Faedred's eyes showed concern as well, but he was more guarded in his expression.

Livia slipped aside to stand near the dining room door while Faedred followed Mother into the chamber. Grundy rose with the others.

"Greetings, honored guests," Mother said, as soft and delicate as her flowing dress, but her tone shifted abruptly. "Joromar, you called to us and we have come. But there is talk among the servants that you changed clothes after your outing on the boat. And by your hair I'm guessing that you took a swim, against my wishes."

Grundy kissed her forehead. "It was for good reasons, Mother, but I'll take whatever consequences you wish to give me later. Please, have a seat. I have some important things to tell you."

She and Faedred took chairs together at the far end of the table. The others sat as well.

"Mother, I know about the poison," Grundy said. Head down, straight ahead was the best way to get through things, he usually found. You might run into a wall that way, but at least you'd know where the boundaries were.

"Who told you?" she said, eyeing each of the others with equal suspicion, only sparing Tiryn in her accusatory search.

"I'll tell you once I'm finished," Grundy said, knowing that by the time he explained what had happened such a detail wouldn't matter. "I also know that Grish was overheard talking to Tellman in a suspicious way the night before I became sick. Despite this, I do not believe it was Grish who did the poisoning."

"You are sure of this?" Faedred said. Though his face remained composed, he had taken off his gloves and kept folding and unfolding his hands. Even Grundy, who was not the most observant fellow, found this odd. He had never seen the marshal demonstrate such behavior before. "How do you know?"

"Because we found Grish at the bottom of the lake."

Mother's eyes leapt to Havrick, reading there the tragic truth.

"How awful," Faedred said, but the coolness of his voice did not seem to match the news.

He doesn't care, Grundy realized. At least not about Grish or even about Havrick. But Faedred had seen death far more often than Grundy. Perhaps his dispassion was understandable. Still, Father would not have taken the news that way. For the first time, Grundy felt the tiniest crack in his rock-hard confidence in the marshal.

"How did you find him?" Mother said. "Did you spot him along the shore?"

"No, Grimbriar can see through the water and even through solid things like rock and wood. It told me where to look."

Mother and Faedred glanced at each other in mutual bewilderment. Neither of them had been told anything about the specific gifts the morningstar possessed, only that, like the other glaives, it could speak to those who had been called and that, in some mysterious way, the bonding between Grimbriar and Grundy had saved his life.

"And how do you know he did not drown by accident or take his own life?" Faedred said. His tone was distant, but it may have just been confusion.

"He was stabbed in the front and we found no weapon near him in the lake. Barazain says that he would not have been able to make it very far with the wound he had, so he must have been killed first and then thrown into the water. Also, with a wound like that, Zinder thinks it must have been done by someone he knew."

Mother rose and knelt beside Havrick. "I am sorry that you have to listen to this, and sorrier still that it has happened. My lord and I have always held your family dear. I fear the Eyre is not as safe as we have always supposed."

"It's no fault of yours, m'lady. All the same, thank you for the kind words. Means an awful lot." He wiped his turnip-like nose with a rough sleeve.

If Faedred shared in his lady's sadness he failed to show it. His eyes had fallen behind a vacant mask, as hard and cold as Grish when they pulled him from Lake Stillmere.

"There is something troubling and dark about the marshal's thoughts," Kithian said.

"Be wary," Barazain said. *"A cornered snake will surely bite."*

"I agree," Nurien said. *"You must question him now, Kion, so that the truth may be known."*

"It is certain that he hides something," Kithian said. *"But whether he is innocent or guilty, we cannot know unless you use the touch."*

After a long hesitation, Kion compelled himself to rise and walk toward Faedred, each step more heavy than the last. Grundy gripped the table. Was this truly happening?

"Marshal Faedred, I have something to say. You welcomed me into this castle and put your trust in me when others did not. I have not one ill thought against you, but I am nonetheless duty-bound to ask you some direct questions concerning this matter. Before I do, you must know that my sword allows me to see the truth of all words spoken by those I touch. May I have your permission, my lord, to lay my hand upon your shoulder and to ask you to prove your innocence in these matters?"

Grundy found it as hard to listen to those words as it was for Kion to say them. Those who served under Faedred loved him, perhaps even more than Lord Namril himself. To suppose that he might have had some part to play in all of this was beyond natural reason. And yet, all of this was so twisted and murky that Grundy no longer knew light from dark.

Faedred's sword flickered in the candlelight with a shrill metallic scrape. One moment he was unarmed and sitting, the next he was standing with his sword across Kion's neck. The snake had struck.

"I will not be convicted by tricks and sorcery," Faedred said in such wild and scathing tones Grundy hardly recognized the voice of the beloved marshal. And in the hissing syllables of the man who now stood before them, the same man who had served his family and the Eyre so well all these years, he heard another sound. The sound of Bramble Eyre's walls crashing down around it. If one so trusted and so true could fall, then the very walls themselves must surely come next. As the old order cracked and splintered and the hot sting of betrayal pierced

Grundy's gentle heart, something surged up from within that wounded place. The old, easy, carefree, winsome path of laughter and festivity, of kindness and good faith, disappeared in the sudden fall of night. Amidst the blind wrath that followed, he took up Grimbriar in his hand and it shone as tree sap in the sun, its spikes tingling with the expectation of vengeance for all the wrongs that Faedred had wrought.

For the moment, Grundy's rising and the resplendence of his glaive checked Faedred's rash, ill-conceived rebellion and the old commanding resonance returned to his voice. "I have no desire to fight you, Lord Joromar. I do not wish to hurt you, or Kion, or anyone else. The poison was not meant to kill you, my lord…It was meant, oh it sounds so foolish now to say…It all stems from a lie my heart told me…" He regarded Valissia with a wild recklessness. "That if I could save Joromar that it would endear you to me, as before. And that with Lord Namril gone, perhaps your own heart would awaken to me at last. For I…I do love you, Valissia. Forgive me for saying so now. You captured my false heart unwittingly and without intent."

Mother seemed to Grundy's white-hot eyes as the sun to Faedred's wisp of shadow. She met his gaze with a look of deep hurt, but also of scorn. For in truth, Faedred had been to her a great comfort in the dark hours of Joromar's sickness, but she saw now that it had all been a cheat, a sham designed to win her affections while her husband was away. And in that scorn, Faedred relived his own wretchedness and hardened his heart anew against his shameful acts and forsook the contrition of his earlier words as the proud, grave warrior within him rose again to contest the field.

"Yes, I had Grish poison Joromar. For I believed his idle boast, blinded by my own passions, that he knew the cure. But in this he proved false. When it seemed that Joromar—whom I have always loved and to whom I never meant any harm—when it seemed that he might die, in a fit of rage I killed Grish for his lies and for taking the life of Tellman, which was wholly against my will and without my knowledge. I never intended for you to die, my lord. You had survived the poisoning before. I only intended that you would be sick for a few days, nothing more. Honor bids that I confess my guilt to you, but now confessed, I forsake my honor and choose to flee. For I spurn both the gallows and the cage. Nor do I desire any further violence, for enough blood has already been spilled from my foolishness. Instead, I hereby banish myself to roam friendless and without hope in a far, unfamiliar country until this miserable vanity which is life should end."

"Murderer!" Havrick shouted, and would have charged Faedred, weaponless, had Grundy not held him back.

"Hold on, Hav," Grundy said.

Faedred took it for a sign that his master's son would let him go as he wished, and made to leave, but in this he was mistaken.

He stepped away from Kion and would have passed Grundy by, but the young lord's frame filled the space and he would not yield. Behind the marshal, Kion drew Truesilver. The crimson glare overbore the feeble light from the candles, but Grundy motioned him back.

"I will deal with this traitor. For it is against my family and against the Eyre that this snake has struck," Grundy said, his skin itching from the inner heat. He wasn't sure whether to bellow like a she-bear or pound this wretched tripe into the ground, but he was sure as the sun not going to let him walk free.

In the midst of this, everyone had risen. Zinder had a dinner fork and butter knife raised threateningly, while Tiryn produced Rimewinter and held it, trembling, toward the marshal. Faedred was trapped and outmatched, yet he refused to lower his sword.

"Joromar, do not make me fight you. For you never took to it, though you might have outstripped us all if you had. I would do my best not to wound you badly, but you have no armor and I cannot promise that you will not regret it. As for you, Kion, you bested me on the sparring floor, but in live battle I may not fight as fair. If you would test my blade, so be it. But I will die before I am hanged or imprisoned." He waved his sword, motioning Grundy out of his way, but Grundy again held his ground.

"Do not fear, glaivebond," Barazain said brashly. *"This fool can do you no harm with a weapon such as that. Whether you choose only to knock him down or bash his head into oblivion is your decision."*

"I may not be half the fighter you are, but no transgressor chooses his own judgment." Grundy wavered between Barazain's two choices, so great did the anger boil within. "I will do what I must to stop you, and if not me, then my friends will do it for me."

"Joromar, no," Valissia said. "You are no match for him." She made to move forward, but Grundy waved her back.

"This is something I must do," Grundy said. "For Father and for the Eyre. Faedred has made himself the enemy of all."

"Even so, I will trust to my blade," Faedred said. He was nothing if not quick, and had fought with the sword since long before Grundy was old enough to wield a weapon. Faedred struck Grundy's forearm, intending to disarm him with one swift strike and then bowl his way past his helpless opponent. Grundy was so unprepared he did not even attempt a block. He winced, anticipating a flash of agony, but the sword bounced off his skin as though Faedred had struck iron. It tore a gash through his shirt, but failed to harm him. Though he still felt the impact, it was more akin to being struck by the flat of the blade.

Astonished, Faedred took a step back. Not even a trickle of blood came from the open sleeve. Faedred struck again. This time Grundy had the sense to attempt a block, but he could not match the marshal's speed. He lunged at Grundy's legs. Again the blow bounced off, only making ribbons of his clothes. It seemed that Barazain's advice was more than metaphorical, and that it was, in fact, literally true that Faedred's weapon could not hurt Grundy at all.

Faedred's right foot swept backwards and caught Kion off guard as he rushed in from behind. It knocked him off his feet and sent Truesilver clattering from his grasp. Tiryn uttered the word "glaivefrost" as a frosty ball sheared through the air at the marshal, but she missed by a wide margin and it struck one of the cabinets, coating the door with bright blue ice.

But Grundy finally struck back. He swung at Faedred's shoulder for all he was worth. And Grundy's arm was worth a fair bit. Faedred parried the spiked head of the glaive, but though Grimbriar had until that moment felt as though it was made of hollow wood, it gained weight with the downward swing so that it sailed through the parry and into Faedred's shoulder. Faedred's steel-plated armor ought to have deflected the worst of the attack, but it was no more than mere decoration against Grimbriar's spikes. The spikes pierced the armor in three places and rent asunder the mail beneath. The sudden outpouring of blood should have convinced the marshal to quit the fight, but he was too wholly in the grip of pride.

He struck Grundy again, this time with a vicious thrust to the belly, the same place where he had gutted Grish. The sword bent and shivered so badly it fell from Faedred's hand. Tiryn's glaivefrost struck again, this time pinning Faedred's leg to the floor and Kion recovered Truesilver and set the point square in the middle of Faedred's back.

"You are bested," Kion said. "This time by your own foolish ambition. I would have served and fought for you gladly, but you are my marshal no more."

Grundy felt the spitting geyser inside him cool. He still loathed the man before him for what he'd done, but he refused to let this newfound anger become his master. His wrath passed away like a fresh breeze upon a sunlit glade.

"You have betrayed your lord and your castle, Faedred. And you will face punishment, though not by my hand. It is prison for you until such time as my father comes and decides your fate." He glanced down at his morningstar, once more light as driftwood in his hands. "Thank you, Barazain,"

"*Yes, well, it was passable. Perhaps now you see the need for practice,*" came the unimpressed response.

Faedred bowed his head, broken at last as the weight of his deeds fell upon him harder than any blow he could have received from Grundy's glaive.

Chapter 42

DUTY DOES WHAT IT MUST

The heat that had burned inside Grundy the day before had long since run its course, leaving a cold hollow cavity in its place. Faedred was in chains locked deep in the dungeons of the keep. Justice awaited him, but a justice no more effective than the mending of broken glass. The cracks would remain. Tellman and Grish were dead. And Bramble Eyre was left with a gaping hole in its defenses with the loss of the marshal's leadership.

Grundy sat in the great hall with the other swordspeakers and his mother. Zinder had gone off to the library to see what he could learn of welnods. The sun stretched its long straight fingers through the high, arched windows, and sparrows whistled songs from the rooftops. The enduring stonework surrounding them seemed as strong as ever and yet the Eyre had been rocked to its very foundations. But Logren was on his way. Perhaps he could begin the process of restoring peace and order to the castle.

"It makes no sense, Mother," Grundy said. "Why did Faedred think that poisoning me would win your heart?"

His mother stared impassively out into the expanse of the hall. Her features remained unblemished, but the radiance of her face was dimmed. Her husband was gone and she had unwittingly been the cause of Faedred's downfall. How quickly life can change and without warning.

"When you took ill with the wraithleaf three years ago, Faedred dropped all his other duties to see that I was attended to while Havrick's father worked to heal the poison. We spent a great deal of time together and perhaps he took my gratitude for something other than what it was. And with your father gone, it seems he thought to turn my heart to him once and for all. Truth be told, I did draw strength from his visits and from his many assurances that your sickness would soon pass, but I see now that his looks and words meant more than mere friendship."

"*A disordered love warps all it sees,*" Kithian said, his voice more somber than usual. "*And will suffer much evil in the pursuit of its twisted good.*"

"Faedred was willing to abandon his duty to pursue a lie." Though Kion spoke the words with firmness, his face betrayed an inability to grasp how it could be that one so noble could have fallen so far.

The clack of booted footsteps resounded throughout the hall, announcing the arrival of Flagmaster Logren. He marched forward with a firm, steady stride and stopped at the base of the stairs and bowed stiffly. He was a fine man, but his youth had long since gone.

"My lord and lady," he said. "You sent for me."

Logren showed no outward sign of concern; such was his way. He never wavered to one side or the other, but always rowed straight down the middle.

"Do you know what has transpired with Marshal Faedred?" Grundy said.

"I know that he has been confined to the dungeon. I presume you have summoned me to tell me why."

While Grundy preferred to be direct, recounting the story of Faedred's betrayal would not make it hurt any less.

"He betrayed his duty to the Eyre. He...hired Grish to poison me in the hope that my Mother would turn to him for comfort. It seems that he had the belief that he was in love with her. When Tellman would not give Grish the cure, Grish killed him, and Faedred in turn killed Grish." At least Havrick was not there to have to endure the horrid details all over again.

For the first time since Grundy could remember, Logren's stern countenance cracked and a glimmer of sadness shone through. He did not allow his emotions to sully his face for long, though, and quickly recovered his old aspect.

"I am glad that you and my lady are safe and that he will threaten you no longer," Logren said. "Still, it is a hard thing to believe."

"None of us saw this side of him, Logren," Mother said. "Faedred was as masterful in deception as he was in the command of his men. The greater the man, the greater his fall."

They gave Logren time to let the news strike home. Logren had served under Faedred for five years. He had lived most of his life before that as the warder of the heralded Valorstand mercenary company, but in his old age he grew weary of wandering and, believing like most soldiers that the time for open war had passed, came to Bramble Eyre seeking a quieter way to live out the end of his days.

"Out of loyalty to Lord Namril, I must choose to believe your word. But I cannot promise that all of the men will do the same," he said. "Some might choose to question the character of his accusers rather than think ill of their beloved marshal. Worse, some might not care about the truth at all, but take his side even knowing what he has done. It will be difficult to maintain unity in the days ahead."

"I'm sure it doesn't help that we've had to reduce the rations and wages these last few months," Mother said. She was wise in the ways of the castle; she often attended Father in his duties and advised him on important decisions. "Their loyalty to us shall surely be tested."

"Shall I double the prison guard?" Logren said.

Grundy looked to his mother for an answer. In truth, he was not prepared to run the castle in his father's place. They were already down a hundred men from what they needed to properly defend the castle. If they took soldiers from guarding the gates or the towers, the defenses would suffer.

"I don't see that we have any choice," Mother said. "Bolster the prison guard with as many as it takes to keep it secure. Now, to the matter at hand." She turned and nodded to Grundy.

Grundy gritted his teeth, trying to recall the words he'd composed in his head beforehand. "Flagmaster Logren, you have served us faithfully for many years and the Eyre has great need of someone to lead its men. We wish to raise you to the marshalship of the castle. Will you accept?"

Logren remained still as a stone and for a moment Grundy feared the worst. But then he bowed as low as his aged frame would allow and said, "Yes, my lord. I will serve Bramble Eyre and the Grundstaff family as best I can."

"We are grateful for your service. No one is more deserving," Grundy said. At that point words failed him and silence spilled over the great hall until he managed to unloose his awkward tongue. "Then, if you have nothing you wish to discuss, you may return to the men and inform them of your new duties." How did his father always manage to know what to say? Grundy should have paid more attention to his lessons in formal courtesies. He would have to learn them as he went now, which meant more uncomfortable exchanges like this awaited him.

"We will confer your rank officially upon you in due time," Mother said. Of course, Grundy had forgotten that part.

Logren gave another bow. "There is one question I had, my lord. Word is that you took several strikes from Faedred's sword before he was captured. And yet by all accounts you fought unarmored. Is this so? And if true, how is it that you survived unscathed? I only ask because the men will want to know."

Grundy had wondered about that himself. But so many other concerns swirled inside his mind after the fight that he had entirely forgotten to ask Barazain about it.

"That is a good question…" was all he could think to say. It seemed an impropriety to address Barazain in front of his mother and Logren since they could not hear his response. It also felt just plain odd. But he had to ask the question somehow. And if that meant talking to a morningstar, he would have to live with the oddness of it. Fortunately, Barazain came to his aid.

"Ah, it is as Kithian says. The knowledge of the glaives has truly faded from the Wards. What a pity. Now listen, glaivebond. Here is the manner of it. When you hold me in your hand, no weapon can pierce your skin, but all will turn aside as if striking bronze. You may still be crushed, however, and your bones broken, or you may be burned or harmed in other ways, but you will never bleed from a wound with me at your side. Such is my common gift, bestowed upon me by the Mastersmith."

Common gift? It did not sound all that common to Grundy. To wade into battle immune to harm was no small advantage. He had always loved hearing stories of battle, but never imagined he would experience them himself. Besides his general disinterest in practicing swordplay, he was the sole heir of the Grundstaff line and too valuable to risk sending into a fight. That was another reason he never put much effort into sparring. But learning of Barazain's gift changed things. He had stood against the marshal of Bramble Eyre and lived to tell the tale and now he knew why. Perhaps there was hope for him as a warrior yet. Barazain certainly seemed bent on turning him into one.

"While I hold Grimbriar, no weapon may wound me," was all Grundy said, and the word went out afterward that he could not die when fighting with Grimbriar, though that was not strictly true.

"Thank you, my lord. I will tell them such. By your leave." If Logren experienced any astonishment at this news, he hid it behind his stony mask. He bowed one last time and departed. Grundy's mother looked upon her son with the contentment that comes when a great fear has been relieved.

"Tell Barazain I am grateful that he chose you," she said. "For he has twice saved your life now, and I suspect he may do so many more times in the days to come."

The great chiseled gem in the haft throbbed once with a mossy green light in recognition of her words.

"Yes, well, duty does what it must," was Barazain's reply.

"He can hear you, Mother, and he is glad and humbled by your thanks," Grundy said. Though it was not exactly what Barazain had said, he nevertheless felt certain that it was true.

After the meeting with Logren, Kion and Tiryn left while Grundy and his mother met with the steward, Adlor, to discuss the increasing difficulties of maintaining the castle while so understaffed. But as soon as his mother would allow, Grundy set out for the lower courtyard and the guesthouse to visit the "swordspeaker company" as he called them, though he supposed he was a part of that company now as well. He was forced to make the journey with two gallants at his side even though he carried Grimbriar and his mother knew that he was well nigh invulnerable while carrying it. But if he occasionally skirted the edges of his mother's wishes while out having adventures with Havrick, inside the castle he rarely dared to go that far. And Faedred's betrayal was too fresh in her mind to allow him to go about without a guard. She had openly wondered whether her son would ever again be truly safe while moving about Bramble Eyre, especially with so many men loyal to the former marshal. In light of that, Grundy was grateful she had let him go at all.

He left the gallants at the door and marched inside, not bothering to knock or announce himself. He was the lord of the castle, after all.

"What are you reading, my little friend?" Grundy said as he arrived in the dining hall to find Kion bent over an open book. The amount of freshly shed wax at the base of the candle showed that he had been there a good long while.

"Little friend?" Kion said. "I like the last part, but I'm not so sure about the first. I don't know that I've been called little since I was half the age I am now, and then only by my mother." The corners of his mouth winced ever so slightly when he said the word, "mother" and Grundy did not miss the unspoken pain.

"Yes, well, 'little' is also a term of endearment. It means that I've taken to you, Furrow-boy, that's all. Now out with it. What book has so captured your imagination at this early hour? For, meaning no offense, you don't look the bookish type."

"True enough. Tiryn is the reader in the family. But this is no ordinary book. It is the personal journal of the bladewarden, Strom Glyre," Kion said. He smoothed the open pages with his hand as though he could absorb some of that renowned warrior's greatness through the ink and paper.

This fellow was full of surprises. "You're serious? But how did one of your standing come upon such a thing? Strom was no mean bondsman and by your own testimony you've no noble blood yourself. I myself don't give half a nick what stock a man claims for his ancestry, but most, as you well know, are not of my mind."

"I took it from someone who stole it. I meant to return it, but Strom died before I could do so. I was there in Roving, you know. I watched him perish by Vayd's hand. A more noble death you will never see. I suppose by one way of thinking I have no business reading his private thoughts, but it seems a terrible loss to let the words of someone so noble fade and be forgotten. I often turn to them when I feel down or troubled."

Grundy unloaded his frame into the chair nearest Kion, causing the aged wood to creak in complaint. "So you're troubled about something, then. But Faedred's in prison, you're the beranskyre, and there's been no ill news from the war. What's weighing on your mind?"

Kion mused a while before answering. "Many things. Faedred's fate. The whereabouts of Vayd Mokán. And the shaydvorn. I don't imagine you've heard of them yet, but they worry me almost as much as Vayd."

"No, that word is unknown to me. What are they?"

"Small, dark-robed men, not much taller than a nyn. They

seem to move only at night or under heavy shadow. They make no sound and do not leave tracks. They fight with abandon, not caring whether they live or die. Tiryn and Zinder managed to kill a few in the woods, but most fled back into the night. No one knows where they come from, but I worry that they may strike again."

"Shaydvorn, you say? Well, if your sister and Zinder could fend them off, perhaps they're not quite such a threat." Kion's description of them, far from producing fear or worry in Grundy, made him all the more eager to see these shadow walkers himself.

"Perhaps. But if they come in greater numbers, it might be a different matter. Don't forget that Tiryn had Rimewinter also."

"You make good points."

"The real cause for alarm, though, is that they appear to be the creations of Shadowriven."

Grundy had never heard that name before, but it sent a tingle of fear down his neck and he instinctively grabbed his glaive.

"Tell me. What is this that you speak of?" Grundy said, unwilling to repeat the name until he knew what it was.

"*Cursed be that foul mockery of a glaive,*" Barazain said, hot with disgust. "*No more than a broken and shattered shiv, that's what he is. If metal were honor he would be made of straw.*"

Kion spoke of many things dark and terrible after that. It was then that Grundy first learned how grave and perilous the threat to the Four Wards truly was. He had of course known of Vayd and the haukmarn armies marching across Inris. But he now learned that Vayd had his own glaive, the fallen axe Shadowriven. He also learned of Kion's own griefs and sorrows. He learned of the death of Kion's mother and of Dunwik, who may have been a swordspeaker himself for a brief time. He learned of their pursuit of Vayd and the emptying of Whitewind and Dunach and of Kion's near death at the hands of the drakyn. But he also learned things that gave him cause for hope. Kithian and Barazain joined to tell of their forging by the Mastersmith's hand

and they spoke of something called the Spark, the source of all life, moving unseen in all things, even those which seemed hard or beyond comprehension.

"*And it is through the Spark that the glaives are given their gifts,*" Barazain said.

"*Yes, I possess the gift of fire and truth. Rimewinter has the gift of foretelling and ice,*" Kithian said.

"*And my gifts are blade turning and thorns,*" Barazain said with the kind of honest pride that comes not from vanity but from pleasure in a gift received.

"Blade turning I have already seen, and I am glad beyond measure for it," Grundy said. "But what is the gift of thorns?"

"*It is my primary gift. Like all major gifts it requires a reagent. Mine is thornbristles. When my handle is filled with them, I can shoot from my head the keenest thorns in the Four Wards, sharp as bear claws and hard as iron. More than that, if you strike my head upon the ground, I can raise thorns up into briar walls or patches beneath your foes. My thistles bite and my spikes rip and tear. With me in your hand your enemies shall fall like chaff at your feet.*"

"*I do not long for battle as you do, my friend,*" Kithian said, his voice more tempered. "*But I will be proud to stand with you when the time for it comes.*"

"*I know that you are always one to advise wisdom and patience in treating with our enemies, but if Shadowriven has returned, surely even you must be anxious for the day of his final defeat.*"

"*In that, we can agree. But to hasten a battle you are not ready to win is only to hasten defeat. There is much we must do ere we are prepared to face such a foe.*"

As foreboding as the talk of Shadowriven was, and despite the haze of dread which yet lingered from the mention of its name, when Grundy set his eyes upon the two glaives the doubt and shadows faded.

"Did not this Mastersmith make all the glaives, even this corrupted one? And a created thing can never rise above the one who created it." Grundy had read that in Luididis, but thought it might sound too lofty to mention where he'd gotten it. "Surely the Mastersmith has not given us the use of these weapons only to see us fail?" In this it may be that the confidence of his glaive had already begun to work in him, though such a thing was easy enough to say within the walls of Bramble Eyre, a place no enemy had ever conquered. His courage might prove otherwise when the enemy was at the gates.

"You are right. Also, we are three and Shadowriven is but one," Kion said. "And that is not all. Only a few days past I was rescued by one of the Mastersmith's servants, the solif."

"The glaives, the Mastersmith, the shaydvorn, and now the solif? You are full of mysteries, little brother. So tell me about these solif," Grundy said.

"Oh, it's little brother now, is it? Fair enough. Now surely you have heard of the golden animals that wander the wild places of the world? They are the solif, though I am sure, like me, that you did not know them by that name."

"No, but I had always longed to see one, though I admit that I never quite fully believed they were real."

Kion told him of his encounter with Cornoc in the depths of the drakyn's lair and of his shining ride through the woods to hasten to the aid of his friends. Hearing this account filled Grundy with the same air of wonder that so often swept over him during nights out on the lake under the unbounded sky or deep in the hallowed wood where the trees bent over him, breathing ancient secrets into the wind. It was said that these golden animals dwelt beyond the edge of the world, in places where men could not tread and there went on about their endeavors unmarked and unchecked since light first graced the land at the Four Wards' dawning. And now—forges and foundries—such things turned out to be real! Well, if glaives could be then why not this?

By the time Kion finished the account of Cornoc's charge against the shaydvorn, Tiryn, Livia, and Mariday had arrived. They brought with them a large carrot bean pie, round sourdough loaves, dried fish, and pitchers of hazelnut milk. Grundy had been so caught up in Kion's tales that he had clean forgotten his hunger. But the wholesome scents re-awakened his slumbering belly as if by a snap of the fingers and he hurried to help the ladies set the table so that the meal could begin that much sooner.

"Zinder's not back from the library yet?" Tiryn said. "It's not like him to miss a meal."

"Well, he took a bag of yurgenbrak and biscuits with him, so I'm sure he'll be fine," Kion said. "This looks wonderful. You outdid yourselves with the pie. I can almost taste it without taking a bite."

"Be sure to leave some for Zinder in case he's hungry," Tiryn said.

"In case?" Kion said.

"It will be a true test of friendship," Grundy said. "It doesn't help that I'm still trying to make up for three days without an honest meal."

"Never you mind," Mariday said. "We'll set out a plate for Zinder beforehand and see that Tiryn defends it from you vultures so that he has something to eat when he returns. A hard-working nyn deserves his provisions."

"It's not as though we've been doing nothing ourselves, you know," Grundy said, trying to remember exactly what they'd been up to. His mind had been so steeped in wonders and revelations over the past hour that he certainly *felt* as though he'd lived a month or two in that short span of time.

"Oh, well now, I don't doubt that you and Master Kion have been hard at work doing some studying of your own by the look of it. Just mind you leave plenty for Master Zinder," Mariday said.

"Ah, Mariday, I'd never deny a man his sustenance," Grundy said with a playful scowl. "Now then, enough talk—let's put our forks to the feast."

They were well into the meal and Grundy was just thinking

what a waste it would be if Zinder never came to claim his plate when the front door burst open and a great shout tore down the hallway.

"We've been infiltrated!"

Zinder, in a perfectly magnificent state of agitation, hat askew, collar ruffled, and mustache out of kilter, bounded through the door as though he'd been launched from a catapult, howling as if the walls of the Eyre themselves had been overrun. And for some reason he waved a leather scroll case wildly in his hand.

"Ho, there, fine fellow, what's this all about?" Grundy said. Though he was naturally concerned by Zinder's distress, no bells had rung out across the castle so this talk of infiltration must mean something else.

"What's wrong?" Kion said.

"Are you hurt?" Tiryn said.

"No, no, not so much as a scratch—unless you count my wounded pride." Zinder rushed up and pounded the table with one fist while raising the scroll case as if he meant to clout someone over the head. "It's him! It's him! He's here in the castle, come to torment me once again!"

"Calm down, old friend." Kion's expression flitted between bewilderment and mirth. "Who is this 'him' you're talking about?"

Zinder regarded Kion as though someone had just struck him senseless. Then, in a single breath, the explanation burst from his lips.

"Why, my Archenemy, the Scribe, you featherhead! That overdressed scribbler is only the greatest threat to my peace of mind and overall contentment that the Four Wards has ever known!"

Chapter 43

QUARRY IN THE QUARRY

Storming with indignation, Zinder expounded his harrowing account to those gathered around the table. He spoke even more rapidly than usual, and that was saying something.

"As you know, I was at the library all morning, flitting from shelf to shelf like a bee in a field of daisies. I found so many marvelous tomes which I had only read about, but I can hardly even remember what they were now for all that happened afterward. I confess that I might have gotten ever so slightly distracted from my main task, which was of course finding out the working of the welnod. Alas, I never did find the answers I sought, but the hours flew by until I looked up to check the time and realized I was about to miss lunch!

"Quick as a spark, I returned the book I was reading and dashed out the door. The hall was empty except for a figure just turning the corner at the far end of it. I only caught a glimpse of him before he disappeared, but in that moment my hat nearly fell off my head. For I would know that ostentatious plume and monstrous headpiece from a mile away. It was the Scribe! I called out to him, but he gave no answer. So I took off running. Now was my chance! He was trapped inside the castle with no way out and I would chase him down and confront him once and for all."

"Pardon me," Grundy said. "But who is this Scribe?"

"Someone who sold Zinder a poem once and Zinder has never forgiven him for it," Kion said with a smirk.

"He also sold one to our traitorous enemy, Tadgart Ilk, I'll have you know, and then gave us up to him in Fennigar," Zinder said, his high-pitched voice rising higher still.

"We can't be sure about that," Kion said.

"If not him, then the moon. That aside, why I needed so desperately to catch him and scrunch a fistful of his frocked neck is a tale for another time. Suffice it to say that I sped down the hall and I swear I've not run so fast since the time my grandnyn accidentally set my pants on fire while trying out his grease squirter too near the hearth.

"Yet as fast as I ran, I only reached the corner just in time to see that ridiculously poofy plume of his disappear ever so easy as you like around another corner. But the second hall was shorter than the first so I knew that I was gaining. The hunt was on! And I was determined that this time I would not be denied. Down hall and stair, through alcove and antechamber, I pursued him, always gaining, yet never quite catching the dastardly scribbler. Such turns he took—always the least expected path— and yet he led me ever down and downward. He never seemed to break into a run, yet he must have known I was following him —but the strides on that fellow! He could cross a river without wetting his toes. He would leave you in the dust, Kion, if the two of you went walking. For all that, I almost reached him once as he slipped through a door. He eluded me at the last possible moment, but at a cost. He closed the door so fast that a leather case he had hanging from his belt got caught in the jambs and snapped clean off. I have it here, as you can see—and you'll never believe what's in it!"

Grundy reached for the battered leather tube, but Zinder was quick to yank it back.

"Pip-pip, not yet! First, the rest of my tale. So, I snatched up the case, but the door was stuck from the strap, which had snapped off. It took me a fair bit to unstick it. Once I finally got it free, I renewed the chase, now following only by the sound of his footsteps, for he had put some distance between us through the affair with the door—a trick of his no doubt, for he is a wily foe.

"But at terribly long last I got close enough to see him pass into the hallway that leads to the quarry. As you know, there is a gate to that hallway and it ought to have been closed on account of today being Vairlin, but whether he picked the lock or by some forgetfulness of the guard, it was open. He slipped through, and in I went. I pursued him down the hall and through the quarry doorway itself, which rather curiously, was also unlocked.

"As I saw him go in, my heart danced inside because I knew then that I had him. For there is only one way into the quarry and one way out. I raced through the doors with a great shout. 'Aha!' I said. 'I've got you at last!' But then my voice died. The quarry was black as the dead of night! Not a sound came back save the useless echo of my own words. Nothing. No shuffling feet in the darkness. Not a sound nor a peep. I snatched up a lantern and lit it, hoping my eyes might succeed where my ears had failed. The tools of the quarrymen lay motionless among the rocks. Not so much as a puff of dust stirred in the farthest corner of the chamber. That was when it came to me that in all this pursuit I had not met another living soul. It was as though the whole castle had emptied. And for a moment I wavered, unsure of myself and wondering if there might not be some reason why the place had been abandoned. But I could not afford to let it shake me, for my quarry was right before me—in the quarry!"

Grundy interrupted. "Even though it's Vairlin, the quarrymen didn't actually take off. They're all in the shop cutting stone. That's why it was empty, though it was blind luck you never ran into anyone else before that and why the doors were unlocked, well, that I can't fathom, and honestly find more than a little troubling."

"Yes, yes, I see," Zinder said, hurrying on. "Now where was I? Oh, yes, into the quarry. So, I ventured into the empty cavern. But as keen as I was to catch my man he proved as elusive as ever. A dozen piles of stone offered places to hide. I checked every one, but no sign of him did I find. And if he had moved from one hiding place to another I'm sure I would have heard him for my ears are quite keen and noise carries easily in that cave. 'Come out, you craven!' I called, and named him 'scoomdigger' and 'squagblotter' and 'scatterslink' and other worse things besides, but the rascal refused to show his face. I had nearly run out of insults by the time I came to a small crevice I had missed and there—to my utter amazement— spotted not the Scribe, but two scoundrels crouching in the shadows!"

Here the storyteller in Zinder could not help but pause for dramatic effect. Grundy, impatient to hear what came next, said, "So what did you do?"

Zinder's chest puffed out. He had his audience right where he wanted them. "Well…Seeing the shifty looks on their two faces, I guessed at once that they did not have good intentions toward me. Several dozen ideas presented themselves to me at that moment, but most of them seemed like they would end with the two lurkers stuffing me into a sack. So in the end I did what anyone with two nicks of sense would do—I fled like a hunted deer. They gave chase, but the quarry is a maze of rocks and carts and pillars so they could not use their superior speed to run me down. In fact, I ran them around in so many circles that by the time I hoofed it up the ramp I had enough of a lead to make it to the door before they could catch me. They would have caught me in the hall, though, had I not happened upon a pair of soldiers who'd come to investigate all the racket. I cried out for help and the two slinks chasing me turned tail and ran, but their legs were already spent from running after me so the guards quickly overtook them. The guards recognized them at once as fellow soldiers by the names of Mord and Prestin."

"Ah, yes, I know them," Grundy said. "Not the best of our men, but fine enough as far as I knew. What were they doing down in the quarry?"

"That I do not know. The guards could get nary a syllable from the two of them. I also told the guards about the Scribe and so after they passed the two sneaks off to some other guards we went back into the quarry to see if we could find him. All we found were a pair of shovels and picks where I'd spotted Mord and Prestin hiding. It looked like they'd been digging at a place that had been sealed up. The guards said the tunnel had accidentally been found a month before and the quarrymaster had it closed off to keep anyone from falling in. 'If that's where Mord and Prestin were digging they were certainly up to no good,' they told me."

"You never found the Scribe, then?" Kion said.

Zinder's whole body went into a standing slump. "Not so much as a thread from his fancy frilled shirt. It looks as though he's bested me again, but I can't see how. Even if he somehow managed to slip from the quarry, he must still be in the castle. The guards promised to look out for him, so I'm hoping it's just a matter of time before he's caught, but that quillgobber is as slippery as they come. I fear he may have vanished once again." Zinder set the leather scroll case down on the table and slouched into a chair.

"Yes, well, you've had more adventure this morning than all of us put together, I can say that," Grundy said. "I'd certainly like to have a word with those two diggers, though. They had no business being there."

"Kithian and I can get the truth out of them," Kion said.

"Right, we'll head over to the prison as soon as we finish eating," Grundy said.

"Aren't you going to tell us what was in the scroll case?" Tiryn said before the meal could get underway again.

"Oh, yes, of course!" Zinder's gaze lingered longingly on his plate of food, but he swallowed his hunger and put on a bright face. "How could I have forgotten? At least there's one good thing to have come from all that running around." He pulled off the top and produced a thick piece of vellum, ancient, but of excellent quality, which he laid on the table next to his plate. A short note on a stylish card with swirls and flourishes around the edges and written in a flowing script had been rolled up within. The small note read: *Belonging to the Grundstaff Library, provided on indefinite loan, to be returned when no longer needed.* "That's his handwriting, by the way, the same that was on the receipt we found in Ilk's bag."

"So, then it's—it's—" Kion sputtered, the thrill inside of him tripping his tongue.

"Another part of the *Lay.* Yes. The third quatrain," Zinder said, less unhappy about his defeat at the hands of his "nemesis" now that he remembered the ancient poem.

"Oh, please read it, Zinder. Please," Tiryn said.

They all leaned in closer while Zinder recited the words.

Then all the world with him was cast
Beyond the smithy's light
A dreadful curse none could reverse
An everlasting blight

In wrath, in bitterness and spite
The fane reforged his gift
Through lightless fire, the weapon dire
Gained edge both dread and swift

To check the coming grievous rift
A champion was blessed
With silver blade, with skill remade
He rose to face the test

Against the strife and grave unrest
He bravely walked the land
Took up the sword against his lord
And nobly made his stand

"That's fine stuff," Grundy said. "The kind of poetry that 'holds its water' as we say in the Eyre."

"It tells us more of the War of the Shattering," Kion said. When Grundy asked what that was, Kion told him of the other parts of the poem they had read, and Kithian and the other glaives spoke of that time as well. One of the Four Lords and the ruler of Verisward, Talinyon, had been the first wielder of Shadowriven and, corrupted by his axe, had turned against the Mastersmith and the other three lords in a dark and treacherous rebellion known as the War of the Shattering.

"So this is not just poetry, but history," Grundy said. "What do we know of the champion who was mentioned? What of him?"

"That must have been your swordspeaker, right, Kithian? That's what the 'silver blade' means, right?" Kion said.

"Yes, his name was Anzel Inverness. He became a great leader of men, though when I was first given to him he was unknown and untested like you."

Anzel. Kion tried to imagine what that first swordspeaker had been like. He had given little thought to such things before. If Anzel had been a great leader, perhaps he had been someone like Strom Glyre. But if he was unknown, he must have been a commoner at one point. Could commoners rise to positions of importance within the Wards? Could they become nobles or bladewardens or even members of the Council of Nine? Kion had never heard of such a thing before, but at least in this case, it seemed to have happened.

"But what did it say about reforging?" Grundy said. "Talinyon was the first fane from what you've told me. This makes it sound as though he reforged his axe? And then the silver blade was remade as well? What does that part mean?" Grundy said.

"It means that Malix was not always as he is now," Nurien said. *"And neither was Kithian."*

"I don't understand. Have you not always been a blade?" Kion said.

"Even humans do not have a singular form. You were quite different as a child and will be quite different when you are old," Kithian said.

Kion did his best to make sense of Kithian's words, but the truth eluded him. "But you're a sword. Swords do not grow and change as men. Neither do daggers or morningstars…do they?"

"Neither do they speak or possess our gifts. You are forgetting that we are not mere creations like those of a common forge. Ordinary weapons are only copies of the true and living ones. To be alive and in this shattered world is to be subject to change. Though not being mortal, we can only be changed through the use of the Spark. Thus did Malix by his cunning trick Talinyon into reforging him and I was remade to oppose him in his new form."

"So what were you before?"

"It is told in the first quatrain of the Lay. *'The reaping blade and hatchet keen. Twin gifts he gave to men.'"*

Grundy, Tiryn, and Kion shared a three-way moment of confusion. Zinder, Livia, and Mariday, who'd been doing their best to follow along, were even more puzzled because they only received what the swordspeakers told them, and, not possessing the same bond to the weapons, did not always grasp the fullness of what the glaives said.

"So, out with it," Zinder said. "What did the glaives tell you now? That the fane wears poison ivy undergarments? Judging from the looks on your faces I'm guessing that's close to it since you all look so astonished."

"Kithian was a sickle." Grundy shook his head.

"A sickle?" Zinder said, raising a dubious eyebrow.

"Well, I never," Mariday whispered in Livia's ear.

"All things have their purpose and their time," Kithian said. *"It was not the Mastersmith's intention for men to go to war. But he provides for all, even to those who turn against him."*

Zinder laid a finger along his cheek. "I don't believe I'll ever fully understand the ways of these glaives."

Kion took Truesilver in hand. It was so perfectly crafted, he could not imagine it had ever been anything else. Perhaps Zinder was right, perhaps as mortals they would never understand the ways of these living weapons. But Kion knew one thing. He trusted them and trust does not depend upon understanding.

Chapter 44

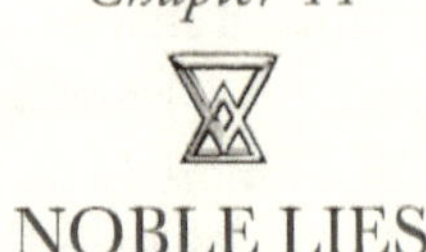

NOBLE LIES

The guards brought in Mord first. He marched into the small antechamber just outside the prison. Shackles bound his hands and feet, the chains rattling with each step. The gallants accompanying him moved off to the side as Mord sat in one of the two chairs across from Logren, who sat behind a desk of withered gray wood. The chamber was dry and well lit due to the flickering glow of two large lanterns, but the air down in the depths of the castle was stale and lifeless.

Grundy and Kion stood on either side of the new marshal. Logren wore the double-barred tabard of his new office, yet seeing it upon him sent a stab of regret through Kion. Faedred had so many masterful qualities. He could have been another Strom. But one false act had doomed him to a life of dishonor and broken vows.

Tiryn had no interest in questioning the men and Zinder was not present. Since he had a hand in catching the two soldiers, they were not likely to be favorable toward him and so he returned to the library to continue his research.

Mord's dark, spiked hair and beard lent a feral aspect to his appearance. His sun-browned face had congealed into a hardened scowl. He looked as though he was ready for a fight or as if he'd just come from one.

Logren's tone was curt. "Gallant Mord, you were found to be off duty this morning when discovered by Zinder Hamryn. Your superior, Tormain Gilliff, failed to report you absent. Further, Gilliff himself has since disappeared. My question to you is simple." He raised a knobbed finger to his chin. "What were you doing in the quarry, and who else besides Gilliff knew about it? Before you answer, the beranskyre is going to stand beside you with his hand on your shoulder. Through his sword, he can tell when a lie is spoken. So be truthful if you wish it to go well with you."

Kion pressed his right hand on Mord's shoulder. It tensed through the prison rags, but Mord held his head high. Grundy frowned as he spun Grimbriar in his hands. The presence of the massive spiked morningstar and how easily Grundy held it caused Mord to bristle uncomfortably.

"This one is trouble," Barazain said.

When Mord wouldn't answer, Logren continued. "You might think we don't know what you were up to this morning, but I have an idea. I believe it has something to do with Faedred. I know that his imprisonment did not sit well with you."

Mord's stillness betrayed the fact that Logren had hit close to the mark.

"I plan on speaking to all the men one by one after meeting with you. If any of them know anything, we will find out the truth. But if you have done wrong, if you speak now, I will grant you a lighter punishment."

Again, Logren's question was treated with defiant silence.

Kion had seen men confined to the stocks, he had even heard of some swine thieves who'd been carted off to work in the mines for the margrave. But he had never been a part of seeing that punishment handed out. Back in Furrow, Fielder Lorris made all the judgments himself and they mostly resulted in a stern talking-to or a small fine. But justice could be swift and deadly in the Four Wards, especially for a common soldier, and to stand and watch it unfold was a sobering thing. Though Mord maintained a surly look, the fearful prospect which lay before him was not something Kion would wish upon anyone except perhaps Tadgart Ilk and others like him who had betrayed the Four Wards in the most clear and evil way.

Logren fixed the prisoner with an impassive stare. "You will answer for your actions, as Gilliff will for his. Someone will give you up. Perhaps Gilliff himself. Is he here now to defend you? No, he remains safe while you are imprisoned. Now speak up, gallant. I will not ask you again."

"*Well said. This is a fellow who knows how to conduct his business,*" Barazain said.

Mord narrowed his eyes and his chin rose to a self-satisfied angle. "What I did, I did for a just cause. Punish me if you want, but you'll not get me to turn talebearer."

"Noble words do not change wicked deeds," Logren said. "Very well. You shall be stripped of your rank and confined to the stocks for two days, after which you will work menial labor under the direction of the steward for one year, or until you confess your crime. You will be given half rations during that time and all your wages garnished to pay your fine." Logren dismissed Mord with a wave.

Mord tensed, but took the news with grim satisfaction and was escorted from the room.

"He always was a bit stiff in the neck," Grundy said. "You really think it has something to do with Faedred?"

"I am almost certain of it," Logren said. "The quarry is not far from the prison."

"You think they would try to tunnel Faedred out?" Kion said.

"It's doubtful. That would take many days," Logren said. "But Mord has been heard murmuring against Faedred's imprisonment and so this business with the quarry is likely connected."

They cut their conversation short as Prestin entered. Other than his dark hair and sun-baked skin, his appearance contrasted sharply with Mord's. He was clean-shaven, with a youthful face and downcast eyes. He had a slight build, made even weaker-looking by his hunched shoulders. He shuffled forward, head bowed low, under a cloud of shame, and sank noiselessly into the chair.

Logren gestured for Kion to place his hand upon Prestin, but as he went to do so, Kithian said, *"I can see the truth of this man's words without the need for your touch, Kion. His mind is clear and without guile."*

"It's all right, Marshal," Kion said. "There is no such need with this man." He remained behind Prestin.

Logren questioned Kion with his eyes, but said nothing.

"Gallant Prestin. This is the first time you have broken the trust of your lord," Logren said. "Yet it is nevertheless a serious offense. You and Mord forced the locks and entered the quarry where you attempted to open a breach that had been sealed by the quarrymaster. For what purpose? Confess the truth and your punishment will be light. Stay silent or speak falsely and it will go hard with you."

Prestin fiddled with the chain binding his wrists, breathing long sighs of regret. His answer came in a whisper.

"I…can't tell you, Marshal."

"Prestin, I can see that you want to do what is right. You have been with us nearly two years. Lord Namril has treated you well, has he not?"

Prestin regarded him warily, as though he expected some trick.

"Yes, of course, Marshal."

"Your wife is well liked among the other washer women. Your son is growing up big and strong. You have never been disciplined before today, not even for tardiness or laziness. Is the price you are about to pay truly worth whatever scheme you and Mord were enacting?"

Prestin looked toward the door, perhaps hoping to borrow some of Mord's stubbornness of heart. But he only shrank back further into his chair and pulled the chain tight between his hands. His whole frame shook and Kion felt certain that the truth would break through at any moment.

"I…I can't tell you that either," Prestin said haltingly. "I'm sorry…"

Grundy laid Grimbriar on the desk and knelt before the crest-fallen soldier. "Think of Nela and Tiv. How will they survive without your wages? For their sakes, Prestin, tell us what's going on."

Prestin crossed his arms and hunched down even further, making himself as small as possible. His love for his family and his secrets fought against each other. He could not honor one without proving faithless to the other. But for all he clenched his hands and ground his teeth, his only decision seemed to be not to make one at all.

"I could send for your wife. Then you could tell her person-ally why it is that you are abandoning her for dishonor and hardship," Logren said quietly. The words had an immediate effect. Prestin thrust himself forward and gripped the edge of the desk, his knuckles going moon-white beneath his darkened skin.

"Please, my lord, no. It would break her heart to see me like this."

"Whether she sees you or not, she will soon be known as the wife of a criminal. Is this how you wish her and your son to be seen?"

"No, no, please. I hadn't thought of all this. I was only trying to help. I meant no harm. But I don't want Nela to see me like this, in chains."

"He is telling the truth," Kithian said. *"It may be that this man was deceived into his actions."*

"And what of Lord Namril—the one to whom you swore an oath to protect and defend? You have failed him as well. You may name deceit and disobedience as allies in your cause, neces-sary to achieve some other good, but in the end all you have done is sully your good name and bring dismay to those you ought to have protected and defended." Logren pursued Prestin relentlessly with his eyes, seeking to find a crack that would open a way to the truth.

Prestin reeled back in his chair. He was not prepared to contend with Logren as Mord had done. With trembling lips and great effort, Prestin forced himself to meet the marshal's gaze. "You are right, my lord. I have done wrong. I…we…Mord and I, we—we were trying to find a way to free the marshal." Prestin winced as he said the words, bitter to his tongue, and yet for the first time, the hunted torment that had marked his face began to lose its hold.

"Very good. And did you plan to dig into the prison?"

"No—we thought we could hide him in the quarry until we could sneak him out later, or that perhaps the cave itself might let out somewhere outside the castle. It was never explored, you know, after it was opened."

"You did not think to free him some other way?"

"It was a foolish plan, perhaps, but we did not wish to try fighting our way out of the castle and killing our own men."

"I see." Logren paused to ponder his confession. "And Gilliff knew of your plan? He was in on it as well?"

Prestin hesitated, but the hesitation itself was enough to give the truth away. The trapped look returned to his eyes. "Yes. Yes, he knew. Though it was Mord's plan, not his."

"Did Tormain Gilliff have some other plan of his own?"

"I—I'd rather not say," Prestin said, hedging.

"He has already mentioned two different plans," Kithian said. *"Perhaps the other one was favored by Gilliff."*

"Did Gilliff want to sneak Faedred out?" Kion said.

Prestin kept quiet, glancing furtively from one corner of the room to the other.

"He wanted to fight, then?" Kion continued.

"No, no, none of us wanted that."

"He is lying," Kithian said, *"to protect his friend."*

Kion, from his place behind Prestin, slowly shook his head, indicating to Logren that Prestin had lied.

"Aside from Gilliff, was anyone else involved in the plot to free Faedred?" Logren said, keeping his tone and expression even as ever.

"No, it was only us," Prestin said hastily.

"Another lie. Again, to protect others. This is what men often claim is a noble lie. But there never has been nor ever will be such a thing," Kithian said.

"True as true can be," Barazain said.

Kion walked around to the side of the desk. He deemed it was time Prestin knew of Kithian's gift for discerning the truth. When he unsheathed the blade, Prestin gave a fearful start.

"Do not worry. I intend you no harm. This is Truesilver, one of the glaives of old. You have heard that it can produce flame, but it can do more than that. It can also tell the truth of a man's words. You have not been honest with us, Prestin. We know that Gilliff favored the plan to fight his way out with Faedred. We also know that there were other soldiers involved in the plot."

Prestin's eyes lit upon the sword as though it had cut him after all. He buried his head in his hands. His whole body was aquiver with shame and regret. He had fallen into a pit from which he could not escape, and all he could do now was look up and cry out for help.

"I'm sorry, Beranskyre. I'm sorry, Marshal. And most of all I'm sorry to you, Lord Joromar, and to your father. I only wanted to save our beloved Marshal Faedred. He has done so much for me. Without him, Nela and Tiv and I would never have found a place in Bramble Eyre. I never wished ill on any of you, nor anyone else, but I see now that I have let my loyalty taint my judgment." He drew himself up at last, doing his best to face his fate with some dignity. He took in all the air his lungs could hold and let it out in a long steady release. Straightening himself in his chair for the first time, he said, "Very well. I will tell you all that you wish to know."

Chapter 45

TRUTH AND JUSTICE

Havrick ambled into the guesthouse after a long day in the garden. His skin was grimy and his poor hat sagged under the weight of his sweat. He dumped an armful of beets into a bowl atop one of the side tables.

"Sorry, I'm late. I'd hoped to have enough time to clean these. But at least you'll have them for tomorrow. This year they turned out sweet as cherries," he said. Grundy, Kion, Tiryn, and Zinder all greeted him with warm words of welcome from around the main table.

"Come, sit and eat," Zinder said. "No one ever needs to apologize if he comes late with food! Especially beets! It's been ages since I had some."

Havrick sat down sheepishly. He tried to leave an empty chair between him and Grundy, but his friend would have nothing of it. "You think I'm scared of a little dirt, Hav? Why, you'd think you didn't know me."

"I was only trying to be mannerly," Havrick said, sliding into the seat next to his friend and taking the plate Grundy passed to him. "Word is you've had quite the day. I never in my wildest dreams would have believed the Eyre had so many rats in the nest. I thought we were all for Lord Namril, through and through." He stuffed his mouth with half a bun, which filled his cheeks to bursting.

"Faedred had a way of winning loyalty beyond the ordinary measure of men," Grundy said.

"It's only when you put the metal to the fire that you find its true character," Zinder said. "And there's been plenty of fire these last few days."

"The good news is, we think we've rounded up most, if not all, of the conspirators," Grundy said.

"Ruwena told me you imprisoned twenty men," Havrick said between munches. "How did you hunt them all down in a single afternoon?"

"Twenty-four. Prestin gave us several of the names, but Gilliff had recruited some he didn't know about." Grundy wolfed down his second sourdough bun, though in his competition with Zinder he still trailed, for the nyn was on his third.

"And Gilliff? Was he ever found?"

"No, but one of the boats was taken and left on the far shore. After Mord and Prestin were caught, he must have stolen it and escaped into the woods. The cunning fox was willing to save Faedred's skin, but not at the risk of his own."

"A bad seed, that one," Zinder said. "I could tell it from the moment I met him."

"Though Gilliff turned out to be behind it all, he left the plans for breaking Faedred free with another of the tormains in the form of a scrap of paper hidden in the fellow's bunk."

"In the bunk! How ever did you find it there?" Havrick said.

"Truesilver spotted it. The same way Barazain spotted...well, you know—through the glaivesight."

Havrick's countenance darkened at the remembrance of that day on the lake when he learned of his brother's death. Grundy's own eyes strayed vacantly toward the other end of the room.

"Have you tried the eggs?" Tiryn said, her chirrupy words aimed at coaxing Havrick out of his sorrow. "I've only ever made them with basil and mushrooms, but Mariday's recipe is quite an improvement."

Havrick's nose gave a twitch, awakened to the rousing scent of the countrified eggs. He willingly fetched a bite with his fork.

"Yes, they're just the thing to cheer a man's soul after a long day under the sun," Havrick said with a halfhearted smile, acknowledging Tiryn's effort, but unable to fully cast aside his heavy thoughts.

"I worry about our defenses," Kion said, hoping, like Tiryn, to move Havrick's mind to other things, but also because the state of the castle had troubled him for some time. "We're down more than a quarter of our men. And we did not have any to lose."

Grundy made a dismissive grunt. "Father will return soon with reinforcements from the fane. But even if he is delayed, the war is far from Bramble Eyre. While we wait, Mother says we will send to Glenwither for new recruits or even hire some mercenaries."

"Do you have the coin for such things?" Zinder said.

Grundy's confidence sputtered and his brow drew taut. "It was a lean winter. Our coffers are drained. I've never concerned myself over such things, but if Mother thinks we should do it then we will find a way. The Grundstaffs always do. Bramble Eyre has never fallen and neither will it fall on my father's watch."

"It is an excellent place for defense with the lake and the thick woods," Kion said. "We could hold out here for some time even with the few men who remain." He knew little of siege warfare, but it did not take much to see the challenges a foe would have to face in order to assault this place.

Zinder shared what he knew about such kinds of battle, but even his knowledge came only from books. In the end, the conversation drifted to other things and the dinner soon wound down and everyone went their separate ways, not a little solemn over all that had happened of late and all that was yet to come.

The next day a party of four soldiers was placed on guard in the quarry at all hours, and no fewer than eight soldiers were assigned to the prison at all times as well. That left only fifty or so to guard the keep, man the walls and towers, scout the roads and surrounding woods, and act as messengers to Rippling, Glenwither, and Madrigal.

Tiryn spent the day in Lady Valissia's company and Zinder resumed his investigations regarding the crafting and repair of welnods. Kion and Grundy toured the battlements, armory, and keep, along with Logren and the new flagmaster, Navrin. Logren and Navrin took charge of working with the smiths and fletchers to increase the supply of arms, arranging the scheduling of the guard, and the sending out of scouts. Navrin was far too young for the position, being only ten years older than Kion, but all the candidates who stood in better stead for the office now passed their days alongside Faedred in dark prison cells contesting with rats and lizards instead of preparing for the haukmar invasion.

Another who proved vital to the battle preparations was Quartermaster Ulvarth. While his chief duty was the management of the arms and supplies of the soldiers, his other duty was far more important. He organized the sparring and training sessions for the men. These happened three times a four-mark and for Kion became the high points of each day. He lived to cross swords with the other men, to test the strength of his will when pushed to exhaustion, and to learn how to handle himself when outnumbered or outmatched.

It took Grundy three days before he consented to join Kion and the rest of the men in the daily sparring. Kion and Zinder decided that it took him that long to finally run out of excuses. Though Grundy had what Ulvarth called a "raw style" which often ended with him tripped up or outfoxed by quicker opponents, whenever he did land a blow, his opponents felt it, usually for several days after. Grundy found, like Kion had when he first fought with Truesilver, that his glaive imparted to him a strange insight and skill beyond what anyone with so little practice could have ever expected. It was not that Grundy instantly mastered fighting with a morningstar, but there was a naturalness to the movements and an ease that had never been there before.

With Grimbriar in his hands, Grundy's training advanced noticeably by the day. It helped that he wielded a morningstar and no one else bothered training with that weapon. It also helped that his opponents knew they could not really hurt him and so they went after him with everything they had. This meant that he received twice as many blows as any other soldier, but it also meant that he learned his lessons more quickly than he would have otherwise.

All the while they prepared the defenses and trained they received news from messengers about the war. Windle had fallen, they learned, not long after Kion had left. Swordswain Forglen had been wounded in the defense, and was rumored to have fled the field, but his final fate was unknown.

It brought Kion great satisfaction to hear that Ganthum and the Fellswords had won great renown in the battle, bringing down several lashtail siege engines and more than twenty haukmarn, including the chieftain of Claw Nakrawn, one of the five great tribes of Haukmar. Even better, the Fellswords had escaped capture and fled with the remnant of Windle's forces south to Rippling where they were preparing for the inevitable haukmar assault upon that city. Kion wished he could have returned to Rippling to join them and to fight for Dalia and her family and the rest of the town, but by the time he got there, the city might already be under siege or have fallen, and there was much to be done at Bramble Eyre.

Every bit of news was of a similar vein. The cities and strong-holds of Inris were falling one by one at a remarkable pace. Charring and Nickling both fell by the end of Arcsand. Nickling had very little in the way of defense and so fell in one day. Char-ring took longer. The haukmarn and Noathryn laid siege to it this time and while Daysman Ilk was no longer there to betray the city into their hands, he had so plundered and sabotaged the supplies before leaving that the Warding forces did not hold out two eight-marks before surrendering.

By the beginning of Falshorn, the fourth and last month of summer, Seabrim had been attacked from the sea by a great Noathryn fleet. Only through the heroism of Waveranger

Menlar, the leader of the Warding navy, had the assault been repelled. However, during the same month, the haukmarn marched against Dunskein, west of Seabrim, and mysteriously, the city fell in a single day. Reports of its demise were scarce and so sparse in their details that none could say how it had happened. Some messengers reported that the city had fallen by some dark curse, others through treachery, like Charring earlier in the war. The only consistent detail was that Vayd Mokán had led the assault and that none could stand against him in battle. And though they did not name Shadowriven, the rumor of his dark axe had begun to spread throughout Inris. Blackstorm they named it and Death Cleaver. And those few who dared oppose it in battle came to a swift end. But again, the details surrounding its fell deeds came not to the ears of those in Bramble Eyre.

The dark news drove Kion often to Strom's journal. There were days when he stayed up reading it long into the night. He wanted to know not only how the bladewarden had overcome the haukmarn in the last war, but how he had overcome his own fears and doubts leading up to the many battles he faced. For many times it looked as if Inris surely must fall. As in this war, the Warding armies suffered defeat after defeat. But the Warding army had won in the end. The haukmarn had been pushed back. And so he read to find out how Strom had persevered through all the defeats and failures. He was surprised to discover that Warding had suffered a betrayal in the last war as well. It reminded Kion in many ways of the recent betrayal of Faedred. Strom wrote:

Meren was a warrior of great renown. We studied his battles back in the Avelar Batal. Yet in the end he was cut down by the haukmar axes like the rest of his men. He was a mere man just as I am. But though it was the axes of the haukmarn that ended his life, it was the betrayal of Sevelius that brought those axes down upon him as surely as the hands that wielded them. For Meren would not have had to make that last desperate charge had Sevelius not let the Noathryn forces into the city.

The men and I spoke of the battle long afterwards and most of them expressed disgust and anger at the varlance's needless death. But I am not of that mind. What good is anger against what has passed? It serves only to bind the heart and stifle our living. Sevelius's betrayal cost the lives of many good men, Meren not least of all. But war is a sword that cuts both ways. None who march or ride into battle are assured to see the setting of the sun.

Sevelius died in the end. He paid for his betrayal. Yet, I can understand the men when they say that his death cannot make up for all the suffering and ruin he caused. There must be some final, fuller justice that truly satisfies, that makes amends for all the evils of this world. We may not see it in this life. It may be waiting in the world beyond, but surely it must exist for there to be any justice at all.

I told the men that this is what we fight for. Not anger at the past, but hope for the future. For that future justice that will be delivered one day, though we may not live to see it. For a world where there is no betrayal or bloodshed. For a time of peace and prosperity when all the injustice of this world is given its due. For a day when the Four Wards will be restored to what they were meant to be.

War is an act of faith. A struggle and a search and a longing for that final justice, for that final peace, when we can lay down our arms and embrace each other, rather than tear each other apart.

That is why we fight. For truth and justice.

Kion read those final words over and over. Truth and justice. Even if our eyes never see it, we must fight on in hope, knowing that our sacrifice, our blood and honor, will have been spent to a greater end. For truth and justice. That is indeed something worth fighting for.

The day after Kion read that entry in Strom's journal, on the twelfth of Falshorn, the peace and assurance those words had given him were sorely tested. For the castle received the worst news yet. Madrigal was under siege. The news was tempered with the report that the margrave had greatly augmented the size of his host prior to the attack, yet Logren made the cold observation that this most likely meant that the forces from the other fallen cities had simply fled there beforehand. From that point on, all news of eastern Inris was scattered to the winds and that land grew dark to them.

Less than an eight-mark later, Bramble Eyre itself began to receive refugees from Rippling, which fell after a brief yet spirited resistance. Kion looked in vain to find Dalia or anyone from her family, or Farmer Marlund, among those arriving, but if they had survived, they had not made the journey eastward to Bramble Eyre. That did not mean he found no familiar faces among those who came, however.

Ganthum and the Fellswords arrived at Bramble Eyre on the sixteenth of Falshorn. Though their number was half what it had been when Kion had last seen them, Ganthum still headed the company. He had been sorely wounded in the left arm, but under Tiryn and Ruwena's diligent care, the hurt was soon mended. Renin and Jalik had survived as well, though Renin had a scar on his neck so vicious it was a wonder he had lived.

"They were less like battles and more like slaughters," Ganthum said after he and Kion had exchanged warm greetings. "But my men held true. It was good to be fighting with honor again. Even in defeat. It's better to die fighting for what's right than win fighting for what's wrong."

"Aye, true enough," Renin said.

Jalik's head dipped in quiet assent. "Thanks for putting us back on the right path, swordspeaker."

"No, thank you. Seeing you lightens my heart and gives me hope in the midst of all the dire tidings of this war." Kion gave the Fellswords a cross-armed salute.

"Indeed. This old heart of mine rises at the sight of you as well," Ganthum said. "We are only eleven in number now, but we offer the lord of this place our blades, chipped and dull as they are."

"From all that I hear, you may as well be offering me a hundred," Kion said. "What do you say, Lord Joromar? Shall we accept this rugged band of former knaves?"

"If they can still put one foot in front of the other we'll take them—and if they don't mind walnuts and sourdough loaves for wages," Grundy said, clapping his waffle of a hand into Ganthum's. He still had no feel for the formalities of the army or of his station, but Ganthum paid no mind and grasped the thick hand eagerly in both his own.

"You have the Fellswords at your service, my lord." He and his men, wounded and battered as they were, bowed before him.

"Now let's see about fixing up those chipped swords of yours," Zinder said. "And it looks like your armor could do with a good deal of help as well."

And so the Fellswords came to join the defense of Bramble Eyre, the best happening in more than a month of that long terrible summer of war. But Kion's mind darkened even amidst the gladness, for he knew that if Vayd came against the Eyre, eleven battle-tested mercenaries—skilled and deadly as they were—would not be anything close to enough to keep the castle from falling.

Chapter 46

SHARED VISION

The arrival of the Fellswords made the training sessions all the more demanding. Though Quartermaster Ulvarth taught the soldiers well, he did not have Warder Ganthum's abundance of battlefield knowledge and so Ganthum took over some or all of the training sessions each day. Ganthum's style had an edge to it. He pushed them harder than ever before and taught them how to fight without quarter and how to use an enemy's strengths against him.

"The haukmarn are bigger and stronger than us. Faster, too," he said. "That just means when they miss, we make them pay double for their mistakes."

He showed them how to avoid a haukmar charge and strike them in the back where they wore little to no armor. He also taught them to weather the haukmar axe blows, which were almost impossible to parry. "If one connects, you're done for. But they're so bent on landing a killing blow that they wind up so you can see the blow coming a mile away. That leaves them open to counter-attack."

"But a single blow won't take one down," Rymir said. "And even the dullest warrior won't make the same mistake twice."

"True. You have to wear them down with multiple blows before you can ever hope to finish one off. But the key to fighting an enemy when you're outmatched, is to outnumber them. Now if you can't do that with actual numbers, if you're left to yourself, you can outnumber them in other ways."

"How so?" Grundy said.

"Well, some might call these tricks underhanded, but I simply call them underused. And underappreciated. It's the unexpected that multiplies the force of an attack. You can throw sand in your opponent's eyes, for instance. Then you outnumber him. You and the sand are more than he is alone."

"Clever," Grundy said.

On that day they practiced with sand, dirt, and gravel and how to follow up and finish off a blinded opponent. The next day Ganthum set up a straw dummy outfitted in haukmarn armor to show them how to strike for the straps on the poorly designed plates. The day after that they worked on leaps and lunges to overcome the haukmarn reach.

On the fourth day came Grundy's favorite day, Vairlin, the day of rest. After he took Kion and Havrick out on the lake during the cooler hours of the morning, they decided to pay a visit to Tapper. Kion had been taking Grundy as often as he could to let Barazain teach him the use of the beast speech. Tiryn often accompanied them, for though she had a good grasp of the language by now, she enjoyed conversing with Tapper and the other animals stabled with him. That day, though, she had gone with Ruwena and Rymir into Fathomwood to hunt for wild herbs for Logren, who had taken ill.

Though he had taken the position of marshal a hale, though somewhat older man, a month and a half in, with supplies running low and the strain of a hundred refugees to house and feed, and not enough hands to fully prepare and man the castle's defenses, he was sleeping only a few hours a night, if at all. After a grueling morning up on the battlements in the hot sun, training the tormains on how to counter siege towers and ladder assaults, he collapsed one afternoon from sheer exhaustion. He would have kept on in his duties after a short rest, but Lady Valissia got wind of it and ordered him to bed. The next day, rather than recovering, he actually got worse, and had been in steady decline ever since.

Kion leaned against the stall door listening to Grundy's

struggles to grasp what Tapper's whinnies meant. Many of the stalls were empty, the animals once in them having been sold or killed to preserve resources. It made the air less foul, but that was where the pleasantness ended. Men and women had to pick up and do the work of the missing animals now and, like Marshal Logren, many of them found it difficult to keep up.

"So that first sound means, 'my hindquarters are…too big'? and the second one means 'but it doesn't matter because I can still…hop the crate'?" Grundy said.

Kion chuckled to himself, not wanting to make Grundy feel too badly for messing up yet again.

"But those two brays sounded exactly the same," Havrick said, giving a puzzled snort. "And how can he say all that in just two short noises?"

"The glaives have a way of making it make sense," Kion said. "Without the glaives we can't understand it either. But Grundy, you didn't get it quite right. 'My harness is too loose,' is what Tapper said. 'But it doesn't matter. I can still haul the cart.'"

"*A good mule can bear an oak,*" Tapper added, trying to be helpful.

Grundy smacked the side of his head. "I'm hopeless at this. It's harder than Celestial Navigation."

"Is that even a subject?" Havrick said. "I've never heard of it before."

"No, I just made it up. Or, I may have read about it somewhere, but it was just an idea someone proposed. If the night sparks were fixed perhaps we could sail upon the open sea or some such nonsense. And right now, the chances of that and me learning this beast speech look about equal."

"You'll get it, Grundy," Havrick said. "Just look at the way you've taken to fighting. You used to trip over your own shadow, but I heard you actually beat Rymir yesterday."

"Three to two, fair and square," Grundy said. "Though he did break another sword."

"If men keep sparring against you, Grundy, the castle will be swordless in a month," Kion said.

"Well, the ones Zinder crafts never break. If a month passes before the haukmarn attack, he'll have made more than enough to make up for my mishaps."

"Do you really think they'll come that soon? Won't Madrigal have to fall first?" Havrick said.

"It would take an early winter to keep them from assaulting us here. With Rippling taken, the western army is sure to march our way," Kion said.

"My father will return well before then. Bramble Eyre will not fall," Grundy said, his eyes straying out beyond the stable doors to the courtyard.

As though borne upon some unseen wind, Ruwena came rushing through the open doors, cutting short their conversation. Her gray-streaked hair was a pure bird's nest of disarray. "Come, Beranskyre, it's your sister—she's fallen in a swoon and won't wake up!"

The lesson with Tapper was utterly forgotten and the three young men quit the stable without a word to the poor, befuddled mule.

"When did this happen?" Kion said.

"Not long ago," was all Ruwena said before waving them on. "Go to her. Now."

Dashing past the winded woman, they thundered across the courtyard. Kion's mind raced even faster than his feet. Tiryn might have been poisoned by some plant, or bitten by a beast, or succumbed to exhaustion. A thousand things could have gone wrong. He had no idea. His thoughts paged back to her bout with the wistering not so very long ago. He'd forgotten how close he'd come to losing her.

The three of them burst into the guesthouse and ran down the corridor to Tiryn's room to find Zinder and Rymir hovering over her bed. Zinder carried a cup of steaming mint tea and was slowly tipping it up to Tiryn's lips. So greatly had fear gripped his mind that it took Kion a moment before he realized that Tiryn was sitting up and that her eyes were staring into his, blinking and full of concern.

"Kion," she said after swallowing the tea. "It's all right. It's passed."

"Fire and ice, Tiryn, but you put the fear of midnight into me," Kion said. "Ruwena said you fainted. What happened?"

Tiryn handed Zinder the tea. "Thank you, Zinder. That helped."

"Of course," Zinder said. "But I'm guessing you'll need more than a few cups of tea to cure you of whatever nightmare sent you into that swoon."

"What's going on, Tiryn?" Grundy said, nearly as spent as Ruwena, who came bounding in just then.

Tiryn folded her hands together on top of her blanket, but Kion did not miss the slight tremble. "I had another vision," she said. Her voice was faint, almost inaudible, as though she didn't really wish to be heard, but each syllable sounded a drumbeat in Kion's heart. She had had visions before, and most of them had troubled her greatly, but her voice was different this time.

"That's what made you faint?" Kion said. How could a vision do that? If it was some fever or exhaustion like with Marshal Logren, that at least would have been something he could understand. But a vision?

"Yes," she said. The word was the loudest drumbeat yet.

"I had the same vision as Tiryn. And at the same time," Nurien said, her voice even more somber usual. *"That is a highly rare and troubling thing."*

"I don't understand," Havrick said. "You had a problem with your eyes that made you dizzy?"

"No, it was a vision—like a dream, only stronger, more real," Tiryn said, her voice gaining strength to assuage the worry she had caused in others.

"Ah, one of those kinds of visions," Havrick said. "I see. I mean, well, not the way you do, of course. Never mind. Go on, tell us what it was."

Tiryn closed her eyes a moment before answering. "The vision came while I was awake this time—while I was in Fathomwood hunting for herbs. At first it didn't feel like anything out of the ordinary was happening. It was only when I remembered that Rymir and Ruwena should have been there that I understood that it wasn't real. The shadow walkers, the shaydvorn, returned. Only this time there were hundreds of them. And they were pouring into the wood through a…through a great wheel of darkness." Tiryn slumped back against the headboard. She seemed to grow faint again, but she pulled out and blinked away whatever spell threatened to overtake her and took a moment to establish herself in the room once again.

"This wheel, I don't understand," Grundy said. "It was in the woods?"

"It was more like a portal than a wheel. It had no substance to it—like a whirling pool of air. Dark streaks stained the edges and it reeked of…oh, Kion, it was the same stench we smelled in Dunach. It was death…"

She stopped to steady herself. "I can't talk about the portal anymore. It's too dangerous. As though thinking of it might rip my mind from all sense. Whatever it was, though, the vorn streamed from it in a river of shadow. They swarmed around me and would have killed me—but before they could reach me, a man came running out of the woods. At first I thought it was you, Kion. But as he drew closer, I saw that it was not you, but… Faedred."

"Faedred?" Grundy said. "Is he in league with these vorn, then?"

"No, he…he saved me from them. He charged straight into the thick of them and in an instant was swallowed by the darkness. Whether he went into the portal, or merely disappeared into the swarm, I couldn't tell. But he drew the shaydvorn after him. They chased him and in that moment I turned to run. I didn't wait to see what happened, but fled unheeding into the forest. I didn't get far before a root snagged my foot and tripped me. I hit my head on something as I went down. After that, I woke up here."

"How long until you were found?" Kion said.

Zinder nodded gravely to Rymir. "Tell them what you saw."

"When Tiryn fainted, Ruwena and I were in the woods with her. We had just come to a clump of bricklestem when Tiryn let out a gasp and began looking around in terror as though she'd spotted some wild beast. Ruwena and I looked in every direction, searching to see what she saw, but the woods were as still and quiet as ever. Then she took off running. I set out after her with Ruwena close behind. Just as I reached her she fell headlong against the forest turf."

"Rymir carried her back to the boat and we rowed to the castle quick as we could," Ruwena said. "She gave me an awful fright, no mistake about it. I'm glad you've come awake, dear. But I don't mind saying you put a few extra gray streaks in this mop of mine." Remembering how unkempt she looked, she did her best to smooth her wild hair.

Kion touched Tiryn's hands. They had not been this cold since he'd nearly lost her in the mines of Regnir. Zinder was right. It would take a great deal more than a single cup of tea to wash away the stain of such a vision.

"It was so real, Kion," she said. "I can't shake it from my mind no matter how hard I try."

"*There is yet another thing you must know concerning visions,*" Nurien said. "*Whenever we experience the same vision at the same time, it is almost certain that it will come to pass.*"

Tiryn squeezed Kion's hands. There was no more strength in them than in the grip of a child.

"*And it will come to pass quickly.*"

Chapter 47

HOPE AND DREAD

All travel along the eastern and western roads ended the day after Tiryn's vision. Only to the south from Glenwither did they still receive goods and messengers after that. Thanks to Logren's efforts, they had managed to muster another thirty soldiers, half from Glenwither and the other half from among the new arrivals from Rippling and those dwelling in the castle. Havrick was among them. Though he, like most of the new soldiers, had little to no skill with any weapon, everyone had to do what they could. On top of their usual work in the garden, quarry, kitchen, or fishing boats, at least part of their day was now spent in training or preparing the defenses of the castle. Quartermaster Ulvarth did what he could with them on the sparring grounds, but mostly they ran errands or shadowed other soldiers as they went about their duties. They did not come close to replacing the twenty-four soldiers now confined to the prison, but what the new soldiers lacked in ability, they made up for in effort and hardiness. They knew how to work without complaint and their help was much welcomed by the other soldiers.

After Tiryn's vision, the scouting parties in the woods were doubled. The mushroom harvesters went always with several guards now. Something was stirring deep within Fathomwood. All the glaives could sense it, not just Nurien.

Tiryn stayed in bed for three days after her vision. She took only a little food and mostly slept so that Kion saw very little of her. Lady Valissia spent at least part of each day at her bedside, attending her along with Livia and Mariday, as if all three were her maidservants. Tiryn protested that she did not deserve such treatment and that a noblewoman should not lower herself in such fashion, but Valissia had the final say in any case.

When Tiryn felt well enough, she returned to working in the kitchen with Mariday in the mornings and in the afternoon with Ruwena in the garden or the healing quarters. Meanwhile, Logren languished in his bed and only grew worse. It was far more than mere exhaustion. He suffered a fever that came and went and he often struggled to breathe and developed a hacking cough. And neither Nurien, Tiryn, nor Ruwena could find a way to bring him back to health.

Regrettably, Navrin was not fully up to the task of replacing him. He often consulted Warder Ganthum for guidance. But though Ganthum knew more than Navrin about defending a castle, he was by nature a fighting man. When it came to the details of managing workloads among smiths and fletchers, coordinating castle repairs with the stonemasons, arranging meals for the men, and other details, Ganthum had little patience or interest. Yet between the two of them, they managed to keep the garrison running and the soldiers working diligently to prepare for the expected attack.

Because Ganthum was so often pulled away from the daily sparring sessions, Kion found them less challenging than before. Grundy, though, continued to improve. On one occasion he mangled Kion's helm and one of Barazain's spikes went through and pierced the underside of his jaw. Grundy apologized profusely and went with Kion to have it bandaged up. It turned out to be a minor wound, all part of the risk of sparring with live weapons, but it could have been much worse. Barazain berated his glaivebond for the rest of the day about learning more precision and control.

"When Joromar learns better control, he will be a formidable warrior," Kithian told Kion before he went to sleep that night.

"For my own sake, I hope he learns soon," Kion said, feeling the tender skin around the bandage. "But power is something you cannot teach and he has plenty of that."

"We will need that strength when the hour comes."

Each night the three swordspeakers gathered for dinner at the guesthouse to discuss the day's events. On most days, Havrick joined them, and Zinder of course never missed a meal. He had long since repaired the welnod. Kion and Grundy went to see when it was first put to the test.

The entire quarry went silent and all the workers gathered round for the trial. Quarrymaster Trimble applied a honey-colored ointment to the welnod's two silvered prongs. He then felt along a great boulder that sat near a wall, tapping the other end of the delving fork against the stone and listening to the faint vibrations. It took several tries before he found a spot that suited him. Sticking the prongs against the boulder, the ointment held it fast. He picked up two metal rods he had laid to the side, fashioned from the same silvery metal as the welnod. He struck the fork on each side, alternating between the rod in his left hand and the rod in his right. The blows came softly and slowly at first, but soon Trimble struck them for all he was worth. It made a hum so deep and harrowing it set Kion's teeth on edge.

"Cover your ears!" Zinder shouted above the din, putting action to his words.

The other quarry workers had already taken measures to protect themselves, though Quarrymaster Trimble continued on without any such precaution. Kion clapped his hands over his ears and it became more bearable, though still unpleasant.

His discomfort was instantly forgotten when the boulder shivered, buckled, and then splintered. Cracks radiated from the welnod in every direction, swift as lightning and in a similar veined pattern. The cracks widened and deepened and within moments the boulder lay in a shamble of smaller stones at the quarrymaster's feet. Many of the stones were still quite large, but most could now be carried by the strong-backed workers and the welnod could be used to reduce the larger ones into yet more manageable sizes.

Everyone gave Zinder a hearty cheer and round of applause. He doffed his hat, taking several bows and soaking in the adulation. Whenever the applause was about to die down he struck the welnod and the cheers rose again. He did this several times, drawing out the cheering and milking the moment for all it was worth.

"Trimble told me that as part of my payment he'd give me the material to make my own welnod," Zinder said afterwards. "They have to be made from trinum, a metal formed from combining several other metals together. I found the schematics and all the instructions in *Guffing's Grand Inventions*. Who knew they had a book by an actual nyn in their library? Nyn rarely write books. Life's far too short to take the time to write things down. But this fellow—Guffing Willsap—was quite meticulous. I look forward to the challenge of crafting my own." Zinder derived the same satisfaction from crafting things that Kion received from swordplay and he took full advantage of his access to the Bramble Eyre forge, spending the better part of his days in the smithy, fashioning his welnod and imparting his knowledge to the other smiths. In little time at all, the armory had more than enough swords and armor for the new soldiers who had joined the ranks.

At mealtime, Grundy and Zinder made it a habit to lighten the hearts of those at the table with their eating competitions and boasting, but as the cloud of war loomed darker, laughter did not come as easily as before. More often than not, long faces and limp smiles greeted their quips and foolery.

"Why, what's wrong with you folk?" Zinder said one evening. "You'd think we'd already lost the war to look at you. Have we not rooted out the scheming scoundrels from the castle and saved Lord Namril's heir from certain death? Is not the welnod working? Is the armory not properly stocked again?

Does the sun not yet shine and the moon rise in her place? Do we not hold three of the Mastersmith's awakened glaives among us? I'm the first to admit that things look dire in this war, but Bramble Eyre has never fallen, and we ought not to consider it lost before the first arrow is fired or the first sword drawn."

When it mattered most, you could always count on Zinder to bring light into darkened hearts and hope amidst the dread.

"It's not the war that scares me most," Tiryn said. "It's the black portal of my vision. How I wish I could banish it from my mind." Though physically Tiryn had recovered, she often went about the castle in a listless half-daze, her mind caught up by things no one else could see. "What if it's not just the haukmarn who attack this place? What if the vorn come? Cornoc said that they have some tie to Shadowriven. What will happen to Lady Valissia and Mariday and Livia and Ruwena and the gardeners and cooks and other servants if they march on the Eyre? This place is so peaceful, and the people here have been so kind. I don't want to see their way of life destroyed."

"I want to see Bramble Eyre stand firm even more than you do," Grundy said. "This is my home. I've lived my whole life on this lake and within these walls. Bramble Eyre will not fall, Tiryn. Not if I have anything to say about it." He pounded his fist into his open hand to emphasize his point.

"Whatever happens because of the vision, there is nothing we can do about that," Barazain said. *"But as for the fate of this castle, we must leave that to the day of battle. There we shall have a good deal to say. And this much I do know: that we will make our enemies pay dearly whether in victory or in defeat."*

"Tiryn does bring up an important concern," Kion said. "What happens if the castle falls? Do Navrin and Ganthum have a plan in place to save the people here? Should we send some away now before the haukmarn come?"

"The castle is barely able to function as it is. We lost too many over the winter. If we send anyone away, it will make defending the Eyre and providing for the soldiers that much harder," Grundy said.

"Well, I will ask Navrin about it all the same," Kion said.

The next day, Kion did just that. Navrin told him that they would send Lady Valissia away by boat in the event the castle was overrun, and that the remaining boats would be filled with women and children. They only had enough watercraft for about a third of the people, though. The rest would have to swim for it. Once they reached the shore, they would make for secret shelters prepared long ago in hidden caves in the nearby woods. The hidden places would provide them food and shelter for a short time before they would be forced to flee to safer lands.

"Could we not craft more boats while we still have time?" Kion said. Anyone forced to swim would be easy prey for the haukmarn army.

"We could perhaps fashion some more, but would have no place to put them. The underground docks are already full."

"I see. Do you think the attack will come soon?"

A shadow passed over Navrin's face. "It will not be long now. The scouts we had observing the western road have not been heard from in two days. We can only assume that they are lost."

Four more men gone, experienced soldiers and skilled at woodcraft. How had they allowed themselves to be captured or killed by dull-witted haukmarn? Even if the Noathryn traveled with them, they were people of the plains and had little knowledge of the woods.

"So the attack will come by way of Rippling, then." It was the most obvious choice.

"Madrigal will not fall easily," Navrin said. "It will hold through to the winter at least, unless Vayd conjures up a second army twice the size of what he's sent against it. He is spread thin, his forces scattered across Inris to hold the towns and cities he has already conquered. It is from Rippling that the attack will come. Keep yourself at the ready, Beranskyre. We will need your fire when the time comes."

Kion found it difficult to fall asleep that night. His mind kept seizing upon the four missing scouts and the inescapable feeling that Vayd, marching with Shadowriven at the head of some great host, drew closer and closer to the Eyre with each passing hour.

Chapter 48

THE HOUR OF HARD PLACES

Several days had passed when a nearby shout pulled Kion from sleep. A thud sounded against the door.

"What's going—" he started to say, but the door sprang open and Tiryn came staggering in before he could finish. Rimewinter's blue crystals cast fractured patterns upon the walls and bathed Tiryn's face in flickering light.

"We have to get out!" she said, grabbing hold of his arm.

He allowed her to pull him a few steps toward the door before resisting.

"Wait, why are we leaving?" he said.

Zinder cried out from the hallway, just before he bounded into the room, still wearing a red-and-white-striped nightgown with matching nightcap. The cap's furry tassel swished down over his eyebrows.

"What's all this racket?"

Tiryn's face wore a hunted look, but no sight nor sound of enemies disturbed the house. "Hurry, before the ceiling falls down on top of us!"

She pulled at Kion again, but this time he held his ground. He and Zinder surveyed the ceiling, but in the light of Rimewinter's blade, it looked as sturdy and intact as ever.

"Do you not feel the ground trembling?" Nurien said, her voice brimming with danger.

"What do you mean? The ground is not moving at all," Kithian said.

Tiryn's head swung about the room. She touched Kion's bedpost, then the walls, and last of all she patted her own shoulders. "I'm not moving," she said. "I'm not moving. Neither is the room. Did it pass so quickly?"

"Did you feel some sort of quake?" Kion said.

Tiryn again surveyed the room, fighting to make sense of her conflicting perceptions. "I thought so…"

"I did as well, but there are no cracks in the stonework and nothing has fallen. Even more telling is that no one else experienced it. It must have been another shared vision," Nurien said.

"But I felt the quake in Rippling. This was just like it," Tiryn said.

"Then perhaps what is coming has some link to that, but whatever it is, it is clear that this time it was a vision and nothing more."

Tiryn slumped against Kion's bed. "It seemed so real…"

"I thought the same. Once again we have had the same vision. Great events are stirring. The dam is about to break."

"Well, let's hope it breaks at a more reasonable hour," Zinder said. "Bother these midnight visions. I was having the most lovely dream. I had lured the Scribe into a net with a particularly stunning poem etched on the highest quality vellum you could imagine. The net had just snatched him up and there he was, dangling from the tree with that ostentatious hat of his in shambles."

The tones of a tolling bell cut short Zinder's recollections.

"Oh, no," Tiryn said.

A second toll rang out, then a third…a fourth…and then came the fateful fifth. Five tolls meant one thing—enemies had been sighted. The castle was about to be attacked. The bells were a call for every soldier to take his post and everyone else to prepare for the worst.

The time had finally come. All those days of practice and preparation condensed into this one dark night. At last Kion would fulfill his duty as beranskyre for his lord, a lord he had never met. Thoughts of Faedred passed fleetingly. The disgraced marshal had believed in him. Or had that been a lie as well? Whatever the case, now was the time to prove himself. "Zinder, you must go with—"

"I'm with you, lad. That's the only request I'll honor. I know you were about to send me with Tiryn, but you can take care of yourself, can't you?" Zinder said.

"I will protect Lady Valissia," Tiryn said, rising and regaining some of the fortitude she had lost from her vision.

Zinder knew Kion too well. That was precisely what he had been about to say. Despite being a swordspeaker, Tiryn was still his little sister and he was responsible for keeping her safe. The natural thing was to keep her from danger and for that she could have no better guardian than Zinder. But she had stood against the snowwinder, the drakyn, and the shaydvorn. And with Rimewinter she was far from defenseless. If she chose to protect Lady Valissia, she could do that without Zinder's help. Still he struggled and might have offered up some resistance but for the urgency of the bells, which demanded an answer.

"Very well. Go to Valissia. Zinder and I will go to the western wall. If the battle goes ill, we will come for you."

"Even though I knew this day would come, I still do not want you to fight," Tiryn said.

"Nor do I wish to leave you. But we have come to the hour of hard places."

"*She does not go alone, swordspeaker. I will be ever at her side,*" Nurien said.

"*Come, now we must hasten to meet our fate. Hard though the hour may be, it is the time we were meant for,*" Kithian said.

"Guard yourself well, sweet Tiryn," Zinder said, stiffening. "We shall see you again soon enough." He embraced her and turned away.

"Yes, soon." That was all Kion could manage without spiraling into a mire of doubt and misgivings. He had to let her go. They had to be swordspeakers now.

After a short but fierce embrace their eyes met.

Tiryn said nothing yet her eyes told him everything. All their work tending the garden and caring for the sheep, all the golden days upon the Tors—days of laughter and days of lack, all the meals they'd shared in the cottage and songs she'd sung by the hearth, together with all their memories of their Mother and Father and the pain of their loss, all this passed wordlessly between them in the span of a moment.

She gave him a cross-armed salute and fled the guesthouse.

"Watch over her, Nurien," Kion whispered after her.

Zinder helped outfit Kion into his armor, then retrieved his crossbow while Kion fastened on his sword belt.

And then they were away. Kion and Zinder sped toward the front gate along with other soldiers spilling from the barracks. Torches lined the walls, blazing a harsh warning beneath a cloud-smothered sky. Kion's scabbard banged against the stairs as he and Zinder rushed to join the other soldiers huddled behind the crenellations along the walls above the front gate.

Flagmaster Navrin and Warder Ganthum spoke together there in grave conference. Grundy stood beside them, looking somehow smaller than he was, and his face had no trace of its usual joy. A paltry twoscore soldiers flanked them to either side. Ganthum's Fellswords stood at the ready, looking every bit as fell as their name. Hard hours called for hard men, and there were none harder. Their presence stiffened the resolve of those around them. But it was not the resolve of the men that concerned Kion at the moment. His eyes fixed upon the dark shapes gathered at the gates at the far end of the bridge.

The pale faces of the haukmarn loomed skull-like in the wispy light of the wanstones embedded into their armor. They howled and raged with voices deep and feral; the discordant noise could be felt upon the skin. The black crowd roiled and undulated, restless for blood.

Behind the bulk of the army rambled a half dozen lashtail siege carts pulled by teams of round-backed musk oxen. The poor beasts advanced dumbly before the harsh whips of their masters. The lash-tail catapults had not one, but five long spindly arms for hurling debris onto their enemies. The arms spread out like a fan behind a central cluster of winches. A chain-link basket dangled from the other end of each of the arcing arms. Small fires which soon turned to great ones lit up the night between each siege engine. Piles of scrap were thrown into dark metal pots and heated upon the bonfires in preparation for the coming assault upon the Eyre.

Kion searched in vain for any sign of Vayd Mokán among the ranks, but if he was present, Kion could not tell.

Navrin waved Kion over and Ganthum saluted him, his eyes gleaming.

"We can rest easy now. The Sword of the North has come," he said.

Zinder's quick eyes surveyed the invading host. "A paltry force. I count less than four hundred. And those lashtails will do little to the castle or its buildings."

"I agree. Something is amiss. There is no sign of Vayd and without Shadowriven's help, such a force cannot hope to conquer the castle," Kithian said.

"Always keep your eyes out for a snake," Barazain said. *"They like to hide in the grass, waiting for their moment to strike. That is ever Malix's way, preferring plans and schemes to open battle—because he knows he would be outmatched!"*

"Yes, Bramble Eyre will never fall to such rabble," Ganthum said.

"I, for one, am glad Vayd isn't there," Grundy said in his honest way. The more Kion got to know him, the more Grundy reminded him of the country folk from Casting Selvedge. Plain and direct, at times painfully so. Though Barazain rested comfortably upon his shoulder and he wore a great suit of thick padded armor, he was ill at ease about what lay ahead. "It is not that I fear death—I would die willingly if it came to it. But even with Grimbriar, I'm not sure that I could help you defeat him."

"Now, none of that talk from the glaivebond of Barazain Grimbriar. You will be ready when the time comes."

"Barazain is right. Learn to trust your glaive and let go of your fears," Kion said.

"Every battle has a cost," Kithian said. *"Wise is the man who measures that cost before he acts. Joromar is not wrong to question himself. His training is not complete, and even if it were, it would be difficult to face Vayd when his forces outnumber ours four to one. For you can be sure that he will not wade into battle unguarded. Shadowriven is far too cunning a foe. No, we would need many men of our own to face him on a day like today. If we faced Vayd now, we would have little hope of victory."*

Grimbriar's spikes gave off a hard sheen. Barazain did not see things the same way, but offered no response out of deference to Kithian. Kion did not like it much either. He wanted to end the war. And defeating Vayd was the only way to do that. But the wisdom of Kithian's words was hard to deny. It would be almost impossible to face Vayd on even footing amidst such a host and Grundy certainly did need more training. Perhaps it was just as well, then, that Vayd was not leading these forces.

Navrin finished surveying the enemy host. "Small as they are, we must bring down the bridge. We cannot let them gain access to the island." Though his voice was measured, uncertainty flickered in his eyes. He was not ready to lead this defense, but he was their leader.

The haukmarn stopped outside the far gate across the bridge. The two gatetowers had already been abandoned. A massive bronzewood trunk, hefted by twenty haukmarn, worked its way to the front of the host. The horns of the haukmarn tainted the air with a mangled chorus of angry notes, each horn blower attempting to drown out the others.

Braaaaaaawwwm! The trunk heaved into the iron gate. The rattling and clanking resounded up and down the lake. But the gate held.

Braaaaaaawwwm! The trunk slammed again into the gate. The wrought iron braids groaned and gave way a little.

Braaaaaaawwwm! The trunk heaved a third and a fourth and a fifth time, until at last on the tenth stroke the gate snapped in twain. With a great roar, the haukmarn surged from behind and shoved the iron bars down onto the bridge. The first harriers trampled over the remnants of the gate and onto the bridge. Navrin allowed them to advance halfway across—some two hundred haukmarn by then—before nodding to the Tormain standing ready at the door of the tower off to his right. The soldier called down and chains and gears shook into motion, operating the hidden mechanisms beneath the bridge. Muffled explosions and grinding noises ran along the paving stones in quivering waves. The stones cracked and shifted, falling away and crashing into the water in a great tumult of destruction. The haukmarn plunged into the lake along with the sundered rock.

"It is quite the sight to behold," Zinder said. "A marvel of stonecraft to take down a bridge of that size in mere moments."

The haukmarn flailed about in the churning water, most swimming back to shore, though a few had the misfortune to get a foot or a leg wedged between the sinking stones and would not rise to the surface ever again.

"So, the bridge is down." A weathered voice drifted across the ramparts. Behind Grundy, and to everyone's surprise, the hunched and emaciated figure of Marshal Logren plodded toward them. He wore the tabard of his office and was girded with a sword for battle, yet he needed a cane and the assistance of another soldier to steady his rickety legs.

"Marshal, what are you doing here?" Navrin said.

"With all due respect, my lord, you do not look well," Ganthum said.

Logren paid them no heed, but went to the edge of the battlements to observe the haukmarn struggling to return to the far shore, their wanstone-studded armor sparkling in the black currents as though a bed of pearls lay strewn below in the dark waters. Meanwhile, upon the land the lashtail crews arranged the five-armed catapults in a line, preparing them to launch the heated piles of metal scrap into the castle.

"He demanded that I bring him," the soldier assisting Logren said.

Logren coughed painfully several times, an awful, wheezing rumble that wracked his frame. "This force is too small. It is a diversion. Have the scouts reported any other movements within the wood?" he said.

"We have not heard from any of our scouts for more than an eight-mark," Navrin said.

"Blast!" Logren's throat seized up with a fit of coughing. Before he could say anything more, bells rang out across the castle once again. Kion counted them. Three, four, five…six. No. The keep was under attack? That was impossible. They could never have breached the walls so quickly.

"How?" Navrin said, panicked. He grabbed the nearest tormain by the shoulder, shaking him as though the bells were his fault. "Do we have word from the watchers where this new attack is coming from?"

"Nothing, my lord," the poor fellow said. "No word at all."

Grundy stepped up to Logren. "I'll go to the keep."

Valissia was there. And so was Tiryn.

"I'm going with you," Kion said. The aftershock of the bells still rang inside him. He had left Tiryn in the safest place in the castle and now it had somehow come under attack.

"I had them bring me in a cart," Logren said, clearing his throat. "Take it."

Ganthum nodded. "This force along the shore is little threat to us. We will send whatever men we can spare after you. It's as good a plan as we will find."

"Yes, of course. Take as many men as you wish." Navrin did his best to collect himself. "Perhaps you should go with the swordspeakers, Ganthum. Marshal Logren and I can direct the defense of the battlements."

Ganthum ordered twenty men—including all the Fellswords—to follow him down the tower. Zinder, Kion, and Grundy hurried on ahead and mounted the cart below as the warder emerged behind them.

"Go on. We will hasten after you," Ganthum said. "With those two weapons of yours, you're already worth a dozen companies as it is."

Zinder drove the horses without thought of peril or sense, but Kion hardly noticed. Castle buildings flew by in the night in a dizzying river of motion until Zinder reined in the horses before the fortress gate. There was no sign of battle anywhere outside the great stone keep, nor along any of its walls. The guards at the gate didn't know why the bell had been rung, but waved them inside. As they barreled into the great hall, a messenger came tearing down a side corridor to intercept them. Of all people, it turned out to be Havrick, dressed in the yellow tabard of a soldier and fitted out in a newly made suit of leather armor, with a short sword flapping at his side.

"Oh, Grundy, you came!" said the gardener-turned-soldier, holding a stitch in his side.

Another soldier came storming up behind him. He barely slowed as he ran past. "I'll alert the front gate," he said.

"What's this about?" Grundy said.

"It's Tiryn and Valissia...They're—they're down...in the quarry. Run to them...I'll catch up when I can...I'm plum spent."

"There's no attack on the keep?" Kion said.

Havrick waved them on. "No, not yet...Find Tiryn...she'll tell you."

They did not wait to hear more. They launched into the castle, retracing Havrick's steps through a twisting maze of hallways, rooms, and doors. They did not stop until they rushed up to the entrance to the quarry, as exhausted as Havrick.

"You came," Valissia said. She stood surrounded by Tiryn and six soldiers. Rymir was among them.

Grundy rushed to embrace his mother and Kion and Tiryn did the same. Though they had only been apart for a short time, a calm washed over Kion in the presence of his sister. In the mad flight from the walls until now, he had feared the worst.

"What happened? Why did they sound the bells?" Kion said.

"The vision I had of the quakes. I had it again after I came to the keep. Nurien did as well. Only this time it was mixed with the vision of the black wheel. The wheel opened up from a crack in a cavern wall and the shaydvorn poured from it."

"You think these shaydvorn have somehow dug under the castle?" Grundy said.

"I can't say for sure. What I do know is that both visions have happened twice, which means they are almost certain to occur," Tiryn said. "Nurien and I think that an attack is coming through the sealed-up hole in the cavern."

"You have men down there watching it?" Grundy said.

"Yes," Valissia said. "We brought in as many as we could. Close to fifty."

"Fifty? But that's half our men. Are you sure this is wise?" Kion said.

"Wait, Mother. We didn't have fifty inside the keep. Most of the men were sent to the walls. How did they arrive before us?"

"We brought down most of those assigned to the keep." Valissia placed a hand upon Grundy's arm. "The rest came from Faedred and his men."

"Faedred?" Grundy withdrew his arm as though she had burned him with her touch. "Mother, you ordered this?"

"Yes, my son. Faedred was part of Tiryn's vision as well, remember? He was the one who fought the shaydvorn. We are in a desperate hour. I chose a desperate course."

"All because of this vision that may or may not come to pass?"

"It comes to pass even as we speak," Nurien said.

A great rumbling beneath their feet and the splitting and crashing of rock below made it sound as though the bridge had come down all over again. Only there was no bridge in the quarry. Something violent and terrible stirred in the cavern below, but it was not at all like the quake Tiryn had seen in her vision. It was something far worse.

Chapter 49

VOICE OF DOOM

The hole was breached before Kion, Grundy, or Tiryn could descend the ramp. Torches and lanterns lit every corner of the room. Twice as many as usual. Faedred, still in prison rags, but armed with sword and shield, stood at the defense, along with a score of other soldiers who had gone to prison for his sake, armed in similar fashion. Next to them, a contingent of armored gallants with spears guarded the opening along with them. But no amount of vigilance could have prepared them for what came through.

Amidst a din of grinding, scraping, and crunching, an immense, bone-plated head pierced the rock. Two thick, three-toed claws burst through after it. Rocks shattered and tumbled into the cavern as the rest of the creature's bulk slid through. Squat powerful legs emerged, pounding the quarry floor with quaking force. Its crusted maw stretched wide, letting forth a deep rending bellow. The men near the front drew back, covering their ears against the deafening call.

Not a single armored soldier, nor any man among those of Faedred's party, nor even Faedred himself, dared draw near as the creature shook a spray of rock and dust from its back and eyed the men arrayed before it. Lizard-like it was, though the plating and coloration were less like scales and more like old yellowed shards of overlapping bone. It was a little more than half as long as a drakyn, for its plated tail was short and thick, but it had enough bulk for two of those creatures together. It might easily have trampled half a dozen men had it chosen to, but instead it shuffled forward, bellowing all the while, and the men gave way. Its two black pebble eyes, close together and embedded into its thick face plate, glared at the assembled men, searching out who it would crush first.

Zinder cocked his crossbow and let a bolt fly. Though it hit the shoulder, the bolt fractured and fell to the ground in useless splinters.

"Horn toads!"

"What is that thing?" Kion said, unsheathing Truesilver and rushing into the midst of the soldiers.

"Another of the dim-touched. Grullits, they are called," Nurien said. *"They dwell deep within the tunnels and caverns which run through the roots of the world."*

Before the swordspeakers or soldiers could test their weapons against the monster's hide, and before Nurien could say anything more, another enormous grullit clawed its way out of the hole. The men fell farther back, their formation wavering.

Taking one of the spears from a nearby gallant, Faedred hurled it toward the open maw of the second beast. It struck soft flesh, drawing a dark line of blood. But the mouth smashed shut, snapping the spear in half. The grullit lowered its head and charged. The soldiers were far enough away to skirt the ground-shaking rush, but the ranks dispersed even more, with some giving ground and others circling to find a chance to strike.

The first grullit bulled its way forward after its companion. At the same time, a third monstrosity burst into the quarry, sweeping away the last of the rocks cluttering the breach. The three grullits plowed through the quarry unchecked, toppling piles of stones and snapping their jaws at anyone within reach, the ground shaking with each thunderous step.

"To me, men, to me!" Faedred shouted. The men collapsed into ranks behind him, using the pillars to protect their flanks. "Spears and swords at the ready. We wait for the charge and strike as it passes." Though disgraced and in rags, Faedred was marshal once again. Despite his failings and two months in prison, the leader within him had not died. He could have attempted to fight his way out of the keep with the sword he'd been given, to win his freedom as he had attempted in the guest-house, but in the face of this threat to the Eyre, he found his honor once again.

"*Oh-rah!*" Faedred shouted. The men answered back with the same cry.

"*Oh-rah!*"

He hurled a rock at the first grullit from behind and his men followed suit, attempting to provoke it. It turned to face them and pulled up, unsure whether to follow the other grullit or thrash the men that surrounded it. For the moment, it let out a bone-shaking roar, hoping to scare them away.

Zinder, standing with Tiryn at the base of the ramp, fired off a bolt into the thing's gaping maw. Though the bolt was no more than a minor irritation, the beast made up its mind and came thundering toward the soldiers.

On Faedred's command they parted, avoiding the rampaging beast and hammering it with blows as it careened past. But the tactic achieved little, save to confirm that their weapons could not pierce the bony plates.

Kion and Grundy rushed into the vacated space near the opening, seeking the best way to get at the third grullit. Its underside was devoid of plates, but the belly was so low to the ground it was impossible to strike it there.

"Glaivefrost!" Tiryn shouted from the ramp. A shower of sapphire darts struck the creature's face. Though most shattered harmlessly, one pierced an eye. The creature lurched ahead, disoriented, flailing about and striking out as it went, forcing Kion and Grundy back.

"*Call for the fire,*" Kithian said.

Kion ran to one side, motioning for Grundy to attack the other flank.

"Glaivefire." Truesilver lit up with a wave of red flame.

The grullit swiveled to face the fiery threat. Unlike most

enemies Kion had faced, the creature was undaunted by the blade's heat. It padded forward on thick legs, attempting to scoop Kion into its mouth. Kion dodged and struck at the same time, but managed no more than to chip away at the bone plates.

The creature's tail whipped in reply. Kion leapt out of the way, but Grundy went down, his feet flying over his head. The creature would have trampled him, but a storm of icy balls crashed against its head and froze, coating its other eye with a shiny blue veil.

"Get up, ironfoot. This is no time for rest," Barazain said.

"That hurt," Grundy said, wobbling to his feet. "I thought I was protected when I held you."

"You will recover. Now strike the ground this time and call for glaivethorns! The creature's soft underbelly looks to be its weakness," Barazain said, his voice bright with the delight of battle.

Grundy may not have had the quickest mind, but he understood his glaive. Hardly knowing what to expect, he struck the ground in the direction of the grullit. A thick cord of woven vines sprang from the floor and ran beneath the creature. Vibrant and bright, the vines multiplied the torchlight as though made from the finest emeralds. Thorns hard as bronze thrust out from the engorged vines, piercing the leathery skin of the creature's underside. The grullit reared back in pain, but failed to dislodge itself from the thorny braid. It whipped its tail again at Grundy, but he saw it this time and dove back. He landed on the ground again, but at least without another set of bruises from the grullit's tail.

By now, the cavern had erupted in pure chaos. Prison-clothed men and armored gallants engaged the first two grullits. A few men lay fallen upon the ground, victims of grullit tail swipes and claws, but the soldiers had failed to wound either beast in any serious way. Only Faedred had managed to whittle away at the plates covering the first grullit's legs, but he had yet to draw blood. Kion and Grundy's beast had foundered, but was still very much alive.

As dangerous as the grullits were, the true threat came next. A noiseless mass of black shapes swelled in from the unsealed opening. The gaping darkness writhed and coalesced into a hundred knots of fury. Shaydvorn spilled into the quarry, a wave of black ichor pouring from the wound in the wall.

Tiryn's vision had come true. Though they did not come through a swirling portal, the end was the same. They spilled in, taking the beleaguered soldiers unaware. Ten men fell to their spiked daggers as the first wave of darkness crested over them. The soldiers fell not by skill or cunning, but by reckless savagery. The vorn flung themselves at the soldiers, heedless of harm. Though they weighed little, when four or five had leapt upon a man, he would topple like a reed in the wind. They fought ferociously, driven beyond all sense and reason, a storm of madness and wrath. Only against Kion did they show any fear, for they hated the light of his crimson flame and did not dare approach.

The vorn rushed Grundy, attempting to pull him down as they had the others, but he felled too many to be overwhelmed, each one perishing at a single blow from the mighty morningstar. Several stabbed him with their daggers, but those whose weapons did not chip or snap were crushed or swept aside by the spiked head of the glittering morningstar.

"We must seal that breach!" Barazain's voice smote like a hammer in the ears of the swordspeakers.

"Kion, drive them back with your flames and give Joromar space to close the hole," Kithian said.

The shaydvorn burst into flames as Kion struck them, set alight like so much midsummer kindling. Their bodies withered in Truesilver's fire, leaving only ashen stains upon the stone. But for every one he struck down, three more came through the opening, driven by a greater fear than the certain death awaiting them at Kion's hands.

"Glaivefire!" Kion waved his blade, spraying flames in an arc before him. This blunted their charge, but only for a moment.

More than a hundred shaydvorn had stormed in against the

keep's defenders. Faedred cut them down like grass in a field. Other soldiers stabbed and thrust and tore them to pieces, yet as easily as they fell to the glaives, it took sometimes five or six blows from the soldiers before the vorn withered away into empty swaths of tattered black cloth. Zinder pierced dozens of them, and still they came on. More and more soldiers fell. The grullit, emboldened by the presence of the vorn, stamped and gored the soldiers with abandon. Kion longed to rush back to help, but first they had to seal the breach.

He swung his sword over and over, filling the space before the breach with a tapestry of flame. But the barren rock offered no wood or other fuel to sustain the fire. Though countless shaydvorn fell to the flames, more and more got past and the flaming shield quickly dwindled. "Hurry, Grundy, stop up that hole!"

Grundy waded forward, having finally pulverized enough vorn to advance.

"Stand back, little brother." Grundy waved Kion away. He struck the ground at the front of the opening and rocks went flying. "Glaivethorns!"

From the base of the opening, emerald vines sprang upward. This time they came not as a single roped braid, but a brambled cloud of thorns, a great briar patch which sprang to life in the midst of the breach.

Thick though the briar wall was, it only came up to Grundy's chin. More vorn climbed the side walls and scuttled over, swelling the numbers of those in the quarry.

Grundy struck the ground again.

"Glaivethorns!"

A thick tapestry of vines shot up, extending the wall even higher and stopping up the remaining space. A handful of shaydvorn sailed over the top just before it closed. The grullit pinned on Grimbriar's thorns broke free with several violent heaves. It scampered away from the wall, bowling over vorn and soldiers alike in a panicked frenzy.

The opening now sealed, Kion waded back into the fray,

seeking to cut through the swarm and fight his way to Faedred. Grundy came alongside him, swinging Grimbriar and crushing the vorn with every blow. But it was not enough.

The other soldiers were forced back up the ramp. Tiryn and Zinder had withdrawn halfway up, firing crossbow bolts and icy darts into the dark churning mass. Threescore shaydvorn fought against only sixteen soldiers, most of them already wounded. Faedred was ever at the fore, but the vorn were too quick and his was only one blade. Several got past him and stormed up the ramp. Other soldiers cut them down, yet there were too many to stop them all.

"Fire and ice, they're going to reach Tiryn," Kion said. He redoubled his efforts, but though the vorn withered before him, the ramp only grew all the blacker.

Tiryn unleashed a flurry of frozen darts and fled farther up the ramp.

"Hurry, lad, we need you!" Zinder shouted. He and Tiryn had stopped at the very doors of the quarry. Valissia's guard stepped in from the hall to protect them.

"We cannot hold them much longer," Nurien said.

Kion swung Truesilver with desperate strokes, but the two unwounded grullits came at him from either side, forcing him and Grundy to leave off pursuit of the shaydvorn. Kion rolled away from one of the thrusting maws and Truesilver bit into the creature's shoulder on the upswing, finding a seam between the plates at last. For the first time, one of the grullits felt Truesilver's fire and it scrambled away, howling in pain.

"Glaivethorns!" At Grundy's shout another spiked wall shot up from the ground on their left. The other grullit reared back, not only startled, but cringing from it, as though the mere sight of it vexed the beast.

"Ha! They are nothing more than overgrown vermin," Barazain said.

"What do you mean?" Grundy said.

"Rats, snakes, and lizards cannot abide thornbristles. It is the same

with the grullits. They loathe the fertile smell, the flow of life through the vines. It is odious to their hateful, twisted spirits."

"Then let us have an abundance of growth within this place," Kithian said.

Grundy laid down more briar walls, one after the other, until he had formed a rough corridor for Kion and Grundy to reach the ramp and keep the grullits at bay. The monstrous creatures were now effectively gone from the battle, cordoned off by Grimbriar's thorny maze.

But the ramp had gone black. Tiryn and Zinder were gone. Though Tiryn had shouted to her brother for help, her cries were lost in the clash and clamor of battle and the roaring of the grullits. Only Faedred, Rymir, and two other soldiers held the top of the ramp. They fought at the very door to the quarry. All four wore their own blood upon their tattered clothes and armor.

Protected from the rear by their thorny blockade, Kion and Grundy had a clear path to the ramp and soon overtook the trailing shaydvorn. Grimbriar and Truesilver smashed and burned the vorn wherever they found them. Their foes showed no fear, nor made so much as a whisper when they met their end. Yet Kion and Grundy were only two warriors against fifty. And several of the shaydvorn, seeing them advance up the ramp, scuttled off the sides and came back around behind them. Soon they were set upon from two sides. And though more than a dozen shadow walkers sold their lives in doing so, enough of them swarmed Grundy at last to pull him down.

"Grimbriar! Glaivethorns!" he cried out as he went down. Sharp thorns exploded from the head of his weapon, piercing four of his enemies and giving him a moment of freedom before twice as many leapt in to replace them.

"Kion, come to the aid of your friend," Kithian said.

"Stillfire."

Truesilver's fire could harm Grundy, but not his blade. Kion struck down the shaydvorn piling on Grundy, sweeping them clear with great, carving strokes.

"Thank you, little brother," Grundy said. He sprang to his feet and lay into his tormentors. But the absence of the fire removed the shaydvorn's fear of Kion and he soon found himself hard-pressed by a new pack of dark men.

Faedred and Rymir were gone now, either having been slain or fallen back. The ramp was a swath of darkness. Kion went down, smothered by a host of shaydvorn. He saved himself only by reigniting Truesilver's fire, sending half of his attackers to a fiery death and the rest scattering back up the ramp. Then whatever held the vorn in check at the door to the quarry broke and the dark men rushed into the hallway with such speed that Kion and Grundy could not catch them until they reached the outer hall.

The battle raged on outside the quarry. The crazed shaydvorn threw themselves against the last defenders with greater fury than ever before. Each fallen soldier enflamed their battle lust and fueled their hunger for blood. Faedred and Rymir were all that remained of the force from the quarry. They occupied a narrow gap in a glistening blue wall of Rimewinter's ice. The vorn had broken through it only moments before. Kion could not see if Tiryn, Zinder, or Valissia yet lived beyond the other side, but took the presence of the ice for a sign that Tiryn was still alive. Faedred and Rymir could not hold against the dark tide that flowed through the gap and fell farther back down the hall.

Kion and Grundy waded in from behind, thinning the ranks of their enemy, but they could not cut through fast enough to reach Faedred. From down the hall Valissia gave a terrible cry and Zinder's voice rose in desperation. Grundy swung more wildly and savagely than ever before, clearing a swath before him. He surged ahead of Kion, only bothering to strike whatever vorn foolishly got in his way, and running past the others.

By the time Kion passed through the gap in the ice, Grundy had reached Faedred. Rymir had fallen to one knee, pierced with many wounds, but somehow still fending off the vorn who sought to finish him off. Faedred had lost his shield and survived now only by his skill with the blade. A dozen vorn threatened Valissia, who lay slumped against the wall near the gate at the end of the hall, defended only by Tiryn, Zinder, and two of her personal guard. Ice darts flew from Rimewinter's hilt, but Zinder had run out of bolts and took up one of the vorn daggers as a last defense. The two guards had suffered many wounds and their strength was fading. Grundy could not reach them before his mother and her defenders would be lost.

They would have perished then, but like ghosts passing through the walls, Ganthum and his men appeared behind them.

They charged in, their swords swift and sure. Ganthum, ten Fellswords, and ten gallants pushed the shaydvorn back down the hall and toward Grundy and Faedred. Kion and Grundy dispatched the vorn before them and fought their way to the beleaguered marshal. With fresh soldiers and the newly arrived swordspeakers, the forces of Bramble Eyre quickly reversed the battle. Kion quenched Truesilver's fire amidst the slash and press of the hallway, but it was no longer needed. Together they made quick work of the reckless vorn. Though two of Ganthum's gallants succumbed to the shaydvorn daggers, not one of the enemy remained.

Grundy rushed to his mother's side, setting down his glaive as he sought to discover how badly she'd been hurt. Though she had only suffered a single dagger thrust, it was deep and much of her noble blood had already spilled on the floor beneath her.

"Something is wrong," Grundy said, working to press down the panic in his voice. "There is something black on her skin around the edge of the wound."

"The shaydvorn blades seem to have some poison or taint to them," Tiryn said as she ripped the fabric in Valissia's dress to get a better look at the cut.

"It is dimyldwyn, the twisted essence of Spark that Shadowriven uses to make the dim-touched," Nurien said.

"Talinyon never used such a thing on humans," Kithian said. *"What effect will it have on her?"*

Valissia winced and clutched the arm of her son. Her eyes veered about, pain marring the usual serenity of her face. "I will be fine. Attend to the soldiers first. Many of them have far worse wounds."

"As the Spark gives life, so the dimyldwyn takes it. At the very least she shall perish if we do nothing," Nurien said. *"Tiryn, place the flat of my blade against the wound. The pure spark of my metal should draw away the taint."*

Ganthum and his men did what they could for the soldiers fit enough to survive. Faedred scorned all aid, though he bled in many places. Rymir lay crumpled on the floor, his life's blood spent. The noble soldier who had given so much, had given to the very end.

Inside Kion railed against all the death and ruin the shaydvorn had left in their wake. If Rymir had possessed a glaive of his own he would still be living. If anyone had been worthy of the call of swordspeaker, surely it was him. But if the call went only to the worthy, Kion doubted he would ever have been chosen.

"Hold still, Valissia," Tiryn said. "I am going to try to draw out the poison from your wound." Valissia shut her eyes, nodded, and forced a smile. She grimaced when the ice-cold metal touched her skin, drawing in a quick breath. Rimewinter shimmered with a pale blue pulse of light and Tiryn withdrew the dagger. The wound was as ugly and deep as ever, but the blackened taint had vanished.

Grundy gripped Tiryn's hand tight. "She will live. Thank you."

Valissia's eyes shone clear and strong as before. "Yes, thank you, dear Tiryn. It was so cold, but the haziness has left me. Please, go now and tend to the others."

"We must draw away Shadowriven's taint before it can do its work," Nurien said.

Tiryn made a hasty bandage for Valissia before withdrawing to tend to the others. Grundy and Kion lifted Valissia to her feet.

Off in the distance muffled snapping and cracking sounds echoed up from the quarry. They were trying to chop down Grimbriar's walls. But the shaydvorn daggers were poor implements for such a task. Were there haukmarn coming in as well, or perhaps even Vayd? His heart quickened at the thought, but looking around him he was reminded of Kithian's warning upon the walls. With so few warriors in fighting shape, they would quickly be overwhelmed if Vayd came with a fresh host of shaydvorn.

"You should never have left the tower, Mother," Grundy said, heedless of the troubling sounds drifting up from the quarry door.

"This wound is nothing. I watched my son grow into a man today." Valissia caressed his cheek. Her natural beauty was surpassed only by the loveliness of her devotion to her son. Yet even the strength of that love could not sustain her against the pain of her wound and she faltered and fell into his arms.

"We must get her to someplace where she can rest," Grundy said, lifting her gently off her feet. No sooner had he taken her into his arms than Havrick came running through the gate, even more winded than the last time they'd met him. Seeing Valissia's bloodstained dress and the fallen soldiers, surrounded by the empty tattered wrappings of the shaydvorn, his eyes blinked in wonder and dismay.

"Oh dear, this is awful," he said. "What in the Four Wards happened?"

"There will be time for that later," Grundy said. "Mother is wounded. Carry Grimbriar for me. We must get her out of the keep."

"Whatever I can do to help," Havrick said, hefting the great weapon. "Oof, how do you manage to swing this thing? I know you're stronger than me by ten yards, but this feels like it was made of stone."

Faedred cut short any reply, hurrying toward them from the

quarry doors. "Something is cutting through your thorn wall, my lord."

"Must be those foul lizard-things that came through the breach," Zinder said.

"No, they cannot abide the thorns," Grundy said. "More likely it's more of the shadow men."

"Rare is the blade that can pierce my thickets," Barazain said. *"The feeble pokers wielded by the shaydvorn are not capable of such work."*

"Only one have I ever known that could sever your vines without being sundered," Kithian said, his voice dark and troubled.

Kion knew at once what those words portended.

"It's him, isn't it?" he said.

"I know your mind on this, glaivebond, but this is not the time. We must get these people to safety," Kithian said.

Kion suppressed all the arguments which sprang to mind. He was not even sure they could defeat Vayd alone, much less surrounded by a host of shaydvorn and the grullits. He had to trust Kithian's wisdom, and so he called out to Tiryn and Ganthum. "Hurry, send any who are able to walk on their own power ahead. We must leave this place at once."

Those able to walk rose and trickled out through the gate, the stronger helping the weaker.

Grundy bowed his head low. "Despite what I said on the wall, I would fight him with you if not for my mother. I cannot leave her alone, not until she is free from danger."

"I will be fine," Valissia said, but her voice was too weak to be convincing. "Do what you must to defend the Eyre."

Kion knew what Grundy felt all too well. If given the choice, he would have done the same.

"We are too few to stand and fight with any hope to win, my lady," Kion said.

"It breaks my heart to leave Rymir and the other soldiers like this," Tiryn said.

"And mine as well."

Snickt, chaaack, snickt, chaaack. The sounds of chopping, snapping, and rending grew in intensity. The bellowing of the grullits rose again as well.

"The barriers are down, and far too quickly," Barazain said.

"With the keep overrun there is no hope of defending Bramble Eyre," Ganthum said.

Faedred moved restively, bursting out in an anguished voice, "I am sorry I failed you, my lady and my lord." Then he sprinted off past them down the hall.

Kion made to go after him, but Valissia's words held him in check. "Leave him be. He has paid for his treachery."

Ganthum, though he only knew Faedred's story secondhand, nodded knowingly.

"And if not," Zinder said, "his own guilt and shame will be punishment enough. He'll have to live with that to the end of his days."

"Perhaps." Grundy shook his head sadly.

Faedred had atoned for the wrongs he had done. He had saved Valissia from certain death, though that seemed a far cry from what Tiryn's vision had shown.

Kion stared hard at the open doorway to the quarry. Vayd was there. Kithian had all but said it. And if so, they were walking away from their chance to end the war. Yet he followed the others down the hall all the same, his feet working against his heart. The one thing that helped was watching Grundy carry his mother before him. Kion had failed to protect his own mother. He would not let Grundy lose his. His place was with the others—for now.

One of the soldiers locked the gate behind them as the last of the party passed through. The thudding steps of the grullit upon the ramp boomed off in the distance.

"I don't think that will stop the grullits," Tiryn said. "Should Grimbriar make another barrier?"

"It would not last long enough for us to waste time creating it," Barazain said. *"My walls only endure as long as they are close, or*

within the sight of my glaivebond. When I am far enough away, they will wither and die."

"The gates will be enough," Grundy said, though there was doubt in his voice.

They hurried on, filing past a second gate at the top of the stairway to the next floor. From within the bowels of the keep came the clang and crash of metal against bone. A grullit had reached the first gate. They increased their pace and rushed through the long inner pathways of the keep, locking each door and gate behind them as they went.

The sundering crack of metal and wood grew closer and closer, no matter how quickly they went. Wounded and beaten, the company could not outpace their pursuers. The great expanse of the keep which had so impressed Kion when he first entered it was now a weight dragging them down, a vast entombment of stone which kept them from freedom.

They paused to catch their breath at the gates to the great hall. There was no point in triggering the gate shut behind them this time for the shaydvorn could easily reopen it since the winch was on the inside. They would have to hope that between the soldiers at the outer gate and the few able-bodied men left, they could hold off the hordes long enough for Valissia and the other wounded to get safely away.

Truesilver flared hot upon Kion's side. Kion could feel the sword even through the scabbard.

"I sense him," Kithian said.

And then came a voice which sent a hollow chill through to the marrow of Kion's bones. It was laced with pride, a voice of ruin, of bitterness and swollen offenses long guarded and nourished in dark and secret places. It hummed with mangled desires running deep and unchecked. It was a voice of doom. It was the voice of Malix Shadowriven.

"At last we meet again, Kithian. This time I will not rest until your metal is torn asunder and your shards scattered to the four winds."

Chapter 50

UNTIL THE BATTLE IS OVER

There upon the dais strode Vayd Mokán, his arms two braids of corded muscle, his neck thick as a bull, and his face, once stone gray, now a dingy shade of pale. His hair was pulled back and no longer held the same midnight shade, but was shot through with streaks of dusty gray. Embedded wanstones coated the blackened leather protecting his shoulders, so crowded there was scarcely a place to fit one more. The stones exuded a sharp, caustic scent that scraped at the back of the throat.

In his hand Vayd held a wide, twin-bladed axe, so black that it shunned all light. Two keen-edged crescents rounded each wing with a jagged, five-pointed gem in the center, dark as well water. A crusted ebony gemstone capped the haft, exuding whiffs of ashen smoke as though it were a burned-out wanstone. Ridges of slagged metal crisscrossed the head in a web of disfigurement. The impossible size of the weapon made it hard to credit that anyone could hold it aloft, much less wield it. Yet there was Vayd, hefting it easily, eager to test it upon the one who had bested him at Charring.

"Nurien and Barazain are with you as well, I see," came the assured voice of Shadowriven. *"Are they prepared to sacrifice their new swordspeakers as before?"*

"We have learned from our folly," Nurien said. *"Though it would seem that you have not. You tear away your thrall's life bit by bit, just as you did with Talinyon."* Her voice held only sorrow, not only for what she had done but for Malix as well.

"All who are not strong will fall away. That is why as glaives we endure, but mortal flesh may not. That is a truth even you cannot deny."

"You are one to speak of truth, Malix Oathbreaker. How many promises have you burned to ash? Now let us clash metal on metal and test and see who shall fall away this time!" Barazain said, his voice bristling with menace.

"You could not defeat me before and you will not defeat me now," Malix said. *"Take them, Vayd. Let us show them the true power of an unfettered glaive."*

Vayd came to himself, as though all that had passed since he entered were some fog or dream and now awake, the wrath within him blazed to life once more.

"Come, whelp," he shouted, his voice clamoring off the walls with the force of an entire host. "Do you dare face me now that I have a glaive of my own?"

Kion unsheathed his blade, the metal ringing in answer to Vayd's challenge.

"The battle has come to us. We have to fight," he said quietly so that only those around him could hear.

"Yes. But we must work together," Kithian said, setting aside his reservations now that the enemy was before them at last.

Tiryn pulled forth Rimewinter. "I will do what I can," she said, though her eyes were full of fear.

"And don't forget me," Zinder added, adjusting his hat to a daring angle.

Valissia gave her son a quiet nod. "You must go. I will be safe with the soldiers at the gate."

Grundy wavered, but assented in the end. "Very well. Duty does what it must." He set his mother down.

Ganthum gave Kion a cross-armed salute. "And the Fellswords will be at your side as well."

They might never get a better chance. Vayd was alone. It was three swordspeakers to one, with a band of hardened warriors at their side. Kion was more than ready to face him. But were Tiryn and Grundy? He would soon find out. As Zinder said, metal only proved itself when tested with fire.

The three swordspeakers stepped back toward the great hall but Nurien's voice held them in place.

"Wait, there is someone behind—" she began.

Before she could finish, a click sounded and clinking chains rattled within the walls. The gate to the great hall came crashing down before them, the iron tips of the bars hammering into the age-worn grooves in the floor with a jarring finality. Kion and the others were trapped outside the hall. From one of the booths beside the gate stepped the figure of someone none of them expected to see. Faedred Alagris. Dark streaks ran down his tunic, shredded by shaydvorn daggers. A purple stripe stained his leg and he had a hitch in his stride. But his eyes were clear and his sword grip sure.

"Faedred, what have you done?" Kion said, pressing his face into one of the open squares between the bars.

"Bought you a little time." Faedred's face was hard, but his eyes more gentle than Kion had ever seen.

"It looks as though they have a traitor in their midst," came Malix's commanding voice. He sounded both pleased and intrigued.

"Faedred, as the lady of Bramble Eyre, I command you to open this gate," Valissia said, her voice high and peerless.

"For the first and last time, I must disobey you, my lady." His face shone with a soft inner light. Whatever twisted selfishness had tainted his love for Valissia was cleansed in that moment. Not since Strom Glyre's duel with Vayd had Kion seen a man bear himself so nobly in the face of death. Even Grundy gave him a nod of solemn respect.

"You send your lackeys to fight in your stead, I see." Vayd strode forward, sneering.

"This is a fight you cannot win," Kion said.

Faedred gripped his hand through the bars. "Until the battle is over, there is always hope."

He pushed himself away and walked calmly out into the great hall, his limp momentarily gone.

Vayd raised a fist in the air. From two corner doorways shay-dvorn emerged, slinking with fearful, graceless steps behind their master. They would not approach Vayd, but fanned out around him and then bolted toward Faedred. It had been a trap. Vayd had not intended to fight alone, and the three sword-speakers would have been overwhelmed had they chosen to meet him in battle. Kion met Vayd's gaze with scorn. Vayd had shown similar treachery in their first battle. But the haukmarn knew nothing of honor. Might was their only rule.

Tiryn's vision had come full circle. Faedred would be smoth-ered by the darkness, but would save them after all.

"Your doom is but delayed," Malix said.

"Run while you can, craven. I will have my revenge!" Vayd yelled.

"Let us make sure that his sacrifice is not in vain," Ganthum said.

Kion gave Faedred a cross-armed salute. "It was an honor to draw swords with you at the end, Marshal Alagris."

"When strength fades, the will grows stronger," Faedred said. He set his guard and waited for the sea of dark men to come.

Kion tore his eyes from the ill-fated warrior and turned and fled with the others.

Despite carrying his mother in his arms, Grundy reached the outer gatehouse first. "The keep is overrun from within! Sound the alarm!" he shouted. One of the twelve soldiers manning the gates flew up the tower. Baleful chimes filled the darkened air for the third time that night. Ringing out in a way that had never been heard in all the years the castle had stood.

*Baaahhhmmm, baaahhhmmm, baaahhhmmm…*Seven times the bells rang out over the horned battlements of the Eyre. "Flee, flee, flee to the woods," they said. "Abandon your posts. Bramble Eyre is lost."

A frightened commotion took hold of the courtyard below.

Men, women, and children scurried from their lodgings onto the pavement like mice driven from the walls of a crumbling house.

"We must find a way to get the people out of the castle," Ganthum said.

"I see no path to safety," Valissia said. "The boats can only be reached from the docks beneath the keep and that way is now shut."

"Without boats, the water is our prison."

Tiryn had been turning the wooden dagger on her necklace over and over between her fingers while the others spoke. Now she held out Rimewinter. The frosted shards of sky-blue crystal on the hilt shone all the brighter in the darkness of the night.

"Rimewinter can get us across," Tiryn said.

"Of course! One of your ice bridges." Zinder was quick to catch on. "But can you make one wide enough for so many to cross at once?"

"*Given enough time, I could turn half the lake into ice,*" Nurien said.

"*Time is against us, old friend,*" Barazain said. "*There are more than three hundred who will need to cross.*"

"*We will save all we can,*" Kithian said.

"Very well, then let us be off," Grundy said. He set his mother down inside the cart. The horses stamped wildly, straining to be untethered from a post beside the wall. Tiryn and the others piled into the cart, Kion last of all. There was not enough room for Ganthum and the other soldiers.

"*If we are to flee, we should first retrieve the glaives,*" Nurien said.

"Yes, we must not leave the glaives behind," Kion said.

"But is there time?" Grundy said. "Our first task is to get Mother and the people down to the lake."

"I will send some men to retrieve them, my lord," Ganthum said. "You and the other swordspeakers must protect Lady Valissia. We will meet you at the southern wall with the glaives."

An uneasiness rose within Kion, but he could not have

carried all of the glaives by himself and he owed it to Grundy and Valissia to see them safely to the wall.

"Very well, but tell your men also to bring the satchel from my room," Kion called out as the cart took off down the pavement. That had Strom's journal and his father's letter. There was nothing more precious to Kion among his worldly possessions.

Zinder did not press the horses much this time, but kept them in check on Valissia's account. Left to themselves, they would have bolted shortly after the ride began.

As they rode away, Kion could not take his eyes off the keep, overcome by Faedred's decision to sell his life for them.

"I can't help but think that it should have been me and not Faedred facing down Vayd in that hall," he said.

"What about the shaydvorn?" Tiryn said. "You could not have fought both Vayd and them all at once."

"Faedred did. And he did not even have a glaive."

"There were too many. If you had stayed and fought, you would not have lived," Nurien said.

"But what if I won? Vayd would be gone and the war would be over," Kion said.

"Nurien is right," Kithian said. *"Faedred's sacrifice was noble. It may save many lives. But not even a swordspeaker could have come out of there alive. If it had been you, you would have saved some lives as Faedred did, but many more would be lost if you were taken from us before this war is ended. Your path lies elsewhere."*

Kion clenched the handle of his sword. Was he not a soldier? Was it not his duty to lay down his life for those he had sworn to protect? Yet the words of opposition withered on his tongue. As always, he could not deny the truth of what Kithian had said. This battle was lost and there was a much larger war to be fought. To face Vayd in that hall would have meant death. It would have meant leaving Tiryn and Grundy to fight Vayd on their own. Yet, it was still hard to accept that it was Faedred facing down his enemy and not him.

They bounced and jostled down the steep path. The lower

courtyard grew more chaotic by the moment. Dozens of people milled about, directionless, with nowhere to go and no soldiers to tell them what to do. Their anxious clamor fueled the mounting panic within the castle.

"Even if we make it across the lake, won't they just track us down in the woods?" Tiryn said.

"Much of their force will stay to take the castle, and Navrin told me of several hidden places in the woods where we can hide. The people will be safe there," Kion said.

"And then what? We can't stay in the woods forever."

"Glenwither is less than two days' march away," Grundy said. "We will make for there once it is safe."

"And what about Tapper?" Tiryn said. "Will we have to leave him behind?"

No one spoke for several moments.

"I don't see any way of saving him," Zinder said with a grimace. "Curse me and my luck with mules! I'm sorry, Marlund..."

They rode on without speaking. One by one the cities and strongholds of Inris had gone dark. And now Bramble Eyre had fallen as well. The ancient fortress now belonged to the haukmarn. All that was left was to escape with their lives and the glaives. They could not even save Tapper.

Kion stared unseeing at the blur of pavement as the cart rolled on toward the courtyard. Despite all their preparation and training, they had failed. In all of Inris only Madrigal remained free. And for all they knew, it may have fallen as well.

Fiery debris rained down on the western wall and the buildings near it. It clattered upon the slate roofs and stone structures, forcing the soldiers upon the wall to crouch behind the crenellations. Volley after volley of burning scrap pelted the castle. How long the battlements would hold would depend on whether the haukmarn came prepared with rafts already made or if they had to make them now. Knowing Vayd, it was most likely they had come prepared.

Navrin and Logren must still be upon the battlements. Ulvarth would be there as well. Those were the men he had trained to fight for. The courtyard was no place for a soldier. But Kion could only fight the battle before him. And his first task was getting Valissia and the rest of Bramble Eyre to the safety of the woods.

The cart came to a stop once they reached the lower courtyard and its occupants poured out onto the pavement, causing a stir amongst the bewildered masses milling outside the servant's quarters.

"Everyone! Everyone!" Grundy's voice boomed over the chattering crowd. Those gathered in the courtyard, many with their children, turned to listen to the giant figure. "Flee to the south tower. Do not return to your quarters except to bring those who may still be there. Bring nothing but yourselves and your loved ones. Move swiftly, as you value your lives!"

A dozen men ran back into the surrounding buildings, but most followed Grundy and the others on toward the tower.

As the tower door opened and they prepared to ascend, Tiryn gave a sudden cry.

"Wait!" she said. Everyone stopped, even the servants behind her who did not know how rare and unusual such an outburst was.

"What's wrong, Tiryn?" Kion said.

"We can't leave Tapper. The stables are right there, Kion. And I'm sure Tapper can climb the stairs. We just need enough rope to rig up a harness and lower him over the side of the wall."

"Yes! Why didn't I think of that? We can use one of the saddles!" Zinder said, hopping with excitement.

"Tiryn, I know you mean well, but are you sure?" Nurien said.

"We cannot risk anyone's life for the sake of a beast," Barazain said.

"That beast carried you here for a large part of our journey," Kithian said. *"If I did not think we had the time I would advise against it, but Tiryn is right. The stables are not far from the tower."*

"I agree, we should save him if we can," Kion said. "Valissia should be safe upon the battlements. Grundy, you go on with her. Tiryn, Zinder, and I will join you as soon as we can."

Grundy's brow tightened, but he had enough sense not to waste time trying to talk them out of it. Porters offered to carry Valissia up the stairs, but he quietly refused and set off on his own.

The stable was only one building down from the tower and they reached Tapper's stall before they could even get up to a full run.

"There's danger in the air, Masters. I can smell it," Tapper said as they flung open his stall.

"Yes, and we've come to get you out of it," Kion said.

The mule's foot set to tapping wildly.

"Yes, let's go. I think today I could gallop as fast as a horse," Tapper said.

"Let's load him up with the saddle and the rope and off we go!" Zinder said.

They gathered the things they needed and in the span of a few moments, were back out in the courtyard. By now, it was even more crowded than before. Word about the flight from the south tower had spread across the castle. But when people saw the beranskyre and the bright gems from Truesilver's hilt gleaming in the darkness, they parted and let Kion and the others through, many murmuring things like, "There goes the Sword of the North," and, "We may yet have a chance."

Getting Tapper up the stairs was hardly easy, but between the mule's urgent desire to flee the castle and Kithian's steady coaxing on how to navigate the "stone rises," as Tapper called them, they caused no impediment to the steady flow of men and women traveling to the top of the battlements. Tapper got a few odd looks, but for the most part, everyone atop the tower was too busy eyeing the courtyard below or assembling ladders to give him much heed.

"It's awfully high up here. Are you sure this is the way out?" Tapper said.

"Yes, though it will take a bit before we're ready to lower you down. Just be patient," Tiryn said, smoothing his flanks while Zinder got to work with the rope and saddle, fashioning him a harness.

Ganthum and the Fellswords arrived not long after Tapper and the swordspeakers.

"I sent Renin and Jalik after the glaives," he said.

Before Kion could answer, astonished cries rang out all around them. A large, winged shape plummeted from the sky.

"The drakyn has returned!" Nurien cried.

The dark presence shrouded the air above them. The drakyn swept in upon a foul wind. It was much swifter and larger than Kion remembered.

"Down! Everyone down!" he yelled, pulling Tiryn to the ground with him.

But dozens of people crowded the battlements and not everyone heard his warning in time.

The supple creature lashed out with unfathomable speed. Its tail carried two men off the walls with terrible cries and the awful crunch of bone against rock.

The swiftness and the shock of it left no time for sorrow or even fear.

"Get down!" Kion shouted. "It's a drakyn!" A pain knifed through his chest at the memory of his last encounter with the beast.

Grundy, concerned with shielding his mother, failed to mark the serpentine outline wheeling around for another pass. But Havrick saw the glistening green darkness barreling down upon his friend and threw himself in front as the tail again raked across the stonework. Havrick was swept over the crenellations along with three others. Grundy reeled sideward in the trailing tunnel of wind as the drakyn roared past and his mother slipped from his arms.

"*Call to me, glaivebond!*" Barazain said, his voice so pounding and urgent that it went past Grundy's mind and straight to his limbs.

With speed rivaling the whiplash tail itself, Grundy leaned out over the gap between the horned crenellations and called out.

"Grimbriar, to me!"

A moment later, the humming emerald sheen of his glaive's gems lit up his face and arms. Kion raced to the edge of the wall and looked down. The great morningstar rested firmly in Grundy's two hands. Strong as he was, Grundy struggled to hold on to it. For two other hands gripped the shaft besides his own. And those two hands belonged to Havrick.

"Kion, help me." Grundy breathed the words through gritted teeth. "He's losing his grip."

Kion wedged himself into the gap and took hold of Havrick's wrists just as his hands slipped from the haft. Together, straining until their arms felt as though they might dislodge from their shoulders, he and Grundy dragged Havrick up and onto the battlements.

"Did I save you?" Havrick said, and then crumpled to the ground and lay still beside them, eyes shut and unmoving.

"What's wrong with him?" Grundy said, his voice half-choking with panic.

Before anyone could answer, Tiryn's voice shouted above the tumult. "Glaivefrost!"

Glittering sapphire spikes pierced the night. Several hit the drakyn, bouncing off the creature's scaled breast and legs, but none struck home.

"Glaivethorns!" Grundy swung his morningstar so that it sent out a wide swath of horned barbs. Several of them tore through the thin wing membrane and the creature listed, the dark form curling into itself with a maddened screech. The enormous shape dropped, slamming into the side of the tower and crashing onto the battlements. The ground shivered as though a piece of the sky had fallen. Several people who had been racing toward the safety of the tower were crushed beneath the beast and the impact knocked several others to the ground. Kion, who had dropped Truesilver to pull up Havrick, called his sword to his hand.

"Truesilver, to me!"

Zinder launched a crossbow bolt at the drakyn's head. It pegged the beast on the side of its snout and skidded off into the night.

"Horn toads!"

The servants fled before the screeching beast as Ganthum came up beside Kion, three Fellswords behind them. Together they wove their way through the fleeing throng. As they closed in, the drakyn was still dazed from its collision with the tower.

Grundy outpaced the others, howling with murderous rage.

"You witless lizard! You killed my friend!"

The drakyn's tail whipped into his side and sent him staggering, but amazingly he kept his feet. Unfazed, he raced forward, rearing back to bury Grimbriar's spikes into the drakyn's head, but the attack was as reckless as it was brave and the creature too quick. It brushed him aside with a sweep of its curtain-like wings. Grundy slammed into the crenellations with a stifled cry.

"Rise up, glaivebond," Barazain said. *"Back to the fight!"*

But Grundy doubled over, clutching at his chest, and did not move.

"Glaivefire!" Kion charged, sword aflame, guarding against another wing buffet, but by now the beast had shaken off its stupor and coiled low, preparing to spring into the air. It would have escaped except that a barrage of ice from Rimewinter struck its clawed foot. The ice formed quickly around it, shackling the beast to the paving stones. Ganthum flared out to the left, seeking a better position to strike and dividing the creature's attention.

The drakyn, seeing that it was cornered and could not attack them both, struck out at Ganthum, who was in the fore. Though his guard was up, and he made a desperate attempt to dodge, the old soldier could not match the lightning neck of the lunging beast. His sword cut into the side of the creature's face, but failed to stop its seeking jaws from clamping around his waist. His armor buckled, then cracked, as the teeth found purchase through the shredded metal.

Casting all caution aside, Kion launched himself at the beast's exposed breast.

"Glaivefire!" he cried out as he struck. His body flushed with rage at this creature that had nearly taken his life and had now taken the lives of so many others.

The drakyn reared back and released Ganthum. It attempted to spring away, but forgot the ice holding it fast. When its leap stalled, the thick green chest came crashing down, bringing its full weight onto Kion's upthrust sword, burying it to the hilt. Rank blood spilled over his hands like scalding oil. His gauntlets shielded him from the worst of it but he instinctively released the blade and yanked back his hands as the creature fell. Flames burst inside its body, filling it with a vibrant glow, as though it had swallowed a bonfire. It writhed briefly and then its great chest collapsed in upon itself. The drakyn let forth one last noxious breath and stirred no more.

"Ganthum!" Kion rushed over to where the man lay sunken on the pavement.

The old warrior's eyes flickered open.

"My days of war and battle are done at last...." He gripped Kion's arm with a feeble hand. "Thank you for redeeming an old soldier who had lost his way...I can die now in peace, knowing I fought with honor at the end..." His grip released and he stared, unknowing, into the deep and fathomless sky.

Tiryn, seeing Ganthum fall, gave out a muffled cry and looked away. But need drove her from the bitter sight to Grundy's side.

"Grundy, are you all right? Are you wounded?"

"Only my pride. I'll be fine. Just had the wind knocked out of me," he said, rising slowly with her aid. "All I could do was watch while Havrick and Ganthum…" He could not finish. After a moment's struggle, he forced his gaze to the other side of the battlement. "And what of my mother?"

"I am here, my son," Valissia said, limping toward him, two Fellswords assisting her.

Tiryn hastened to where Havrick lay. The fire in his usually ruddy cheeks had gone ashen. Grundy hovered nearby, the color in his own face draining by the moment.

Tiryn's eyes lit up when she touched Havrick's neck. "His life blood is faint, but not gone."

"It is poison," Nurien said. *"But the wounds from the barbs are small and grundrak poison is not fatal. He will recover."*

"Oh, Nurien, I can't tell you what those words do to my heart," Grundy said.

"Dear old fellow!" Zinder said, patting Havrick on the shoulder. "He's got lots more beets to plant."

The servants crept around them, still wary of the drakyn, fallen though it was.

Kion motioned to one of the Fellswords. "Let's get those ladders down—now!"

"Yes, Beranskyre," the man said.

The soldiers finished assembling them with all speed. While the ladders took shape, battle erupted on the western wall. Haukmarn had found their way up and quickly outnumbered the soldiers there. And yet the men refused to yield. With great acts of courage and sacrifice that would never fully be known, they held the enemy in check—for now—and gave the rest of the Eyre the precious time it needed to escape.

Livia and Mariday arrived with the last group of servants, rushing to their lady's side.

"You've been hurt, m'lady," Mariday said, her old face looking even older as she took in the sight of her mistress's bloody dress. Livia clung to Mariday's side as though the old maid was the one thing keeping her afloat amidst a sweeping current.

"It is only a little cut," Valissia said. "I am safe now."

The Fellswords sent the first of the ladders over the side of the castle. Long, rickety things they were, looking no more stable than spider's thread, but the first one held when a soldier tested it. He shimmied down to where the foot of the ladder anchored itself in the rocks below and called up for others to follow him down. No more than an arm's length separated the ladder's feet and the dark waters of the lake but he did his best to steady it for the next person down.

As one of the servants, a young child strapped to her back, snaked her leg onto the first rung of the ladder, one of the Fellswords called out a warning from the other side of the battlements. Kion rushed over to see a dark wave sweeping down the path from the keep to the lower courtyard.

The shaydvorn had escaped. Faedred was dead. But he had held them off far longer than any of them could have hoped. More and more vorn skittered across the castle grounds, a dark plague eating up the pavement. The pale figure of Vayd Mokán raced before them, leaving the shadowy train behind with his long, powerful strides. The edge of his axe, blacker than night, shimmered with a grim and hollow light.

"*We will not be able to get everyone down the ladders in time,*" Kithian said.

Panic rippled through the masses gathered upon the wall at the sight of the advancing sea of shadows.

"*No matter. As you said before, we save as many as we can,*" Barazain said. "*We can hold them at the door to the tower until we fall.*" Far from showing any dismay, he relished the idea of fighting to the end.

With great reluctance, Grundy turned to one of the Fellswords. "You must take my mother down the ladder. The swordspeakers and I will stay and fight." By now, three ladders were in place and the women and children were rushed to be the first to descend.

"No, there is another way," Nurien said, her words coming like a fresh wind to disperse the cloud of fear gripping the battlements. *"Tiryn, hurry down to the bottom."*

"You want me to go? Shouldn't I stay and help them fight Vayd and the shaydvorn?"

"No, you must save these people. This is something only you can do."

Against such urgency in the voice of her glaive, Tiryn put up no further resistance, but held on to Kion's hand perhaps longer than she should have.

"Truesilver will protect me," he said.

"Don't fight him unless you have to."

"I will come back soon," Kion said, unwilling to promise that he would not take the chance to defeat Vayd if it came.

She turned and went over the battlement, her eyes never leaving his until she was gone.

"At least she will be safe," he thought.

Kion questioned what Nurien had planned, but now all his thoughts turned to the shaydvorn horde. It split in two as half of them headed for the front gate and half headed to the south tower.

The courtyard below was empty, save for two lone figures laden with weapons, making for the southern wall. The loads were too cumbersome for them to break into a run and Kion chided himself for not telling Ganthum to send more men, but everything had happened so fast.

The guesthouse seemed a mile away.

"They won't beat the shaydvorn to the tower," Zinder said.

"Then we have to go down and fight," Kion said.

"Yes, we must. We cannot allow the glaives to fall into the hands of our enemy," Kithian said.

The time had come. They were going to face Vayd after all.

Chapter 51

A TEAR IN THE FABRIC OF NIGHT

Kion started for the tower door, but stopped when Zinder made to follow.

"Not this time, my friend," Kion said. "Your crossbow will be of better use from up here."

Zinder's face tensed in protest, but he made no outward plea. He knew Kion was right and there was no time to argue. The walls were the best place for an archer. Several soldiers were already running to unloose bundles of arrows and bolts and string the bows which could be found at intervals along the walls.

"Horn toads," Zinder said. "Tell that sword of yours to take care of you. And keep an eye out for that big oaf who's going with you. I've grown rather fond of him."

"I will." Kion nodded and slung his sword over his shoulder. It was good knowing that Zinder would be safe.

Grundy kissed his mother and raced after Kion.

"Guard my mother," he said, looking back.

"You have my word on that," Zinder said.

"And protect my son," Valissia called after them.

"That I will, my lady," Kion said just before the door banged closed behind them.

They took the stairs two at a time, but it wasn't fast enough. The tower seemed to grow and stretch as they went, so that the bottom would never come. And the worst part was that they were blinded to what was happening outside. Would Jalik and Renin reach the tower before Vayd? Had the haukmarn overwhelmed the western battlements? Were the people descending the ladders quickly enough? How did Nurien plan on getting them all down? The few sounds that rumbled from without over the noise of their stampeding feet came as if through deep waters, telling them nothing.

The first thing Kion saw when he finally burst from the bottom of the tower was Renin and Jalik, running like mad across the courtyard. The glaives clearly weighed them down. Renin had the enormous claymore and staff, Veleros and Kelgrist. He also had Kion's satchel slung over the staff. Jalik bore the great hammer Gorven in his hands and Falskein the double-bladed sword strapped to his back. They were more than halfway to the tower.

But haukmarn can outdistance any man when they choose. And few among them were swifter than Vayd. He outran the dark mass of vorn trailing after him. As he closed in, a spray of five or six arrows rained down from the ramparts. This caused him to swerve and slowed him briefly and it looked like it might have been enough for Kion and Grundy to reach the soldiers first.

But something else caught them instead.

Vayd gave a great cry of pain, and for a moment Kion thought that one of the arrows had pierced him after all. He swung his great axe and a wave of darkness spread before him. It was as though the blade of a monstrous scythe passed over the courtyard, rending a tear in the fabric of night. The black swath cut through Renin and Jalik and swept past them, rolling over Kion and Grundy like a thick fog. The arc had no substance to it, but they staggered in its wake. A spell of weakness passed over Kion, as though he'd been dealt a blow. Images of dark, gibbering faces, contorted and grimacing, their toothless lips chomping together in insatiable hunger, smothered his mind for a moment and then were gone. It left him struggling for breath, but the dark wave left no mark or hurt that he could see or feel. Neither did Grundy show any sign of harm.

Renin and Jalik suffered a far different fate. Shadowriven's dark swath dropped them to their knees and the glaives fell from their hands. For a moment their faces contorted in horror. Writhing strands cloaked them in nethershade. The dark mantle consumed them and whipped its way back toward Vayd where it sank into the ground at his feet, dragging the two Fellswords with it. Two pits opened up before him—like the ones in Whitewind—and from out of these black circles crawled a pair of shaydvorn with hooked noses and fingers and dark robes wrapping their short frames. No sign of Renin and Jalik remained.

"This is what your twisting of the Spark has wrought?" Kithian said. It was the first time Kion had heard him so utterly lost and dismayed.

"Beasts are not fit to remake a world. That can only be done through the hands of men, but men lack strength and often rebel. I was shackled in my designs until I learned to use the dimyldwyn to perfect their impurities. Behold now, the result of all my labors." Malix's words rang with a cold triumph, as if he had just unveiled some great invention, years in the making. But all his cunning was merely corruption with a clever face, taking that which was good and right and transforming it to suit his own fell purpose.

The dismay in Kithian's voice vanished, burned away in the heat of anger. *"For many purposes you were forged, but never this. I do not relish seeing justice meted out, yet neither can I be true to my own purpose and fail to seek it. Go, Kion, finish him quickly, before he can inflict more of his taint upon this land."*

"Now, Joromar! Let us bring a forest of thorns down upon this tainted shiv!" Barazain cried out.

"Truth and justice!" Kion shouted. "Glaivefire!" He ran with his sword upraised, its crimson fire bathing the courtyard in a defiant glow. Grundy thundered alongside him. Images of the orphans of Whitewind, of the dead boys in the stable at Dunach, and the smoldering ruins of Furrow, blazed through his mind. In that moment, he counted no danger nor did he give a thought to whether he might win or lose. His heart so enflamed within him that all he could think of was dragging this monster down into the dust once and for all.

Vayd let forth a roar to the sky, a fusion of anger and pain, as though some horrible thing was trapped inside of him, desperate to escape.

"Come! Yes, come!"

For all the fury within Kion and the intensity of his desire to vanquish Vayd and end this war, he stumbled as he ran, for a touch of weakness from Shadowriven's dark swath yet remained.

Another round of arrows let fly from the battlements, but Vayd used his great axe head as a shield and the two arrows on the mark clanged off. A cry of "Horn toads!" rang out from the battlements.

Vayd slowed, willing to let his enemies come to him. The two newly created shaydvorn were not so patient. They sprang at the swordspeakers in a maddened dash, running at them as men run from a house on fire. Vayd's eyes flickered with a terrible delight as his dark servants flung themselves at his enemies.

Kion slowed as well, wishing he did not have to fight them, for though all traces of Renin and Jalik were gone from these creatures, he held out hope that something of them remained within those dark forms.

But in the end, the vorn were too swift to avoid. They skirted Truesilver's flames and threw themselves at Grundy instead. Their withered hands reached for his throat. Grundy had no choice but to pound one into the pavement, flattening the vorn with a powerful stroke. The other clawed at his arm, but Grundy shrugged him off and swung his weapon back around, impaling the shadow walker so that its chest collapsed like an empty husk. Both bodies blew away like ashes in the wind.

While their attention was diverted, Vayd sprang. Kion and Grundy had only a moment to react before he was upon them. They veered to either side as he came barreling through.

Vayd swiped at Kion as he passed. Though Kion deflected

the stroke, the force of it trembled through his shoulder. More than that, it came with another arc of darkness. This was but a fraction of the blast Vayd had sent before, but it went through Kion's chest and he faltered once again under the sudden spell of exhaustion. As before, the worst passed within moments, but some of the feeling lingered.

"Make haste. With each stroke he drains your strength and increases his own. You must finish him quickly," Kithian said.

"You like Shadowriven's sting?" Vayd said. The mass of wanstones on his shoulders had a hazing effect on Kion similar to the axe's dark waves, though not as strong.

The two enemies circled each other. Kion held his guard up and Vayd pressed the attack. Grundy came in awkwardly behind him, but Vayd caught his blow on the haft of his weapon and quickly reversed to land a blow that would have severed Grundy's arm had it gone through. Instead, the force of it knocked Grimbriar from his hand.

Panic flashed in Grundy's eyes. He was no longer under Grimbriar's protection.

Vayd reared back for a vicious swing. Grundy's arms flew up to brace against the blow.

But Kion lunged, forcing Vayd to fall back or risk being struck by Truesilver's fire and steel.

Vayd altered his attack and came back with a whirlwind of strikes upon Kion. They had none of his old cunning and skill. He fought now as one who did not fear hurt or even death, striking wildly, fighting as the shaydvorn fought. Yet while they were small and weak, Vayd towered over Kion and came at him with unrelenting blows. Kion could only dodge and parry. He tried to move in such a way that he did not drift too far from Grundy, but the attacks came so quickly, he had little choice. Vayd drove him steadily toward the oncoming shaydvorn.

"Shadowriven gives him unmatched strength. You must use the fire if we are to have any chance," Kithian said.

"I can hear you now, you oversized knife. And I know what

tricks you play," Vayd said. Though his breathing came loud and heavy, he had yet to pause to recover.

On his next dodge, Kion spun away and sent a blast of fire that caught Vayd in the face. His hair lit up like a torch and the awful stench of burning skin and hair spread across the courtyard.

Vayd howled, yet kept up the attack. Purple welts broke out across his skin and his hair went up in smoke, yet he would not stop. With each of his strikes, the dark, sapping waves drained Kion further of his strength. Grundy had regained his weapon and moved to flank Vayd, but he was cautious now, and did not move quickly enough to get in a strike. All the while, the shaydvorn came on.

"Use the thorns, swordspeaker! Strike while you may!" Barazain said, but Grundy held back, unsure of how to hit the haukmar without hurting Kion.

"Glaivefire." Kion breathed the word from his heaving lungs. Desperation spread through his frame. He struggled to swing his sword now, light as it was. But he refused to give up. He sent fire across Vayd's arm, then his chest, and finally his head again. Vayd's screams filled the courtyard and he clutched at his eyes.

"Fool, you are greater and stronger than these fleshlings. I will not allow you to be defeated by a mere child," Malix chided Vayd with obvious scorn.

Enraged, Vayd sent dark swaths in every direction, each one released with a howl of pain. Kion's sluggish feet managed to dodge a few, but several more hit him, and some swept over Grundy as well. They shook Kion's frame and sent him down on one knee.

"You have done all you can," Kithian said. *"Vayd is blinded, but the shaydvorn come. Seize the glaives and run for the tower before you are overwhelmed."*

Kion's heart sank like a stone in his chest. They were winning. Burns ran all across Vayd's face. He could no longer see. His hair was all but gone. Some of his armor and even some of the wanstones had been scorched by the fire. Kion may have faltered for a moment, but he could feel his strength returning.

"No, we have to finish him! Victory is within our grasp."

"Joromar, rouse yourself. You must retrieve the glaives," Barazain said, crestfallen, but even the fiery-hearted glaive knew when to trust Kithian's wisdom above his own.

But Grundy's big feet dragged upon the pavement. He looked dazed, horrified by the sea of oncoming shaydvorn.

Kion rushed at Vayd. The end of the war drew near. He could feel it. Vayd swung his axe wildly, but the dark blasts had ended. Summoning what was left of his strength, Kion evaded the reckless blows and landed a searing strike on Vayd's side, slicing through the leather armor and eating into the flesh. Vayd bellowed and leapt back.

"Use the glaivesight, fool. Your mortal eyes are weak, but mine never fail," Malix said.

Vayd listed for a moment and then, though his eyes were still swollen shut from his burns, his head swiveled toward Kion and he advanced on him with singular purpose.

"Glaivefire!" Kion swung his sword and unleashed another fiery burst, but this time Vayd held up his axe and used the massive head to shield himself from the worst of it.

"Fall back, Kion. This is not our time," Kithian said.

Kion shuffled backwards, but Vayd came on too swiftly. Vayd braved Truesilver's fire as though it were nothing. He struck from the left. When Kion blocked it—barely—he swung from the right. Kion blocked that blow as well, but his sword had grown heavy and Vayd's blows came with more bone-jarring force than ever. He was not near defeat as Kion had believed. And the shaydvorn were almost upon them.

"A warrior gains no honor by throwing his life away," Barazain said, so unlike his usual brazen tone.

Though he could see the war's end slipping once more from his grasp, Kion turned and ran. He exposed his back to Vayd, but he had no choice. He could not trust that he would be able to block Vayd's next blow. Vayd would have cut him down, but Grundy's shout of "Glaivethorns!" sent a briar wall thrusting up between Kion and Vayd.

Grundy ran to Kion and together they bolted for the tower.

"Cravens! Your heap of straw cannot stop me!" Vayd shouted. He rounded the wall and charged after them, but by then they had separated from him and Kion's strength grew with each stride. If they did not falter, they might just have time to bar the tower door against Vayd and the shaydvorn. But as he ran he spotted the pile of fallen weapons.

"What about the glaives?" Kion said. Their flight would take them right past them. His satchel with Strom's journal and his father's letter was there too.

"If you stop for them, Vayd will overtake you. We must leave them to their fate," Kithian said with deep regret.

But for the second time that day, Kion followed his own instincts over the counsel of his glaive. He may have failed to defeat Vayd, but he could not allow the glaives to be lost as well. At least he could save one. He slowed to scoop up the staff, the lightest of the weapons and the easiest to catch. To his amazement, hooked at the end of it was the satchel. He threw it over his shoulder and kept on running, staff in one hand, sword in the other.

"I shall have my vengeance," Malix said, his voice pounding in Kion's ears.

Grundy, who had outpaced Kion when he slowed to grab the glaive, turned to look back. "Hurry, Kion, he's going to—look out!"

Kion saw the warning in Grundy's eyes before he heard it in his voice. But even if Grundy had warned him in time, it would have made no difference. The great black axe spun through the air and lodged in Kion's right arm, cutting clean through his armor. Truesilver and the staff fell from his hands. He tumbled to the pavement, a rush of pain coursing through the right side of his body.

"No, lad, no!" Zinder called from the tower.

The world flashed red, then black, then red again.

"Shadowriven, to me!" Vayd shouted.

With an agonizing, wrenching twist, the axe tore away from Kion's arm and a thousand daggers of needle fire delved deep into his flesh.

"Kion, get up!" Grundy shouted. But it sounded as though it came from the far side of the lake.

Kion's mind nearly went black again, but by some grace his eyes fluttered and he held on.

Kithian called to him. *"Steel yourself, swordspeaker. Doom comes upon you. Vayd is here!"*

Though the words were enough to rouse him, the pain wracking his body pinned him to the ground. He could not avoid Vayd's second strike any more than he could the first. The pale giant brought down his fell weapon for the killing blow. The axe would have split his head from his shoulders had a massive shape not loomed over him and taken the blow for him. Shadowriven landed square on Grundy's back. A mangled cry came hurtling from his lips.

Terrible as the blow was, the axe failed to pierce his skin. Grundy, driven by fear for the life of his friend, had found his courage. He was tested in the fire and found true. He rose up and slammed his shoulder into Vayd's chin. The haukmar leader staggered back, his arms flailing. He nearly lost hold of his glaive as he toppled over onto the pavement.

"Glaivethorns!" Grundy cried, slamming his weapon on the ground. A nest of spikes erupted beneath Vayd, skewering him in a dozen places. Vayd roared, but could only writhe in pain like the grullit down in the quarry.

Grundy might have ended the haukmarn leader's life at that moment had the shaydvorn not swept in. They raced toward him and Grundy only had time to cradle Kion under one arm before dashing away. Several vorn reached him, but Grundy beat them down with great heaving cries, swinging his morningstar left and right, sometimes felling two at a blow.

"Kion, do not leave me behind," Kithian said.

Gritting his teeth against the pain, Kion reached out his hand and called out, "Truesilver, to me."

The handle leapt into his hand and the fire extinguished. Only the bond between them gave him the strength to keep it from slipping away.

"You of all the glaives are the last one I thought would turn coward, Barazain," Malix shouted with unmasked loathing. *"Rise, Vayd. A little pain is a small price to pay for vengeance long delayed."* But Kion did not see how the haukmar responded. For the dark horde and his own pain enclosed him in a prison, capturing all of his senses.

For all Grundy's strength, he could not run full speed while carrying Kion. A large pack of shaydvorn ran past him and reached the tower first. By the time he arrived, he and Kion found themselves surrounded by a storm of dark figures. A fence of spiked daggers enclosed upon them, as if the razor-toothed maw of some ancient monstrosity had opened wide to swallow them whole.

Chapter 52

THE BATTLE IS NOT THE WAR

Shots peppered down from the battlements, thinning the shaydvorn tide. The arrows gave Kion and Grundy a moment of protection, but Zinder and the handful of archers could only do so much. Grundy broke through the gauntlet where it was weakest, but that took him farther from the tower. He soon found himself with his back against the outer wall. More and more of the dark men surged in from every side. He leaned Kion against the wall in order to be able to swing Grimbriar freely. Grundy cut them down in droves, but still they came on. The shaydvorn daggers bounced off his skin, but they clawed at him, scrambling, tearing, yanking, pulling, trying to bring him down and wrestle his weapon from his hands.

Kion's right arm hurt too much to move. His armor was smeared in his own blood. The pain came in waves, each one threatening to pull him into oblivion.

"Stay strong, swordspeakers. While we are together there is always hope," Kithian said.

Zinder screeched from above. "Get in the tower, you fools!"

Unlike Kithian's, Barazain's voice had a note of defeat. *"There are too many. Here is where we make our final stand."*

"Glaivethorns!" Grundy shouted over and over again, sending showers of spikes into the dark masses, but the tide never thinned. A pair of vorn leapt onto his back while another three latched on to his arms and legs. He slammed into the wall, crushing those on his back before pounding the ones on his legs. "Kion, what do we do?"

Kion wished he could help, but he could barely think. He had just enough strength to keep up his guard with his sword in his left hand and protect one flank with Truesilver's flames, but if the vorn ever mounted the courage to test him, he would quickly be overwhelmed.

They were surrounded. Even if they fought their way into the tower, Grundy could not carry him and fight so many at once, especially on the stairs.

"I come for you, worms!" Vayd bellowed, wrenching himself at last from the bed of thorns with a terrible shout. Black blood stained his armor and his face was scarred and mangled from Truesilver's fire, but he rose a pale shambling mound of flesh.

"Use the thorn wall," Kithian said.

"They'll just climb over it," Grundy said, smashing through more oncoming vorn.

"No," Kithian said. *"Not a wall around us, a wall beneath us."*

"Brilliant, Kithian!" Barazain said.

"A what?" Grundy said.

"There is no time to explain," Barazain said. *"Pound the ground and you will see."*

Though as usual he didn't understand what he was doing by half, Grundy struck the ground as another wave of shaydvorn swarmed in upon him.

"Glaivethorns!"

A dense block of thorny vines sprang up beneath their feet. One of the vines pierced Kion's boot, giving him another spike of pain, but he did not wholly sink into the bramble. Grundy tore away three more of the shaydvorn clinging to him, sending them off the side of the thorn carpet into the pack of enemies below. As the vorn struggled to mount the wall, Kion swung his sword with his offhand, lighting the edges of the briar. The flaming barrier kept the shaydvorn down on that side, but forced Grundy to back away from the heat.

"Agh! Glaivethorns!" He struck the bed of briars once more. The patch of thorns shook and pushed them higher up the wall.

Kion saw what the glaives meant now. He sought to bypass the tower and bring them to the battlements upon the rising pillar of thorns. The flames bit into the bramble beneath them and it was not clear whether the pillar would hold all the way to the top, but they had to try.

Grundy fought off the last of the shaydvorn grappling him. One by one he tossed them back into the seething crowd below. He showered the sides with sprays of thorns until the top was clear again. Cries of "Glaivethorns!" rang out as he struck the bramble pillar over and over, causing it to rise with sudden thrusts. It was a dizzying ascent. Kion felt certain the great heap would topple, but it soon crested the horned crenellations, some three stories above the courtyard. Shaydvorn still crawled up along the places without flames, but only a handful made it even halfway.

Grundy leapt onto the battlements while Zinder and the soldiers hauled Kion over.

"Cravens! Wherever you run I will find you!" Vayd shouted from below.

"*No one will escape the night to come,*" Malix said. "*Soon the world shall be ordered according to how it was meant to be, freed from the curse at last.*"

"*You cannot undo a curse which you brought upon yourself,*" Kithian said.

"*Enough of your lies, Malix,*" Barazain said. "*Your words are ever as one grieved, yet who has caused more grief and woe than you?*"

"*Heed my words. All will be remade through the spate of darkness.*"

Nurien's voice came to them from outside the castle as a crisp, piercing wind. "*He is only baiting you. Trying to give his forces time to ascend the tower. Come, join us below before the shaydvorn can gain the battlements.*"

In his pain and weakness, Kion failed at first to note that the battlements were all but empty. Even Tapper was gone. Only Zinder and the archers remained.

Kion leaned out over the edge of the wall and set fire to the top of the thorn pillar. He kept his sword there until the entire thing was ablaze. As the flames ate into the brambles, fiery chunks peeled away and the pillar sank and began to crumble. Shaydvorn still clinging to the sides fell into the masses below, meeting their end on the pavement or within the reckless horde.

Vayd shouted up at them from the tower door, heedless of the falling embers.

"Unlike your craven race, the haukmarn finish what they start. I will come for you, whelp, and for that fool coward you fight with. The time of the haukmarn has come!" He disappeared into the tower door and his hammering footsteps echoed through the stone.

"Hurry, we must get to safety," Kithian said.

Grundy and another soldier helped Kion to the outer edge of the wall. The ladders they had placed before were only just visible beneath a thick layer of deep blue ice. An enormous frozen ramp ran over and past them, wide enough for ten grown men to slide down at once. It swept off into the lake where it transitioned to a gentle curve and became an icy road across the surface of the water, smooth as sanded wood.

"So this is how they all got down," Grundy said, still huffing from the battle in the courtyard.

Down on the surface of the lake, the servants and soldiers walked tentatively across the ice, strung out in a long line from the castle to about a quarter of the way to the shore. Toward the rear, one of the soldiers led Tapper, who trod even more carefully than the rest, and whose legs shook as though he bore the Clarion Toths upon his back.

"Is Kion all right?" Tiryn said, calling up from the base of the ramp where she stood with several of the Fellswords. She tried to keep the note of panic from her voice, but she clearly suspected the truth.

"No, he is sorely wounded and in need of your aid," Kithian said.

"Send him to me!" Tiryn shouted, panic setting in.

"And the glaives? Did you recover them?" Nurien said.

"They are lost. We could not overcome Vayd before the shaydvorn came," Kithian said.*"Joromar, fill the top of the tower with thorns and let us be gone from this place."*

"Come, glaivebond," Barazain continued. *"Let us lay a nest in this tower thick enough to keep that thrall and his servants at bay until we are well out upon the lake."*

"Put a thousand barriers in my way if you choose, but they will not save you." The proud voice of Malix Shadowriven came to them as though the dark axe were right next to them. *"The world is changing. You can feel it, can you not? The old order is being swept away and upon its ruins I will rebuild and remake a new one—stronger, greater, grander than ever before. The Age of Might is coming."*

"Enough of this." Grundy ran inside the tower and began pounding the morningstar against the top of the stairs, calling out, "Glaivethorns!" many times.

Kion did not stay to see him finish. Two soldiers helped him onto the ramp and slid down with him on either side. At any other time, Kion would have found the descent thrilling, for by the time he reached the bottom he was going faster than he could run. But now, with his arm screaming and weakness seeping into every part of his body, he could do little more than grit his teeth and cling to the hope that Tiryn would do something to ease his pain.

Zinder and the other soldiers stayed atop the wall firing as many arrows and bolts as they could into the mob of shaydvorn. A shattering crash sounded from inside the courtyard as the tower of thorns, weakened by Truesilver's fire, toppled over completely.

"Ha, it landed in front of the tower!" Zinder called out with glee. "See if you can hack through that with your little needles, you dim-witted shades!"

"Glaivethorns!" Grundy called out for the last time.

"Let Shadowriven chew on that for an age or two," Barazain said.

Everyone on the battlements came down, Grundy first, then the soldiers, and last of all Zinder.

"My, what a ride! If you'd made it any steeper, I might have slid all the way to Lowerwyn!" Zinder said as he came barreling down the ice to where Kion lay. All who came traveled a good distance from the castle before they slid to a stop.

As Tiryn bent over him, the paleness in her face made Kion think that the moon had finally broken through the clouds.

"Your wound has the same dark taint around it as the blades of the vorn. Be strong, this might hurt a little." She placed Rimewinter's blade on his skin and for a moment the pain stormed so fiercely that Kion nearly passed out. But then a quiet coolness invaded the fiery tempest and overcame it. Tiryn withdrew the dagger and swiftly cleaned and bound the wound with strips from the tabard of one of the nearby soldiers. Grundy, Zinder, and several men had all gathered around, anxious to see if Kion would pull through.

"That's better," Kion said, his voice so feeble it barely sounded in his own ears. His arms were just as weak, but he touched Tiryn's hand and held it for a moment. They were together again. Despite the bitter losses in the courtyard, he drew comfort from that. "This ice, though, is bitterly cold. Help me up."

With great care and much concern upon her face, she and two of the soldiers helped Kion to his feet.

"Can you walk?"

"I think so. But wait—"

He felt for the satchel hanging at his hip. By no small mercy it was still there. He fumbled with the fasteners and Tiryn helped him when he struggled. Inside were Strom's beaten journal and his father's letter tucked inside the middle of the pages.

"They saved it," Tiryn said.

"Yes, but Renin and Jalik…they did not make it." The horror on their faces, the way the shadow marred and contorted them into the dark, shriveled creatures—he could not banish the image from his thoughts. It was a nightmare that his pain-wracked mind could not fully penetrate. Yet, this much was clear: from Whitewind to Dunach to the rest of Inris, Shadowriven and Vayd had raised an army of these shaydvorn and there was nothing they could do to keep them from swelling its ranks with thousands more. "They gave their lives to recover the glaives and we lost them all the same." If only he had listened to Kithian, they might still have them.

"Gorven and the others will be sorely missed," Barazain said, remorse filling his voice.

"Indeed, of all the defeats we have suffered in our battles against Shadowriven, none have been so grievous as this. I fear we shall never see our brothers-in-arms again," Kithian said.

"He cannot destroy them. Nor can he awaken them against their will," Barazain said.

"Before today I would have agreed with you," Kithian said. *"But if Malix can twist men the way he did, his power has grown beyond anything any of us ever imagined."*

"He will not destroy them," Nurien said. *"For while they have no swordspeaker, they are no threat to him. Instead, he will try to corrupt them if he can. We must hope that they stay true."*

Tiryn smoothed Kion's sweat-soaked hair. "We may have lost much, but not everything."

Yes, he had lived. And Tiryn as well. And Zinder. And Grundy. They had found a new swordspeaker, and he had shown his true mettle this day.

"Thank you, Grundy," Kion said. "I owe you my life."

"I may be the one with the iron skin, but you're stronger than steel to take a blow like that and live," Grundy said.

Zinder took his hat off and dropped his head in a show of respect to the young lord. "You saved him, Grundy, and for that I am ever in your debt."

"If only I was a true warrior like Kion, we might have beaten Vayd once and for all," Grundy said.

"I'll have none of that, glaivebond," Barazain said. *"You showed your courage when it mattered most, and for that I am proud of you."*

Grundy stood for a moment in stunned silence at the unexpected praise.

"I couldn't have stood against Vayd for one heartbeat if not for you, Barazain," he said finally.

"Tell that weapon of yours that I...that I'm..." Zinder's voice caught with emotion and he fixed his eyes on the morningstar. He leaned in and addressed the weapon in a loud whisper. "...that I'm grateful."

"Tell him I'm not hard of hearing," Barazain said, but Grundy only chuckled.

"He heard you."

"And Grimbriar not only saved Kion, it saved you. I saw that blow you took. It would have split a tree," Zinder said, shaking his head in wonder.

Grundy winced at the memory.

"Are you hurt at all?" Tiryn said.

"Just sore. I imagine I'll have an awful bruise, but nothing like what Kion suffered."

Kion's pain had drained away by a good measure now that Rimewinter had removed the taint from his wound. The clouds enveloping his mind began to clear.

"I will recover. You know Tiryn's skill as a healer. Go to your mother, she needs you now."

"Yes, of course." Grundy paused before leaving. "It was an honor to fight beside you, Beranskyre."

"The honor was mine as well, Lord Joromar," Kion said. He placed his good hand into Grundy's.

"It's just Grundy, remember?"

Grundy set off across the ice and several of the soldiers accompanied him. Two stayed behind to assist Kion. He would have protested against all the attention if he had been strong enough. But his weakness came from more than just his wound. The words of Shadowriven still haunted his thoughts. What new and glorious order did Malix envision? And how could they ever keep it from coming to pass?

"We must take down the ice now so that they do not follow us that way," Nurien said.

"Yes, I had forgotten about that," Tiryn said. She walked back a little way to the bottom of the ramp and pointed Rimewinter's tip toward the massive rise of ice. The ramp shook and then cracked all along its length. With a wrenching roar, it came crumbling down in great sheets. Most of it fell into the water with a torrent of splashing, but Tiryn remained dry, for the ice, even in its broken state, obeyed Nurien's will.

"We lost the glaives and we lost the castle," Zinder said, plodding along the icy path as Tiryn rejoined them and they made their way toward the far shore.

"I thought you said you were going to put two bolts in his eyes," Kion said, managing a strained smile.

"Between you and that big oaf I never got a clean shot," Zinder said. "And when you went down…well, let's just say my aim went off a bit. I thought for sure you were finished. It was all the soldiers could do to keep me from jumping off the wall or running down the tower to save you. Promise me you'll never turn your back on a filthy false-hearted cheat like that again. He may have enough strength to juggle a family of bears, but he doesn't have one honorable bone in his body. That axe went clean through your armor."

"I wasn't ready to face him after all. I thought I was, but I failed," Kion said.

"No, Kion," Tiryn said. She pointed at the ragtag file of servants and soldiers before them. Far ahead, the giant figure of Grundy had picked up his mother in his arms once more. Mariday and Livia kept close to his side. Elsewhere, mothers and fathers cradled their children or led them by the hand. Almost three hundred of them trekked ahead along the ice. "By fighting Vayd you saved all these people. The castle is just a heap of stone. Their lives are what matter."

That was true. And that was no small victory. Every battle had its cost. And they had paid heavily in this one. But Vayd could not follow them across the lake. And they could survive in their hidden shelters within the woods until it was safe to journey south to Glenwither. For many, life would go on. Broken and fractured, but it would go on. The wounds would heal in time.

"They may have won this battle, but a battle is not a war," Kithian said.

Tiryn touched the necklace at her throat, drawing strength from the kindness of the two little children, so far away, who had made it for her.

For the first time in many days, Kion took hold of his own necklace, stroking the carved wooden sword with his fingers. He thought of the small hands that had made it and the innocent hope in which it had been made. Pinna and Skol had sent him off to win this war. And that hope, simple and unadorned as it was, had not died. The cost of battle was indeed great, but a battle was not a war. And this war was not over.

www.ingramcontent.com/pod-product-compliance
Lightning Source LLC
Chambersburg PA
CBHW020343310726

48979CB00015B/2488/J